Huntress Rising

by

Lee Roland

Angel of Death, Book 1

This is a work of fiction. Names, characters, places, and incidents are either the product of the author's imagination or are used fictitiously, and any resemblance to actual persons living or dead, business establishments, events, or locales, is entirely coincidental.

Huntress Rising

Cover Art by *Debbie Taylor*

The Wild Rose Press, Inc.
PO Box 708
Adams Basin, NY 14410-0708
Visit us at www.thewildrosepress.com

Publishing History
First Black Rose Edition, 2019
Print ISBN 978-1-5092-2887-4
Digital ISBN 978-1-5092-2888-1

Angel of Death, Book 1
Published in the United States of America

Dedication

For Woody.
I still miss you and think of you every day.

I would have to kill the kids, too. The two playing in the moonlight below didn't know death hovered over them. A full-grown werewolf might have spotted me, but the boy, seven or eight, and the girl, no more than five, couldn't perceive the danger. His claws gouged make-believe roads in the sand as furry little hands pushed a tiny toy truck along. I'd have to kill the human watching over them, too. By law and moral imperative, humans harboring weres received a mandatory death sentence. No judge, no jury. I'm the executioner. Maat Athena Ferris, werewolf hunter extraordinaire. I was born during my mother's Goddess period according to the aunt who raised me. Maat is a simpler version of Ma'at, the ancient Egyptian goddess of justice and order. Mom also stuck me with Athena, the mythical Greek warrior goddess.

I'm no goddess, but this Maat demands justice for our dead and maimed. I stand for the victims and survivors of the obscene beasts ravaging the land. Vengeance is my life. It's also my livelihood. I must eat and buy ammunition.

I'd arrived before dark and found a high spot overlooking the meadow. Now I huddled in a pile of stone where two boulders leaned close and formed a tight, primitive cave. The reek of rotting vegetation and living green moss rose around me. My rifle, high-powered and loaded with silver, rested against the rock while I waited. The full moon overhead brightened the landscape like a massive floodlight. Not that it mattered to me. I'm blessed with exceptional night vision. Shades of gray, but I can see most everything.

The Green Valley AG Commune farmers had hired me to kill a sheep-stealing werewolf. I'd searched for a week until I spied vultures circling an old carcass dump with distinct signs of monster feeding. I knew weres had a habit of returning to sites of previous kills. Faint tire tracks in the sand led to this steep rocky rise overlooking the meadow. For the last seven days, I'd slept on the ground at a creek-side camp over a mile away. Nights I spent here, waiting, watching, hoping the creature would make a return visit. I hadn't expected a whole family.

The day's meager warmth had faded as the sun descended and night's chill set in. The golden promise of October died last week in a punishing rainstorm. Early winter stalked the hills, and frost would cover the ground by morning. I should have worn more clothes.

The family had arrived in a ragged pickup truck. The kids, already shape-shifted and furry, jumped out and rolled on the ground, growling and yipping like playful puppies. Mom and Dad, still in human form, followed them. Werewolves are born human. It takes another were's bite for them to become monsters. They're also sterile once it happens, so these parents either carelessly or deliberately infected their own little kids. This was the first time in all my years of hunting I'd seen children turned so young.

Mom stripped off her clothes. She stood motionless

for long seconds, until her form blurred in the moonlight and she changed from wife and mother to savage beast. I swallowed the bitter taste creeping up from my stomach. Tiny fingers of terror slithered along my nerves. My unique, psychic ability to sense werewolves kicked into high gear. It hissed and danced and demanded that I flee. I forced it down. I would not run.

Monster Mom walked upright like a human. Two arms, two legs, but her hands and feet lengthened. Fingernails extended to claws and body hair thickened and grew longer. Bones and muscles stretched. That incredible increase in body mass—the one that defied the laws of biology and physics—finally dragged her down. She rolled, kicked, and tore at the earth. Dad grabbed the kids and hauled them out of her deadly reach. This bitch was young and new to shifting. I'd seen older creatures morph in mere seconds, as if they had materialized out of thin air.

It must have hurt like hell. She shrieked when her jaw stretched and sprouted killer fangs. That shriek ended in a nerve-shredding howl. I bit my lip and drew in as deep a breath as I dared.

Some people called it magic. Some fools said disease. I say fuck magic and disease. I will, until my last breath, strive to exterminate them.

I might have taken her then, but she stood near the limit of my rifle's sure-kill range. One myth about werewolves held true. Silver. Sure, you can slow them down with lead. It hurts. Lead would only kill with a close brain-blasting head shot. Silver tears massive holes in the body that refuse to heal. Silver bullets do have issues—shorter range, reduced impact, and piss-poor accuracy. But hey, all I had to do was get my ass closer. That's all. Ignore the tearing claws. Ignore the piercing fangs, blinding speed, and super strength. Just get closer.

She finished her transformation and rushed away to hunt. She had a wild animal's enhanced sensitivity, and if she'd hung around a few minutes longer, she might have detected me.

The man below carefully tended his children, his freak anomaly of a family. The little girl whimpered. He gently lifted her, held her in his arms, and stroked her furry back. She licked his face with a long tongue, a hungry child with knifepoint teeth so close to his throat.

Fucking waste. With human populations dangerously low, we needed all our children.

By 2035, World War III and the plague they called the Devil's Dance leveled all the large cities and killed most of the world's humans. Then the creatures who had lived hidden among us for thousands of years thought their time had come. The vampires and werewolves declared war. They woefully underestimated us. Only the strongest men and women like my grandparents survived war and plague. *Survivors of a species that could eliminate ninety-nine percent of its own kind could certainly hold out against a bunch of hairy beasts and bloodsuckers.*

Werewolves came first, striking as individuals as well as in packs. Far more devious, the vampires killed too, but were always fewer in number. Vampires were selective and isolated. They knew how to hide. Maybe when I'd rid the world of all the nasty two-legged dogs I'd investigate that situation. Meanwhile, the battle for our world raged on.

Idiot farmers! This was taking too long. I told them to leave a few sheep unguarded for an easy kill. They grumbled about my fee and said they'd already lost enough livestock.

I rubbed my fingers against my jeans then slipped them into my arm pits to keep circulation going. Careful, slow, silent, I lifted each foot occasionally and twisted it at the ankle. To let my limbs grow cold and slow my reaction time could be deadly.

A movement across the meadow caught my eye. Oh, yes. She'd returned. I'd take her out, then do the man and fuzzy little beasts. I carefully lifted the rifle from its resting place and steadied the stock against my shoulder. Cold metal brushed my cheek as I sighted her head in the scope. She shambled closer.

Oh, yes! Come on bitch, come to Maat.

Bent, moving slow, she staggered and hunched over her kill. Her low, painful moan drifted in the still air.

Wounded!

Not a killing shot, but greed had turned one of the AG Commune farmers into a hero. If they'd killed her, they wouldn't want to pay me. She'd heal soon, but I wasn't going to let her live that long. She straightened, lifted her burden, and trudged on. I kept her head tight in the crosshairs of the scope and waited for her to close the distance.

Closer, closer… Now! She was mine.

She froze. Her head popped up. Yellow beast eyes searched the land around her. Long, pear-shaped ears twitched.

I held my breath.

She stared straight at me. Bright and sharp, her

eyes filled with the terror I so longed for her to know before I killed her. I squeezed the trigger.

The bullet smashed into her face. It blasted out the back of her head, so blood and pulverized brains burst in a cloud across clean meadow grass. The fierce explosion from the rifle echoed off the rocks and danced away into the night. She collapsed across her prey. I shifted the barrel to the man and kids as she hit the ground.

Gone.

They must have spotted me before I nailed her. I laid the rifle down and snatched my Rudra handgun from its holster. I had to keep the man away from his truck.

I'd diligently scouted this pile of rocks and dirt all week and knew every path, every escape route. He made distinct noise as he scrambled through the boulders. He chose a dead-end trail. I caught them within a hundred yards. He stood with his back against a rock, the little girl in his arms. The boy huddled against his leg. I braced myself and aimed. One shot for him and the girl, one for the boy.

His heavy breathing turned to choking sobs. "Please. Please don't."

Shit! I hated it when they cried and begged. "You know the law, dog fucker."

"They're only children." His arms tightened around the girl as if it would protect her. "It's not their fault."

No, it wasn't their fault. But the only cure for rabies is to kill the dog. *Grim brutal reality of life in 2075.* The grim reality of my life every day and every night I could remember. Nits made lice and puppies would grow into savage killers. The world grew silent.

Even the chill wind held its breath. Damn men and damn werewolves. Children! God, God, what a cruel insane world.

The boy made a hesitant step forward. I lowered the barrel to him.

Shoot, Maat. Damn it, kill him.

Another step. He lifted his arm. He opened clawed fingers and held out the toy truck he'd pushed across the sand a few minutes ago. A gift for the executioner, the only thing he had to offer for his life.

I lowered the gun. *God forgive me. I knew better.* "Get out of here. I'll kill them when they're grown." I had to force the words out.

The man lurched and staggered toward me. He kept his eyes focused downward, offering no challenge. When he passed me, he pressed himself tight against the rock as if I were the monster, not his wife and children. Fifteen feet from me, he twisted back with a pistol in his hand.

Our guns flashed fire.

His aim was off.

Mine wasn't.

My bullet slammed into the girl in his arms and punched on through his body. The impact knocked him back among the rocks. Fire, white-hot, blade sharp, skimmed the side of my leg. I jerked the gun barrel down to the boy.

Gone.

One step to follow him… My leg gave way. I collapsed and howled like one of the beasts I hunted. Muscles quivered, and pulsing nerves sent an excruciating web of agony racing from the wound. Curled into a tight fetal ball, I lost my mind in blinding pain for dangerous minutes. When rational thought returned, I rolled onto my back and focused on razor thin clouds drifting across needle sharp stars above.

Count the stars, Maat. Concentrate. Stay awake.

The pain gradually subsided to a heavy thudding ache. It throbbed in perfect harmony with my beating heart. Blood seeped from the wound and spread down my jeans, black and wet in the moonlight. Not enough to kill me immediately, but it needed to stop.

I'd managed to hang onto the Rudra, so I holstered it and dragged myself over to the man's body. I ignored the stink of bloody slaughtered meat to perform the necessary tasks. A few tugs and his belt came loose. I cut off an unstained part of his shirt for a makeshift bandage and cinched the belt tight for compression. It would do for a while. I dug in his pockets and found the truck keys. I'd walked here, but I'd drive back and sell the truck. Lucky, too, given my leg.

The werewolf girl's body sprawled across the man. Daddy's sweetheart, her furry little chest blasted open by the silver that passed through her. Damn silvers made a mess. *Stupid, stupid bastard! I'd gone temporarily insane. I was letting them go.*

I drew a deep breath, squeezed my eyes shut, and used a rock to lever myself to my feet. Clinging to the rigid stone, I waited until the sharpest edge of agonized movement passed. The toy truck the boy had offered me lay on the ground by my boot. He must have dropped it when he ran. I picked it up and stuffed it in my pocket. I'd keep it to remind me of the idiocy of compassion for monsters.

The farmers wouldn't pay me without proof, so I limped across the grass to the dead were. The bullet had ruined her head, but clawed hands would be enough. While the silver myth is true, the one about a werewolf changing back to human form when you kill it is bullshit.

When I reached the were's body, I saw what I hadn't seen in the narrow focus of the rifle scope. A little girl, barely older than the werewolf girl I killed, lay under the creature. She had long black hair, and someone had loved her dearly. Hand embroidered flowers and butterflies decorated her plain white cotton nightgown. The farmers had locked up all the sheep. The werewolf bitch found different prey. Thank God the child had died of a broken neck and not gutted alive like many I'd seen.

I knelt beside them. My trembling fingers brushed silky strands of hair from the girl's face. I closed her glazed eyes. An unguarded moment and another human child lost. *And Maat Ferris, a weak fool filled with a false sense of compassion, had allowed a killer to escape.*

I'd seen cougar tracks earlier in the day, and the odds were against the boy surviving without a protector. But it was the slaughtered girl with her dark hair and lovingly embroidered gown who would haunt me, along with memories of all the others I couldn't save.

I drew the toy truck from my pocket and stared at it for a long time.

Chapter One

Ten Years Later, May 18, 2085 A.D
Avalon Agricultural Commune
Appalachian Mountains

Christopher worked his way down toward paradise. His tongue flicked in my navel and his fingers had already reached the gate. The lantern's golden light played across our warm, flushed skin. I twisted my own fingers in his thick red hair, urging him on to the heart of gratification. He stopped, raised his head, and stared at me.

"What?" I didn't expect him to answer. Christopher never spoke. One of the other members here at the AG Commune told me he could speak but wouldn't because he was a Prime Oracle. His prophecies always came true—and he hated it.

To my dismay, Christopher rose from the bed, grabbed his robe, and drew it over his head. A frantic knock sounded at the door. The knock came again, this time accompanied by the voice of Julia, our leader Anolia's young assistant.

"Maat? Maat, are you there?"

I glanced at Christopher, but his face remained impassive. The dark night terrified Julia. What was she doing at my door?

"Maat? Maat, please." Each word came with a

higher and more desperate note.

Christopher gave me one of his sweet smiles. Yes, I knew I had to answer.

"I'm coming, Julia." I rose, grabbed my own robe, tossed it on, and went to the door.

Julia jammed herself inside before it completely opened. She stood gasping, eyes wide, and pale hands clenched tight around her lantern handle. She shivered, even though summer had almost arrived and it wasn't cold outside.

"What is it, Julia?" I touched her arm. She jerked. She closed her eyes and whispered a broken version of the serenity prayer. She didn't seem any calmer when she finished.

"Anolia wants you in the chapel dining room right now." Julia blurted out the sentence like a single, multi-syllable word.

"Why?" Anolia often sent Julia on errands, but she wasn't cruel. What caused her to send the girl into the darkness she so feared?

Julia shook her head, unable to continue. She glanced over her shoulder toward the door. "I have to go."

I wouldn't get anything else from her. "Tell Anolia I'll be there soon."

Julia nodded. I opened the door and watched her lantern sway as she hurried up the path and over the hill. After I closed the door, I turned to Christopher. "Something's wrong. I better go see what she wants."

Christopher seized my shoulders with hands made strong by his work at the forge. His fingers squeezed in a savage grip, and his striking face twisted in anguish.

"Take your guns, Maat. Take your guns."

He spoke with a gravity that stunned me. He gave me a sweet kiss, and he too hurried out into the night. Seconds passed while I recovered from the shock of hearing him speak for the first time in over a year. Then I took his advice.

I dragged my old suitcase from under the bed and threw it open. The scent of gun oil and saddle soap filled the room. All my weapons lay there as they had for the past two years while I'd lived in peace here at the commune. Regularly cleaned, they patiently waited for the once familiar killing urge to strike their mistress again.

I pulled on well-worn, black denim pants and a knit shirt, both softened with age. The supple boots that allowed me to tread softly across most terrain still fit comfortably.

I'm tall, lean, and have a moderately androgynous face. I'm not beautiful. Beauty is a blessing for women who need it to survive in this dangerous post-war, post-disease world. I've never envied them, those lovely things with their smiles and sparkling eyes. All I needed was a gun, a blade, and a little luck. I may even run out of luck, but I kept my blade sharp, and my well-oiled guns didn't age. The bullets retained their devastating punch.

I pinned my mass of unruly and not so lovely brown curls at the nape of my neck and wedged a small sheathed knife into the knot. The .44 Magnum Rudra, loaded with high impact silvers, the only ammunition I used, went into the unwieldy and uncomfortable holster at the small of my back. A more accessible shoulder holster carried a .45 caliber Aries under my left arm. I strapped a leather knife sheath to my left forearm, so I could grab the hilt with my right hand. I'd seen sheaths that buckled to the thigh, but I preferred my legs free, so I could run better. Knowing when to run had saved me more than once.

Running hadn't saved me one vital time. Rearming myself brought back vivid, agonizing memories. By 2080 to 2081, we hunters had mostly exterminated werewolves east of the Mississippi. I'd become bored and overconfident, so I decided I could hunt vampires I'd heard about in the ruins of New York City. They caught me within minutes. A month later, a rescuer carried me out of that crumbling concrete dungeon, clinging to the bare threads of life and sanity.

One good thing had come from my time in vampire hell, though. I'd been able to psychically sense the presence of werewolves since I was twelve. In the shattered remains of New York, I'd learned how to sense the presence of vampires, too. No way could the monsters hide from me now. Not that I hunted them. I'd learned my lesson.

New York had left my body, mind, and soul twisted. Life had worn me to a bare nub. I was twenty-seven and didn't think I could continue another day. The hardworking, peace loving men and women of this agricultural commune had chosen to accept me despite my obvious violent nature. Avalon and its gentle residents had repaired much of the damage of my past life. Now twenty-nine, I found myself strapping on my weapons again. I kicked aside the braided rug Loretta had given me at the solstice festival and opened the trap door to the crawl space beneath the cabin. My scuttle hole would let me exit into the thick woods. Maat's rules of survival—make sure there's more than one way out of a building, and never use the front door if there's even a hint of a problem. Christopher's warning to take my guns screamed significant problem.

The ageless aura of the living Appalachian forest surrounded me. As always, my exceptional night vision, which had also sharpened in New York, served me well. Insects sang their hymns to the warm night without marking my passage. Tall trees loomed like black tents and allowed only the occasional peek at the stars. A fitful breeze brushed fingers through the treetops, flitting from one to the next, but never made it to the ground. I eased through the woods, avoiding any obvious paths. In less than five minutes, the single fieldstone building that housed Avalon's kitchen, dining room, and chapel, came into view. Lantern light blazed through the dining room windows, but the rest were dark. I saw why Christopher warned me to go armed.

Two armored cars with the U.S. Army logo painted on the side and a long sleek limo parked in the drive. Well-armed troops stood guard at the chapel front door. Others had spread out into the yard. Two hid in the bushes close by the path I would usually take from the cabins to the chapel. I counted eight soldiers, but no telling how many inside or behind the building. It must have taken hours to get the vehicles up the atrocious mountain road to Avalon. We deliberately kept it rugged to discourage intrusions like the one now before me.

I didn't know what they wanted, but professionally speaking, I'd done a few things in my life to piss off the U.S. Army. They were sensitive bastards when people stole their hardware and munitions. Werewolf hunting was an erratic and eventually vanishing profession. I moved on to make a living as a mercenary and a thief. My success served me well when I became a black-market trader of whatever I managed to steal. Of course, Avalon was an unsanctioned and illegal agricultural commune. That alone might warrant the soldiers, but why did they want me? Why not immediately round up everyone and sort us out?

And if Christopher knew I needed to take my guns, why didn't he warn me about the troops before they became entrenched?

One of the troops stepped away from the others and lifted a night scope to his eyes. I dropped flat, scuttled behind a tree, and lay there with my face close to the rich-smelling loam. I waited a few minutes, then slipped away and skirted the building at a safe distance.

Two soldiers stood guard at the back door, so I had to go to the side. Since Anolia insisted that every aspect of the chapel complex be in working order, the small basement window in the stone foundation opened with no more than a whisper.

A tight squeeze for me and my weapons. I scraped a thin bloody line down my arm. Soft, careful steps up the stairs, and I eased through the door into the warm, dark kitchen where the aroma of fresh baked bread, cooling for tomorrow's meals, filled the air.

Muted voices drifted from the dining room. I wedged a straight, wooden chair under the kitchen door to the outside. It wouldn't hold long. Anyone coming through would make a hellacious noise, though. With the Aries drawn and gripped in my hand, I stepped into the narrow hallway separating the kitchen and dining room. The door from the hall into the dining room stood ajar, and like the basement window, it made no sound as I nudged it another inch to give me a better view. I never jump in, guns blazing, until I checked things out.

Well, almost never.

There were only twenty of us at the commune, and we enjoyed our meals at a single, long table in the spacious dining room. Rugs covered the stone floor to dampen the sound of footsteps, and wall-mounted oil lanterns cast a peaceful golden light over the stacked rock walls.

Anolia Dupree, our amazing leader and moral guide, sat in her place at the head of the table. She had an arrow slim body, and her auburn hair hadn't faded despite her fifty years. Rage narrowed her green eyes on this dangerous night. It had turned her usually tranquil face to a taut, defiant mask.

The handsome, silver-haired stranger sitting beside her had a bearing of importance—a man who gave orders and expected others to jump and obey. If I could take him, I could use him as a hostage. I'd drag him into the woods, the soldiers should follow us, and I'd lose them in the forest. I knew the land around the mountain as well as I knew my own cabin. Anolia could escape and… But what about the others in their cabins? Surely Christopher would warn them, too and they would already be gone by now.

Not a good scheme, but I'm a fighter, not a planner. My life is full of failed plans.

Anolia glared at the silver-haired stranger. He smiled and spoke in low soothing tones. It didn't pacify her. Julia was nowhere in sight.

Two of the armed troops guarded the front door.

Another man stood by the table. Dark hair, golden amber skin, that one wore jeans and a leather jacket. No uniform, but he had the tight, broad-shouldered look of a professional soldier. A big man, maybe six-five, he carried solid bone and muscle on every inch. His open jacket revealed a shoulder holster and significant weapon. I drew a sharp breath and tightened my grip on the Aries when he turned toward my hiding place.

A savage red scar ran from jaw line to ear on one side. The mark of a devastating injury, it stopped shy of a generous, sensual mouth. His dark eyes stared straight at me and he stood incredibly still. He couldn't see me, but he *sensed* something.

"Xavier?" The silver-haired stranger spoke. "Perhaps you should fetch her yourself."

The scarred man's gaze moved from my hiding place to the speaker.

Xavier. An interesting name, maybe an interesting man, but careless. He'd sensed something important and allowed himself to be distracted. I've made mistakes, but not that one. My focus on the immediate situation reigned.

Anolia laid a hand on the arm of the man beside her. "Please, let me get her."

He gave her an indulgent smile but shook his head. Xavier's twisted expression proved he was anything but indulgent.

"Where's the little mouse you sent before? She can show me—"

"No! You've frightened that child enough." Anolia tried to stand. The stranger restrained her with a hand on her shoulder. Her fists clenched. She jerked and gave a fierce twist. He didn't release her.

17

Xavier's voice carried a violent edge, but oddly enough it didn't seem directed at Anolia. He focused on the man giving him orders.

The silver-haired man kept his hand on Anolia's shoulder as he stood. "Anolia will tell you which cabin. Take those two." He nodded at the door wardens. "Go, and politely request that she come."

Xavier stood straight and still. "And if she won't?"

The man holding my friend captive gazed down at Anolia's auburn hair. His face expressed regret—and determination. "Bring her."

He released Anolia's shoulder and sat in his chair. He spoke softly, "You don't understand." He sounded gentle, so sincere.

Anolia sighed. She glared at Xavier. "Down the left path, third cabin on the right." Even at her angriest I'd never heard her use such a hate filled voice.

Third on the right? That one was for storage. She'd known I'd see poor frightened Julia as a warning. Was she buying me time to run away? Too bad. Running was often an option, but not this time. *Anolia had saved my life. She'd given me sanctuary, comfort, and time to heal. I would not abandon her without taking action to be sure she was safe.*

Xavier headed for the door. He stepped swiftly, his movements lithe as a sleek, deadly cat. So surprising for such a substantial man. Every inch of his body radiated energy and screamed danger. I'd seen so many men, but this one... Ah, too bad. But good for me. Once he left the room with the guards, I could act. He stopped short and turned back. His eyes searched again for something he could sense, but not see. He'd decided to listen to instinct. Time was up. I had to move before he came closer.

I threw the door open, dashed to the man sitting next to Anolia and grabbed him by his silver hair. Hair that was, thank God, long enough for me to get a grip. I jammed the Aries' barrel in his ear. He drew a sharp breath but didn't try to pull away. Maybe he'd had a gun in his ear before. I have. Turns your guts to concrete.

The door guards jumped forward, guns ready. Xavier made a single sharp slash in the air with his hand—they instantly stopped. They couldn't shoot me without killing my captive.

I offered Xavier my best smile. "You want to bet who can pull a trigger faster?"

He hadn't moved, except to stop the guards, hadn't even drawn his gun. I saw death in his icy, dark eyes. Death, so familiar, my old companion, my inevitable friend.

I kept the gun barrel in my captive's ear and a grip on his hair. He'd die with me when the violence came. He didn't move, but he spoke in a calm, articulate voice. "Ms. Ferris, we only want to talk to you."

"Sure. Everyone needs a small army for conversation."

"The troops are here to guard me, not harm you."

"So, who are you?"

"Lowell Parr."

He had my attention. For what little it was worth, I occasionally read the official government approved newspaper. Now the army made sense.

"The vice president?"

"Yes. Won't you at least listen to me? Violence isn't necessary." Such a smooth creamy politician's voice. I almost believed him.

The Vice President of the United States wanted to talk to me—and I was holding a gun on him. Deep shit coming down. Virtually all the good, God-fearing citizens of this country had one thing in common with vicious, low-life criminals like me. We hated our President and Dictator Aaron Gannett. He and his army were as popular as stomach ulcers and butt boils. His vice president was a bit of a mystery, but he was, of course, guilty by association.

I swallowed hard and tried to make the best of the situation. "Okay, Mr. Vice President, if you'll tell *perro feo* to back off, I might loosen up a bit."

Xavier's ferocious dark eyes narrowed. I'd called him an ugly dog. I don't speak Spanish, but I'd memorized a few choice insults. It's not nice to make fun of deformities, but I'm not always a nice person. Other than me, he was the greatest danger in the room. The soldiers at the door didn't count. The idiots had relaxed. I'd kill both before either could raise a barrel again. Nothing relaxed about Xavier. He'd be on me in an instant.

"Xavier, will you please come and sit with us?"

Xavier held steady, long enough to show defiance, even though Parr had technically made a request. *Was there some power struggle between these men?* With easy, graceful steps, Xavier came to the table and sat across from us. He laid his hands on the wood in front of him.

"Put your hands on the table, too," I told Parr. He did so, slowly and carefully.

I hooked a chair with my foot. It clattered and popped across the floor as I dragged it to a spot where I could sit with Parr's body between Xavier and me. I released his hair and lowered the gun, but my hand rested on his shoulder to remind him it pointed at his brain. A tremor rippled through his body, but then he relaxed. I touched his neck with the barrel, and he tightened up again. He needed to pay attention, because somebody was probably going to die in the next few minutes.

I glanced over at Anolia, who'd watched the scene without a word. Her eyes remained tight with fear. My soul vomiting confessions had often left her kind and gentle nature shaken bare as trees in winter. Did the soldiers and guns here frighten her? Or was it the instability and capacity for violence, for absolute carnage, she knew still lived in me?

Xavier and the troops had done a piss poor job of guarding an important person. They should have made certain they covered all entries, no matter how insignificant. Typical of soldiers, though, to believe firepower was everything. I had faith in my weapons, but I never let them substitute for caution. The soldiers of today were pale shadows of the last generation's military—men like my Uncle Jake.

"Gentlemen." Parr called to the men guarding the door. "Please wait outside. Colonel Xavier and Ms. Ferris have sufficient arms."

They immediately obeyed. How odd. They hadn't looked at Xavier for permission to leave the room. Parr required words to gain the compliance Xavier had obtained with a single hand.

I suppose Parr was trying to make me feel less threatened, but if I were in his position, I'd never have sent my guards away. It slightly improved my odds, though. If it came to a fight, it would be Xavier and me. He was big and tough, but one bullet could change that.

Xavier's eyes had not left me since I entered the room. He gave me a twisted smile that said his time would come, and I damned sure wouldn't like it when it did. I smiled back at him all bright and perky, like I couldn't wait for us to meet, one on one. I'm not stupid. I planned to run like hell.

Parr turned to me. That put the gun barrel inches from his nose. Steady breath, relaxed position, his eyes radiated intelligence and humor. "Ms. Ferris, is there any way we can defuse this situation so we can talk?"

"Sure." I was easy on that one. "You defuse Xavier and I'll back off." My words sounded like a truce, but I had already realized I could possibly be in the middle of a dangerous power struggle between these two men.

Xavier continued to offer that feral smile, and a challenge on his ruined face. He radiated a deep, fearful energy. It tempted me to forget the dangerous situation and gaze into those dark eyes to discover…what? That he wanted to kill me? I already knew that.

He slowly rose from his seat and carefully drew his gun from beneath his jacket—his thumb and forefinger on the grip. He laid it on the table and shoved it toward us. It slid across the wide expanse of polished wood and stopped, slightly out of my reach. A larger version of my Aries, but made for a sizeable man's hands.

What the hell was he doing? Did I believe he was unarmed now? Hell no. After all, I still had the Rudra at my back. He couldn't have seen it, but he had to know I wouldn't give up my only weapon.

Xavier returned to his seat, his hands clasped in front of him. For the first time, he looked relaxed.

Relaxed? Bullshit!

I drew a deep breath. I laid my Aries down and pushed it across the table toward his. It slid and bumped its bigger twin with a soft click. "Oh, look—" I chuckled like the situation was truly funny. "—I think they like each other."

Parr's gentle laugh, however, felt and sounded genuine.

My knife was easily visible in its sheath on my forearm. I sat close enough to use it on him. I'm fast and could kill Parr in the few seconds it would take Xavier to draw another weapon. Xavier appeared barely interested, not threatening at all. Baiting me. I shrugged and tried to look innocent. Innocence is not natural for me. I've always had to work hard to get it right.

"Very well." Parr spread his palms flat on the table. "Ms. Ferris, I've introduced myself, but you should know that Colonel Xavier is the president's Chief of Security."

I tried to keep a straight face as the shit got deeper.

Parr studied me. "It took a long time to find you, Ms. Ferris. You leave few tracks."

"Thank you. Get to the point."

"You're a legend among werewolf hunters. They call you Suriel, the Angel of Death."

"Oh yeah. I'm a real nightmare."

Parr smiled. "Tell me, hunter, we haven't seen a werewolf in over three years. Have you lost your touch?"

I grinned back at him. "Don't think so. I dodged your soldiers and stuck a gun in your ear." Bragging is one of my many faults.

Xavier drew a deep, hissing breath. "She wouldn't

have if I had *my* men with me." Parr glared at him. *Yep. A testosterone fueled power game.* Parr turned to me. "Ms. Ferris—"

"Just Maat."

"Maat. What about your reputation?" Parr wasn't letting up.

"I'm a competent killer." My skin prickled like someone had wrapped me in a blanket of tiny needles.

"My reports say you've killed over a hundred weres." Parr's eyes were wide and bright. "And that you can psychically sense them at a distance."

I shrugged. "Your reports are wrong." The number was closer to four hundred. Maat Ferris, queen of mass extermination. That I could psychically sense them was not common knowledge, though my success would point to my having an unusual skill.

"Why ask questions, Mr. Vice President, if you know so damn much?"

I'd been holding my right hand near the knife on my forearm. Would Xavier notice if I inched it toward my back to snag the Rudra?

"Don't!" Xavier snarled. He stood, body rigid and hands at his sides. Yeah, he was ready and poised to obliterate little old me. Certainly, he had another weapon, probably a pistol hidden in the jacket.

I jumped up and grabbed the knife handle. I'd throw it at Xavier rather than stab Parr. Of course he'd dodge, but it would slow him down and give me time to draw the Rudra. Then I could shoot them both.

"Sit down, Xavier." Parr snarled the order between clenched teeth.

Xavier stood tight and still for a moment, then slowly sat, but on the edge of the chair, ready to pounce. I waited a moment, then dragged my chair back so my legs wouldn't be under the table. I was farther away from Parr, but I could still take him with the knife—maybe.

I'd come in this room with the idea that I might not leave alive. Parr had presented me with a tiny bit of luck. *He wanted something.* I might survive if Xavier didn't attack before I could learn what it was the vice president desired.

"I want you to come to New Washington with me." Parr answered my unasked question. "That's all I can tell you now." He turned toward me, and his jacket fell away from his body. He too, wore a gun in a shoulder holster. With my attention on big bad-ass Xavier, I'd missed it. I was screwed. I'd never draw the Rudra in time.

Parr smiled, as if to reassure me. "I'm delivering a personal invitation from President Aaron Gannett. I know it's unusual and—"

"Unusual? Bizarre is the word. How many soldiers does an invitation usually take?"

Parr's mouth tightened. "Your reputation is such that the president believed you would decline."

"No shit!"

Parr nodded his head at Anolia. "I give you my word, I mean you no harm. I don't want anyone here injured. We can leave, right now."

In our world, we valued a person's word. There were no written contracts because there were no civil courts to record and uphold them. Your word was the basis for what manner of person you were. I'd always kept my word, but Parr and Xavier were part of a dictator's high-power structure. What was the word of a man aligned with a tyrant worth?

I leaned back and relaxed. I'd lost my advantage—if I ever had one. Choices? Die fighting or go with them and let them kill me at their leisure. Maybe if they killed me here, Parr would leave Anolia alone. At least she'd know what happened to me. I wouldn't just disappear. Or maybe I had lived in peace at Avalon for too long and couldn't resist the temptation to indulge in combat. I'd faced werewolves and vampires. These were only men.

"What about Xavier?" I grinned. "Who does he want to hurt?"

"You have to ask?" Xavier's savage words cut the air. He remained poised for action.

"Xavier will obey the president's orders." Parr's voice held firm. "The men outside obey me." He was looking at Xavier when he said that.

It didn't comfort me. "Poor helpless Xavier, all by himself without his own army."

I didn't have a logical reason to bait him. It just felt good. Conceit, egotism, two of my many faults. I'd made my decision on how to die. I would fight, as I had my whole life. Xavier was a worthy opponent.

"Maat!" Anolia drew in a sharp breath.

Xavier tightened his hands into fists. "You fucking bitch, I'll—"

"I'm a fucking bitch?" I chuckled, knowing how it would end. I held my hands out palms up. "Okay. I give up. I guess you know a bitch when you see one, don't you *perro*?"

Xavier hurtled himself across the table. *Across the fucking table*! Shit! I'd never seen a human, a man that big, attack from that far, that fast. I threw myself out of my chair. Too late. His solid body slammed into mine. We crashed to the stone floor. At least I'd managed to move enough to stay out from under him. With a desperate burst of energy, I kicked free and drew the Rudra. I didn't have a secure grip when he grabbed and wrenched it out of my hand. Ah, shit, shit. Acute pain spread up my arm from my fingers. Broken? Maybe not.

Xavier tossed the gun away. It clattered across the floor, far out of my reach. I jerked away from him. Frantic, I scrambled backwards on my butt. Not fast enough. He grabbed my upper arms, hands clamping down like an iron vise. I couldn't draw the knife. He swung his leg over me, straddled my hips. With unrestrained fury he pinned my back to the floor. Damn, he was heavy.

Xavier's substantial weight sent shock waves of outrageous agony up my back and down into my legs. He caught my wrist, snatched the knife from the sheath, and tossed it away. He outweighed me by at least ninety to a hundred pounds, had a longer reach, and way more muscle. I stopped my struggle and forced myself to go limp pretending to submit. He smiled. Evil anticipation filled his eyes.

He grabbed my throat with both hands. His fingers tightened in a homicidal grip. My right hand throbbed where he'd torn the gun away. The left hand was fine. If he moved his head a little lower, I could punch his eye out with a finger.

Good plan—at least as good as the plan that got me here. I struggled against an unmovable enemy. My throat burned as my lungs fought for air. The world blurred. His hands tightened—and then suddenly released.

I gasped, desperate for oxygen. My breath whistled like a winter wind through cracks in the wall of an abandoned house.

"Xavier! Stop!" Parr loomed over Xavier with a gun pointed at his head. "I don't want to kill you." Parr's voice gritted with determination. "But at this moment, *she* is more important than you."

I was more important than Dictator Gannett's Chief of Security? The shit was deeper than I could have imagined.

Xavier's eyes never left me.

"Another day, bitch." He spoke in a conversational tone, not threatening at all.

My chest heaved. "I can't wait…" I started to call him a dog again, and…no, not a good idea. He pushed his weight down hard as he lifted himself off me. It was all I could do not to scream. I ignored my leg and hip muscles' agonized protests and rolled on my side. I reached back and snagged the small knife I'd tucked in my hair earlier. I wanted to stand, but my leg muscles cramped. The best I could do was struggle to sit up. I kept the knife hidden at my side.

"Help her," Parr demanded.

Muttering under his breath, Xavier stalked toward me. Just as he got within range, he saw the knife and reeled back. I did what I could from the floor. I lunged forward and jammed the four-inch blade into his left leg, right above the knee. He never made a sound.

I released the knife and tried to scramble away. Could I get to my gun? He seized my hair in one hand, and wrist with the other. He jerked me to my feet. I balled up my uninjured fist and drove it straight into his face as hard as I could.

Anolia screamed. Parr shouted. I didn't pay much attention. Suddenly airborne, I flew across the room. Brilliant white light flashed across my eyes as the stone wall terminated my flight. Then, thankfully, everything went black.

****

Pain stomped in first. That meant I wasn't dead. I kept my eyes closed and tried to sort things out. Exquisite waves of agony in my head ratcheted up a notch when I remembered. Oh, yes. Colonel Xavier and the wall. A burning spike streaked across my lower chest. Cracked ribs? Or broken?

"She's awake." Xavier's voice—flat and cold.

I opened my eyes. The hushed roar and sway of the vehicle made me think we were on the highway. The ride was far too smooth for Avalon's rough road. I'd been unconscious for a few hours. The limo's two long bench-seats faced one another, with about four feet between them. Parr sat on one seat, with Xavier beside him. They'd laid me out on the other.

Xavier looked like hell. The scarred side of his face had swollen until it closed his eye. Oh, yes, a respectable blow for Maat. The leg I'd nailed was stretched out in front of him with a heavy bandage around the knee. Too much to hope he'd bleed to death. My injuries, head and ribs, seemed to be internal. Did that mean I'd won?

Parr moved forward and dropped to his knees beside me. He held a small bottle of water he tipped gently and let a few drops fall on my lips. "Lie still. I think you have a concussion. Do you think you have any broken bones?"

I had to work my mouth and swallow the water before I could answer. "Ribs," I croaked.

He patted my arm. "Try to rest. We'll be at a hospital soon. Dear God, woman. What did you think you were going to do? Take on the army with a knife and two guns? Are you completely fearless? Or just crazy?"

Crazy? Probably. I'd been called insane enough times to believe it possible. Fearless? Oh, no. I have my fears. Parr's army and the sweet freedom of death are not among them.

Xavier continued to stare at me, his eyes dark as sin. Pure hatred filled his gaze—until it didn't. I couldn't define what changed. Certainly, his flat expression remained in place. What then? I watched and stared into his eyes, until I could no longer keep my own open. I don't remember much after that. Except, as I drifted in and out of consciousness, I could have sworn I heard Parr say, "You want to know what he told me? He said if she dies, he'll bury *us* with her."

Chapter Two

New Washington, Virginia

Aaron Gannett, President and Dictator of the United States, glared across the desk at his Chief of Security and Vice President. The study's book-lined walls loomed over the three men sitting in a pool of light cast by tabletop lamps. Maat Ferris, the enigmatic werewolf hunter Gannett had spent over a year searching for lay upstairs in a coma. He gritted his teeth. Damn! If they'd screwed things up… He forced himself to relax. Tension and pain etched Xavier's eyes and swollen, scarred face. He wore a brace over his bandaged knee.

Xavier shrugged. "I lost my temper."

A statement of fact, not an excuse. Xavier never made excuses. The bitch had hurt him though. Few others had ever managed to do so.

Gannett turned to Parr. "What about you?"

Parr smiled with the calm self-confidence that both fascinated and enraged Gannett. Over the past three years, that self-confidence and diplomatic demeanor had smoothed many a rough spot in Gannett's uneasy rule. Parr drew adoring crowds as he carried out presidential edicts, making all but the most egregious seem palatable. The rage came because Gannett wasn't entirely sure he had his vice president under his command. If it weren't for the insistence of other players in the game, he'd eliminate that danger.

"Aaron," Parr said, "I do not control Xavier. He was provoked. That woman is—"

"Vicious? Volatile?" Gannett slapped his palms on the desktop. "That's precisely why I sent Xavier with you. He was supposed to back you up, not engage in a full-scale assault. One woman. You'd think she was an army of Amazons."

Xavier stood and stalked out. He barely limped despite obvious pain.

"Strange man," Parr observed.

Gannett grunted. Xavier wasn't just strange— Xavier was dangerous. Not that he worried. He owned Xavier—and Xavier understood that fact.

"What's the latest from Seattle?" Gannett leaned back in his chair and changed the subject. He hoped for good news, but he knew it wouldn't be coming.

"Same thing. Free Seattle, Capitol of the new United States. Elections are set for November." Parr shrugged his shoulders. "It won't get better."

"And Atlanta?"

"Deteriorating. They're trying to negotiate, however. You need more troops there."

"What's the latest population count?"

Parr tossed a piece of paper across the desk. "Eighty thousand or so east of the Mississippi. There were twenty or so people at the commune where we retrieved Ferris. Multiply that by a hundred... conservative, but I'd guess about eighty-five. Anything in the deep south and west of the Mississippi is speculation."

Gannett stared at the faded wall map of the United

States. His mind traced the blue lines, the tenuous veins of the interstate highways he controlled—north to Chicago, south to Atlanta, and west to Memphis and St. Louis. Except for New Washington, those were the only population centers left east of the Mississippi. The frail, treacherous capillary leading west from Missouri to Utah, and on to Seattle, the one that he did not control, felt like blood poisoning, inching toward his heart.

The wonder of CLT, Century Life Tarmac, remained. The almost indestructible paving and support structure material had replaced regular asphalt and concrete on the interstates. CLT held Gannett's country together, because the rest of the major roads he'd allowed to deteriorate or deliberately made impassable. If he kept the diminished population confined to the cities and surrounding agricultural outposts, and left great swaths of wilderness between, he could maintain his stranglehold on power—maybe.

Again, he cursed his predecessors. After the war ended, during the plague years when millions died, the succeeding presidents began an insane and systematic purge and destruction of all military arms. Those they couldn't destroy they hid and erased everything pertaining to records. As if those acts of stupidity would end all conflict. Nukes were deactivated, guns hauled out and dumped at sea, equipment rusted with no replacement parts produced. When the weres and vamps arrived, and the war of monsters began, humans had to fight with a mismatch of small weapons—and the enormous amount of silver lying in homes and banks around the country.

"Tell me Aaron, do you expect this werewolf hunter to save you?" Parr broke through Gannett's musing on his country's desperate condition.

"No. Maat Ferris is the coin I'll spend to save myself."

****

I woke in a four-poster bed and stared up at the white shroud of a canopy. I lay there for a while, sorting memories. Oh, yes, the remarkably robust Colonel Xavier had tossed me into a rock wall. I had a tube taped to my wrist. The tube snaked up like an obscene umbilical cord to a bag hanging on a pole. Except for that, my arms were free. I moved my legs to see if they had chained me to the bed. Nothing. The fingers on the hand Xavier twisted were purple and swollen. I flexed them and each joint begged me to stop. Not broken, though. I could hold a gun—if I could find a gun. On the third try, I managed to sit up.

I gazed around the room. Rich. Picture book elegant. Celery-colored, damask drapes hung ceiling to floor and framed tall windows. Heavy ornate furniture crouched on dark curved legs like toads, ready to hop away. Ivory carpet blanketed the floor. Carpet so thick I'd sink up to my ankles. If I could stand, that is.

My blood clots fast, so only a few drops stained the sheet when I peeled off the tape and removed the tiny tube. *Ow, ow!* The damned tape took a patch of skin with it, leaving a raw pink splotch. When I shoved the covers away from my legs, I found another tube. This one hung over the side of the bed. It stung a little as I pulled the catheter out, but at least they hadn't taped it down, too.

I eased my legs over the bedside. I sat there long minutes as muscles quivered and tempted me to give up and lie back down. Okay, time to move. A deep breath…one…two…three…I forced myself to stand. My body lurched sideways, so I hit the floor on my hands and knees, my ass exposed by a gown that opened in the back. I sucked in deep breaths of air. Another struggle, but I reached over and used the tall bed poster to drag myself, inch by inch, to my feet again. I held on and swayed for a minute but didn't fall.

Then the world went marvelously weird, spinning and shifting around me. Probably the blood leaving my brain after lying down. Or worse, they'd hit me with a spectacular drug. I wobbled around the room, snatching out drawers looking for my guns. Time shifted, and I found my clothes—or somebody's clothes. I didn't find my boots, but that was okay. I wiggled my toes. Soft carpet would do.

Panic hit me when I headed for the door. Even in my deranged state, holding on to the wall to keep from falling, I sensed a werewolf close by—and I didn't have my guns. It had been years since the sensation had shredded my nerves, but there was no mistaking that psychic hook in my guts. My brain danced, weaving stray thoughts into a bizarre tapestry. Physically I could walk. My mind had to crawl.

After three tries to push the door open, I remembered that it opened inward. I pulled it back, stumbled forward through the opening, and went sprawling into a hallway. Thankfully, it had carpet, too.

I remember specific events after that, but the time between them stretched into a foggy haze. Someone shouted words I couldn't understand. Strong hands grabbed my arms. My body moved involuntarily by instinct, and I found myself on my knees with an unconscious man in a black uniform lying beside me.

Another lay not far away. Had I taken them down? Wow!

Gun. He had a gun. I dragged it from its holster. The world jittered in an angry dance…spinning, spinning, damn why wouldn't it be still?

The werewolf remained in my sensory range, but its exact location eluded me. I lifted the gun, desperate to find the monster.

"Maat?" My nemesis, the inestimable Colonel Xavier, knelt beside me. "Maat, give me the gun before you get hurt."

My arms suddenly gave way. The gun's weight dragged my hands down to my knees. But I didn't release my weapon. I stared at Xavier—into his dark eyes. At Avalon, he'd wanted to kill me. Now, something different rested in their midnight depths. What had changed? His mouth turned up in a slow, warm smile. How odd—and how beautiful.

I drew a deep quavering breath, one I could feel stuttering in my chest. "Werewolf. You kill it for me? Please?" My voice sounded far away, as if it came from another room.

My hands relaxed, and the gun hit the carpet with a gentle clunk. I reached up, and my fingers brushed Xavier's scar. I traced them down to that perfect mouth.

"You have beautiful eyes."

I collapsed into his arms. He held me tight. My face lay against his warm throat and, exhausted by my escape attempt, I fell back into a deep sleep.

Chapter Three

Blue Ridge Mountains

"Maat?"

The voice sounded like Anolia's but it couldn't be. I opened my eyes.

She poised on the edge of the bed, holding my hand. It took a while for the thought process to make the circle of my mind, but I squeezed her fingers.

Anolia released me. She pressed a damp cloth against my lips, and I sucked enough moisture to help work up a viable bit of saliva. In a few minutes, we'd progressed to her holding my head up while I sipped from a glass.

"You...why...happened." I croaked like a frog. She was supposed to be safe at Avalon.

She brushed a gentle hand over my forehead. "Lowell—the vice president—came back for me the day after they took you away."

Lowell? The best I could do was raise my eyebrows.

Anolia smoothed her skirt with her hands, and I realized she wore a dress. I'd never seen her in anything but Avalon's cotton and linen robes. The soft, mint-colored fabric flattered her and made her look years younger.

"Everyone okay?" This time my words came

easier.

"At Avalon? Yes. They're all secure."

I tried to sit up and couldn't. Knowing I wouldn't cease to struggle, she grasped my shoulders and lifted me. The room appeared expensive, but it didn't give the plush impression of my first one. The polished wood and leather furniture spoke to comfort rather than opulence.

My bladder sent me an urgent message. "Help me. Bathroom."

Anolia helped me rise, stand, and totter across the room like a baby. It wasn't long before a bit of strength returned, and she suggested a most welcome shower. The long mirror on the back of the bathroom door gave me a nasty picture of fading bruises running from shoulder to hip. At least the swelling in my hand had eased.

She had brought me clothes I'd never seen before, and had stacked them on the toilet seat. I don't know where or when she obtained them. Denim pants and knit shirt—only I would have gone for gray or black, not blue. When I came out of the bathroom, she and Parr sat at the table by the window. I wobbled, but I made it across the room. My strength level improved with every step.

"Maat." Parr stood and pulled out a chair for me. "Are you feeling better?" His smile seemed warm and friendly, but I remembered he was my kidnapper. Worse, Anolia's kidnapper, too. I plopped down and slapped my palms flat on the table so I wouldn't fall off the seat. "I'll be fine once I get off this boat." Important things come first, even if I knew the answer to my question. "My guns. Where are my guns?"

"In a safe place. You may have them back soon." Parr, sitting beside me, had such a pleasant note to his voice.

"Soon? How about now?" I didn't feel pleasant at all.

He shook his head. "I'm sorry. That's not possible."

"Why?" This shit was getting old.

"Please understand."

"Understand? Seems clear to me. I…we…were kidnapped from our home. Oh yes, right after a bully bounced me off a rock wall. And you're sitting there grinning like everything is okay. Like it was only a misunderstanding."

Parr didn't reply for a moment. He cocked his head. He had the look of a man choosing his words carefully. "Very well. The president gave me a mission. To go to Avalon and bring you safely to him. I failed. I failed to give credence to your reputation for evasion of authority and your propensity for violence. I failed to consider the possibility that the veteran soldier who accompanied me might suddenly go utterly mad." His hands rested on the table with his fingers laced as if to keep them from betraying an inner secret. His eyes twinkled, though, and he gave me a charming smile that would probably melt most women. "I sincerely apologize for your injuries."

I had to laugh, even if it hurt my head and guts. "Wow. How shrewd. Accept the blame while carefully pointing out it wasn't your fault. You should consider a career in politics."

I understood the situation. I was a prisoner and no, they were not going to allow me weapons. The *following orders and bring you safely* shit was questionable, but I had no way to determine whether it was the truth. His words seemed to satisfy Anolia. I'd heard her voice when she said his name, and he gazed at her with eyes soft as a lambskin. I did remember that he'd threatened to kill Xavier to keep him from strangling me, so maybe that made her forgive him for what happened.

"How long have I been here?" I stared around the room. "And where am I?"

Parr spoke, but kept his eyes on Anolia. "Since yesterday, you've been here at the president's mountain retreat. You spent two days in the hospital and then four days in the presidential mansion in New Washington. You had a severe concussion and fractured ribs. Your recovery time is amazing. You surprised everyone."

People deserted Washington D.C., as they had the larger cities during the plague years. In a vain attempt to reconstruct a constitutional democracy, survivors built New Washington close to I-81, between the ruins of Lexington and Roanoke, Virginia.

Memory jumped up and slapped me in the face. "The mansion. There was a were."

"How did you know there was a were?" Parr's eyes were bright with curiosity.

"I just know."

"And you wanted to kill it." Parr leaned forward with interest. "Tell me why."

I stared at him as if he'd grown a second head. "Because they're monsters. Bloody killers and predators." Seemed simple enough to me.

Parr sighed. "Is there any possibility you could consider them afflicted with a...disease...for want of a better word?"

"Not a chance in hell." I stood and immediately plopped back down as the floor shifted under me. "Disease be damned. They need to be fucking exterminated."

"Maat!" Anolia sounded dismayed. "I had hoped we'd cured you of cursing."

"Nothing to curse about at Avalon," I muttered…lied, really. I just didn't curse out loud there.

Parr offered one more thing. "Okay, I'll say this, and I beg you to think and consider the idea. I've seen new science reports on the plague, the Devil's Dance. They suggest that the Dance was considered responsible for causing some, but not all, of the werewolves who had lived peacefully hidden until that time, to go crazy and crave human flesh. That it changed their fundamental nature and that change carried into many created since then. The science report offered credible evidence."

I didn't know what to say to that bit of…garbage.

Parr must have decided my expression meant it was time to shut up about werewolves. He cocked his head and smiled a smile I'd bet women swooned over. "You certainly created a stir at the mansion. Do you remember?"

"Some. Did I do any damage? Do I care?"

Parr kept smiling. Obviously, my actions made him happy. "You flattened a couple of Xavier's prize security guards and terrified the other staff."

Oh, that. Whoa! What the hell kind of drugs did they use on me? Another memory slugged me. I winced and rubbed my hands over my face. "Oh, fu…"

"What is it?" Anolia leaned forward, as if ready to

grab me.

"I told Xavier he had beautiful eyes."

After a moment of silence, Anolia sighed.

"How unfortunate." Parr spoke gently. "Now you'll have to kill him." He stood and laid a kind hand on my shoulder, just as he had Anolia's when he restrained her at Avalon. "You need to rest. I'm sending my car and driver to pick you up in the morning. It takes two hours to get down the mountain and another to reach the mansion, so it'll be here before seven. You have an appointment with the president at ten."

"And my guns?" I wasn't about to give up on that one.

"After you talk to the president." He walked to the door. He stopped and seemed to hesitate. "Did you know…?"

"What?"

Parr sighed. "Not only do your fellow hunters call you by that name, but werewolves do too. Suriel…Angel of Death."

My body went tight. The ache doubled. "You talk to weres?"

Parr nodded. "In human form, and with reluctance, I have. The madness that overcame so many did not touch all. You have much to learn here, Maat. Don't let your past or your prejudices blind you. That could be as dangerous as any monster."

My past. I closed my eyes, and the image of my brother Donnie came to me as it had so many times before. Six-year-old Donnie lying in torn, bloody pieces while two weres fought over scraps of flesh. I opened my eyes. *Werewolf victims populated my memories like deadly poison mushrooms scattered across a damp forest floor.*

Anolia followed Parr, and he kissed her on the cheek as he left. Oh, what a change. His actions and words, whatever they were, had certainly tamed her. She returned to me and held out her hand. "Try not to think too much about it today. Could you walk? You need exercise, and I'd love for you to see this place."

The house perched on a mountainside and gave visitors a magnificent view of the valley and New Washington below. It was a spacious place with armed guards every ten feet or so. They'd provided ample manpower to watch over two women, even if one of them was me.

Dressed in black fatigues, sharp-eyed and competent, each guard had a small white eagle embroidered on one shirt pocket. Xavier's men? I'd bet they wouldn't overlook a basement window. More interesting, I'd occasionally catch sight of one in lighter gear, one who could spring instantly into the woods, if required, to track and follow me. While I wouldn't call it impossible, I'd pay hell escaping from here, especially in my weakened state. Anolia's quiet maternal nature had charmed them, so they smiled and opened doors for us, but at the same time, they always made us aware of their presence.

The resident chef served us a splendid dinner on the western deck. We watched a glorious pink and gold sunset, then gazed down over the lights of New Washington, twinkling below. Only a few cities, New Washington, Atlanta, Memphis, and Chicago, claimed the luxury of electricity. I'd heard talk of stringing lines along the interstates between them, but talk is only talk. Empty words with little value. This house had electricity courtesy of a gasoline generator.

Anolia told me about sitting by my bed when I was in the hospital and at the mansion. She explained that Parr had taken her to lunch when I made my aborted mansion getaway. She'd heard about it second hand.

Anolia laughed. "They said it was impossible for you to move so soon. To do what you did. But I knew better. You have a remarkably strong, resilient body." She studied me for a moment. "I wasn't the only one who watched over you. Colonel Xavier spent time there, too. It's hard to tell, but I think he regrets what happened."

That disturbed me because she was a keen judge of people.

"Regrets? He's probably thinking of ways to torture me." Xavier was my enemy. I wouldn't be foolish enough to believe otherwise.

Anolia shook her head. "He spoke to me once. He apologized for his behavior toward me and Julia at Avalon. He also seemed genuinely shocked at your ability to provoke him to a rage. I think he's disturbed at his personal loss of control."

"I can piss off a brick wall. You know that." I'd carefully cultivated that talent. Blind rage equals mistakes. Mistakes can kill you. Provoking Xavier had almost killed *me*. A mistake? Oh, yeah. But I'd do it again.

"How's his leg?"

"Healing. I imagine it hurts, if that's what you're looking for."

It was.

"What's with you and the VP?" I had to ask, but I tried to sound casual.

Anolia sipped her wine and let it linger in her mouth before she swallowed. "What we have is a beginning. Lowell and I find each other attractive. We don't quite know what to do with it yet. Do you object?"

"No." That they liked each other was okay by me, but nothing about this situation was clear.

"It troubles you." Anolia's voice carried a note of dry honesty.

"Yeah. Did you ever think…I mean…" I didn't know how to say it, and I wished I'd kept my mouth shut.

"You think I'm a hostage? He's charming me in an effort to control you?"

"It crossed my mind." Actually, it had more than crossed *my* mind. I'd bet money on it. If it weren't for her, I'd find a way out of this house and be on my way before morning—or maybe not, given the guards. Anolia set her wine glass on the table. A range of emotions flowed across her face so quickly I couldn't pin one down. When she spoke again, it was barely a whisper. "I think Lowell can and will protect *me*. But I'm not important. You are. I don't know what they want with you. That terrifies me. He either can't or won't speak of the reason you are here."

Anolia reached over and grasped my hand. Her fingers were rough and calloused because she had worked beside us in the fields. "They're waiting on something, or someone. They reek of anticipation, even Lowell. It's not likely you'll have a chance to escape, but if you do, leave me. It won't be easy. There's a steel guard tower out front you haven't seen. More soldiers, too."

I leaned back and weighed my options. Could Parr protect Anolia? Would he? She had more faith in him than I did. But, no, I wasn't going to leave her.

Thunder rumbled in the distance, promising rain before morning. A breeze brought the fresh scent of wildflowers blooming in a meadow not far away. A few insects hummed in the night, and in the distance, a small animal screamed.

Wilderness had returned to these mountains after the war, as it had throughout the country. Wolves, bears, and panthers walked the forest, and I'd heard that lions, tigers, and leopards from a wrecked zoo hunted wild cattle in North Florida.

I poured myself another glass of the dwindling supply of wine. I'd enjoy it while I could. I drained the glass and gave serious thought to asking for another bottle and getting drunk.

Avalon was behind me, now. It's just as well. The commune saved my life, certainly, but boredom grew like a weed after the first year. Anolia, Christopher, and the others I cared for kept me there longer. My nature allows me to take only so much peace and quiet, and I'd have left soon anyway.

A wolf howled in the forest below the deck. A true wolf, not a monster. Lower, toward the valley, another answered...and another. Stillness crept through the woods as the pack fell silent. The hunt had begun. A terrified animal would die tonight, and they would feed. Tomorrow I'd find my own hunt. A werewolf in the president's house and the vice president called it a disease. I'd been curing *that* disease since I was twelve.

****

Aaron Gannett tried not to breathe too deeply,

since the musty, dead smell had come back, the smell of burned meat. He'd ordered the study cleaned, but the stink always returned.

The door opened, and two men entered. Herman Grant Borden, General of the Army, and Lowell Parr quietly occupied the chairs across from his desk.

"Mr. President." Borden licked his lips, a habit Gannett found annoying since it forecast unwelcome news like a barometer predicted dangerous weather. A small man with a balding head and poor posture, his shaking hands betrayed his age. Gannett wished he had a decent replacement for the sly-eyed old bastard, but Borden did have a few redeeming qualities. The man had been with him since the militia years. His unquestioned loyalty was his greatest value, followed by a shrewd, but fading mind and cunning military tactics.

Gannett acknowledged him with a nod. "Get on with it, Borden."

"Yes sir." Borden licked his lips again and began a monotone drone citing numbers of troops, equipment, and the pathetic output of the weapons and vehicle factories in Chicago and down the corridor through Ohio.

"How much of that reaches the troops?"

Borden drew a deep breath. "Maybe fifty percent."

Gannett shook his head. He squeezed his hands into fists. "In spite of the fact that a battalion of troops is stationed at the factories, and every convoy is guarded, thieves are siphoning off that much?"

"Yes, sir."

"Are we any closer to getting an airplane up?"

Borden hesitated and rubbed his hand across his

mouth this time. "Another year. The last test flights crashed."

Gannett silently groaned. "Tanks?"

"Two will be ready in about six months. Armored cars are the best we can do. But we can keep control with armored cars, and we've made great strides in mobile artillery."

He braced himself when Borden stared him straight in the eyes. Whatever his faults, the general wasn't a coward.

"The problem, Mr. President, is labor and disruption, not capability."

Gannett had started his weapons rebuilding efforts right after he abolished Congress. The problem was always labor—and sabotage. *Disruption* as Borden so cautiously called it, adequately described the situation. Despite his anti-homesteading laws, people were drifting away into the vast reaches of empty territory. The wilderness swallowed them, further testament to his eroding grasp on power. One day hordes would surge up to challenge his rule. He had to be ready.

"Very well, General, you may go."

The door closed behind Borden, and Gannett turned to his vice president. "You brought…what's her name?"

"Anolia Dupree." Parr smiled with calm confidence.

Gannett preferred Borden's jittery disposition. Parr made him feel so God damned inferior. "It's a convent?"

"No. It's actually a farming commune with a loose, earth-centric, agrarian religious base. No weapons, no aggression. She and Maat are at the mountain house. I thought it best to get them away from the city."

"Good idea. You think this Anolia can keep our hunter under control until it's time?"

Parr shrugged. "Maybe."

Gannett's mouth twisted in a wry smile. Even drugged, the bitch flattened two of Xavier's handpicked mansion guards. Xavier had accepted the event with amazing fortitude. How utterly weird and out of character.

"Aaron, I'd like to talk to you about allowing a few radio broadcasts."

Gannett shook his head. "No. The only radio contact is between army bases. Any other receiving or broadcasting equipment is to be confiscated—and the owner executed."

"But if you control the broadcasts, keep it to local news and music." Parr lifted his hands in an appeal.

Gannett knew the request was reasonable. He would allow it, but only when he had better control. "No, Lowell. I can't. Local news, music, means a proliferation of radios. The next thing you know someone will have found or fabricated broadcasting equipment. Once they have that, I'll have to deal with pirate stations springing up all over the place. If they believe there's an available audience…"

Gannett allowed only one official newspaper, carrying stories approved by his staff. In such a sparsely populated country, information and misinformation often served his purposes better than Chicago's weapons and ammunition factories.

"It's amazing isn't it, Lowell." Gannett leaned back and closed his eyes. "Something of this and something of that. We've managed to hang onto things like antibiotic formulas, vaccines for diseases, minor electronics, trucks and smaller vehicles, but I can't get airplanes and tanks."

Parr gave a gentle nod of his head. "Yes, it is amazing. All that technology to give life, save life, but so little left for killing. I'm sure you'll manage, though. You do remember the small, but excellent artillery storage bunker you found last year."

Gannett laughed. Parr did have a dry sense of humor. "Pacifist. Such a pacifist. That's all for tonight. Go. Rest. Tomorrow's a big day."

After Parr left, Gannett mused on the day's events. He glanced at the wall clock. Almost time. He poured another glass of whiskey, drained it, and filled the glass again.

Chapter Four

Anolia came to my room before daylight. I'd slept, thanks to the wine, and while I didn't feel great, my pain level had decreased. I'd gained strength and was ready to go on. She carried assorted pieces of clothing across her arm. She described her shopping trips in New Washington, and I had the largest wardrobe in my life. The beige knit shirt she gave me was softer than anything I'd ever worn. It wasn't tight, but it did cling to my shape. Everything fit, but the shirt stretched across my breasts and you could see the nipples. I'm not substantial in that area, so it didn't appear vulgar. I never wore a bra. She also provided a cream-colored linen jacket to cover the blouse. I plopped down on the bed and pulled on my boots. She'd managed to rescue them from the hospital they took me to when they first brought me to New Washington.

"Maat? How do you feel?"

"I'm okay."

Anolia gave me a warm smile. "Oh, I almost forgot. Before I left, Christopher went to your cabin and picked up your suitcase. He insisted I pretend it was mine and bring it with me."

Oh, Christopher, my sweet oracle, what the hell did you see in my future?

"Where is it?"

"In the closet."

I ran to the closet, grabbed the case, and carried it to the bed. A single thumb push and it popped open. I scooped out a haphazard assortment of old worn clothing. Christopher had found my gun cleaning kit and wrapped it up tight inside a shirt. I pried out the suitcase's false side to reveal my old Sparks .44 semi-automatic. The gun was my first, given to me by my crazy Uncle Jake on my thirteenth birthday.

The Sparks felt heavy in my hands compared to the Rudra and Aries. The smooth cold metal still gave me a high. I'd wedged four clips of silver bullets into elastic straps on the bottom of the case. The Sparks wasn't as accurate as the Aries or Rudra, and it had a shorter range, but it was a damn good gun. The newer high impact silvers wouldn't work in it either, but the four clips of regular silvers could do severe damage when they hit their target. The leather holster creaked when I picked it up.

Anolia held out her hand. "Let me," she said softly. I handed her a tin of saddle soap from the gun cleaning kit. She knew nothing about guns, but she could care for leather. We sat at the table as I cleaned the Sparks and she rubbed holster leather back into a supple harness. We worked in silence for a while. Then curiosity got the best of me.

"What's changed?" Anolia hated guns.

Anolia sighed. "Everything's changed. The only werewolves I've ever seen were dead, killed by the militia. I've isolated myself and everyone at Avalon too long. Denied the world. Peaceful yes, but careless. Lowell says… You heard him, a disease."

"Yeah, I've heard it before. It may be a disease. But I'll bet none of those disease talkers ever stood toe to toe with seven feet of fangs and claws." I forced my fingers to move faster. I had to finish and load.

Anolia stopped her work for a moment before forming a question. "You're sure there was one in the mansion?"

"Oh, yes. It's been years since I felt one, but it was there all right. I thought they were all gone, too. I'll bet a lot of people think that. I don't know how bad the situation is yet. I know it's incredibly dangerous."

"Maat, I know you care for me. I love you too. But I believe this situation is not a simple apprehension for your supposed crimes. That's why I'm telling you again. You must escape if you get a chance. Find me later. I was promised I could go back to Avalon."

I didn't bother to answer. I would not leave her.

The multitude of guards at the mountain house were there to keep me prisoner. They had decent weapons, but I doubted they carried silver. Only five years of diminishing attacks, and they'd forgotten the danger. And yes, so had I. I'd put my guns away at Avalon. I slipped the holster over my head and secured it under my arm. I buttoned the jacket up so I wouldn't accidentally flash the weapon. I wedged the other clips in the inner pockets. Anolia sprayed me with a light perfume, hoping it would cover the scent of saddle soap and gun oil. A good thing, since right as we finished our subterfuge, Colonel Xavier arrived to escort me to meet the president.

Anolia stepped up to face him when he walked in the door. Anolia Dupree was not a coward. She had implied earlier that she thought a little better of him, but it was clear she wasn't overwhelmed with trust.

"Lowell said he'd send his driver." She had that

stern mother look, the familiar one she used at Avalon on the rare occasion one of us earned a scolding. I had sorely tried her patience my first weeks there—and most weeks thereafter. Hell, I was pretty much a pain in the ass my whole time in residence. Christopher calmed me down eventually.

"The president changed his mind. He considers her a security risk." Xavier's deep voice was firm but polite. His dark eyes focused on me. Although hard to tell, I don't think he was any happier about the situation than she was.

I walked up beside her and wrapped my arm around her shoulders. She was such a small woman to be so strong. "I'll be okay."

I wasn't so sure about the okay, but I wanted her out of the line of fire.

Xavier had exchanged his jeans and leather jacket for black fatigues like the guards. He still had that dangerous animal presence. A tactical holster carried his Aries on his thigh.

"Don't worry." He spoke to Anolia, but he kept his eyes on me. "I've been warned how sanctified her ass is. She's safe."

He didn't favor the leg I stabbed, so the knife must not have gone deep—or he had enormous self-control. I'd bet it was self-control. Was this the man who caught me in his arms when I passed out at the mansion? Did I really see him smile? More like a drug induced delusion.

I hugged Anolia again to give her assurance that I didn't feel. Xavier opened the door, but he made sure I went out ahead of him.

The rising sun barely touched the top of the thirty-foot steel guard tower watching over the two-hundred-foot circle of the gravel parking area. Behind the tower sat a massive square concrete pad, though I couldn't say what its use might be. It had rained during the night, and the cool morning air promised a beautiful day. The *car* they sent for me was not another limo but a big, flat, shit colored box set on four enormous tires. The brilliant piece of military hardware was lovingly nicknamed the *turtle*.

Turtles happened to be highly popular vehicles because they, pickup trucks, and transport trucks, were the only ones currently manufactured in the country. I'd liberated a turtle from the Chicago Army Base four years ago and traded it to a stupid Memphis ammo dealer for five hundred rounds of silvers, which, for me, was the best use for the clumsy mechanical beast. Had to admit they were *turn-the-key reliable*, and Army models were bulletproof for medium caliber rounds.

Xavier opened the back door and lowered a step for me to climb in. I had one foot on the step when he reached out and caught my right arm just below my elbow. Not bone breaking pressure, but enough I knew it was a possibility. It was a defensive maneuver to keep me from drawing a gun.

"What?" I stared straight into his eyes. I forced myself to relax.

Xavier shook his head. He released me and stepped back. He didn't touch me again as I climbed in the turtle.

The driver and his companion in the front bucket seats turned to study me. Oh, my. Young men, too young, barely eighteen or so, they wore black army fatigues like Xavier. Drafting kids now? Were recruitment levels that bad? Both were handsome enough to make an adolescent girl, or a grown woman, squirm and get her panties damp. The driver was gray-eyed, blond, and Nordic looking. His partner had black hair and darker skin, but brilliant blue eyes. He had a little boy grin that tugged at me. Bet both would have their choice of females through the years. I gave them my best smile as I settled on the seat. The blond smiled back and turned his attention to the front. The dark haired one smiled but studied me longer and with more interest.

Xavier lifted the step and climbed in to sit beside me. I tried to relax and watch the scenery as the vehicle inched away from the house.

The green hardwood forest surrounded us, with only an occasional break in the trees to expose the valley below. A rough, single-lane, gravel road coiled in tight, steep curves cut into the mountainside. At times, the mountain skimmed by inches from the open window on my left. On the right, it dropped straight down. The freshness of the forest after a rain always soothed me. Bird song and the sound of rustling leaves accompanied us on our journey.

The turtle engine whined as the driver maneuvered it at a crawl down the slope in low gear. We made twenty miles an hour in the best sections. The bucket seats in front had a three-foot gap between them, so I leaned forward to talk to the boys. "Hi, I'm Maat. What's your name?" I spoke first to the darker one riding shotgun.

"Corporal Daniels, ma'am." His blue eyes twinkled. I chose to believe he called me ma'am out of respect, not age. I turned to the driver. "How about you?"

"Corporal Sanders, ma'am." He gave me a quick glance, flashed a smile, then his eyes went back to the road.

Daniels grasped an automatic rifle between his knees.

"That's a nice piece," I pointed at the rifle. "You carry any silvers?"

"No, ma'am." He slid his hand down the gun barrel.

"What do you use for weres?"

"Never saw one." He shrugged. He didn't meet my eyes, and I'd bet he was lying.

"You mean you never saw a *fuzzy* were." I turned my head and grinned at Xavier. He knew there was one in the mansion.

"Shut up." Xavier snarled through clenched teeth.

I laughed and turned back to Daniels. "Is he always such a grouch?"

Daniels didn't answer, but his eyes widened and his mouth tightened, as if he tried not to smile. Uncle Jake taught me to play tag with diamondback rattlesnakes, and I wasn't about to let up on Xavier. I wanted to make him as miserable as possible.

"How about you, Sanders, you ever see a were?"

"No, ma'am, but my father was in the Freak Squad and one of them...have you killed..." Sanders' hands gripped the steering wheel so hard his knuckles turned white. He wanted to ask but was afraid of Xavier. I didn't give a shit about Xavier.

"I didn't keep count, Sanders, but I killed a lot of them."

Sanders relaxed. "Thank you," he said softly.

I didn't know what to say, so I leaned back and studied the landscape again. In all the years I'd been killing weres, few people had ever thanked me. Griped about how much I charged them, yelled at me because I didn't work fast enough, but thank me—almost never. They simply looked the other way, anxious to forget their terror and get on with their lives.

The Freak Squad. Long time since I heard anyone speak of them. I enlisted in the Freaks, the official branch of the military designated to kill werewolves, when I was sixteen. Uncle Jake lied about my age. *Mature for my age he said.* He was wrong. Yes, I could handle weres, but I had trouble with authority. I had trouble following orders. After one great disaster, the Freaks kicked me out eighteen long months later. The entire squad died an unnatural death when a pack of weres stormed their barracks one moonless night, five years after my departure.

The vehicle slowed as the road turned super rough and full of holes. My list of options wasn't exceptionally long. Even if I escaped, they had Anolia.

I glanced at Xavier out of the corner of my eye. He sat with the scar turned away from me, and I could see something of what he had been before the injury. A gorgeous face, ruined, but he was still graceful, with a powerful body, strong, long-fingered hands…whoa! Best not to think about his hands. They'd been around my throat choking my life out of me not long ago. For a perverse and unfathomable reason, I wondered how they would feel on my skin and—he turned to me as if he heard my thoughts. Although his gaze didn't hold antagonism, those dark eyes were intense as he stared at me. "Where did you get a weapon?" His words sounded indulgent. Curious, too. Not hostile—yet. Maybe secretly speculating about how hard he'd have to fight to get the Sparks.

I didn't answer. He'd probably smelled the gun oil.

"Give me the gun, Maat."

"No." He would not intimidate me. I leaned back against the seat, crossed my arms. "What *is* your problem, Xavier? Don't you understand my insecurity in this situation? I was minding my own business at Avalon when a bunch of thugs kidnapped—"

"Shut up." His voice deepened, and tension vibrated the air. Hot damn, another fight. I lost the last round, but I might do a little more damage this time. Especially since he'd been warned *how sanctified my ass was.*

He turned toward me, so I scooted away and jammed my back against the door. Turtles are exceptionally wide in girth, so I had room to kick at him.

"Maat, the Vice President of the United States…." Xavier stopped and glanced at the front seat. He didn't want them to know what happened. Too bad.

"Yeah, yeah. The Vice President of the United States came in person to officially kidnap me. I snuck past you and the guards and stuck a gun in his ear." And for spite. "How's the leg? Do you have my knife? I hope it didn't break when it hit bone."

His fists clenched. He drew in several deep breaths. Then, with a visible effort, Xavier relaxed. "You're insane."

"That's what they tell me." I always ignored opinions on the condition of my mind. So why did I suddenly have a hollow space inside me? You'd think he hurt my feelings.

We rode on in silence. For a few minutes, anyway. The turtle rocked and tires splashed up water as we crossed a shallow, clear mountain stream. The forest grew close to the road here, enclosing us in a cool emerald cave.

Xavier drew a breath, held it, and then released it as he spoke. "Maat, I can't let you take a gun into the mansion. It will get you killed." He'd turned to face me again. Those beautiful hands stayed relaxed, one on the seat and the other on his knee. He must have decided to try reason. Reason worked on me occasionally, but I refused to compromise when it came to my weapons.

"Stop being such an ass, Xavier. There was a fucking werewolf in the mansion. A live were. And no one seemed excited about finding and killing the thing."

"And that's exactly why you can't have a weapon." Xavier's voice sounded tight.

"So I won't kill a were? Now who's crazy?"

His hand lashed out with lightning speed and grabbed my right wrist. If he'd been closer, he might have had me, but he had to lean over. That gave me a chance to scrunch my body up and get one leg up between us. I planted my foot on his stomach and managed to keep a respectable distance between us.

We struggled, but pound-for-pound, he outweighed and out muscled me. Colonel Xavier was too strong. A wrestling match wouldn't work. I battled with my left hand, while I stretched my free leg out across his knees. I hooked the turtle's door handle with my free foot.

One of the turtle's many appalling design flaws allowed its doors to open with a single inward pull of a handle. I jerked the foot hooked in the handle. The door popped open. Xavier cursed. He reached to close it, but I still had my foot in his stomach. I pushed—hard. He slid off the seat and out the open door. He still held my wrist so, of course, he dragged me with him.

Jumping out of a vehicle on the side of a mountain isn't an optimal exit strategy, even at the turtle's slow, crawling speed. Xavier hit the ground first. I crashed on top of him. I heard the whoosh of his breath as my weight forced it from his lungs. Excellent! He cushioned my landing. The impact broke his grip on me, too.

I rolled over. The ground dropped beneath me. Oops! Gravity, that old bastard, tried to haul me off the narrow road and down the steep mountainside. Xavier suddenly appeared and had my arms in a muscle-bruising grip.

"Shit!" He summed up the situation with one word.

His fingers dug deeper as he tried to stop my descent. We balanced on the road's edge for what seemed an indecent time. Then my weight dragged both of us down.

A thick carpet of nut-brown leaves, wet and slick from last night's rain, coated the steep angled slope. I slid ten feet, hit a tree, tried to grab hold, and missed. I clawed at leaves and dirt and dug in with my boots in a desperate effort to slow my descent. Another ten feet glided under me before I could catch a protruding rock and brace my foot against a tree. Leaves plastered my face, and pain spread from my hand where the rough rock scraped off skin and tore off part of a fingernail.

Xavier cursed. He'd caught a tree. A line of blood trickled from his nose, and his holster was empty. I fumbled under my jacket for the Sparks and found it tucked in tight. Another twenty feet below us, the mountainside dropped off to a sheer rock ledge.

Xavier tore his way from tree to tree, straight toward me. His intention was clear. Breath hissed through his teeth, and he had that *I'm going to kill you* look on his face again. The only tree *I* could reach was in his direction.

Choices? Shoot him or grab him and take him over the ledge with me. Neither option was particularly appealing. Salvation arrived in the form of Daniels and Sanders who rappelled down ropes toward us. Fast work. You'd think they practiced this every day.

Daniels came parallel with me and wrapped his arm around me. "Are you okay?"

He pulled me a little closer than I thought necessary for a simple rescue. I relaxed against him. I could see the laughter in his eyes. "I'm better now than I was a minute ago."

Xavier cursed again. Nope, no one needed to rescue him.

We started back up toward the turtle, but it was a tedious process. I think Daniels had the idea that he would have to carry me. I had to convince him that I could climb any mountain if I had enough rope. Unfortunately, the discussion allowed Xavier to get to the top first. He held the advantage of bending over a woman hanging from a rope. I might fight, but if I let go, I'd fall. Daniels solved my problem by quickly hauling himself up and thrusting his body between Xavier and me. I dragged myself up over the edge and scrambled to my feet. I backed up, careful where I stepped. I didn't need another slide downward.

"Give me the gun." Xavier shoved Daniels out of

the way.

"No."

"You're outnumbered."

I shook my head and bared my teeth like a pit bull ready to brawl. I held up two fingers. "No. Just you and me. It's personal. You bounced me off a rock wall." *After I stabbed you in the knee—but what the hell.*

Daniels stood beside me, and Sanders stood behind and to the left of Xavier. I think the boys liked me, but when it came down to specific orders, they would obey him. At least they'd left the automatic rifle in the turtle. Xavier took another step and I moved back. Daniels made no effort to stop me. Good boy. It might have come to Xavier chasing me down, but it didn't. My monster sensors suddenly screamed a warning.

Werewolf.

Not the gentle bump from the mansion but an appalling shriek that shredded my nerves.

It must have shown on my face, because Xavier stopped.

"What's wrong?" he asked.

"Weres. More than one." I searched the area trying to determine their approach, where I could get my best shot. "Coming fast from behind us"

Xavier hesitated, and then shook his head. "No. You're stalling. Now give me the gun."

It didn't matter whether he believed me or not. I drew the Sparks. Danger closed the distance behind him. Three werewolves, all large males in full fur and fang, charged around the curve in the road.

Chapter Five

My actions, automatic, ingrained by years of discipline, kicked in. My heart rate rose to meet the instinctive reaction to fight or flee. My attention focused on the threat. The Sparks' accuracy range is only twenty feet with silvers, so I ran toward them. Striking the offensive with weres occasionally worked. They expect their victims to run away. Run away? No human can outrun a werewolf.

My first shot blasted the leader's chest open. *Go Sparks!* He staggered. Forward momentum carried him another ten feet before he collapsed. The second were was closer. He caught the silver in the stomach. He slammed face-down on the road, still alive, claws digging in the dirt. Two quick shots require time, and the third were went for the closest available body.

Sanders twisted in a hopeless attempt to ward off the attack. Three-inch teeth locked in his shoulder and four-inch claws slashed through his uniform. He screamed when those claws tore at his chest, digging for the heart. Precious seconds raced by as I stepped in close enough to kill the were and not hit Sanders. I already knew I'd have done Sanders a kindness if I *accidentally* killed him, too.

I pulled the trigger again. The silver sheared off the top of the monster's deformed head, blasting blood and brains to eternity. He reared up, arms flung out, and backpedaled over the edge of the road. He disappeared down the mountainside where Xavier and I had clung to the trees minutes ago.

Xavier and Daniels ran to Sanders. "Get the bag," Xavier ordered.

Even slightly deafened by gunshots, I heard in his voice what I already knew.

Sanders, so young and handsome, with all his life ahead of him, would be dead in minutes. I kept the Sparks ready, but I knelt beside him.

"Are there more?" Xavier asked.

I could feel a disturbance in the distance. "Yes. Not close."

Parr had spoken of my ability to psychically detect monsters. Had Xavier not believed him until I proved it?

I glanced at the paralyzed were. The second one I shot. Only one bullet in his stomach wasn't killing him fast. He still struggled against the venom of silver but was no longer a threat. Daniels returned with the medical supplies. He dropped to his knees and tore the case open. Xavier ignored it—nothing inside would save the boy.

"Maat," Sanders choked out as blood poured from his mouth. The bloody mass of his chest quivered as he gasped for air.

"I'm here." I knelt close beside him.

"Be...come.... were?"

"No, sweetheart. You won't become a were." I laid my hand on his cheek. I wouldn't cry. I'd spend a million tears on monster victims. I had no more of those in me.

"Kill..." He choked again. "Kill...for...me."

Sanders' back arched. His fingers scratched shallow furrows in the dirt road beneath him. His last breath escaped his lungs as he left this world.

I'd seen kills where weres had torn men and women apart and scattered the bloody remains across the yard like broken dolls. I'd helped bury half-eaten children. *Kill them for me, the survivors said. Kill them for my wife, my husband, my child.* And kill I did, until I could find no more to butcher.

I stood and walked to the paralyzed were. Brown fur ruffled in a slight breeze, and his dog-like muzzle wrinkled, and he bared his teeth. He growled—a rumble filled with blood. With a mouth never made for spoken words, he croaked, "Suriel."

I'd never heard a were in fang and fur speak before. Of course, I was smart enough not to give them the chance. My hands don't shake, but they did now when I aimed the barrel between his eyes and pulled the trigger. That shot exploded the loudest of all. I drew a deep breath and holstered the Sparks.

I turned to find Daniels behind me. Tears leaked from his eyes and ran down his cheeks.

"Weres killed my mother," he whispered.

"Mine too," I told him. "Daniels, I—"

"My name is Ty."

"Ty." I reached out and my fingers gently brushed his tears away. So much violence and hurt in our world. Had the monsters not come, my little brother Donnie would be close to Ty's age, almost a man.

Xavier knelt by Sanders, but his eyes gazed into the forest. After a moment, he rose, walked to the turtle, and came back with a blanket. He and Ty wrapped Sanders' body and placed him in the turtle's back hatch.

The radio up front beeped. Ty raced to it and picked up the earphones. After a few seconds, he turned to Xavier and me. "Back at the house…weres." He jumped in the driver's seat and started the engine. I climbed in the backseat, and Xavier went to the front. He checked the automatic rifle Ty had carried earlier. No silvers so it was almost useless.

The narrow road left no room to turn around. Ty backed up the mountain in reverse. Had to give the boy credit, he could drive looking over his shoulder.

"How much silver do you have?" Xavier asked me.

"Three clips of nine, minus four." Was he going to try to take my gun again? "Do the troops at the house have silver?"

He shook his head. "Is there any other way?"

I shrugged. "Fire."

"Fire." Xavier climbed between the seats and crawled into the hatch behind me. He lifted a full gas can from a compartment near the fender well. We had a weapon, but no way to deliver.

"Ty, did they say how many?" With a surprise attack, three or four werewolves could wipe out the troops at the house if they didn't have silver.

Ty's voice carried the strain of looking over his shoulder and twisting his body to drive. "Don't know. Transmission cut off too soon. They radioed headquarters for help, though."

Help? Parr said it was a three-hour drive up the mountain. Help would arrive too late.

Xavier cursed and climbed past me back to the front.

"Hey! Come on, guys. I'm the hunter. Get your guns and stand beside me. Lead will slow them down.

Give me time to aim. I'll kill the fuckers."

Ty grinned at me. Xavier muttered under his breath.

We came to a wider place in the road, and Ty jerked the wheel and whipped the turtle around. He rubbed what had to be a stiff neck. "About a mile to go. What next?"

"Stop the car." I glanced at Xavier. His gaze met mine, and I hoped he understood.

"What?" Ty frowned.

"Stop, put this thing in neutral, and set the brake." I approached each battle with the idea I was going to die. Having seen young Sanders slaughtered minutes ago, I'd try to save Ty.

Xavier understood. As soon as the turtle stopped, he jammed himself against Ty, opened the door, and shoved the boy out. Ty yelped and rolled as he hit the road. Xavier slammed the door, settled in the driver's seat, and released the brake.

"Stay here," he shouted out the window.

Ty ignored the order. He jumped to his feet and snatched at the door. Xavier thrust him away with one hand and threw the turtle into gear. I locked the back doors, so he couldn't get in that way, either. Then I climbed into the front seat. This strip of road had less incline and fewer holes, so we moved out faster than before.

The young soldier ran behind us. Ty kept up with us for a minute, screaming curses. That boy put wonderful obscenities together in a way I'd never heard, and he used a few words I didn't know. If I lived through the next hour, I'd have to have a little talk with him.

I thought I'd better ask. "So, Xavier, do you have a plan?"

"No." His voice was tight and furious. And yes, bitter. "You're the one-on-one werewolf expert. I haven't fought them in over ten years. I had silver and a militia behind me then."

I glanced over my shoulder. Ty raced after us. He'd stopped wasting his breath cursing.

"Okay," I said. "How about we soak this rolling casket in that gas. They usually gang up close together, at first, if surprised. Get as close as you can to them. We'll set this piece of junk on fire, and then jump out and shoot. If we keep our backs to the fire…shit! Do we have any matches?"

"No, but there's a flare gun kit back there."

"Wonderful. We can jump out *before* we light up." I wasn't sure of the effect of a flare on a werewolf, but it would ignite the gasoline.

I removed my jacket so I'd have free access to the Sparks. Then I crawled back and found the flare gun and shells. Maybe the odds wouldn't be too bad. *Not too bad.* That mantra had served me well in the past. Sometimes.

I opened the back hatch so the fumes wouldn't overwhelm us. The gas can top unscrewed, I turned it on its side. It would soak everything. Sanders' body would burn too, but I didn't think he would mind. We'd send him off in style.

I crawled back to my seat, opened the flare gun, and loaded it with a shell. I reached over and stuffed the other shells in Xavier's fatigue shirt pocket. Steady breathing, no excessive tension, I didn't like him, but I did admire his nerve. And his amazing ability to adapt to an unusual situation. To *actually admit* that I knew more about werewolves than he did made the man resilient. He saw me as a warrior, not a woman. I'm drawn to strength like his. But he drew me from the first moment I saw him. Why did he have to be such an ass?

We came around the last curve. The jump-out would have a hard landing, but I wasn't a virgin with those. At least ten weres gathered together near the front house.

"Damn it! Damn it to hell!" The words exploded from Xavier.

It stunned me too much to speak. How were there so many when everyone believed they'd become extinct? Would I have caught on to a resurgence if I hadn't hidden at Avalon?

Bloody, black uniformed bodies littered the yard. At least I didn't see Anolia's lying among them. The surviving troops had climbed the steel lookout tower, and I prayed she was there too.

One trooper must have had werewolf experience, because small piles of burning material lay scattered around the tower's base. Dropping burning clothing on weres would discourage them—for a while.

Okay. We needed a plan. Sort of. "Those in a bunch over there. By the house. Can you ram them? We'll do them first."

"Yes." Xavier's bleak expression said he understood the odds. He steered the turtle toward the house. The automatic rifle Ty had held earlier lay between the seats. He drew it over his knee and between his legs. It didn't have silvers, but he could slow them down for me—if we survived the leap.

Two hundred feet.

I opened my door and he did the same. Like most weres in full fang and fur, these weren't too bright. When they saw the turtle coming at them, they drew closer together in a pack.

One hundred feet.

I tightened my grip on the Sparks. Xavier picked up the flare gun.

Fifty feet. We jumped.

I hit the ground hard but rolled to my feet. Blood leaked from my elbow, and outrageous pain spiked in my hip and shoulder. The turtle plowed into the weres straight on. It smashed into and over at least four before it crashed into the house's front door. It also carried two on the hood into the collision.

On his knees, Xavier fired the flare gun. It popped like a firecracker in the back hatch. The turtle exploded. Hot air gave us a punishing slap and flames swelled into an inferno. It engulfed everything around the turtle with licking orange tongues and whirls of billowing black smoke.

The four weres left standing near the house headed our way.

Xavier struggled with the flare gun. His fingers fumbled trying to reload. His left arm didn't seem to be working right. My first shot cut the closest were down. The other three stopped. They hesitated.

My partner in death finished reloading. He aimed, pulled the trigger, and I learned that I should add a flare gun to my arsenal. The flare hit the were mid-chest—and stuck. He brushed it away. His hair kept burning. He snapped his jaws. Clawed hands beat at the flames. He gave up and ran howling toward the woods. The other two followed him and in an instant, they moved out of the Sparks' range. No point in wasting silvers.

Xavier managed to stand, but he clutched his arm close to his body.

"Are you okay?" I'm always polite to people who help me kill weres.

He nodded. Otherwise, he ignored me. His attention was on the black uniformed bodies lying around. I'd bet he was the kind of leader who knew each one personally. The kind who would count each loss as the loss of family. Uncle Jake was one of those. He'd told me stories of brave men and women under his command.

I looked up and saw Ty running toward us, waving his arms and shouting. I caught three words—ammo, powder, and backseat. Xavier must have heard him too, because we raced away from the burning house at the exact same moment. We made it to a shallow ditch fifty feet away. I went down, and Xavier threw himself on top of me, covering me with his own heavy frame.

I twisted and tried to get away. "What the fuck are you doing?"

"Shut up and be still." His ground out words, ragged in my ear.

The turtle exploded. The heated blast sent pieces of metal and burning wood whisked and whistled over our prone bodies. A second deeper explosion came from inside the house. When a reasonable calm returned, I shoved Xavier off and forced myself to sit up.

The president's summer home burned like what it was—an outstanding funeral pyre for young Sanders. It shuddered and groaned. The supports underneath had to give way under the assault. A whirlwind of smoke raced into the sky as the unburned timbers of the building snapped. It slowly collapsed inward and began the inevitable descent down the mountainside. Last night's rain should thwart a forest fire.

Ty staggered up and dropped to his knees beside me. He gasped for air. "That…shitty…do to me."

"Sure was. Deceitful, devious, sneaky—and dastardly." This charming boy was alive and uninjured. I pushed him away when he tried to help me stand, so he went to Xavier. Anolia ran up to me as I rose. She slammed into me and almost knocked me down as she wrapped me in her arms.

Xavier embraced Ty with his good arm and Ty hugged him back. I saw expression and a taut embrace of pure love and relief. Only a moment, but not your usual commanding officer/young soldier relationship. So, that's the way it was with Colonel Xavier. He preferred the boy. That *wasn't* disappointment I felt. It was the cool-down reaction to a chaotic dangerous event.

An odd thumping sound filled the air, like a giant beating on a drum. I seemed to be the only one surprised as the helicopter rose from the valley below. How incredible. I'd never seen any machine that could fly except in books or Uncle Jake's photos. They hadn't survived the war and military deconstruction.

"Go." Anolia hissed the word in my ear. "I'll be okay. For the love of God, go now."

She released me while everyone's eyes were on the flying tin can. I'm sure it fascinated them, even if they'd seen it before. I stepped back and slipped away into the woods. A shame to leave my guns behind, but I had the Sparks. Once I got a head start, I'd bet they couldn't track me. I found a nice little animal trail— I whirled and snatched out the Sparks. Something crashed through the woods behind me. Another werewolf? No.

"Maat." Ty called out.

Shit! Just what I didn't need.

"I want to go with you. I want to learn how to kill weres and—"

"No! And if you—"

The biggest, blackest werewolf I'd ever seen rose out of the brush behind Ty and grabbed him by the shoulders. *This was not one of the weres we'd chased away from the house.* With my monster sensors on overload from close contact, I'd rushed right by him. I aimed the Sparks in an instant, but the were held Ty between us. Ty's eyes widened as he stared at the claws clamped on his arms.

We stood there, frozen. Things got worse. Three more weres, two males and—that rarist of creatures—a female with fur as auburn as Anolia's hair, stepped soundlessly out of the woods. The males started forward but stopped at a growling bark from the female.

"Suriel." The female's rough growl came through her fangs. Her yellow eyes bore a look of intelligence I'd never seen in her kind before. My only vision of weres involved ripping, tearing beasts. Now I stood surrounded by four who made no move to attack. "Suriel." The female spoke again.

I aimed the Sparks at her. "What do you want?"

In all my life, I never dreamed I'd speak to a werewolf. The weres I'd killed on the road and at the house behaved in a typical manner—these did not. The female said another word I didn't understand.

Bodies crashed through the forest above us. Xavier had missed us and sent the troops. The weres whirled and disappeared into the forest down the mountainside. Suddenly released, Ty staggered and fell to his knees, then face planted in the dirt.

I ran to him. "Are you okay?"

He shook his head and grinned. The day's violence hadn't taught him a damned thing.

The troops arrived and surrounded us. They held their guns ready, but seemed unsure where to point them, especially with Ty so close. I holstered the Sparks and steadied him as he struggled to his feet.

"I'm sorry," he said softly. "I just wanted to go with you."

We trudged back up the hill surrounded by the troops. The day that began with a cool morning after a rain had pushed to an after-battle swelter. Sweat pooled under my arms and on my neck. Ty stayed close to me, as if he thought I might break and run again. I would, but not today.

God gave birds and butterflies wings. I doubt he ever meant werewolf hunters should fly. This one damned sure wasn't. Probably the only operating helicopter in the world, and—lucky me—it belonged to the president who'd made me a prisoner.

They wanted me to fly to New Washington, and Maat Ferris always kept both feet on the ground— unless tossed at a wall. "No. Get another turtle. Or I'll walk."

"It's not bad." Anolia appeared disappointed I hadn't escaped but tried to soothe me. "I flew up here with you. You slept, but—"

"That's enough of this shit!" Xavier marched up.

Hot damn. Another fight. His arm was in a sling. He also limped, favoring the leg I'd stabbed. Wonderful, I might have a chance. I smiled and whirled to meet him head on.

Three of the black uniformed troops jumped me from behind. Sneaky Colonel Xavier certainly had that planned. One on each arm and the third grabbed the Sparks.

Time jumbled and danced as it always does when I fight. I broke a nose. It flattened under my fist. My boot made a respectable impression on two sets of balls before multiple arms hauled me up and slammed me to the ground.

Gravel cut into my face, but when they rolled me over, I filled multiple eyes with a handful of dirt. Overwhelming odds, but I had one advantage. They were trying *not* to seriously injure me.

The melee ended with me cuffed at the wrists and ankles and in considerable pain. The ribs Xavier had fractured at Avalon protested every movement. My right eye swelled shut because one of the troopers I'd kicked in the balls slugged me after they cuffed me.

I lay on the ground, my head cradled in Anolia's lap. She cried while she bathed my eye with a cool rag and wiped my mouth as I drooled out nasty mouthfuls of Virginia soil. I could see and hear Ty argue with Xavier. How amazing. This boy liked me to the point of defying orders. And Xavier accepted that defiance stoically, without a word of censure.

I made the best of my respite until they picked me up and loaded me in the helicopter like a side of beef. Xavier refused to allow either Anolia or Ty to go with me, which was fine in a way. They didn't get dirty when I vomited. The helicopter held eight, and they had strapped me in a middle seat. Anolia had made sure I'd eaten a hearty breakfast earlier. I slung my head and put plenty of energy in heaving. I decorated quite a few. I hit Xavier too, and he sat up front. Of course, I leaned sideways to have better aim.

A were knocked me off a bridge once. It saved my life because I was losing the fight. I remember the sensation of falling before I hit the water. That's my impression of a helicopter ride—harrowing, falling forever. If Xavier wanted to torture me, all he had to do was keep me in the air. The flight finally did end. The vomiting, too, by way of an empty stomach. I kept gagging and the disorientation stayed with me. The troops hauled me out of the copter and tried to walk me across the tarmac toward a limo. My legs kept giving way and they gave up and carried me.

"No! Get a truck." Xavier issued the command. He sounded irritated. I wonder why.

The truck had a covered back with benches for hauling troops. My maltreatment continued. They hoisted me in, and after a while, the sound of other vehicles told me we'd rolled through town. I couldn't see because I lay face down on the floor with several combat boots firmly planted on my body. I struggled occasionally, but the boot pressure jammed down and I couldn't breathe. That worked. Every time the truck hit a bump, a fresh wave of anguish racked my body. Losing my breakfast left me dehydrated, but Xavier fixed that when we reached our destination.

I'd never been to New Washington, at least while I was awake and not under the influence of drugs. I'd seen pictures. The precisely manicured bright green lawn stretched out from a multistoried brick building that had to be the presidential mansion. So formal, so fastidious, I longed for the forest.

"Hold her." Xavier commanded. Like they were doing anything else. I figured he had a wicked deed in the works, and he confirmed my suspicion when the bone chilling water hit. I don't mind being wet, but having the bastard hose me down like a yard dog who tangled with a skunk—oh, I would make him pay for that evil act.

Once finished, they lifted me to face him. He was safe enough, since the previously attached cuffs still secured my hands and feet. Bruised and battered, if they weren't holding me, I'd have collapsed.

I hurt. God, I hurt.

Xavier came in close. His mouth twisted in a sneering smile. The wicked furious gaze that had glared at me across the table in Avalon sparked with vengeance. "The Angel of Death doesn't look so tough now, does she? You're right about one thing. I know a bitch when I see one."

A little water had worked wonders in rehydration. I spit in his face.

Xavier's hand shot out, and his fingers locked in my hair. He twisted. I'm resilient, but that was one pain too many. I didn't scream. A wretched moan was all I could manage. The abuse finally overwhelmed me. I sagged in their hands.

My mind spun near the edge of unconsciousness for a moment, but when it cleared, I found myself staring at a vastly different man. Unadulterated horror filled this Xavier's face. He backed up a couple of steps, then turned and staggered away.

"Bring her," he called over his shoulder.

I struggled. It's my nature. I fight as long and as hard as I'm able. In a futile gesture, I tried to plant my feet for resistance. Up marble steps, inside, across a polished wood floor, carpet, doors, it all slid by in a blur. The troops picked me up and dropped me, sopping wet, in a large, soft chair. Two of them clamped a hand on each shoulder so I couldn't rise. A joke I guess, since I couldn't walk, let alone run away.

Not far away, Xavier stood toe-to-toe with a tall, thin, fair-haired man who had to be President Aaron Gannett. The few newspaper photos I'd seen made him look older.

It was to my advantage and Xavier's detriment for me to play the victim.

I moaned and struggled against the cuffs and hands holding me. Swollen eye and lip, scrapes and cuts, torn clothing, soaking wet, you bet I made a wretched sight. I didn't have to pretend to shiver.

Gannett left Xavier and came to kneel beside me. Xavier limped after him, and shouted, "Not so close, she's—"

"Shut up." Gannett yelled over his shoulder. Damn, he looked worried.

Play the game Maat.

I let my teeth chatter. "Xavier hurt me. Help me. Please."

It didn't ease the pain, but I drew comfort from the chaos unfolding around me. Gannett screamed at Xavier, and Xavier roared back. Moderately gentle hands removed the cuffs and wrapped me in a blanket.

One of those hands held a fucking needle. The last thing I remembered was Lowell Parr's handsome, elegant face hovering over me. He smiled. I hadn't fooled him. His voice was barely above a whisper. "Maat Ferris, you are an evil, evil woman."

****

I woke up with Anolia holding my hand. She sighed and shook her head. "This is getting to be a habit. What am I going to do with you?"

I licked my lips to work up a little saliva. "It wasn't my idea."

She helped me sit up and propped pillows under my back. At least I was clean. I couldn't help but wonder who had washed and dressed me. I ached, but it wasn't bad. I did worry about the drugs pumped in my body so often. They'd dressed me in pants and shirt this time, instead of a ventilated gown. This room contained more practical furniture and not the antique horror of my first presidential mansion accommodations.

Anolia sat close beside me and gently brushed my swollen face. "That's going to turn a pretty shade of purple."

"Yeah, then dirty yellow. Drugged me again." The black room windows spoke to it being night. "How long have I been out?"

"About ten hours. It's nine o'clock now. How do you feel?"

"I'll live." At least until I ran into Xavier again. The door opened, and Parr walked in. I know he's the vice president, but he should have knocked. He settled by Anolia on the side of the bed.

"Aaron—the president—would like to talk to you in the morning. Do you feel up to that? He's furious with Xavier. I don't think I've ever seen him quite that angry."

"Will Mr. President tell me what's going on?"

"I presume he will." He grasped Anolia's hand. His eyes held the look of a man in love, but I caught an impression of fear. Possibly, because she was a hostage for my agreeable behavior, and he was afraid he couldn't protect her.

****

Aaron Gannett studied his vice president, who relaxed on the other side of the desk. A shrewd analytical mind worked behind Parr's pleasant face. Gannett had reliable sources of information, but Parr had resources he couldn't touch.

The once comfortable study grew smaller and more suffocating each day. He had often come here to relax, read, and remove himself from the madness of the power he'd gathered. Now he wanted nothing more than a night that swiftly passed on to the safety of sunrise.

Xavier entered the room and sat in the chair beside Parr.

"Well." Gannett's mouth twisted. "At least you didn't do as much damage this time, Colonel."

Xavier didn't speak.

Gannett nodded for Parr to begin his report.

Parr offered several sheets of paper across the desk and said, "I've received information from reliable sources, but the real Maat Ferris is elusive as ever. Not sure where or when she was born, but Anolia says she's twenty-nine. She grew up on an AG commune in North Georgia. We know nothing about her father. He left the family about the time she was born. A were attack, she was ten or eleven years old, killed her mother, stepfather, and brother. The Southern Militia files thoroughly documented the incident in reports and photos. There were a few survivors, mostly children hidden by their parents, and she wasn't among them. Next place she shows up is at her uncle's in the Western Pennsylvania mountains. We have no idea how she made it there."

"What about the uncle? The one who raised her." Gannett cursed to himself. He'd allowed himself to accept information from one source, and thanks to Parr, he'd discovered that source wasn't always truthful. No small part of that information came from stories Maat herself told. Now he raced to gather bits and pieces of her life and arrange them like a bizarre puzzle.

Parr turned another paper. "Jackson Holder Ferris, known as Bull Head Ferris in the Army, and Crazy Jake the last twenty years of his life. Army Special Forces in the war, weapons specialist. Wife of many years, Eleanor, once a college professor. No children. Eleanor died of cancer in 2057. After that, his instability increased. I have an interesting firsthand account of how he died. Would you…?"

"By all means." Gannett refilled his glass from a bottle of Tennessee bourbon sitting on the desk in front of him. Parr sipped from his single glass, and Xavier, of course, refused to drink. Gannett had long since given up trying to make a dent in Xavier's taut nature. What worried him was his Chief of Security's sudden inability to control his temper. It was as if Maat Ferris had driven him mad.

Parr lifted his papers. "You remember your presidential predecessors' devotion to destroying and hiding the remaining weapons in the country? Crazy Jake discovered a massive underground arms bunker in southern Pennsylvania. The likely source was the old Letterkenny Army Depot. He used it and his Special Forces training to educate our marvelous werewolf hunter. Her aunt greatly contributed to her formal education. She is impulsive, and while she does, at times, act ignorant and uncultured, she is neither. Her actions, her performances, are just another weapon for her."

Gannett sighed. He'd long since given up hope of finding such a weapons cache like the one the uncle had.

Parr continued. "Maat joined the Freak Squad after her aunt died. She was sixteen. Jake lied about her age, told them she was eighteen. She was nineteen when the Northern Militia discovered Jake's weapons hoard. She'd been away and returned and had to watch Jake and five acres of Mother Earth get blasted to brown powder. There was a damaging rain of rocks involved, too.

"My informant said she begged the militia commander to let her go talk to her uncle before it happened, but the commander, Russel Jenks, refused. He took her prisoner and raped her." Parr frowned and pulled out three photographs and handed them to Gannett.

"God damn," Gannett muttered.

"Indeed. That's what was left of Jenks when they found him secured with silver-coated chains carefully covering the vital areas. He was staked out in front of a den of completely regressive werewolves who never took human form. Tourniquets at his shoulders and hips kept him from bleeding to death while they ate him.

"After they finished with the arms and legs, they

had to dig the rest out through gaps in the chains. At some point he would have gone into shock, but the doctor's report said Russell Jenks was probably conscious through a good part of the beasts' meal."

Gannett huffed out a breath of skepticism. "Don't be so sure it was her, Lowell. It sounds likely, but I knew Russell Jenks and he had more than one enemy." He glanced at Xavier who met his eyes straight on. Gannett offered him the photos. Xavier shook his head.

"Oh, Jenks had enemies." Parr chuckled softly. "I heard there were a number of celebrations when news of his spectacular demise—and these photos—circulated. However, that entire were pack was slaughtered within days after they finished their Jenks meal."

Parr lifted another paper and laughed softly. "These are official records. She didn't last long in the Freak Squad. In the spirit of youthful fun, Privates Maat Ferris, Ajax Sanuri, and Cormac McClellan, placed a dead werewolf in the commanding officer's private bathroom. Unfortunately, the commander's staff assistant discovered it first. The staff assistant fled from the building in such terror she neglected to don her clothing. The first person she ran into on the way out was the commander's wife, who immediately discerned the true nature of the situation.

"McClellan was reported to be Maat's lover. He died in a major attack. She suffered serious injuries in the same battle, but she managed to kill all the weres before she went down."

"What else?" Gannett had a keen interest in how the woman's mind worked.

Parr smiled and drained his whiskey glass. "The

same conflict. She's a saint, a whore, or both, depending on who's talking. Everyone agrees she's spectacular at killing werewolves, and she's respectable in an old-fashioned fist fight." He cut his eyes at Xavier. "Once she commits herself, she's considered loyal. She keeps her word. There are significant gaps in the report because she can come and go without detection. Were it not for her loyalty to Anolia, I'm sure she could have escaped from Avalon and the mountain house."

"And what does your lady friend say?" Gannett had Anolia brought to New Washington to use as a lever and it backfired. Many of the town's beautiful young women had invited the charming vice president into their beds. How was Gannett to know he'd succumb to a woman his own age?

"Anolia betrays no one's confidence." Tension ridged Parr's voice.

Gannett turned his attention to Xavier. "You and the bitch almost killed each other at the commune. You hurt her, though not as seriously, today."

"It won't happen again," Xavier said.

He wanted to believe him. Gannett still needed Xavier, but occasionally, he couldn't remember why. Often, he couldn't remember many things he was sure he should have known.

After Xavier and Parr left, Gannett gathered the report and photos, stuffed them in Maat's growing file, and locked it in the desk drawer. No point in getting distracted by the woman's adventures. They might be interesting, but she was a critical tool, nothing more. She'd do quite well. Unless Xavier killed her first.

Chapter Six

Anolia refused to leave, so I woke with her beside me. For the first time in a long time, I thought about my mother. I'd slept with her until she married my stepfather. I didn't like him because he made her cry at times during the night. Mama would come to my room mornings though, and we would talk, mostly about what life would be like when I grew up. How we had hope for our violent world, hope for safety and a better life.

The first hints of gray wove through Anolia's auburn hair, and tiny lines outlined her mouth. I'd never noticed them before. She opened her eyes.

"Good morning." She smiled like an angel. Her fingers touched my face. "The swelling's almost gone. I have a salve to cover the bruises."

This woman had humbled me. In a time of despair and self-loathing she'd found something in me worth saving. "Anolia, I always wanted to ask you...I never had the nerve...why did you let me stay at Avalon? I'm so different from all the others. Crazy, disruptive... dangerous. The first person I met when I arrived on the mountain was Elaine. She told me to leave. I turned to go, and she stopped me. I don't know why. Then she went to get you."

"I remember it very well." Anolia laid a hand on my cheek. "Elaine's exact words to me were, 'There is a woman and she wants to stay. I'm afraid of her.' "

"I should have covered my guns."

"No, love. It wasn't your guns. Elaine is eighty-nine years old. She's a tough old lady who's lived through war and plague. Guns don't bother her. A purely religious woman, she said the devil had your soul clutched in his hand. That frightened her."

Oh, yes, fierce decisive Elaine. "What did you think?"

"When I saw you, I was afraid, too. You literally reeked of power and violence. Guilt and sorrow weighed upon you so heavily I wondered how you lived. Avalon was the work of a lifetime for me. I was deeply concerned you'd destroy everything."

"But I did. They came for me and now everything's changed."

"No, Maat. Like Elaine, I feared you, but then I became more afraid of what would happen to you, and my world, if I turned you away. Now look at this situation. I can't see the future like Christopher, but here in this place, in this time, you are playing a dangerous, world changing game with powerful, brutal men. *You have no idea how formidable you are.*"

"Maybe I just needed a rest. At Avalon I rested."

"Perhaps." Anolia bit her lip then said, "When you finally learned to trust me, you said you were evil, vicious, and a wretched excuse for a human being. You told me things you'd done. You spoke of your failures, for which you carried a great unjust burden." Anolia stroked my cheek with fingers made rough from farm work. *"You are not evil. You're ferocious, whether you love or hate. You have a brutal sense of justice, a massive ego, and the courage of a lion."*

"So, does that mean I'm okay? I'm okay for you?"

Anolia's eyes said more than words. I wrapped my arms around her—for a few precious moments.

I was supposed to officially meet with the president soon. My first encounter, yesterday, pinned down by soldiers and soaking wet lasted only a few seconds. A man in a black uniform and white eagle patch brought us breakfast an hour later.

Fortunately, most of the wardrobe she'd optimistically purchased for me while I was in a coma had not gone to the mountain house when they took me there.

She had me decked out in soft, honey-colored pants and a cream blouse. A blouse, not a shirt, made of material, not sheer, but far softer and more unsubstantial than anything I would have chosen. The fabric molded to my breasts. Did she think it would make me seem less aggressive—or turn him on? That way he might not kill me?

Anolia slathered sweet-smelling oil on my hair and brushed it until it had as much shine as coarse, curly brown hair could have. She pinned the curls up, then let them fall across one shoulder. I had it cut super short when I arrived at Avalon and would have kept it that way, especially working on a farm. She and others persuaded me to let it grow. Good thing I guess, since it let me hide the knife I used to stab Xavier. That was good—wasn't it?

"You look lovely." She tugged on a curl and let it spring back.

"Acceptable. I look acceptable. I know what I look like."

"You are not unattractive Maat. You are rare,

exotic, unique."

I tried to draw the line at make-up, but she insisted on painting my mouth a rich amber color. I gave in since I could lick it off before I got where I was going.

"Thank you for staying with me last night," I said. "Did the VP mind?"

"I don't sleep with him, Maat. He's asked me to marry him, and I might, once I get to know him better. There's no rush. For me, anyway. I'm cautious for a reason. I told him I will take no personal action until your issues are resolved."

"Oh. Sorry." Celibacy wasn't required at Avalon. She knew all about Christopher and me.

"Maat, my life is not like yours. You've lived with danger so much you're quite right to take pleasure when and where you can. If that troubled me, I'd have run a convent, not a commune."

"Have you met the president?"

Anolia shook her head. "Not yet. And that's probably for the best. I was informed that it was his idea to rudely summon you—and me."

I started to suggest that her precious Lowell wasn't completely innocent. I decided it wouldn't make a dent in true love. If it wasn't true love, Anolia was smart enough to figure things out on her own.

****

Parr came and led me into the hallway. Two armed troopers stood at attention on the opposite wall, and I figured they had been there all night. Black fatigues and an eagle patch on the pocket—Xavier's men. Each had an Aries in a tactical holster strapped to his thigh, and an automatic rifle in hand.

We walked down a hallway to an elevator.

Mattress-soft carpet lined the hallways and tugged at my feet. "Your room is on the fourth floor." Parr spoke as the door closed. "Most of the guards are on the first and second floors." That sounded like a warning. "The soldiers in the brown uniforms are regular army. Those in black are Xavier's handpicked troops. I think you've realized there is a vast difference in skill—and whom they serve."

Black shirt, brown shirt, I didn't like any of them. Thanks to Aunt Nell, I knew my history and the implication of their description.

President Aaron Gannett greeted us when the elevator door opened on the second floor. Two more of Xavier's armed black shirts, both women, narrow-eyed and alert, stood behind him.

Gannett's intense ash gray eyes studied me. I suppressed the urge to shiver. This thin, angular man wore a mask of civility, but inside…details would come later.

"Maat." Gannett gave me a thin-lipped smile.

"Mr. President."

"I'm glad you weren't seriously injured yesterday. You looked and sounded bad in the brief moments I saw you. But I'm told you helped with a spectacular defense."

I didn't know if he was talking about my battle with Xavier over the helicopter or the weres at the mountain house, so I said, "Sorry about your house."

He waved a dismissive hand. I don't think he gave a shit about the house. My body stiffened. I turned, scanning the area around me. Werewolf. Close…but not deadly close. My hand rubbed my side where the Aries should have been.

"What's wrong," Gannett asked.

"A were pretending to be human. In the building or right outside."

"Let's go, Maat." Gannett nodded to his left. "You can deal with it later."

I looked away as the implication sank in. He had not questioned my monster detection ability. Not only did the President of the United States have a werewolf in his home, he sanctioned its presence. I bit my lip, and for once, kept my mouth shut.

We walked a short distance and stopped at one of the multitude of doors lining this hallway. The floor here was slick polished wood, not carpet. Gannett opened a door and ushered Parr and me inside. The two black shirted guards took up position on the opposite wall facing the door.

Three walls of books reached to the high ceiling of the room we entered, and nubby brown rugs spotted the polished wood floors. Two slate-blue couches and two chairs centered the room, but nothing changed the cold unsociability, especially with small, high windows striped with steel bars set into one wall. One-way in, one-way out. Library? Well, it did have books.

Gannett moved closer to me than I liked anyone to be without an invitation. He grasped my arm above my elbow. Brown age spots I associated with a much older man dotted the parchment skin covering his bony fingers. My nostrils flared. He had the faint odor of something familiar. Some uncomfortable scent I knew but couldn't pin down.

Gannett's fingers tightened. "Before we begin, Maat, I want us to have an understanding. Do you know how many assasination attempts I've survived in the last ten years?"

"Never heard of any." Not true. I'd heard rumors from people I trusted.

"There have been twelve. My very competent Chief of Security foiled them all."

"Good thing I never tried to kill you. Right?" I cocked my head and grinned. Score one for my ego.

"Maat, you need to understand." Gannett's fingers tightened to the point of bone bruising pain. "Do you know what it means to be a dictator?" A thin smile turned his mouth. His eyes twinkled.

"Yeah. It means you can perform numerous evil deeds until someone knocks the king off the hill."

"Exactly. Now, if you were in my position, and a renegade infiltrated a few secure army bases, stole precious equipment, and sold it on the black market, helped deserting troops cross the Mississippi, and—"

"Maybe you should hire that renegade to guard your vice president so no one will stick a gun in his ear again."

Gannett's eyes widened for a second, and then he relaxed and released my arm. "Maat, when you catch a werewolf, do you put it in a cage, or kill it?"

"Kill it."

"Well, that's what I do to people who cause me problems."

I wanted to step back, but I didn't. I desperately wanted to kill him. It interested me, though, that he felt the need to begin any dealings we might have with an *or else* warning. A smarter man would have begun gently. Elicit cooperation, and then if it didn't work, use the whip.

Gannett frowned and glanced at his watch. "Wait

here." He quickly released me and walked to the door. That left me alone with Parr.

Parr sat on one of the couches. "Come sit by me." He patted the cushion next to him.

I walked over and sat. He reached out and grasped my hand, then turned it over in his. His fingers traced the calluses earned with years of farm work, plus drawing and shooting practice.

"You spit in the tiger's eye," he said.

"No. Not a tiger. He's the one who orders the tiger to attack. He wouldn't get his hands bloody. Something's wrong with him, though. Yeah, he's a psychopath but…something else is off. It's familiar, but I can't pin it down."

Parr ignored my statement. "Anolia loves you. People don't usually heed unrequested advice, but for her sake, you're going to get mine. This world is changing, Maat, and you must change—if you want to survive. You're quick, intelligent, and extraordinarily resourceful, but your single-minded obsession may destroy you if you don't open your eyes and see what's happening. You've made killing werewolves an art form. It's set you apart." Parr squeezed my hand. "Tell me, what do you do when you think you're walking into a trap?"

"The unexpected. Change the plan, make different moves, run away." I understood his warning, but I suspected the trap already had me. "I guess running away isn't an option."

"No. If it were, I'd grab Anolia and go with you."

Do the unexpected, change the plan…how? I had no idea what I would be facing.

The president returned. Xavier followed him.

Gannett spoke to Parr first. "Lowell, will you excuse us, please."

Parr froze for an instant, then he nodded pleasantly and left the room. But not before I caught a flash of concern in his eyes.

Gannett and Xavier sat in chairs across from me. Gannett leaned back and relaxed. Xavier did not. He remained as stiff and ready to strike as always. Eyes focused directly on me, he almost dared me to try a foolhardy act of violence.

"Suriel. Angel of Death." Gannett's mouth pursed like he was going to kiss someone. "Isn't that what they call you?"

"Who calls me that? Weres? I don't listen to fucking monsters. Do you?"

Gannett clasped his hands together and shook his head. "I'd hoped to reason with you."

"You want to reason with me? Give me my guns. I'll play nice then." A totally brazen lie. I'm malicious even when I'm armed—especially when I'm armed.

Gannett's bogus *trying to be nice* persona disappeared. "I know you're not a patient woman."

"I'm patient—when I'm waiting to kill."

Xavier's breath hissed through his teeth.

Gannett glared at me. "Maat, you're here for a reason."

"And that reason is?" I held out my hands as if in expectation of an answer. It didn't come.

The president went on with his speech. "Unfortunately, the person who was supposed to be here, to speak with you, explain things, has not arrived. I learned only moments ago that he's delayed. A bit of patience on both our parts is required. I want to personally reassure you—"

"Fuck! Personally threaten me."

"You're a peculiarly elemental person, aren't you? Very well. I'll be more specific. I have a file on you. It's four inches thick and full of truth, outright lies, and fairy tales. You're an expert at getting into tight places, killing, and getting out. They called it guerilla warfare in the twentieth century. You've applied it quite successfully to werewolves—and to me. I'd say it's earned you a firing squad many times over." He spoke slowly, sounding so sincere. "And such criminal charges could cover Anolia Dupree for harboring a fugitive."

The threat, always understood, had become more blatant. I liked it better that way. No cozy vice president to soften blows. And no sudden moves. Killing this man would take a cool head and quick hand. It wouldn't happen in the next five minutes. Especially with Xavier sitting there staring as if he could control me by his will alone.

I shrugged. "And you want me to…?"

"Wait."

Sure I would. I nodded to let him think everything was cool. And all the time I waited, I'd be looking for ways to escape. I'd also try to think of a way to do my country a favor and kill this son-of-a-bitch of a dictator before he killed me.

"I think you understand me, Maat. I won't pretend to understand you. I would prefer your cooperation, so I'm not going to lock you in a cage. But, if one of the guards tells you not to go somewhere, don't go."

I nodded again. I smiled…sort of smiled. He should have started with that proposal, not the threats.

A sense of wrong surfaced again. Was I sensing an illness or an injury? A man didn't rise to his level with the perplexing manner he'd shown me. It could be an act, but he wasn't playing it well. This was, by rumor, for all his evil, an intelligent and focused man.

"That's not a good idea." Xavier spoke in a low angry tone.

Did he want me locked up? Put me in a cage. Interesting. I couldn't stop myself, even if I'd barely recovered from my last encounter. I perked up and grinned at him. "What's the matter, *perro*? Worried I'll get past you—again."

Xavier's eyes narrowed. His face formed that, *I'm going to kill you* look, that I was getting used to. He jumped up and reached for me.

"Xavier!" Gannett shouted. Too late. I dropped to roll. Not soon enough. Xavier's hand clamped on the back of my neck. Why did I always underestimate his speed? I jerked forward, twisted sideways. I escaped the hand, but fingers latched onto the fine soft blouse Anolia had me wear. It tore and buttons popped on the front. In a desperate and reflexive motion, I shrugged my arms out of the garment to escape. Damn, why did the room have so much fucking furniture? I tripped and flopped to the floor, face down. I rolled over and scooted backward, while trying to hold my arms over my breasts.

I'm not shy. I'd once stood on a table in a Memphis bar and stripped naked when I lost a bet. Almost naked—I kept my guns. I had no weapons now, and the rare and unpleasant sensation of vulnerability surged through me.

Xavier stared at me as if he'd found a werewolf

under his bed. Gannett's eyes were wide, and his mouth open. They'd seen the savage, intricate chevron pattern of deep red burn scars across my entire back. *Appalling but artistic*, a former lover had once called them.

Xavier quickly unbuttoned and stripped off his black fatigue shirt. He dropped to his knees beside me and draped it over my shoulders. His bright white T-shirt stood out against darker skin and thick muscles. In one smooth movement, he wrapped his arms around me and lifted both of us to our feet.

I wasn't thinking about fighting then, because Xavier's presence overwhelmed me. Not just his considerable size, but he had a sweet scent, masculine but clean and fresh. His chest rose and fell against me as he breathed. If I laid my cheek against his throat, as I had when I passed out in the hallway, I could feel his heartbeat and...my body stiffened. This couldn't happen.

He released me. Overwhelmed, I said, "Some scars show, Xavier. Some don't."

It troubled me that I found myself thinking of him from a woman's perspective, especially given his obvious personal relationship with the boy, Ty. Damn, I can usually read people better than that. Xavier nodded and looked away.

"Maat...who?" The president reached out a hand to me.

I stepped back. I drew Xavier's shirt tighter around me, as if I could use it as a shield. "New York vampires play rough, Mr. President."

Gannett continued to stare, but I don't think he saw me. I think his mind turned inward to a place where all the clues in a mystery fell into place. Not a good sign.

I carefully slipped my arms in Xavier's shirt. As I did, I suddenly realized that, like werewolves and vamps, I'd sense Xavier's presence anywhere within my psychic range. Why? I glanced his way and wondered if…no, it wasn't possible. Had he somehow marked me, too? He anticipated my actions, but he might just be skillful at reading body language. *How in the name of God or the devil had this impossible situation come about?*

Xavier left the room without a word.

Chapter Seven

Parr escorted me back to my room where Anolia, pale and obviously terrified, walked the floor and waited. He had returned to the library immediately when Gannett called him, so I knew he hadn't gone far. The vice president asked no questions about me wearing Xavier's shirt. He simply seemed grateful that I'd survived the encounter. Anolia started to ask but stopped when I shook my head. I didn't want to talk about it yet. She dug through a seemingly bottomless closet and found me a more practical T-shirt, and thank God, a pair of jeans. Under other circumstances, my surrogate mom would probably have my ass covered with silk and lace. My Aunt Eleanor managed to educate me in proper behavior, even if I rarely succumbed to such. Uncle Jake's training, however, negated any ideas she might have had about making me a dress-up doll.

I removed and laid Xavier's black shirt on the bed. The fabric, rough as a penitent's hair robe, slid through my fingers. I'm drawn to power, and Xavier was as powerful a man as any I'd seen in years. Too bad he preferred a young pretty boy. I'd bet he had reserves buried deep, ready to rise when needed, and he was excellent for a fight when I got bored.

At least the werewolf, wherever it was, had left the building before I came out of the library. Before we had reached my room, the vice president had extracted a bizarre promise from me that I wouldn't try to kill any non-violent weres. My experience with the talking weres on the mountain, even speaking single words, remained an amazing and deadly puzzle. I wasn't ready to concede that the non-violent sort existed. I'd built my life on the opposite sphere. Parr had even asked me again to reconsider werewolves. I wasn't sure I was capable of anything remotely resembling a promise or plea.

Anolia produced another pretty shirt for me, and Parr escorted us to a luncheon he hosted. He'd invited me and I followed, mostly out of curiosity. I did concede to another promise to behave myself. Anyway, I could explore the layout of the building. The VP and Anolia certainly made an attractive couple. They seemed ideal for one another as he graciously led her around the elegant room, introducing her to people who thought they were important. She seemed as comfortable in her soft, cream-colored dress as she had wearing cotton robes at Avalon. What was her life like before she founded Avalon? No one at the commune knew, and I hadn't asked her. Parr wanted to know how he should introduce me. I suggested he call me his minion, but he didn't agree. I finally reminded him of my easily activated predilection toward violence and my uncompromising asshole attitude. He wisely backed off, accepting that I would behave as promised, but participation was too much for me to stomach. I followed them around and refused to make eye contact.

Lunch was okay. The pile of grass they called a salad wasn't appealing and the chicken tasted like leather. I'd eaten far worse. Dessert was a tiny odd-looking cake with no flavor. It got me longing for Avalon's fruit pies.

More wandering and more talking—shit I was bored. Every time I eased toward a door, several black shirted guards casually closed in. I was testing them, feeling things out, and they understood. Xavier had his troops well trained.

Ty came up behind me and slipped his arm in mine. Another surprise. The terribly young soldier at a vice-presidential function? His sweet smile tugged at me, drawing out congenial emotions. He wore the black shirt fatigues and eagle patch, but no gun. "Would you like a tour? I've got a card that will get us in almost everywhere."

"You can actually get me out of this circus? Oh, you are my hero."

"I'm a big man in the mansion. Watch me." The guards let us pass without challenge. However, I could tell from the looks they exchanged they'd be reporting to Xavier soon.

He did have a card. Pre-war technologies, electronic door locks and such were, like the helicopter, picture-book relics from another age. They did, however, pop up occasionally in unusual and interesting places. Ty shocked me with the calm, almost educational way he led me on an excursion through Aaron Gannett's Presidential Mansion. He evaded guards with ease. His knowledge of the building extended to connecting rooms and alternate hallways. His *little card* proved to be a veritable magic wand. He carried a small key ring, too. Xavier didn't strike me as the type to allow a young boyfriend such latitude. Of course, Xavier didn't strike me as the kind who would have a boyfriend.

"Ty, how old are you?"

"Is it important?" His voice lowered and was suddenly edgy, tight.

"No." Had I offended him? It wasn't intentional, but I have a natural talent for such things.

"I'm eighteen. How old are you?" He shoved his hands in his pockets.

"Twenty-nine." For two more months, anyway.

He said nothing else, and I decided to drop the subject.

The mansion was four stories, but Ty said there were other floors below ground. He didn't offer to take me down. "That's where the president goes when people start shooting at him."

"Shooting at him?" *Sounded delightful to me.*

"Yeah. Sometimes people—"

"People? Citizens? Patriots? You know, men and women who love their country and want democracy again?"

Ty chuckled, tried not to, but then laughed out loud. "Yeah. Those guys too."

Lord, what a delightful boy.

I suspected this fortress housed a few escape tunnels under the silky-green grass lawn outside. I doubted I'd get close to one of them. I saw little traffic above the second floor. The third and fourth floors, including the area around my room, could double for a museum/art gallery. Our dictator and his predecessors must have plundered the few surviving art galleries and museums to amass such a hoard.

I lingered in a room filled with the most superb collection of ancient weapons. Body armor, shields, swords, and knives in every length imaginable decorated the walls, floor, and filled glass cases. I drooled over a case containing particularly well-honed, silver-plated steel blades, forged in the early days of war against werewolves.

Finally, we walked back down to the main floor, and outside to a patio filled with great concrete urns full of blooming flowers. Everything baked in the sunshine, and a breeze cooled the air making for an ideal spring. I hadn't been outside in the open air since that one evening Anolia and I spent on the deck overlooking the city. At least peacefully outside. From the outside, the mansion was a rectangular brick box, dotted with white framed windows. It sat on a slight hill, and a tall perimeter fence a quarter mile away across the neat green lawn circled the complex. Other than well-maintained grass, no vegetation marred the line of sight from the fence to the mansion walls.

Open turtles patrolled the fence line at three to four-minute intervals. Enough for me to get over the fence if I could cross the lawn without a guard spotting me—and there were no landmines. Anolia would never make the distance. Having met and measured Gannett, I wasn't about to leave her with him or Parr.

The mansion's only exterior adornment was the flowered patio and a long narrow pool of water that stretched fifty feet across the lawn. The pool cumulated in an odd-looking, pink marble fountain. Such a weird sculpture, it made me want to cock my head to see if an idiot installed it upside down. Ty sat with me on the grass at the edge of the pool, and we watched gold and white fish swim among purple and white flowered water lilies.

"Is there a Mrs. President?" I realized I hadn't thought of that during my confinement.

"Sabrina? Yeah, she's out of town today."

Sabrina? First name basis for Ty. "What's she like?"

"Beautiful. Intelligent." Ty spoke, but didn't meet my eyes. "And strange. People don't understand her. She's always nice to me."

"Do you…" My senses went on alert and jiggled my nerve endings. Prepare for action they screamed. I twisted to search the area around us. *It wasn't possible. My extrasensory perception only worked on werewolves and vampires. This was neither a fuzzy nor a leech.*

"What is it?" he asked.

"Xavier's coming."

Ty reached out and clasped my hand in his own. Turning serious, he said, "You know, he's angrier with himself for losing his temper than he is with you."

Sure he was. Xavier appeared on the patio, hit the steps, and bore down on us. I rose to meet him. I glared at Ty who sat relaxed, grinning at me.

"What the hell are you doing?" Xavier directed the remark to Ty, so I bit my tongue.

"Showing Maat around the mansion." Ty stood and faced him. He acted as if he was accustomed to Xavier's moods. Did Xavier think I was poaching? Trying to steal his boy lover?

Xavier turned his fury on me. He stood feet planted and fists clenched.

I grinned at him and held out my hands, palms up. "Don't worry, Xavier, your little boyfriend is safe from me. I like mine a bit more…mature."

Xavier stared. I won't say he looked confused, but

he did appear as blank-faced as a man with a scar like that could…until he burst into laughter. Damned if Ty didn't laugh with him.

It didn't make me happy. "I've been known to shoot men who laugh at me."

Not exactly true, but I'd done damage once or twice. Since I didn't have my guns…damn I hated being defenseless.

Ty's eyes sparkled. Another way too hearty laugh bubbled from him. Xavier rubbed a hand over his forehead as if fighting to control himself and go back to his iceman posture. Then he lost it and fell into derisive chuckling again.

I lost something too—my temper. I slammed both hands against Xavier's chest and shoved him toward the pool. The bastard grabbed and took me with him—again. I knew I probably wouldn't drown in three feet of water, unless he held me under. Of course, he did. The next thing I knew, Ty had his arms around my waist and dragged me out. The little shit sniggered while he hauled me to the side and rolled me on the grass.

Xavier marched toward me. I kicked up and outward. I missed my target, but my foot connected a bit lower. Not the knee I'd stabbed at Avalon, but close enough. He staggered backwards and landed on his ass.

I scrambled away, jumped up, and whirled to run—only to slam into a couple of the president's brown-shirted soldiers. By that time, a bunch of Xavier's black shirts had arrived, too.

"Help me, please," I cried to the brown shirt I ran into. "He's going to hurt me." I knew I wasn't going to escape, but I had a plan. Maybe it would work better than the last plan I had involving Xavier. I counted on a bit of rivalry between the two sets of troops. More brown shirts arrived. I ducked behind the lead brown shirt as Xavier came limping toward me.

Xavier snarled orders and the brown shirt, either confused or a complete idiot, politely argued with him. Black shirts and brown shirts, all armed and ready for a fight. It looked like it would come down to an opportune mini-war at the presidential mansion when Gannett and Parr came running out the door and across the lawn.

Parr ordered the brown shirts to back off. Gannett controlled Xavier and the black shirts. While that circus developed, I snagged a carelessly holstered pistol from an irresponsible brown-shirt. No place to hide it, so I stuck it in the front of my pants and tugged my shirt down for cover. I wrapped my arms around my middle as if in pain. Parr grabbed me by the arm and dragged me toward Gannett—and Xavier.

Gannett's eyes blazed. "What the hell are you two doing?"

"Xavier tried to drown me." I faked my distress. It had worked once.

The president sighed. "You need new lines, Maat. Are you always this much trouble?"

"Only when I'm kidnapped." Indignation seemed appropriate. Ow! Parr jabbed a finger in my back.

Gannett glared at me. "Go to your room and stay there."

Xavier stepped in front of me, narrow eyed, and angry. He kept his distance but held out his hand.

"What?"

He didn't move. I knew a lost cause when I saw

one. I sneered and laid my purloined pistol on his palm. Parr smiled when he saw the weapon. Well, it was a worthy effort. Four black shirts escorted me back into the mansion. Ty tagged along. His clothes were wet from the waist down, and his boots sloshed like mine did.

"Isn't Xavier going to be pissed at you?" I punched him in the arm.

"Yeah, but it was worth it. And he'll forgive me."

"You sure about that?"

Ty grinned. "Yep. He's my father. He always forgives me."

Oh, shit!

****

Anolia paced back and forth across my room like a big cat in a cage.

"Maat, I had this beautiful outfit for you to wear."

The president had planned a formal dinner party for us this evening. But now he'd forbidden Xavier and me to attend. Me, I understood. I'd use any excuse to cause turmoil. Xavier? Not so much. The guy in charge of security is important. Why keep him away?

I was lying on the bed, in my comfortable new jeans, trying to relax. By *beautiful outfit* Anolia meant a dress. I hadn't worn a dress since before my mother died.

"The *president* wants to show me off like a freak."

"Yes! But I wanted to show you off as the person I know you are."

"Oh, the guilt thing again."

Anolia stopped pacing and planted her hands on her hips. "Okay. Sit here and be bored. You know there are guards outside the door."

"When haven't there been guards outside the door?"

Anolia nodded, and her mouth pinched tight. I'd truly troubled her more here than all my time at Avalon. She came to the bed, kissed me on the cheek, and left the room. A few minutes later, Ty opened the door and walked in. What the hell? Forget relaxing.

"Polite people knock, Ty." Not that I would be polite and mind my manners with my captors. Oh, Aunt Nell taught me manners along with my history, science, and language lessons. I learned and occasionally—in a place with people I liked—behaved myself.

"Polite. Yeah. But I'm only a kid. I don't know any better." He unbuttoned his black fatigue shirt and stripped it off to reveal a rope tightly wrapped from armpits to waist.

"Ah…That must itch like hell. A new kind of body armor?"

He managed to look indignant. "No. I know a fun place in town, and we can go tonight." He tied one end of the rope to the bed frame and anchored it around a heating radiator by the window. "The room below is empty, so at nine o'clock, open your window, climb out, and drop down one floor. I'll be waiting."

"I don't think I'm supposed to leave the mansion."

"We won't be gone long. They'll never miss us."

The boy had already fascinated me with the ease he navigated a secure mansion. Going out with him was better than sitting here doing nothing but planning my revenge on Xavier. Well, if nobody shot me for trying to escape.

"Are you sure we can get out and back in? Don't you think they watch the outside of the building?" How interesting.

"Yeah, but I have a friend who's going to create a diversion. Climb out when the noise starts."

"Okay. You're not going to the big dinner party?"

"That's for grown-ups." Ty sniffed, pretending offense over the slight. "They didn't invite me."

Chapter Eight

Ty's diversion proved simple but adequate—a moderate explosion. I learned later his compatriot rolled a barrel of oil across the lawn on the other side of the mansion and set it on fire. I put skepticism aside and that's how I found myself hanging from a rope, thirty feet off the ground, outside a closed window. Ty stuck his head out a window four feet to my right.

"Sorry, wrong room. Come on." He leaned out and stretched a hand toward me.

"This plan of yours better be damned good." I grumbled while he hauled me in.

"Maat?" Ty caught my arm with a gentle hand.

"What?"

"I'll be in trouble, *real* trouble if…you will come back, won't you?"

"Yes, I'll come back. I promise. I'll wait until I can escape on my own. More fun that way." I didn't tell him the woman I loved like a mother was a hostage to guarantee I didn't run. I figured Anolia would be safe for a while, though, and I needed to look around outside in case the opportunity to get both of us away presented itself. That's what I told myself anyway.

Ty led me through back hallways, down dark stairs, and to a service door where a turtle stood waiting. I crawled into the back and covered up with a blanket. Ty wore his black fatigues, and the perimeter guards waved him through at the gate. *Such sloppy security. No wonder I got by them at Avalon.* The black shirts were valuable, but apparently limited in number. They'd lost quite a few at the mountain house, too. Those left apparently concentrated on guarding people on the first floor of the mansion.

After I crawled to the front seat, I discovered I liked New Washington. I'd walked wide around the place in the past. Too much military. Ty drove the turtle down new streets, between new buildings and brightly lit sidewalks full of people, most of them young.

The few cities I'd walked in my life were ruins where humans lived off the corpse of a dead world. Prudent folk on the fringes of what remained of civilization didn't have the luxury of pleasure-walking after dark. Wild and native animals, escaped or released from zoos, had made secure homes in the wilderness. Wilderness bumped the edges of habitation, always ravenous. Avalon? We had no livestock, so we were less a target for wild predators, but I see now how careless we were. But that was Avalon's enticement, that sense of peace. Our neighbors barricaded themselves inside when the sun went down.

I knew better than to think New Washington was typical. I'd been to Memphis, Chicago, and Atlanta, and I'd traveled the few roads between. There weren't as many vehicles in New Washington as there were in Chicago and Memphis. Chicago and southeast through Ohio had the gun and ammo factories, the forges and steel mills. Memphis had the army. Horses, mules, and wagons dominated agricultural Atlanta.

Ty parked the turtle on the street in front of a row of brick and stone buildings. He reached out and grabbed my hand. "Ahem...since I got you out for the evening, I was wondering...if..."

"I am *not* going to screw you."

A beguiling grin turned his mouth up, and a clever gleam twinkled in his eyes. "I was just going to ask for a kiss."

"I might go that far." Oh, hell. I liked this kid. How had Xavier managed to produce him?

"A *real* kiss? Please."

Oh, oh, too much excitement in that voice. "Real is the only kind I do. No tongue, though." I leaned over and kissed him. I thought it was good enough for a beginner.

He wanted more—a lot more. "Ty, I..."

"It's okay, Maat. I know I can't have you. But that's not going to stop me from trying." He quickly opened the turtle door and jumped out. A boy with a crush on an older woman? *Get over it, sweetheart. That's not me or my nature.*

I like my music loud and my beer cold. The club Ty led me to offered both. A band on the small stage blasted twentieth century rock and roll and couples writhed on the dance floor. Tables crowded close together created accidental and deliberate body contact as we wound our way through the dim light to the bar. Ty bought me a fine dark-amber draft beer from a bartender with a patch over one eye and a gapped-toothed smile. A couple of men eased up to me, but Ty glared at them until they went away. Interesting. A certain power came with the black shirt and eagle patch.

He led me around the room introducing me to his friends like a prize he'd won in a contest. They stared speculatively. Ty was obviously a virgin. He wanted them to think he'd made a real conquest. I'd bet they wondered what he saw in a rough older woman like me. The music slowed, and I danced with him. He held me too close, but the beer had improved my mood a bit.

"There are lots of pretty girls here. Why don't you find one?"

"But they're so ordinary." He nuzzled my throat and nipped my ear.

"Stop that!"

He laughed and spun me around in his arms.

We left near midnight, when I reminded him that someone who paid attention might miss me. As he drove back, I figured I'd pick his brain while he was in such a good mood. "How did you come to live in the mansion?"

"Xavier's been with Aaron since before I was born. They were in the militia together. My mother and sister were killed in a werewolf attack when I was seven, and Lilly, Aaron's first wife, took care of me after that. Aaron's my godfather. Lilly, she..." Ty's voice broke. "Lilly died five years ago. I use my mother's maiden name and don't call Xavier father because it's supposed to be safer for me if no one knows I'm his son. That was Lilly's idea."

"Does Xavier have any other name?"

"Sure. Antonio Ramon Xavier Chavez. My great grandfather was the last ambassador to the U.S. from Spain before the war. He stayed on during the war but died in the plague."

I understood then. Because he grew up with them, he'd been protected as a child. Ty saw too many deadly people as players in a game. You'd think, living in the same sphere with his father and a dictator he'd know

113

better. "Ty? You've seen werewolves before those on the mountain, haven't you? Around here? Recently?"

"No…well…yes." He drummed his fingers on the steering wheel.

"Make up your mind."

He shrugged and grunted. Irritation filled his voice. "Okay. I've met a couple here in human shape."

"In my line of work, we call any humans who harbor werewolves, dog fuckers. And we kill them if they stand between us and the monsters we need to exterminate."

He didn't speak, but the way he studied the road made me believe he had heavy brain work in progress. I recognized the dilemma. Someone he cared for was a werewolf. What would I do if a monster bit someone I loved but didn't kill them? I didn't know. How could you allow a person you love to slaughter others? Thank God I'd never faced that situation.

Ty slowed the turtle to allow pedestrians to cross, though we were virtually alone on the road. When we rolled again, he asked, "You don't think that there are different weres, good and bad? I mean, isn't it how they act? Just because they can change shape…"

"Ty, I hunted and killed one of your so-called *good* weres once. He was careful. He lived, went to work every day, loved, and supported his family—until he lost control one night. He got pissed, tore his wife apart, and ate his kids."

Werewolves had killed Ty's mother. Was he told, or had he witnessed the slaughter? His grief for her passing was certainly genuine. Yet, what he'd seen on the mountain hadn't taught him a lesson. When the big werewolf grabbed him, he hadn't reacted as he should have, either. Oh, there might be a bit of truth in Parr's disease talk. A rabid dog might be a dog, a beloved family pet, but the only cure was, hopefully, a swift death.

"Vampires are worse than werewolves, aren't they?" Ty's question came with surprising intensity.

"Yes, vampires are worse." His interest worried me. I decided to tell him about New York. "Ty, once upon a time I was young, cocky, overconfident—like you. Five or six years ago, I'd run out of weres to kill. At least I thought I had. I'd heard about vampires in New York, in the ruins, so I decided to add a couple of bloodsuckers to my extermination list. They caught me within minutes.

"They took control of my mind and body. I couldn't move. Glamour, hypnotism, enchantment, call it what you want. They subverted my will, and I didn't raise a hand to fight. I thought they'd kill me. I wasn't that lucky. Then I begged them to kill me. You hear hunters brag about staking vampires, but it's all lies. I know. They're almost impossible to kill. Please, please, if you think a vampire is going to catch you, kill yourself while you're still in control."

"You escaped."

"Yes, I escaped. I had help. Otherwise, I'm sure I would have died there."

"Tell me about them." Now he sounded eager. Too eager. "Does silver kill them? A wooden stake? Their blood, is it magic? Can they have sex? I heard they can't do it because…well, I heard. I mean, they're dead."

"No. They're monsters, different, but no more *dead* than werewolves. Silver hurts them. It cuts deep, better than any other metal. But it's not poison like it is for weres. A wooden stake is a toothpick. Ingesting their blood helps heal human injuries. I don't know if you'd call it magic or medicine. And yes, they can have sex."

The New York vampires had made a vicious art of rape, too.

"Did they bite you? Did it hurt?" He reached out and brushed my arm with his fingers.

"No, Ty. They didn't bite me. God knows why. I've never been bitten by a vampire." *Tortured to insanity, yes, but no bites.* Lucky me.

Ty didn't say anything else, so we rode back to the presidential mansion in silence. We arrived at the perimeter gate, and the brown shirts challenged us, but they recognized Ty and let us through. I didn't have to hide. It seems the only reason I had to go out the window was to get past Xavier's black shirt guarding my door. I guess the president had assumed, correctly, that if he kept Anolia close, like at his party, I wouldn't escape. Ty drove around to the service area at the end of the public wing. We hurried past the startled kitchen staff and eased our way down a back hall. The workers looked finished with clean up, so the party must be over.

A few steps on, recognition hit so brutally I grabbed Ty. My fingers dug into his arm.

It's hard to explain a psychic hit to someone who's never had one. This one was far different from werewolves. Coming after years of enjoying Avalon's peace, it struck clearer and sliced deeper. It made a hollow preternatural punch low in my guts and crawled across my skin until it forced my mind to accept its persuasive message.

"Maat…what…God, you're…you're white! Don't faint…"

No! I would not faint. I drew deep breaths and forced myself to be calm. The most important game of my life had suddenly become more immediate. I'd hoped never to play this hand again.

"What's in that room?" I nodded at the door.

"The main salon. That's where the party is. Or was. Everyone's probably gone." Ty stared at me, confusion in his eyes. He'd never seen me afraid.

"There's a vampire." And I knew this one personally.

Coincidence be damned. *It did not come down like this by chance*. Bits of the puzzle of a kidnapping at Avalon were moving together now. The vampire in that room was a familiar monster. *He had carried me away from the torture chamber in New York.* He did it for his own reasons, not to save one human. He'd never explained those reasons to me. What I learned about him later would disturb and give me nightmares forever. *That knowledge and the insight I'd gained here, required that I act tonight.* I couldn't get to my guns, but I wouldn't face this fight unarmed.

"Ty, how far is it to that weapon room?"

"Not far." He grinned as if we were having great fun. And he *damn sure didn't seem shocked* when I said there was a vampire in the house. The little shit had known—he'd asked questions—and said nothing! I'd deal with him later—if there was a later for me.

There were more black shirts evident this time, probably because of the party. We evaded them twice, then Ty used his plastic card to open a door—and another door beyond. "This is the president's study. My card isn't supposed to open these doors. Mistakes happen."

Books lined the dark-paneled walls, and nut-brown carpet muffled our footsteps across the floor. The air carried the fragrances of leather, alcohol—and the dead stink of the vampire. I'd have known it instantly if Gannett had brought me here instead of the other room he called a library. Ty headed straight for a closet, opened the door, and entered.

"What are you doing?"

"There are passages in the walls."

"Secret passages?"

"Yeah. I accidentally found the blueprints one day when I was…exploring."

"Accidentally?"

Ty shrugged. He pushed on one corner of the closet's back wall with both hands, and it silently slid to one side. "I don't have a light, so you'll have to lead the way."

"Who told you I can see in the dark?"

"Sometimes I listen when I'm not supposed to. I like living. Information can save your life. Xavier taught me that."

And little Ty always shared his information with Daddy, I'd bet. Such a clever boy. Unfortunately, he'd been selective with the information he'd provided *me*. My fault. I'd misjudged the artful naiveté of a young man raised in a savage world for immaturity. It was one of his weapons for survival.

The stairs going up were narrow and branched out at each landing. Though constructed only twenty years ago, the musty smell of time gathered in these secret passages. When we reached the third floor, we exited from a hall storage closet only two doors away from the weapons room. No guards, so we slipped in without a problem.

"I have to break it." We stood over the glass case. He nodded and stood back while I picked up a hatchet and smashed the glass. The silver-plated steel blade I chose was too long for a knife and too short for a sword. I touched the edge with my finger. Sharp. Nothing else in the room presented itself as an appropriate weapon.

We hurried back the way we came to the door of the salon. I opened it a crack and peeked into the room. Gannett and the vampire stood there alone, talking. So serious appearing, that conversation. Were they waiting for something? Or someone?

The vampire? Perfect as ever. Long golden hair cascaded down his back in soft curls. His tall, slender body had the muscular grace of a man in the prime of his life. He was a beauty all right, and as deadly as any viper that ever slithered across the earth.

With time, planning, and help from my demo expert friend, I'd eventually gone back to New York and reduced blocks of ruins to broken concrete slabs, twisted steel, and crushed vampires. I'd warned this vampire, the one who had carried me out of that hell, to stay away. I told him it paid in full my debt for the rescue. I also told him what I had learned about him and his dreadful acts of evil, and promised the next time I saw him, I'd kill him, too. He laughed at me then, and every time I'd seen him since.

Unfortunately, much as I desired to do so, I realized it was unlikely I'd get to kill him tonight. That would require enhanced weapons. A flamethrower or a cannon. *The blade would have to be for his puppet, Gannett.* The vile bloodsucker had ambitious plans for this world, and I'd seen the gruesome, failed outcome of one of his visions. If he wanted to use Gannett to start an American Vampire government, I'd set him back a few years. I could give the revolutionaries out there a chance and time to act. Maybe Vice President Parr would take over. Oh, yes, Xavier had foiled assassination attempts in the past but, like me, Gannett had grounded him tonight. I knew Xavier might kill me for my act. For some odd reason, that idea filled me with sadness, not fear.

I leaned back and whispered in Ty's ear. "You stay here."

Killing Gannett would royally piss off the vampire. He might kill me. He might not. I'd take the chance. I had royally pissed him off before and he'd let me live. I think I amused him. This is one of the things that defined me, defined my life. I killed monsters. This one monster, this dictator, this human, needed to die. The bigger monster would have to wait.

Ty snatched my arm. "But I want—"

I grabbed his jaw in my hand and squeezed hard. He squeaked like a mouse.

"If you don't stay, I'll never let you go with me again."

He stood frozen, wide eyed, then nodded, so I released him. Well, that had worked. Not that I ever planned to let him go anywhere with me, even if I survived the evening.

I held the long knife straight, slightly behind my leg. The vampire might see it, but he understood I was always armed. Certainly, it didn't threaten him. I threw open the door and marched across the marble floor. No time for subtlety. Besides, he had most likely heard or sensed me outside the door.

The salon, a generous open-floor design, had warm lighting and exquisite brocade seating lining the walls. Perfect for a president's dance party. The vampire's eyes sparkled, and he had what looked to be an indulgent expression as I approached. *His favorite toy, his entertainment for the evening, had arrived.*

I stopped directly in front of him. "Hello, suck face. Which sewer did you crawl out of?"

His breathtaking smile welcomed me like a dear friend—or a lover. "Ah, Maat. There you are. I've been waiting for you." His voice had a musical tone, so pleasing to hear. "I see you're as sweet-natured as ever."

"Oh, yeah. Despite my trials and tribulations, I've managed to retain my girlish charm."

The vampire chuckled, shaking his head. His golden curls danced across his shoulders. He wasn't tall for our time, five-ten or so, but he would have been a giant a thousand years ago when he was born.

Gannett stepped closer. He stated the obvious stupidity. "I take it you two are acquainted."

"Acquainted?" I resisted the urge to spit on Gannett "Sure. He's a thousand-year-old vampire who goes by the name Ruelle San Nicolás."

Ruelle spread his arms expansively, that charming smile growing wider. "And she is Suriel, Angel of Death, the Grim Reaper who taught the vampires of New York to embrace mortality—and the dearest love of my extremely long life."

I held the long knife in my right hand and tried to

relax. I judged the distance between myself and the malicious pawn, Gannett. I needed to be closer to him and further from Ruelle. Less chance of Ruelle being able to stop me.

Ruelle's body suddenly stiffened. His vampire grace vanished. He froze, one hand clenched into a fist over his heart. "Maat...run!" He hissed the words full of panic and strain under his breath.

Only one thing frightened Ruelle—and it was too late to run. Another vampire had entered the room. She thrust her vile aura ahead of her like a spectral tidal wave. Either his presence had masked hers, or she had just arrived.

Emanis. Vampire Queen of New York. A creature who had held me in her arms as her subjects laid hot irons on my back in their vile form of entertainment. Emanis, who forced her own blood down my throat so my body would heal during the day—to endure another night of anguish.

"Guess I missed one in New York." I didn't bother to turn and look. Failure. Dismal failure. All that fire and explosive fury and my primary objective had escaped.

Ruelle stepped between me and her. He staggered one step and fell to his knees. Whatever magic she held, despite his power and beauty, Ruelle remained her servant.

Sweat chilled my body, and I could smell the stink of my own terror. Acid burned my throat as I remembered. Shrieking agony, hopeless prayers...let me die...let me die.

I turned to face her. An instant of pure joy, one brief exultation filled me. My spectacular New York lesson in mortality had brushed her with fire. Once a great beauty, her skin now twisted and stretched in hideous red whorls pitted with dark craters. Little remained but a burned, scarred husk. If she lived ten thousand years, she'd never heal. But fire hadn't destroyed her vampire power.

Ruelle struggled and tried to rise. Why was he fighting her? Surely not for me. He knew the price he'd pay for defiance. Emanis hissed and flashed her fangs. He lowered his head to the floor and choked on a scream. She turned her attention to me. A rasping growl came from her throat.

"My children...dead." She must have breathed in the fire as she burned.

What did she want? Sympathy?

One second, that's all I needed. I had to keep a touch of self-control. Kill her? No hope for that. I had to cut her, to commit a single act of defiance. I prayed that would enrage her and make her kill me quickly.

Her call, her psychic demand, slammed through my mind. It reverberated and wrenched me, dragged me toward her. I fought but had to obey. My feet made those first tenuous steps. She waited so patiently. Vamps are patient. They think they have eternity, so they're rarely in a hurry.

"Yes," she croaked. "Come." She raised her hands. Her fingers tried to stretch into claws. A pathetic gesture since she'd lost several fingers. Others were blunt nubs. Her gown, torn and crusted with filth, made an obscene contrast to the fine silk and diamonds she'd adorned herself with last time I'd seen her. A wig perched on her head like a vulgar yellow hat. What foul tomb had she crawled in to sleep that day? Under a whiff of the grave, I caught the scent of seared meat, as if the fire still smoldered in her flesh.

Emanis intensified the familiar psychic flood that would enslave my will. Pure agony, it forced me forward.

Wait! What's this? Something had changed.

Impossible. Had the fire ravaged her power too? How could that be? She'd sent Ruelle to his knees. The vampire enchantment—the one that should have made me a mindless creature, stripped of all personal resolve—washed over my consciousness like water poured on coarse, dry sand. It stood for an instant, then seeped away. *She could tear me apart with her finger nubs, but she could not control my mind.*

In the ruins of New York, by their blood and power, amplified in torture, Emanis and her monstrous children had made me immune to their glamour, their best weapon. I'd never dreamed they'd given me such a reward for my suffering.

I fought down astonishment, lowered my face and trudged on. I pretended to struggle against the wall of the now absent extrasensory energy.

Emanis hissed. She sure sounded happy. I grasped the long knife in both hands. She saw and ignored the blade. She couldn't imagine I'd be able to hurt her.

When I got within four feet, I stopped, my face focused on the floor, so she wouldn't see my anticipation. Bizarre, crackling laughter wheezed in her throat. "Look at me, Suriel, and I will show you the true Angel of Death."

I raised my face. I had to meet her gaze, eye to eye. I held that connection with cold clear detachment. My mouth formed the only genuine smile I'd ever give her.

"You have no power over me, Emanis."

A single swift step forward. The blade flashed. Years of memory, years of nightmares, drained from me into the silver in my hands. It met little resistance when it sheared her neck. She blessed me with a wide-eyed stare of complete and utter shock. Her body collapsed. Her head dropped at my feet. It thumped, nothing more than a repulsive ball of meat and bone. The wig popped off and revealed thin strands of wire-like hair protruding from a scar-ridged scalp.

I'd killed a vampire.

No special weapons. No fire or massive explosive blast as in New York. Only Maat Ferris with a sharp silver blade. I stared at her body, locked in time, filled with an unimaginable sense of wonder.

I bent, grasped those remaining strands of wiry hair, and lifted her head. Blood slowly drizzled from the neck in thin ropes. Crimson fluid, thick and viscous, slowly drained from Emanis' body and spread across the floor. I stared into her open, dead eyes. I prayed she could hear me in hell.

"I win, bitch queen. I win."

Chapter Nine

With Emanis' head in my left hand and the short sword in my right, I stalked back toward Gannett, focused on finishing my original task. Too late. Ruelle, released by Emanis' death, stood between us. He gawked at me. Only one time before had I ever surprised him. The night I warned him about my planned destruction in New York.

Gannett's face mirrored the vampire's shock. Ruelle's stunned expression quickly transformed to one of supreme satisfaction. Satisfaction? Him? I'd done all the work.

I held up Emanis' dripping head. "Look here, Mr. President. This lesson is for you. Vampires are not gods." I stared straight at Ruelle. "They are not immortal. They are not all powerful, all knowing. They can be exterminated."

My monster senses suddenly roiled. I tightened my grip on the silver blade. A woman—a werewolf in human form—entered the room. With all the vampire shit surrounding me I had been blind to her presence. I recognized her. I recognized her eyes. This tall red-haired beauty in a formal black gown coming toward me was the female were who had spoken to me on the mountain.

She stopped and stared at me standing there with my bloody knife and the vampire's head. If I ever personified an Angel of Death, it would have been then. She turned to Gannett, obviously confused. Gannett went to her, slid an arm over her shoulders, and drew her close.

"Maat, this is my wife, Sabrina."

Sabrina nodded, graceful as a vampire herself. "Maat…Suriel, I'm honored to meet you."

Such a velvety musical voice, so incredibly far from the single rough word she spoke on the mountain. *Honored to meet me?* And so my world twisted again. The President of the United States was married to a werewolf.

Gannett realized I could kill her. That's why he held her so close. Not that it would help. I'm that good. I'd kill him and punch the silver knife in her heart before she could change shape. Only one person in the room could stop me.

Ruelle. And stop me he did. Not by force, but by the sense of anticipation he projected as surely as Emanis projected evil. Cunning and devious, with a thousand years of blood and treachery behind him, he wanted me to kill the president's wife.

Whatever his reasons, whatever the vampire desired, he wouldn't get it from me.

For the first time in my life, I greeted and spoke politely to a monster. "I'm pleased to meet you, Mrs. Gannett." A bit of a hard voice, but within the bounds of good manners. I even smiled. "I'm sorry I made such a mess on your floor." I tossed Emanis' head toward her body. It bounced with a wet smack and rolled a respectable distance.

Eyes wide, she said, "Oh no, I'd say the room is much cleaner now." Her mouth pursed, and then changed to a smile as if she thought I'd performed a good deed.

The president loved his werewolf. I could see it in his eyes and the touch of his hands. Unless she attacked me, I'd let her live for a while. I didn't have to kill this werewolf anyway. Ruelle would do it for me, eventually. Gannett's obvious love for her was a threat to his control.

"Should I ask what you're doing here?" I glared at Ruelle. "Running the country?"

Ruelle's playful smile showed no fang. "I'm only the president's advisor. An excellent position, until Emanis arrived last month. It complicated things. I, too, believed she'd perished during your spectacular bit of vengeance in New York. She wasn't supposed to be here tonight."

Emanis' dripping head had already bloodied and ruined my jeans, so I swiped the long knife on my leg. Complicated? *Ruelle, she sent you to your knees only minutes ago.*

"Maat?" Ruelle's voice hummed around me, gently tugged at me, brimming with power. Yes, he was top dog vampire now that I'd killed his mistress. If Emanis failed to control me, how could he? I couldn't deceive him. I stared him straight in the eye. "Bullshit, Ruelle. Try something else."

I spoke without malice because I didn't want to provoke an attack by him. I'd lost the element of surprise. Even with the ability to withstand his psychic power, I had no chance of surviving a face-to-face conflict. I had tried it once and he hurt me. And let me live.

The door crashed open, and Xavier charged in—

followed by a contingent of black shirts, all armed and ready. Bet they had silvers this time. Xavier's eyes scanned the room, assessing immediate threat and for clues on what he'd missed. They locked in on me. Me, not his president, not the living and dead vampires. The troops spread out behind him. *They* focused their attention on Emanis' headless corpse. Ty followed them in. He'd left me to get Xavier.

Xavier held his Aries in both hands, ready to fire. He ignored Ruelle standing so close beside me. His gaze traveled down my body, taking in the long knife and bloody clothes.

"You're late." I allowed myself the luxury of relaxing. I grinned and winked at him. "You missed the party."

"I misbehaved earlier today. I wasn't invited." The corner of his mouth twitched. Fighting a smile?

"Same here. I crashed it anyway." He really did have beautiful eyes.

Xavier holstered his Aries. He turned and went to his men and calmly gave orders for a cleanup. With an expression of contempt, Xavier then zeroed in on Gannett. Yep. Gannett had kept his security chief away from a place, a scene, where a security chief should have been in control. Had Ruelle ordered the president to do so?

Xavier grabbed the president by the arm and dragged him aside. They spoke in fierce whispers and finally left the room. Sabrina nodded at me as if we'd had a pleasant conversation, then she left, too.

Ruelle walked to Emanis. The black shirts had donned rubber gloves as they prepared to mop the vampire blood from the marble. He ignored them and knelt beside her, carefully avoiding the pool of blood. The black shirts backed away. Ruelle spoke softly to one. The man hurried over to one of the couches lining the wall, removed the blanket sized covering, and brought it to Ruelle. Ruelle tenderly wrapped Emanis' body and head in the covering. He picked her up and, as if placing a child in bed, laid her on a cart they had brought in. He watched as they rolled it away.

What bonds formed between creatures like Ruelle and Emanis, those who had lived so horribly long? Beings that had left humanity so far behind. Love, hate, servitude? The inevitable struggles for power? Not questions that I would ever answer.

Ty came from where he'd been standing at the side of the room observing, and thank God, not interfering.

"I didn't need to be rescued, Ty."

"I know." Ty leaned closer and spoke softly. "But if I hadn't told him, and you died, or were hurt, if he had lost you, he'd never forgive me."

"What do mean? Lost me? I'm not... He can't lose something he doesn't have."

He smiled, but I saw sadness in his blue eyes. "He's in love with you, Maat. Don't you...can't you feel it? Can't you see? I've watched him. I watched him sit by your bed while you were unconscious. I've never seen him behave this way."

Ty was making assumptions about Xavier's emotions and behavior—and my own—based upon his youthful inexperience. I'd known Xavier barely two weeks. Yes, he disturbed me. He'd almost killed me. For a few brief moments in that time, he'd also treated me with respect. Then he'd driven me crazy with more bullying.

I'm an emotional coward. I've always tried to avoid close relationships. My love for Anolia had already made me a prisoner. I did not wish for Xavier's love. Yes, I might find him attractive in a bizarre way, a violent way, but love? Not possible.

"Was that a vampire?" Ty nodded toward the cart carrying Emanis away.

Good. Change of subject.

"Yeah. And the blond too." Ruelle still stood staring at Emanis' wrapped body as it rolled out the door. "Stay away from him, Ty."

"I will. Xavier warned me about him. I've never seen the other one before."

Did Ty know Sabrina was a werewolf? I'd bet he did. I wanted to smack him.

"So, Ty, my friend, my buddy, you didn't think I needed to be told that blond-headed leech was hanging around? Like when we talked about vampires earlier? A little, *bloodsucker ahead, watch your ass* warning?"

"I'm sorry. I was afraid you'd leave if you knew." He gave me one of those woeful blue-eyed little boy smiles. I was tired of his schemes.

I thumped his chin hard with my finger. "You don't get to manipulate me. I'll leave when I get ready." And I was ready to leave—at least this room—before anyone cornered me for more bloodletting or worse, earth-shaking discussion.

I'd hesitated too long.

Ruelle blocked my way. "I wish to speak with you." He stared at Ty.

I couldn't escape. "Go on Ty, we'll talk tomorrow." Tomorrow—in the sunshine. Ty grabbed my fingers for an instant, then left us.

"I don't want to talk to you, Ruelle." I tried to make my expression show him how much I didn't want conversation. "In fact, I remember telling you that the next time I saw you, I'd give you a *lesson in mortality*, too." Threats were useless, but I'd never let him forget what I learned about his evil.

"Yes, Maat. And I have respected your wishes on the matter."

"*You* had me brought here, didn't you? Why?" I battled the urge to lift the silver blade again. *My hand held it in a fierce grip. I knew though, if I tried to slice him, he'd take it away from me. I'm fast, but not as fast as a vampire—or at least not this one.*

"Yes, Maat. I wanted to talk with you over a year ago. To my amazement, you had vanished. I have had others, not just the president, searching for you. I can usually locate you with ease, but this time... It's late now. I will explain tomorrow night. While I did not expect Emanis tonight, I went to your room several times this evening, to warn you she was here in New Washington. You were not there."

"Lucky you."

He laughed softly under his breath. It sounded like a broken sigh. "Oh, my love, Emanis woefully underestimated you. Time and adversity have increased your considerable power and intensity."

"Why me, Ruelle? For once in a thousand years, tell the truth. Why can't you either kill me or leave me alone?"

I wanted to threaten him, shake him, and somehow make him answer the questions he'd never answered over the years. Not only why had he made Gannett bring me here from Avalon, but why did he rescue me from New York? He'd risked Emanis' wrath even then. Why had he threaded his horrific existence into my life since that time?

Ruelle didn't speak. He reached out as if to touch me. I stepped back. I wanted to be gone from this place. I wanted the peace of Avalon. In that moment, foolish and self-deceiving as it was, I longed for the boredom, the dirt grubbing work. *Oh, what a misguided fantasy, Maat.* I'd never have that again.

"We will talk tomorrow night." Ruelle turned his eyes toward the door where they were trundling Emanis away. "I must go and be certain they keep her head away from the body and burn her."

I shivered. "You can put a head back on?"

"I doubt it, but we won't take any chances." Ruelle walked away, leaving me with the disturbing idea it might be possible to reattach a head and bring her back into this world.

The whole thing was out of my hands. I'd done my noble deed for the day…year…lifetime. With adrenalin rapidly draining from my body, I was going to have a bath and go to bed.

When I left the salon, Xavier's troops standing guard inside the door opened it for me. One asked if I needed anything. Fancy that. Killing a vamp got you more respect around here than killing the fuzzies.

Chapter Ten

Aaron Gannett laced his fingers around the whiskey glass. He watched Ruelle browse the books on the study walls. The barbarous scene in the salon kept replaying in his mind. The egotistical, ferocious bitch, the so-called Angel of Death, had killed the insane vampire who had so suddenly arrived to plague them.

And Sabrina, damn it! What possessed her to enter the room at that precise moment? Maat could have...but she hadn't.

It had taken him an hour to soothe Xavier. Gannett had begged for forgiveness and meant every word. He'd wanted to forestall conflict by keeping him and Maat apart and away from the party. Such a ridiculous idea. Maat Ferris personified conflict, and would until it killed her.

Ruelle had wanted to talk to Maat earlier, but when he went to fetch her, he couldn't find her. Damn. Ty, too. The boy had spirited her out of the mansion. He laughed softly at the irony of his own words about her. *You'd think the woman was an army of Amazons.*

The vampire chose a book and then came to sit on the couch. The creature moved with the assured grace of a powerful predator creeping through the forest.

Gannett found his voice. "Emanis...she was more powerful than you. Did you think that Maat could kill her?"

Ruelle smiled like a mildly amused aristocrat. "No, I did not. I wanted to enlist Maat's aid, and together we could formulate a plan and attack. I thought I could distract Emanis and hope Maat's hatred could drive her to kill. It never occurred to me our extraordinary hunter could do it alone. Although, she did have an unusual element of surprise."

"How? How did it happen?"

"I can only guess. I remember how she fought in New York. Each night Emanis forced her own blood down Matt's throat so she would heal for another night. Since our hunter is what you call psychic, she may have absorbed a degree of Emanis' power. Or she had it all along and didn't know."

Gannett shuddered, remembering the thick ridges of living flesh that had scored Maat's back. He frowned. "Vampire blood? It healed her?"

Ruelle shook his head. "It worked for a while. But she was close to death when I managed to get her out of the city. Still, with what she endured, it should have killed her sooner, or at least driven her mad."

"Mad? She's sane now?" Gannett drained his glass and reached for the bottle again. "And death? Ruelle, I swear, when it's time, the devil will have to come in person for Maat Ferris, tie her up, and drag her to hell. If he doesn't, she'll live forever."

"Indeed." Ruelle sounded so pleased, as if he'd had some hand in her vitality.

"You told me you rescued her, saved her. Got her out of New York." Here was the thing Gannett didn't understand. "She doesn't seem significantly grateful, does she?"

"No. For Maat, hatred for vampires overrides

personal gratitude. She suffered. She fought when she could have given up and died. That courage drew me to take a chance and rescue her. That and the desire to spite Emanis. She received her power eons ago from something best not spoken of, or otherwise revealed in this world. We are all well rid of her."

"Does that make you top vampire in the country? Did her crown fall to you?"

"It would seem so. Although there is another of great power in the west. Fortunately, he cares nothing for us and what we do here."

Gannett studied the vampire. "Are you in love with her? The Angel of Death?"

Ruelle's eyes glowed in the lamplight. "What makes you ask that?"

He shifted under the vampire's gaze. He couldn't take back the question, so he continued. "A dangerous woman to humans. Now you know how dangerous she can be to those of your kind. If you didn't love her—"

"I'd destroy her. And I may do so eventually. But I wouldn't call what I feel for her love."

Gannett shrugged. "I'm the man who loves a werewolf."

"A werewolf who sorely tempted fate tonight. A werewolf who loves you only a little more than Maat loves me, which is not at all. At least Sabrina allows you in her bed."

Ruelle's eyes focused on him. "Tell me, aren't you afraid your lovely red-head will change some night? Rip you to shreds?"

"No. Sabrina and I have an agreement."

"Agreement? Like your agreement with Colonel Xavier? He serves you because you *protect* his son. She behaves and you don't take the army and slaughter her pack?"

"Yes. Exactly." But if he could go back, if he could change things…

Gannett tossed down the last of his whiskey. He stood and walked out of the room, leaving the vampire reading a twentieth century novel of love and war.

Chapter Eleven

I woke when dawn's first light brightened the windows. Barring the occasional inconvenience of a few spectacular hangovers, I had always marveled each morning that I was still alive. After the incident of violence and triumph last night, I found unique delight at this day's rising sun. Much evil walked this world. I couldn't kill it all. Last night, though, when it came to the balance of good and evil, I'd dropped a solid coin on the good side.

I'd slept on the floor for the night, to keep the bed clean. Dressed in my bloody clothes, with the silver knife in my hand, I remained ready to fight. The battle had a greater impact on me than I realized. Exhausted as I was, once in my room, the specter of Ruelle coming in on me wouldn't let me get undressed and into the shower that I so desperately needed. I'd postponed it until daylight.

The door flew open, and Anolia raced in. Parr followed close behind her. I must have been a little addled since I arrived here, because it now occurred to me that my room door didn't have a lock.

"Maat!" Anolia rushed over and dropped to her knees beside me. She grabbed me, trying to lift me into her arms. Oh, sweet hell, I'd frightened her again.

Once I got her calmed down and rose to stand, I told her there was a vampire attack. I told her that I'd killed the creature. I said nothing about Ruelle. Parr had to know more, but he didn't ask questions. Nor would he meet my eyes. He had to have known about Ruelle, too. Like Ty, he'd offered no warning. *God save me from my friends!*

After I convinced Anolia that none of the blood on my clothes was mine and that I had no new bruises, she dug through drawers and produced clean clothing for me. *Had she found time to shop again?* Oh, well. As I had chosen her as a surrogate mother, she'd chosen me as her child. Dressing me up delighted her. She left only after I promised I would join them for breakfast downstairs once I washed and dressed. I tossed my bloody clothes in a trash basket, went into the bathroom, and gloried in the luxury of hot water. The welcomed sunshine through a tiny bathroom window helped ease my shredded nerves, too.

I was still enjoying my shower when Xavier moved within my psychic range. I turned off the water, dried, and then wrapped the towel around me. I was glad I'd taken that precaution because I damned sure didn't expect to find him sitting on the foot of my bed when I opened the bathroom door. I started to step back, but then where would I go? Damn it, if I could face Emanis, I could face a single man, even this one.

He stood, his gaze straight on me as it had been when he rushed in the salon last night. "I came for my shirt."

Man in black—big, tall, powerful, well-armed and…oh, hell. Now what do I do? Ty said Xavier loved me. We had something between us, emotions far more complex than love or hate. I couldn't explain it, even to myself.

I tucked the towel tight and walked to the closet, opened the door, and dragged his shirt off a hanger. I turned and offered it to him. Before I drew a breath, his heavy hands had a fierce grip on my shoulders. He drew a deep breath as if to speak, and—the door popped open.

Shit! From now on, I'd barricade the damned thing with a chair.

"Maat." Ty surged into the room. "I want to ask you." He thrust a short sword into the air. One of the silver-plated ones from the museum case I'd rejected as too long for me. "Is this enough silver for—" He stopped. His eyes widened, and a range of emotions played across his face. They settled into dismay.

Oh, well. It had to happen eventually. I tossed Xavier's shirt at him, marched up to Ty, and held out my hand for the sword. He lowered his eyes and obediently laid the hilt in my palm. I threw it out the open door, where it bounced off the wall between the man and woman in black shirts who had been guarding my room. I'd bet Xavier would make them pay later for letting Ty in. At the risk of losing my towel, I slammed both hands against Ty's chest and shoved him back a few steps.

"Listen to me." I had to shout. Nothing else would do. "The word is *no!* I will *not* teach you to hunt werewolves. I will *not* teach you to fight vampires. I want you to grow up, get married, and have children. *I want you to live!*"

"But, Maat…" His eyes flicked from me to Xavier.

I rarely explain anything. This time I had to try. "Ty, I can't endure it. I had two apprentices, once. Two kids who wanted to be hunters. They were skilled and fast, but not fast enough. My utter failure. I couldn't protect them, and I buried what a were left of them in western Kentucky." My body shook at the intensity of that memory. When I lost those two kids I loved, for the first time in my life, I asked if there might not be another path for me. It marked a signpost on my journey to Avalon.

Xavier moved in, grabbed Ty by the arm, and shoved the unresisting boy out the door. He glared at the black shirts. Then he slammed the door shut. He turned back, caught my shoulders again, and moved me to the bed. The bastard shoved me down on my stomach and lay beside me. Rage filled me, but I knew his strength, and I didn't waste energy fighting him. I'd been raped and survived. Only I didn't want it to be rape with him.

He gently drew the towel down to expose my back.

A feather touch of his fingers traced each scar. Delicate as a whisper, or a kiss on a child's hurt to make it go away. "Tell me about this." There was nothing delicate about the rage I heard in his voice.

I shivered, but I wasn't sure if it was his big warm body so close to mine, or the memory of New York. "They heated an iron bar and burned me. I screamed, cried, and begged them to kill me. Near dawn, Emanis—"

"The bitch you killed?"

"Yeah, that's her…was her. She made me drink her blood. The next night they started it all over again."

"Ruelle rescued you."

I had no idea how much Ruelle had told Gannett, or what Gannett might have told Xavier. "Yes, Ruelle carried me out of the city just before dawn. Hid me, then came back that night to carry me again. I don't know why. He took me to Ajax, a friend of mine, to heal. Ajax is a demolitions expert, so he and I went back a year later. We blew a few blocks of New York City's ruins to hell. We dumped a fuel tank of gas, so it would burn, too. I thought I had killed her." I didn't speak of how Ruelle gave me his own blood to save my life. He came every night until I was out of danger.

Xavier lay beside me for a moment, his breath in my ear. Just as I decided to turn and wrap my arms around him, keep him with me, he rose and left me alone. When I finally rolled over, I saw what I hadn't noticed before. My guns, the Aries, Rudra, and Sparks, holsters, ammo, and my silver knife in its arm sheath, lay on a chair across the room. The only thing missing was the small knife I'd stuck in his leg at Avalon. I bet he kept it as a souvenir.

Xavier...damn. What was I going to do about the man? I'd had the occasional companion over the years. I'd never considered any of them serious since my first lover, Mac, was killed in the Freak Squad. Sweet, kind Christopher was a friend, but he never roused emotions like Xavier. Xavier and I were like big raging cats. Our foreplay involved brutal shrieking battles full of teeth and claws. We'd get around to fucking eventually, if we didn't kill each other first.

I dressed, strapped on the Aries, Rudra, and the knife. Oh, yes! I felt like the true Maat, the Angel of Death, again. I stored the Sparks in a dresser drawer. I decided to wear the Rudra at my hip, and the Aries in the shoulder holster. The Rudra didn't have the Aries' range, but it handled the soft silver bullets better. I could be reasonably sure the bullet wouldn't go too far after it hit and punched through the target. That was always best indoors. Arm sheath strapped on, short knife in place, I purposely left the blade that killed Emanis in the dresser with the Sparks. When I opened the door, the two black shirt guards grinned at me.

I sneered in return. "Wasn't daddy bear a little pissed?"

"Yeah." One of them laughed out loud. "But it was worth it."

"Where'd Ty go?"

They grinned even more.

I had my guns, but I wouldn't have much freedom. If I could get outside the fence and walk around a bit, I might find Ruelle's lair for the day. Not likely, but I'd always been lucky that way. Drag that vampire out, let him burn. I would. I owed him nothing.

I caught a glimpse of Ty on the second floor.

"Ty, wait."

He stopped. His mouth turned down in a pout. He wouldn't look me in the eye.

I rarely explain anything, but for him I'd try. "Ty, it isn't what you think."

"Sure." He bowed his head as if to acknowledge an inevitable event.

I laid a hand on the rough black fabric of his shirt to get his attention. "Look. My guns. He brought me my guns."

Ty's eyes brightened, and his attitude changed instantly. For survival sake I needed more information. I could only think of one person who might be forthcoming enough to freely offer any. "Will you take me to Sabrina. I want to talk to Mrs. President."

He eyed me with interest—and a bit of suspicion.

"I swear I won't hurt her." I raised my hands, palms out. "I promise."

He appeared a little nervous. He didn't trust me. Damn it. He'd known things he should have told me, but instead used them in an attempt to manipulate me, to keep me here. Did he not recognize that Anolia was a hostage for my behavior?

"Okay. But come with me first," he said. He slipped his hand in mine and squeezed. "It won't take long."

He led me up to the third floor and ushered me into an apartment. The scent in the room told me Xavier lived there, too. An orderly place, not as lavish as the rest of the mansion, and conspicuously lacking any feminine ornament. Ty went to another room and came back with a picture frame. He handed it to me.

Easy to recognize him. He looked about six or seven in the photo. He had the same shy smile he'd given me on the first day I met him. The woman with the baby on her lap was pretty, but no great beauty. Xavier stood behind them. Xavier passed beyond handsome and into the realm of angelic. His eyes were on his family. I doubted he was ever narcissistic about appearance, nor did his scar concern him now. Ty looked like his mother but had a touch of his father's perfect face.

"This was taken about six weeks before my mother and my sister died," Ty explained. "I wanted you to see her because you'll understand. I had Lilly, but I missed Mama so much."

"Yeah, I miss my mom, too. It still hurts. Come on. Let's go talk to Sabrina."

Ty led me to the second floor and down a hallway

to an unguarded door. When he knocked, a comfortable looking woman with dark skin and darker eyes opened it for us.

"Maat," Ty said. "This is Mama Ann. She and Lilly made sure I ate all my vegetables while I was growing up."

Mama Ann hugged Ty and stared nervously at my guns. At his request, she went to ask Sabrina if she would see us. In a few minutes, she ushered us into a room with a wall of windows and a view across the city toward the mountains. To my surprise, Anolia sat on a couch with a cup of tea in her hands. Oops. I had promised to go to breakfast with her before Xavier sidetracked me bringing my guns. And lying beside me on the bed. And leaving before I could grab hold of him.

Sabrina rose to meet us. She wore an ivory dress that set off her green eyes and gold streaked, copper hair. An exquisite beauty—but still a werewolf.

"Welcome, Maat." She seemed genuinely glad to see me. I turned to Mama Ann. "Ty looks a little thin. You should take him and feed him. Keep up his energy."

Mama Ann grinned and dragged a mildly protesting Ty out the door. Maybe there wasn't another secret passage where she was taking him. His snooping was dangerous. He'd probably been doing it for years, but if he used information to attempt to manipulate the wrong person it would hurt him. Xavier couldn't protect him from everything.

I sat by Anolia. She leaned against me, shoulder to shoulder. "Please, please, listen Maat. This is important." Her voice was so soft I could barely hear.

Sabrina sat on a couch facing us. She clasped her hands tightly on her lap. "We must speak quickly, before someone realizes you're here."

Who realized? Her husband? I'd take whatever information I could get. "What were you doing on the mountain that day?"

Sabrina leaned forward. She seemed so earnest. "My pack received word of the planned attack, and we went to help you. It wasn't necessary. You fulfilled all expectations for the Angel of Death. Please tell me though. You recognized me last night in the salon. How?"

"I'm not sure. Your eyes, I think. And the shade of hair. Why come to help me?"

"Maat, there is far more here than you know, and more than I can tell you in the time we have. Watch, and in God's name, don't take anything for granted. You have a vital task to complete. More important than killing werewolves and vampires." She softly clapped her hands and laughed. "A vampire! For the love of God. Impossible, but you killed a vampire."

Gannett walked in. If she wanted to tell me something without his knowledge it was too late. He scanned the room, and his mouth formed a dictator's facetious smile. Sabrina rose and went to him, slipped her arm in his, and kissed his cheek. He kissed *her* on the mouth. He so obviously loved his werewolf wife. No wonder Ruelle wanted me to kill her last night in the salon. She had to be a significant threat to his influence over the president. Dangerous game. A werewolf married to a dictator didn't need lessons in danger from me, though.

"May I join you?" Gannett's insincere smile

widened. "Or is this just girl talk?"

I tried my best to look evil. "You see any girls here?"

"No, Maat, but—" This time his eyes widened when he noticed my guns. Xavier had obviously not informed his boss that he was rearming me.

"Don't worry." I reassured him. "I'll behave myself. I was going to ask Sabrina to tell me what I *don't know* about weres. She's the first one I've ever spoken to. I'm a kill on sight hunter. No conversation required. You can listen if you want."

"Why, thank you." A flash of anger crossed Gannett's face. An irreverent scruffy werewolf hunter had told him what he could do in his own house. I had more vital concerns. Like survival. Ruelle wanted me, needed me for something. His pet president wasn't going to hurt me. Not yet, anyway.

We sat together in that pleasant room, and Maat the werewolf hunter, the Angel of Death, received a lesson of a lifetime.

My first question? "Weres and vamps. Are they related?"

Sabrina leaned forward, with an earnest expression. "We are alike in only one thing that I know of, but I know little of vampires. We were all once human. I believe more of that humanity remains in werewolves."

The dismay on the president's face was evident, but the hypocrite kept the King of Wickedness as an *advisor*.

I shrugged. "More humanity? The lesser of..." Anolia shot me an exasperated glare.

"The lesser of evils." Sabrina finished for me. "Am I evil?"

"I don't know. Tell me why you're different?"

Sabrina visibly swallowed. She folded her hands on her lap in a complete non-confrontational pose, as if she suddenly realized she faced serious peril in her own home.

"There are few survivors of a werewolf attack. I think you know that. But when there is one, there are still incredible odds against a victim successfully making the first shape-shifting transformation. It's devastating. Have you ever seen a were change shape?"

"A few times, yes. But I didn't stand and watch. If one goes fuzzy in front of me, I'm in serious trouble. I usually shoot it numerous times with silver bullets."

She brushed the side of her head with her palm, smoothing hair coiled in a flame color braid. "Most bite survivors who also survive the first transition retain human characteristics. The ability to reason, understand cause and effect. Good or evil, whatever our nature before the attack, remains. Mostly we try to live unnoticed in the population, in the cities."

In the cities I avoided. "Mostly?"

"There are criminals among us, too, Maat." Her face filled with sadness. "Unfortunately, a few survivors become dim-witted, as if the trauma damaged their minds. They're harmless and need protection. You've probably never seen one of those. Then there are the rogues. As I understand it, you've fought them most of your life. They are our enemies, too. Aggressive wild animals, attacking in packs, never or rarely ever taking human form again. Those are, rightfully, your prey."

Rightful prey. Not words I would have chosen because it suggests that some of my kills were unjustified. They were not. More men and werewolves would die before all the battles for our world ceased.

"So, Sabrina, you think the next time I see a werewolf I should ask if it's good or evil before I shoot?"

Sabrina gasped, plainly unnerved by the suggestion. "Not if you want to live. Those who *do not* want to fight will remain in human form and certainly avoid you. Justice is well served by your guns, Suriel."

Sabrina breathe rapidly. Gannett looked like he'd break into hysterics, but she grabbed his wrist. "Sorry. This disturbs me, but I must go on. We're not true wolves. I think you know that. We're no more or less an animal than anyone in this room. We're shape-shifters. A biological anomaly. We should not exist. And yet we live."

"Biological anomaly. And that's how you're like a vampire?"

Sabrina shook her head. "As I *understand it*, a vampire must drain and replace a human's blood to make another vampire. Werewolves only require an open wound, or in recent times, a hypodermic syringe. The needle removes the danger of trauma from an injurious bite, but not from the change itself. It might kill when it takes hold, even on a willing participant."

"Willing! Who would...?"

"Want to be a werewolf? The average life span of a werewolf who survives the initial change, with mind intact, is four hundred years. That would be tempting for many. There's also the rapid healing ability with non-silver weapons, absence of disease and probably other things I've never experienced."

Four hundred years? I raised an eyebrow at that

assertion, but I had to go on. "Why are most weres male?"

"Most women who are bitten die during the first transformation. I don't know why. I survived, but I couldn't walk for weeks afterward. A werewolf who thought he was in love and wanted to keep me with him bit me thirty years ago. I made the transformation successfully, bided my time, then I tore him to pieces. Did you know female werewolves are physically stronger than males? Even in human form, though, all werewolves are faster and stronger than regular humans."

Gannett started to reach for her, then hesitated. She sat there with her incredible beauty, speaking of violent actions like the deadly creature I knew her to be. A werewolf indeed.

I sat back to think about what she said. Sabrina and Ruelle looked and acted human on the surface, but danger lay beneath it all. I could certainly kill a were easier than a vamp. *And part of what she told me didn't exactly sync with my werewolf experiences.* The major revelation was the extra strength and speed in human form.

"So, Sabrina, do you call it magic? Or disease?"

"I don't believe in magic, but I understand why a person would use the word. The transformation itself defies the so-called laws of physics and biology. Disease? Not in the truest sense. Infection? Perhaps that's the best word for werewolves."

More information for me to consider, although I wasn't sure how useful it would be. While I'd dealt with *psychic* abilities most of my life, I'd never seen any proof of true magic. She was right. The change in shape defied laws of biology and physics. Slapping a name on the process changed nothing. She'd said nothing about Parr's so-called *scientific reports* that the Devil's Dance plague caused supposedly peaceful werewolves to go wild and crave human flesh.

"Sabrina, do you ever have the urge to kill something?"

"Maat!" Anolia jerked.

Oh well, I'm not known for my respectable manners.

Gannett stiffened and started to rise. "I don't think—"

Sabrina caught him by the arm and dragged him back down. "It's an honest question, Aaron." Her intense, green eyes suddenly changed to animal amber and gazed straight into mine. "I'm primarily a carnivore. I prefer meat warm and raw. If I get it from the butcher, it's nourishing and palatable. My preference is to run a deer down occasionally. The thrill of the hunt is exciting, too." She gave me a smile that embodied the essence of things not human.

Sabrina slowly stood. I rose to meet her. No werewolf would have the advantage of standing over me. The room air charged with tension—killing tension.

"Draw your silver knife," Sabrina said.

Problem. I had my hand on the Rudra. If I released it to draw the knife, I lost my advantage.

"Maat." Anolia called to me, her voice calm.

I sighed and drew my knife from the forearm sheath. I held it out to her, blade first. She could strike me dead, but I stood close enough to take her with me.

Sabrina shivered. She reached out a trembling

hand, touched the razor edge with her forefinger, then snatched it back. The barest touch of silver opened a substantial wound spurting blood.

With crimson running down her arm onto her fine dress she said, "I swear to you, upon your silver blade and my life blood, I have never harmed a human. Will you accept that?"

Should I take a were's oath? The oath had caused her genuine fear and pain. But I had my life's experiences to deal with.

"Accept? I will certainly try, Sabrina."

Anolia and Gannett jumped up to tend to her wound. It would heal, but she'd made a sacrifice touching the blade. She insisted that we sit and continue talking after they bound the cut.

"My pack is very peaceful," Sabrina said. "Others are not. We thought things had settled a few years ago, but there's been a sudden dramatic increase in the number of werewolves. I can't conceive of how many have died during first transformations to reach those numbers. We're trying to find out where those who attacked the mountain house came from. They were not rogue. It required too much planning.

"The alpha of my pack believes your exceptional reputation has frightened the other packs in the area. They knew Aaron was looking for you, and they feared the possibility of you forming an alliance with him. There's a revenge factor, too. You have killed so many."

I rubbed the back of my neck, suddenly weary. "Two years. Monsters we thought we'd eliminated were reproducing while I lazed around at Avalon."

Anolia squeezed my hand to offer comfort.

"Have I made you think any differently about werewolves?" Sabrina's smile was too bright, too eager.

I stood. "Well, I'm going to leave here with you alive, Sabrina. I don't know if you've seen or experienced the slaughter or agony that made me a hunter. But I do love something more than I love killing monsters." I nodded at Anolia.

Gannett hissed like a snake.

Sabrina laughed—a soft musical sound of genuine humor. At him? Or me? Okay. This lovely monster had a sense of humor and more than a little courage. Ty had managed to get back in the room. I figured the conversation would drop to a mediocre level, so I grabbed him and left.

Chapter Twelve

"This one." I offered Ty the silver-coated steel blade. But only after we left Sabrina and I made him procure me a private lunch. He had friends in the kitchen, so we had tasty food and laughs. He'd mostly grown up here and called it home.

After that, he'd persuaded me to return to the weapons room. To soothe his injured ego, I agreed to help him choose a knife. I warned him again against hunting monsters. I don't know if he truly accepted that warning or agreed to placate me. The shattered glass case stood as we'd left it last night. Obviously, the mansion had more guards than maintenance workers.

"Why?" Ty grasped the hilt. The blade's deep silver luster reflected light from the high windows. It was too long for me, but it fit him. He had Xavier's height, and if he ever bulked up, he'd make a whopping man.

"Most of these are either pure silver or only have a thin plate. I like a solid steel core with a thick plate. Heavier, but worth the added weight."

"You can fight with a knife?"

"I can, but I avoid it when possible. A blade's useful to have at times. Sadly, if you manage to get close enough to cut or stab a werewolf, you're dead. The same is true with a human unless you're highly trained. A gun's faster, better. And you might survive."

He chuckled and laid an arm across my shoulders. "The troops who brought you in the helicopter said you fight dirty."

"Of course I fight dirty! Sweetheart, I'm tough. I'm strong and fast and know a few respectable moves. But men outmuscle me twenty to fifty percent. If I can't use my guns, I'll use what's available."

"Oh." Ty frowned. "I guess I didn't think of it that way. When you came up here last night, how did you know what to choose? I thought silver didn't work on vampires."

"I didn't *know* anything except that Ruelle was in that room and I was unarmed. I didn't know Emanis was here. I guess his presence covered hers. Or maybe she'd just arrived."

Let him believe I was attempting to kill Ruelle. I didn't plan to tell him the head I'd gone to remove belonged to Aaron Gannett. The president as front man for a power-mad scheming vampire equaled incredible danger to everyone.

"Since I couldn't get to my guns, I chose the best available weapon. Everything else in this room is too big or too small. Silver doesn't work on vampires like it does weres—unless you cut their heads off. In this case, it was pure luck."

A change in the air around me sent a warning signal. I drew a sharp breath. "Shit."

"What is it?" Ty lifted the blade.

"Xavier's coming." Yep, psychically attuned. How had it happened? And why?

Ty's gaze drifted nervously around the room.

"Is there a problem?" Was he looking for an escape route?

"Well, we're kind of stealing pieces of the president's collection."

"Right! And who did he steal them from? Which museum did he loot?"

Ty stared at me and flashed his little boy grin. "I guess it's okay then. I mean to steal stolen stuff from a thief. Like the *Treasure Hunt*."

The *Treasure Hunt* he referred to was current slang for the ongoing search for the magic pot of gold. At some point during WW III, the gold of the US Treasury disappeared. Since we currently live in a barter or gold coin society, it would be a prize if located. I won't say I saw it, but vampires like gold too, and they sat on incredible piles of it in New York. Of course, my friend Ajax and I had buried it and them under a million tons of steel and concrete when our plan for revenge went sideways. No one would be getting to it soon. Not a problem, since neither I nor my demo man had ever craved that kind of wealth.

Xavier walked through the open door. He glared at me. "What are you doing now?"

Smart-ass me, I couldn't resist. "Figuring out the best way to piss you off."

"You have to work at it? That's a surprise." Xavier stared at the knife in Ty's hand and then turned hard eyes on me. "You're teaching him to steal."

"I'll teach him to survive."

The tone of Xavier's voice didn't match the message I received from his rigid body. My ability to perceive his presence had swollen into a haunting specter with a life of its own. I could sense his confusion and anger, too.

"He's only seventeen." Xavier didn't seem

reassured by my words on survival.

"And the big bad werewolf hunter might corrupt him, right?"

Great. Ty had lied to me about his age.

"Stop." Ty ground out the word through clenched teeth. "This is so…stupid." He stalked to the door and marched out. He took the knife with him. Was that a tear I saw in his eye?

Xavier and I stood there as time swelled into an awkward silence. For the life of me, I couldn't think of a single smart-ass remark. I opted for the truth.

"I won't hurt him, Xavier. I swear, I'll do my best to protect him while I'm here. I won't let him follow me when I leave."

Xavier watched me with those raven eyes. The armor lining the walls mirrored his shield of silence. But he stood closer than he needed for casual conversation. He wasn't moving away, and neither was I. In fact, we seemed to be drawing together. Could he feel it, that dark energy swirling through the room?

He reached out, and his fingers trailed down my arm. Were those his lips on my throat, my fingers against the rough, black cloth of his shirt?

The slight brush of a sound received an instantaneous reaction from us both.

Ty stepped into the room, and immediately stopped when he found himself staring at the barrels of two pistols. Shit! Xavier could out-draw me.

Xavier and I eyed each other, relaxed with a sigh, and lowered our guns.

"I…Aaron…" Ty stammered. "Aaron wants both of you."

"And how did that come about?" Xavier shoved his

Aries back in its holster. Ty shrugged, but the little shit's mouth twitched at the corners.

Xavier's breath hissed through his teeth. He stalked out the door. At least he wasn't pissed at me this time. After he left the room, a grin split Ty's lips. Or at least it did until I punched him in the stomach. Not hard, but he felt the blow. He grunted and wrapped both arms around his body. Since I'd been summoned too, I followed Xavier to the stairs.

Ty was on my heels. "You hit me."

"Oh, shut up. Baby. Whiner. If I'd wanted to hurt you, you'd be on the floor."

He lowered his head, accepting defeat. I cared for him, but he made it difficult because one minute he was a little boy and the next he...well, damn it, he was always a little boy.

Xavier didn't look back as we trooped down the stairwell to the first floor. When we got there, he received his orders from the president. Sabrina and Anolia were going—of all damned things—shopping. They had insisted I go with them. Monsters might eat us alive, the president might shoot us, the world might end, but let's go shopping first. Someone responsible, someone skilled, had to go and be sure Anolia, and by default, Maat, returned. If she and I were together I might find a way to grab her and escape. Mr. President, evidently, considered Xavier the only one competent enough to restrain us from fleeing.

After Xavier formed a special guard, he resorted to his default attitude and blamed me again. I had to give myself credit. I didn't laugh at him. I did cover my smile with my hand. Well, I used my fingers, so he'd be sure to see. Why did I enjoy pissing him off so much?

Ty didn't laugh, since Xavier refused to let him go with us.

New Washington looked modern in the daylight. Young emerald-leaf trees lined the roadside, and we rode round-a-bouts with pink and white flowers in center islands. The early afternoon late spring air smelled sweet. I ached for the freedom of the mountains where wild azaleas and mountain laurel would be in bloom.

I stared out the limo's window. A few trucks and turtles passed, moving in the opposite direction. Two troop carriers, each loaded with well-armed black shirt soldiers, went before and behind us. I considered the show of arms a bit excessive, even for little old me.

Sabrina had dressed for the occasion in plain slacks and a shirt. She'd bound her glorious hair in a scarf. Anolia dressed the same, but she'd twisted her auburn hair into a bun at the nape of her neck. My jeans and T-shirt were good enough for me. And I had the Aries. Xavier wanted me to leave my guns, but I argued and he left me with one. He did confiscate all of my ammunition except the clip the gun held. It was either agree with his demand or stay locked up in the mansion.

Anolia patted my hand. "I've been told about this market. You'll like it. I hear there's lots of chaos."

"What? You think I like chaos." I was being cynical, of course. Chaos was fine by me. Unless I had a stake in the outcome, I could stand apart, and enjoy the general mayhem.

An odd thought nagged me. We'd been in the car for over twenty minutes, and Anolia hadn't mentioned Parr. She'd seemed to be growing closer to him. I started to ask, and then decided not to. I think she wanted to talk to me alone, but we hadn't had the chance. And we had no idea who might be listening.

We rode away from New Washington into what might have been a small town before the war. The single-story buildings without windows and doors weren't ruins, only victims of salvaging, to create the new city. The limo parked in an open red clay field among dozens of trucks and turtles. The doors stayed shut until Xavier's troops surrounded us.

Uncle Jake taught me to shoot, hunt, and defy authority. Aunt Nell taught me history. They both hated the military. Uncle Jake's fury came from experience and seemed general and all-inclusive. Anyone in uniform was a criminal and/or a coward. Aunt Nell called soldiers hired guns of tyranny and assassins of democracy. My aunt's passion, her love of country, would have quailed before what I saw when I climbed out of the limo.

"Is that why…"

Sabrina came to stand beside me. "Yes. This is the Bell Market. I've asked Aaron to do something about it, but he won't budge. It's not important in his world."

I heard sadness in her voice.

The Bell Market. The Liberty Bell Market. I'd seen pictures. The object sitting on a concrete platform, aged almost beyond recognition, had to be the original, cracked bell. Thank God Aunt Nell couldn't see this travesty.

During the last heaving gasps of the war, low-level nukes had blasted Old Washington to gravel. Patriots were supposed to move the most important historical documents and artifacts out and hide them in a safe place. Gannett had a valuable stash of art in his mansion, but I didn't see anything remotely political. Not likely the bastard would display the Constitution anyway, unless he could make it a rug on the floor.

Xavier was suddenly at my side, his hand firmly grasping my arm. I guess he'd seen the look on my face as I stared at the bell.

"Let it go, Maat." Anolia crowded close on my other side. "Save your anger for greater things. They will appear soon, I'm sure."

I relaxed. Xavier released me.

I didn't look back as we entered the Bell Market, surrounded by a troop of the black shirt soldiers.

Sabrina's arm made a wide sweep at the scene before us. "The market is run by a group of...merchants...for want of a better word. You can buy, or sell, *anything*." The last word came out with a touch of a monster snarl.

Carts of fresh vegetables, stacks of linens and hand-crafted items lined what had once been commercial streets of a small town. Men and women scurried among the carts and tables, carrying merchandise. I'd been to similar markets, and this one seemed ordinary—until you looked closer. A few of the buildings had boarded up windows and armed guards standing beside the doors. Whoever bartered there didn't want daylight on their transactions.

I had to ask. "What's the *anything* here? What's for sale? Sex? Kids? Not much I haven't seen, Sabrina." I'd often encouraged myths and wild stories of my fighting prowess to bolster my reputation. Several of the true tales involved wreaking havoc on certain monetary transactions I deemed totally wicked in nature.

"It wasn't always like this." Sabrina's voice sounded sad. "A farmer's market. That's how it began. Then the others moved in and no one stopped them." She cut her eyes to Xavier. "Decent people have tried to clean it up," she said softly. "But a few powerful merchants make considerable money here."

And the president didn't give a shit. He likely got a share of the take to turn his head. Not that I could throw stones. Wait. Yes, I could lob a few. While I never robbed regular people or small merchants, I had stolen and sold hard merchandise, much of it from the militias and Aaron Gannett's army. I occasionally persuaded a rich asshole to share a reasonable chunk of his fortune with me, too. No, I wasn't a virtuous person. I never pretended to be, even at Avalon. I did, however, try not to hurt innocent bystanders. The words *collateral damage* drove me to fury and precipitated many a battle.

"Why did you bring me here?" I rubbed my hand over the Aries, secure in its holster. This was not comfortable. Every breath, every step, intensified a sense of danger. "Not just a shopping trip?"

"No." Sabrina lowered her voice. "My pack leader is often here, and I wanted you to meet him if possible. It's difficult for me to contact him. He's much older than I am, and exceptionally wise. He could tell you much more about us than I can, if we can manage time."

Pack leader? I'd asked her about werewolves—while sitting in the sunroom of a mansion—but a meeting went a little too far. A werewolf, mature, intelligent, an alpha leader was a level above a biology lesson. Despite her beauty and the friendship she seemed to be offering, it was incredibly difficult to trust a werewolf. I'd built my life around killing the fuzzy things. It would take more than a cheery hello and a warm smile to change that.

Xavier had moved away from us. His eyes searched the crowd, and he stopped occasionally to speak to one of his men or women. He had a sharp-eyed female sergeant who glared at me as if I was the devil incarnate. Jealous, I'm sure. I'd bet news of the incident in my room earlier in the day traveled fast in the mansion. The fact that nothing happened with us didn't mean shit.

The market goers watched with wary eyes and stepped out of the black shirts' way. They didn't panic, so I'd guess they'd seen them before on occasion.

We passed alleys and I could see more trading, but the number of guarded doors increased. I wasn't surprised to see a few mercenaries I knew standing as guards. I also recognized a couple of merchants I'd dealt with before, peddling their wares in the alleys.

Sabrina stepped close to me again. "My pack leader doesn't seem to be here today. I want to ask you to have patience. There are things you don't understand, but it will become clear soon."

More wait and see garbage. Mystery bullshit. *This wasn't a fucking game!*

Anolia glanced around at the soldiers. "I need to talk to both of you later, too," she said softly. "I've learned something that profoundly disturbs me. I don't understand it, but Maat needs this information. It's important, imperative, that she know."

Sabrina nodded her agreement. "I'll make sure

we're alone."

The president's wife stopped at a table of woven clothing. Red, yellow, and blue shirts hung from stick hangers, and thick rugs draped the table. She and Anolia exchanged pleasant words with the vendor, a thin man who launched into a lengthy speech about wool from sheep fed solely on a weird diet.

To my surprise, I felt the presence of another were as we approached a sizeable crossroads. I'd thought being close to Sabrina might deaden my senses, but this one hit me strong and true. A high-pitched wail came from ahead of us. The sound cut the air, wavering, agonized, and inhuman—like a shrill winter wind cutting through cracked glass. Sabrina clutched her hands to her chest and moaned.

Xavier acted quickly. He ordered the black shirts to close ranks and turn around. Sabrina would have none of that. She shoved them aside as she forced herself forward. I followed in her wake. I almost plowed over her when she staggered to a stop.

A substantial metal cage, wrapped with a few strands of thin silver wire on the bars, sat on a trailer twenty feet in front of us. Inside, a young werewolf boy, about twelve or thirteen years old, whimpered and curled in a ball on the floor. He was naked and in human form. He moved only when a man jabbed him with a silver pointed stick. The man looked like a farmer, with dirty hands and big booted feet.

"Change, damn you!" the farmer shouted at the were. "Show em' you're not human." He jabbed the stick again, this time hard enough the silver punctured skin. The werewolf boy screamed in agony. A sign leaning against the trailer proclaimed that the boy was for sale. A curious crowd stood around and stared, but others shook their heads in disgust and walked away.

"Come on," the farmer shouted at the onlookers. "Caught it in my sheep pen. Make me an offer and he's yours. Use 'em for target practice."

A full-grown werewolf would have torn through that little bit of silver, then ripped the cage and the man apart. The boy, young, inexperienced, and starving, couldn't. A mature werewolf would have gone for the farmer first, and then taken the sheep. Oh, I didn't like it, but I'd seen it before. It was not my business. If I'd caught the boy, I'd have ended it right there before he reached maturity and started killing humans.

The black shirts closed around us and forced us away. I thought Sabrina might resist, but Anolia seized her arm, and she stilled. That was Anolia's greatest gift, the ability to instantly soothe and calm in dire situations.

Gunshots, I counted five, erupted in the distance. The arrangement of buildings, alleys, and streets wouldn't allow me to pinpoint the exact location.

"Back to the car," Xavier's tight voice ordered.

The black shirts turned and surged forward, forming a tight shield around us. I guess shopping was over. Tears ran down Sabrina's face as they hurried us along.

Anolia held Sabrina's arm. Sabrina leaned toward me. "Maat, please. Is there anything we can do for him?"

Why ask me? She was the president's wife for God's sake.

"What did you have in mind, Sabrina?" I eyed Xavier, who walked along the perimeter of our guard.

And he was watching me for sure. While the kid's torment made me uncomfortable, and Sabrina had shown me a new perspective, I was a werewolf hunter, not a savior. Certainly not a liberator. The vivid memory of the young Corporal Sanders who died on the mountain not long ago asking me to kill his murderers for him, remained.

Anolia dug in her pants pocket and lifted out a purse that jingled in her fingers. "There's twenty full golds here. Will it buy him?"

"I don't buy monsters." I wasn't being nasty, just stating the facts. Even if I bought him, I'd never be able to free him. The mob would expect me to kill him immediately. If I didn't, one of them would.

Sabrina turned angry eyes on me. "Then steal him."

"That's a bad plan." The worst plan I'd heard of since I challenged Xavier at Avalon. "You've never offered me any harm, Sabrina, but—"

"He's a child, Maat."

Damn. She knew better. "And when he grows up, who will he kill?"

Sabrina's eyes turned wolf yellow, and I knew that was a precursor to a shape change. I hope she had control of herself. If she did turn full were and tried a rescue, people would die. Her secret exposed, they'd kill her too. That would create an unbearable disaster when Gannett came to avenge her. He had a reputation for slaughter.

Anolia's eyes met mine, and I saw the challenge there, too.

Uphold your reputation Maat. The Angel of Death come forth. Avalon's peace is gone forever. Carnage rules. Fuck!

Xavier had moved ahead of me now. How long since my last fight? Long enough. I edged closer to Sabrina. "Okay. Watch me. When I rub my hand over my mouth, you and Anolia get their attention. Don't make it *too* obvious. Unless you can get Xavier to trip over you."

We walked on, and my opportunity arrived. Fate, luck, or coincidence, several things happened at once. A group of armed men, mercenaries by the look of them, shoved though the crowd toward us. Probably a merchant's bodyguards, but the black shirts immediately lowered their gun barrels and prepared to fight. As they did, I rubbed my hand over my mouth. Sabrina stumbled and fell to the pavement, taking Anolia with her. So much for *not being obvious.*

I punched my way through the black shirts and dashed down the alley. Two of them were immediately on my heels. I'd bet Xavier had given them orders to stick with me if I broke away, no matter what the circumstances. My game though, and I was ahead. They carried more equipment than I did. And go me. I'd had experience running from soldiers.

I ducked behind a display table and shoved it over in front of them. The table's owner pulled a knife, only to have a black shirt punch him in the stomach with the butt of an automatic rifle as he passed.

I gained running room before they pounded after me. What fun. I'd missed this action. These guys were good. I loved a challenge, especially since they weren't shooting at me. Time to change tactics. I turned a corner and dashed in the first open door—right into the middle of a dogfight. Men stood around the short, fenced circle, cursing and urging two four-legged beasts to tear each other apart.

I'll admit I have a fondness for watching two evenly matched humans pound the shit out of each other. It was a familiar part of my violent world. It usually involved a choice. Animals? No way. Two muscular, short-legged dogs, a brindle and a gray, both sheeted with blood, tore at each other. The brindle had won, although he bled from mortal wounds himself. True to his nature, he savaged his barely living opponent.

I ran for an open window. I stopped, drew the Aries, and put both animals out of their misery. I'd have felt better if I could have shot their owners, too. Aries holstered, I dove out the window headfirst, rolled, and raced away.

I left turmoil behind me as the black shirts chasing me charged into the room. They were big boys, and they could take care of themselves. The sound of automatic weapon fire chattered behind me. Ah, justice for the poor doggies.

I headed back toward the market center at a fast walk. The dogfight gunfire had stirred the crowd, but they couldn't pinpoint its location as the shots echoed through the alleys. Random gunfire on a normal market day event? No panic—yet.

So, I was down by two bullets. My own insecurity descended, and I felt the immediate need for more ammo. No telling what I problems I might run into. I hurried on toward the area where the werewolf was caged. What luck! There was a merchant I'd unfortunately dealt with in the past.

Bemon Belcher sat his fat ass on an oversized stool

and watched me approach. His piggy little eyes narrowed a bit, but his pale face remained neutral. A wide assortment of clips, ammunition, knives, and other hand weapons lay on a table between us. The bigger guns were behind him, guarded by two mean looking brutes lounging against the wall.

"Belcher." I nodded cordially. "Long way from Memphis."

"I could say the same to you." Belcher's fleshy lips quivered as he spoke. It didn't surprise me that he was here. He was a traveling merchant, scavenging and thieving as he moved along. Some merchants spent their profit on alcohol, some on sex, corpulent Belcher consumed great quantities of rare gourmet foods.

I casually scanned his wares. Then I met his eyes. "You owe me."

"I owe you," Belcher agreed and held out his hands in an expansive gesture.

He had two clips for the Aries. Neither were loaded. I stared at him and raised an eyebrow. He signaled one of his brutes, who dug around behind him and came up with a couple of boxes of silvers. He knew that's what I'd want. They weren't the high impacts, but they would do. He set them on the table. I picked them up and swiftly punched bullets in the clips. Belcher sat on his stool, silent and unmoving, until I finished.

"Are we even?" Belcher asked softly.

"What?" I quickly stuck the extra clips in my pockets. "Your ass is worth more than a little ammo." I'd saved his life once. A gang of rogue militia troops had a noose around his neck and was prepared to relieve him of his debauched existence and steal his merchandise. Belcher is disgusting, but they could have robbed him without killing him. Belcher drew a breath to speak, but then stopped. His guards straightened and went on alert. I knew what it was without turning. Xavier had entered the alley. Walking, not running.

"Slow him down, Belcher, and we're even." I jerked my head in Xavier's direction. "But don't hurt him, or you'll find your neck in *my* rope."

Belcher nodded, a slow smile spreading over his face. There was a considerable bit of commotion behind me as I raced away. In seconds, I was at the silver wrapped cage. I drew the Aries. I shot the farmer in the toes, right near the tips. Painful but not fatal.

He plopped to the pavement and howled, much like the boy he'd tortured with silver moments ago. My second shot smashed the cage's lock. I jerked it open, snatched the stunned were boy by the hair and dragged him out.

I jerked him to his feet and released him. "Run. Don't change shape until you're away from here."

It was all I could do. At least he was smart enough to listen. He stumbled away and disappeared in an alley. He'd be naked, but anyone who didn't know him for what he was might hesitate to shoot him on sight.

The crowd around me stirred, then fell silent. It parted to allow Xavier to stalk through. His dark eyes focused on the scene. The empty cage, the rough farmer lying on the pavement moaning, and me—standing there with the Aries in my hand.

Xavier turned to the crowd. He drew a breath and spoke loud enough to carry, but he didn't shout. "Troops are coming. If anyone's interested."

The crowd sighed collectively. Individually, they

melted away. Xavier turned, ignored me, and went to stand beside the farmer. He dropped a half-gold coin on the pavement in front of the man's face. "That's for your were." He tossed two more coins, both full golds. "For your foot. Don't come back here."

I eased closer to Xavier. His aura radiated like a slow fire, dark on the outside and white-hot underneath. He let me approach. Oh, God, I could smell the anger, the rage. And yes, the desire. Even seeing and knowing his fury, I clenched my fists to keep from grabbing him.

"The others are waiting for us." He turned and walked away, leaving me alone.

It would be easy for me to slip away then. Ruelle would come after me, but I'd be ready for him. I'd done Sabrina a big favor. Could I trust her and Parr to protect Anolia? Probably. Maybe.

Who was I kidding?

It was Xavier I followed. He drew me after him like he had a hook in my guts. Worst of all, he knew it too. I caught up with him and walked at his side. Vendors were the only people left at the market, and they were packing up—fast. Nothing like a few gunshots to ruin your day.

I passed Belcher. He glared at me and bared his teeth. He pointed at his guards lying prone on the ground. They were moving, though, crawling, obviously wishing to leave such a dangerous place. Xavier had won again.

Xavier slowed his pace. "So. Since when did Maat Ferris become a—"

"Dog fucker? Hey, I just wanted to shoot something. It's been a while."

Xavier stopped so fast I outpaced him and had to

turn back. "What do you think?" He asked with no anger, no malice. "Are werewolves monsters? Or humans with a disease?"

"I don't think anything. I…" I gasped and staggered. A substantial number of werewolves had come within my range and changed shape, all in a single moment. Xavier didn't wait for me to explain. He dashed off in the direction of the vehicles. I was right behind him.

"Your men have silver?" I called to him.

"Handguns. Couldn't get any for the rifles."

We pounded along the pavement. He went around a woman, and I shoved a man out of my way. *Damn, why was it so far? Hadn't we walked this way a few minutes earlier?*

If attacked, the black shirts would fire rifles first and let the weres get too close before they went for the silver in the smaller handguns. The sound of rapid gunfire confirmed my guess, but the single shots of pistols soon replaced the larger weapons.

We dodged and shoved the now panicked vendors out of the way. We burst into the parking lot, and a wounded were staggered in front of us. We both fired. Ahead, by the vehicles, lay black shirts and werewolf bodies. Strewn about on the ground, Mother Earth's red clay accepted the profuse offering of human and monster blood without prejudice.

Xavier's troops had shown their skill and courage, but it cost all their lives. Only two attacking weres remained. The pair had Sabrina and Anolia trapped against the limo. Sabrina's clothes lay in rags on the ground where they'd fallen when she changed shape to fight. Her shift had to wait until all the troops went down or they would have killed her, too. Snarling and slashing, she kept the two attackers at bay.

Anolia backed up against the limo behind her. I'd seen plenty of weres fight from a distant hidden place, and skill is not a thing I'd associated with them. Throw the arms up and slash down was the preferred attack method. Speed, force, and fury, no expertise required. Sabrina, however, had mastered an alien battle form.

The two attacking weres had their attention focused on their victims as Xavier and I edged around, trying to get a clear shot. Both our guns packed a reliable power, and at this range, a silver could easily blast through the weres' body and kill Sabrina and Anolia.

One of the weres, a big male, lashed out at Sabrina. She slashed back. He howled and jumped away. Xavier picked him off. As the sound of the shot faded, the last were, a rare slate-colored female, ignored Sabrina. She charged straight in. Three-inch claws punched deep into Anolia's stomach and up toward her heart. Sabrina's clawed hands caught the female's head. Fangs flashed as she tore the female's throat out. A deluge of blood soaked her fur.

The female collapsed across Anolia, dragging her down, impaled on her claws. Sabrina bled from multiple gashes across her breast and stomach.

No. No. No. I ran to Anolia and shoved the were's body off hers. My world collapsed into the metallic smell and thick sucking sound as claws tore out of human flesh.

Anolia's feeble movements slowed as I hovered over her. Blood ran from her mouth and oozed from the stomach wounds. Everything disappeared as I dropped to my knees and touched my fingers to Anolia's cheeks.

I whimpered like a child hiding in the dark.

"Maat." Anolia struggled. She choked on blood in her throat. I carefully turned her head and strained to listen, to understand.

She gasped. "Lowell. Warn." She released her last breath.

"Please don't leave me. Anolia...Mother...please. I need you." I doubt she heard my plea. I gathered her limp hands in my own and closed my eyes. Images gathered in the dark. Anolia leading prayers, thanking God for our lives, asking that we go on to better days. My surrogate mother, my sister, my friend. I don't know how long I knelt there before I consigned her to my memories, locked tight in the special place reserved for those I loved. Mother, brother, lover, friends, all lost to monsters. How many more could I bear? My heart raged and cursed. I genuinely wanted to die, to end the pain of human existence.

A soft growl drew me out of my grievous daze. Sabrina, still in were form, crouched on the dirt beside us. Her wounds had almost healed. She stared up at Xavier, who had his Aries pointed at her heart. Xavier's scarred face, rigid with fury, spoke to his intent.

Sabrina relaxed. There was nothing she could do. This close he'd cut her down before she could reach him. I understood. Standing there amidst the torn bodies, I'd might have wanted her dead too, just because she was a werewolf. Anolia trusted her, though, and there were too many mysteries. If Xavier killed Sabrina, Gannett would kill him. What would happen to Ty?

After what seemed an eternity, Xavier lowered the gun. He glanced around. He, Sabrina, and I were the only living beings in sight. Those who could run, did so when the shooting began. Xavier holstered his Aries, and, as he had done for me in the library, stripped off his fatigue shirt. He tossed it to the dirt in front of Sabrina. "Change back before someone comes." He knelt beside me. He reached out, grasped my hand, and held it tight.

So unexpected. I leaned against him, needing his presence, needing his strength. He kissed my forehead and stayed close, offering comforting intimacy that surprised me. Was this the same man whose fury almost killed me? I should leave this place—get away while I had a chance. Nothing held me now but his hand. He'd not hold me if I pulled away, nor would he stop me if I ran. I would not. Anolia had wanted me to do something here. *Important*. Twice she'd stressed that. Two trucks pulled up and brown-shirt soldiers poured out. Xavier had to leave. His last words to me?

"Guard Sabrina."

Chapter Thirteen

Sabrina and I rode back to the mansion in the back of a troop truck, surrounded by armed brown shirts. Yes, I needed to guard her. I glared at any of the brown shirts who stared at her. Most of them were as young as Ty and had probably never seen a fuzzy werewolf, dead or alive. However, they had seen the bloody battlefield and Xavier's slaughtered men. I kept the Aries drawn, ready to fire. I was sure the smarter older troops in the truck with us realized what Sabrina was, and that men and women had died protecting her.

When we drew close to the mansion, a turtle came from behind and passed us at high speed. Black shirts met us at the mansion door. Xavier had managed to make it back before us.

The troops, all grim-faced and angry, knew how many of their brethren died that day. They herded Sabrina and me down steps, into a sizeable but bleak basement room. Low ceiling, no windows, poison green and brown furniture, four walls created a place as claustrophobic as a coffin. Ty, Gannett, and Parr were already there.

Gannett embraced and led Sabrina away, but he quickly rejoined us. Parr sat in a chair by the wall. He had the silent, inward stare of a man unwilling to face the knowledge that a precious part of his life had ended. I could find nothing to say to him, offer no comfort.

Things didn't get any better when Xavier came in.

"Why weren't you and Xavier with them?" Gannett started the apportioning of guilt with me. I stood with my feet apart and my hand on the Aries at my hip. "What are you so pissed about, Gannett? You didn't lose anyone you loved today. Your wolf can take care of herself."

That was my blustering, my anger to relieve my guilt. Suriel, the Angel of Death, had been out in the market playing games with Xavier. My shame—my burden for life. I'd failed Anolia, the woman who had loved and trusted me.

A spasm of fury jerked muscles in Gannett's face. "*I'd* like to order a firing squad for you."

"Really? I bet you would. But the vampire with his finger up your ass has plans for me. You've seen what he can do when he's pissed, haven't you?"

I leaned back against a mud-brown chair. Gannett stood, fists clenched, knowing his impotence where I was concerned. He turned on Xavier.

"How many did you lose?"

"Twenty-seven." Xavier stood straight and held steady, always the soldier when he faced Gannett.

"How many weres?" Gannett's eyes jerked, searching the room. His elbows jabbed into his sides. Was he having a seizure? He suddenly relaxed and went to a Mr. President pose.

The tiniest of frowns touched Xavier's forehead. He'd seen the weirdness, too. "Eight werewolves. They died in were shape, so we can't identify them. Witnesses all had the same story. Two turtles and a truck pulled up, fast. Five men and three women jumped out and changed shape. They attacked just as the troops with Sabrina and Anolia arrived at the limo."

Gannett ran his hand through his thin blond hair and shook his head as if to deny what happened. "Xavier, get everyone in their rooms and under guard. Then we'll talk."

Ty came to me and laid a hand on my shoulder. "Maat? Are you…"

"I'll be okay, Ty. I need time." He nodded and stepped away.

The black shirt escorted Parr, Ty, and me back upstairs into what had become a fortress. Men and women with flamethrowers stood at every first-floor door, and others guarded the windows. Ty and Parr huddled together in quiet conversation, and then eased away. Despite Gannett's orders for guards, no one, least of all Xavier's black shirts, followed them.

****

When I got to my room, I rearranged my belt and added the Rudra back to my arsenal. I packed as much ammo as I could. I'd have added the Sparks if I had a decent way to carry it. I watched by the window while the sun painted the western sky behind the mountains purple and gold. Would it have made a difference if Xavier and I had been with the troops or would we have gone down, too? Could I have reached Anolia in time? If we hadn't stopped to talk?

I wondered if Xavier would blame me for delaying him, but we seemed to be beyond that kind of gamesmanship. The black shirts died doing the dirty work. Xavier and I had the element of surprise, coming from behind.

The compelling facet of guilt for me was that I had gone to Avalon in the first place. Yes, I would have completely burned out in another year. I'd have put a silver bullet in my own brain to end the agony.

Werewolves started clawing through my life before I was out of the womb. What happened to my family happened to thousands of others.

I was barely eleven years old. Little Donnie and I had huddled under the porch where Mom had hidden us. A woman screamed. My brother jerked out of my arms and ran. I started to follow but froze in terror when I saw the two werewolves snatch him up like a rabbit. He shrieked as his small body tore apart in their claws. Mama ran toward him, but a were caught her and threw her to the ground. He tore her clothes off, gouging great red streaks in her flesh. There is a point where the conscious mind shuts down and other survival instincts take over. I reached that point for the first time that day, as I watched the slaughter. As I grew older, that disconnect of the mind became my friend, the source of my so-called fearlessness.

I ran into the house and found my stepfather's long knife, the one he'd had plated with so much silver it was awkward to carry. With the blade gripped tightly in both hands, I ran to my mother. I shrieked my rage. The were hovering over her gawked up at me. Animal madness filled his eyes. I stabbed down. The blade sliced his throat, and the hot blood of his life pumped out and soaked my clothes.

The line between sanity and madness is thin—I'll never be sure which side I walked on then. My mother, my beautiful loving mother…the were had chewed on her face. Her eyes jerked back and forth, frantic in pain, terror, and the knowledge that death was coming. Or she may have welcomed the peace it would bring.

She'd seen what happened to Donnie.

The wailing sound of sirens came from below the hill. The militia had arrived too late. They had standing orders to kill anyone injured by werewolf bites. They would shoot Mama as she lay on the ground. Then they'd drag her body in the house, loot any valuables, and burn the rest. Since werewolf blood drenched me, I'd get a bullet, too.

"Maat." Her lips were almost gone, and I could barely hear her.

"You...kill...not...them," she gasped. "Please ...run away."

I wailed and cried, but I knew what I had to do. I was *never* indecisive, even in my youth. Mama had no eyelids, so she had to see it coming. As I knelt beside her, she grasped my free hand and squeezed. I placed the knife under her chin. "I love you, Mama. I'm going to kill them, all of them. I promise." One vehement thrust and the knife pierced her brain. I left it there when I raced away to hide in the woods. Oddly enough, I didn't remember anything after that, until I woke up on Uncle Jake and Aunt Nell's front porch. I know by my thirteenth birthday, thanks to Jake, I was on my way to becoming a premier monster killer.

I set my life's goal the day I killed my mother. That appalling act of bloody mercy sealed my oath of retribution. Now there was Sabrina. She'd tried to save Anolia, but she changed shape, grew fangs and claws, just like those I'd slaughtered since I began to hunt. Was there a difference in monsters? How could that be? I'd walked through the blood of hundreds of butchered families. Could I break my vow or forget my dead for one who claimed friendship?

Darkness had fallen when a tap hit the door. It opened and Parr entered. Weariness and sorrow etched lines in his face. I went to him and he wrapped his arms around me and held me tight. Taking a deep breath, he released me.

"We have to be stronger than this—for her sake. Come. They want you downstairs. I won't be there, so…"

So, I should behave myself. I nodded.

The elevator whisked us down to the first floor, and the doors opened into a hall of armed black shirts. Parr held my arm as we waded through them.

We stopped at the president's study. A stern-faced guard informed me that I was to leave my guns and knives outside. I didn't argue. I simply unbuckled belt and harness and handed them over. Parr hugged me again and kissed me on the forehead. I drew a deep breath and entered the room.

I'd been through the study before. I reminded myself that Gannett didn't know that, and I wouldn't compromise the closet escape route. The president sat behind his desk glaring at Xavier, who stood, arms crossed, glaring back. Great. I'd walked into a piss-off.

"Sit down, Maat," Gannett ordered. His gaze never left Xavier.

I sat in a hard chair facing the desk. I gazed around the room for a weapon. Not much available. I suppose I could throw the books lining the walls. Lighting came from a single lamp on the president's desk, and it left the rest of the room in shadows.

"Xavier?" I heard a threat in the Gannett's voice. "I know you understand. I will act. I know what I want, and I won't allow false sentiment to get in my way."

Xavier slowly relaxed, but I saw his eyes. Not as bad as when he threw me against the rock wall, but close. Gannett was pushing his Colonel hard. He'd regret it eventually. Xavier came and sat in a chair beside me.

A vampire moved within my psychic range. Ruelle had entered the building.

I decided to offer Gannett one chance. It wouldn't make things right for all the crimes he'd committed, but it would give him a few points.

"Mr. Dictator?"

Gannett raised his head.

I leaned forward. "Do you know where that bloodsucker sleeps during the day?"

The corners of Gannett's mouth turned up in a brief smile—a cautious smile. "Not exactly. He's careful about such things."

"I bet. Point me in the right direction. I can feel him when I get close. Come sunrise, I'll go find him." I glanced at Xavier. "Then me and Xavier will dig him out. Show him the light." My laugh sounded feverish and vicious in my own ears. "I'd do it by myself, but I got to kill the last vamp. I don't want to hog all the fun."

Xavier stirred and drew a deep breath. "She's offering to save you, Aaron. She's probably the only one on this earth who can. In God's name, let her."

"I don't need to be saved." Gannett's voice quivered.

"Sabrina does." I knew that for a fact. "You don't think Ruelle is going to let anyone who influences you live, do you?" Gannett stilled. His eyes narrowed. He acted like I planned to kill *her*, instead of the vampire. I knew the uselessness of my plea. "He'll kill Sabrina—and you too, once he's finished with his grand master plan. Humans are animals. Ruelle's trained monkeys. What a show."

Ruelle walked in.

He'd heard the last few minutes of conversation. I'd mouthed my brutish threats for years. He had ignored them. He could take me anytime he wanted and we both understood. But now I'd killed Emanis, and she was much stronger than him. Did he feel a little vulnerable? Not a chance in hell.

"Thank you for coming, Ruelle," Gannett welcomed him with a smile.

I gritted my teeth. Stupid bastard talked as if he was the one in control. Ruelle ignored him. He held out a hand to me. "Maat, I know you blame me for much evil in this world. I am guilty of that and more. But I swear I did not order, nor did I have prior knowledge of today's attack. I had no reason, no desire to kill your friend."

I stared straight into his eyes. I couldn't tell if he spoke truth or lie. "Maybe you didn't, Ruelle, but you can find out. Do it. If you had left me alone, hadn't ordered me brought here—"

"No!" Gannett shouted. "We have more important matters."

Of course, Ruelle didn't speak. He would act as he wished, but for an odd and perverse reason, his game required that Gannett pretend to be in charge. He went to sit in a third chair facing Gannett.

Gannett's forehead formed a slight wrinkle of a frown like he was trying to find a lost memory. He drew a single breath. Then another. It was as if his brain paused, leaped forward, and launched into action again.

"There's a pack of werewolves in the mountains north of here." He stared directly at me, so I presumed Xavier and Ruelle already knew the game. "Those weres have something I need. If I send any obvious force, they will destroy it. Ruelle says they can detect him, so he can't go."

Gannett shuffled papers on his desk. He handed me a small map drawn and labeled in perfect script. Ruelle's hand. I'd seen it before. He'd drawn the mountains to the north in detail and labeled the roads passable and impassible. He'd marked trails leading to a small circle in a valley.

The president leaned forward. "Maat, you and Xavier are going to retrieve the target. He's trained a small, covert force to do the job."

"Why me?" I had a fair idea, but I wanted to see how much he knew.

"You have night vision." Gannett's expression said I was stupid, and their choice was obvious. "And you can sense werewolves at a distance."

I could do more than that. Ruelle knew. Had he not told the president? I'd not speak of it in this place. "How many fuzzies are we talking about?"

"Uncertain, but observers have never seen more than six." Gannett flipped a hand like six werewolves equaled a pack of puppies. Eight had killed over twenty armed troops at the Bell Market earlier. He sounded so sure of himself. "I believe part of that pack guarding our objective was behind the attacks at the mountain house and today. I'm sure they meant to kill you. Sabrina was probably a target today, also."

"Sure." It didn't make sense. None of it made

sense. Eight werewolves at the market, at least that many at the mountain house? Yeah, I had a reputation, but I wasn't a god-like fuzzy-slaying hero. Did anyone but me have sense enough to know that?

Gannett placed his hands on the desk, as if he heard my unspoken doubt. His eyes focused on the far wall. He suddenly had the look of a man who was present only in body. What the hell?

"Aaron?" Ruelle called, as if his president had merely slipped out of sight, not dropped into a semi-coma.

Gannett jerked at Ruelle's voice. He sighed and continued his instructions. "Xavier's ready. He has a plan and he's the leader, Maat. You follow. I know you're not adept at following. You'll manage. You leave in the morning."

Anolia was dead so he didn't have a hostage, and he still expected me to obey him. Why? Well why the hell not? Ruelle was close enough to catch me now if I ran away. I turned to Xavier, and his dark eyes met mine. Hatred flashed there, but I knew it wasn't for me this time.

It only took an instant to understand. Gannett held Ty hostage to keep his chief of security in line. Yes, I'd come to care for Ty, too. The boy had touched something in me. Gannett wasn't the only threat to Ty. Another one sat a few feet from me.

I stared at Ruelle. "Got your pet dictator trained good, haven't you?"

Ruelle's sly smile acknowledged my facetious praise.

"That's enough!" Gannett surged to his feet. "Go back upstairs, Maat. Be ready to leave before daylight.

You may go too, Xavier."

Maybe I could take a precipitous action to relieve one part of the problem. I tried to give Ruelle a non-verbal message, and an almost imperceptible nod of his head said he understood.

Xavier walked with me to the door, opened it for me, and followed me out. He stood silent while I picked up and strapped on my guns.

"I'll have plenty of ammo." Xavier spoke without emotion as we moved toward the elevator. "All you need is what you'd carry if you were going hunting." We stopped in front of the elevator doors.

Xavier laid a hand on my shoulder. This new familiarity unnerved me, but I didn't pull away. He squeezed tight. "What happened? Something between you and the vamp. You—"

"I'm going to talk to him." Damn. How *did* the man get so sensitive to me?

The elevator door opened.

Xavier shook his head. "Maat, don't try to kill him. He'll be expecting you."

"It's my life. I'll spend it as I see fit. I'm impulsive, but I always know the odds."

Not that the odds being against me would stop me when I decided to act. I drew away from him, stepped in, and the elevator door closed behind me.

****

I was lying on the bed when Ruelle silently slipped in the room right after midnight. I suspected it was too much to hope he'd used his glamour on the guards outside to come in secret. It wasn't important to me, was it? Secrecy? I was no one's property. Specifically, no man's property. Any bargain I made was by my own free will. I'd been telling myself that lie for hours. It didn't change anything.

I'd already undressed. The lights were off, but both of us could see in the dark. He sat on the bed beside me.

"I always keep my word, Ruelle."

"Yes, you do indeed, my love."

"I hate it when you call me that." My breath hissed through my teeth. He was not human. He could not love me as I understood love, nor would I accept it knowing the vile acts he'd committed.

His laugh was low and seductive. "You hate me so much what I call you cannot possibly be of importance. What do you want?"

"You know things about this situation that you're not telling. I'll deal with that. I've done it before. But I want to save Ty. I'll give you my word. I'll do my absolute best to get this…thing you want so much. To bring it to you." I touched his chest to remind him of our connection, the blood from his veins that saved my life after he carried me, near death, out of New York. "But if I get killed, I want to know the boy is safe." Ruelle would know, would feel it when I died. I was sure of that.

"Your absolute best is spectacular at times, my love. I swear I won't touch him."

"I want more, Ruelle. If I get killed, Xavier likely will be too. I want you to take Ty away somewhere. *Take him from Gannett*. It's a small thing for you. For his safety, I'll give you this one night."

I'd bargained with Ruelle before. I'd stolen for him. I'd killed for him. Yes, the men I'd killed were vile, homicidal specimens of humanity. Only they died because they were in his way, not for justice, not for crimes they had committed. I'd once stayed with him for ten long nights in exchange for aid saving the life of my only friend.

He laid his hand on my stomach and slid it down between my legs. He was not among the vamps who raped me in New York. After he rescued me, he'd always bargained when he wanted me. I would never go to him by choice. The idea that he valued me, a human woman, was incomprehensible. I'd long since stopped questioning, because I doubted I'd ever receive an answer.

Vamps aren't animated corpses. Another myth. They simply have slow beating hearts and thick warm blood. Only Ruelle's mouth tasted of the grave. I'd let him kiss once before. Never again.

"Is it different?" He lay beside me. "Now that I have no power over your mind." His long hair teased my skin. I brushed the lustrous curls away and watched him for a moment, then said, "Let me see your fangs."

His head came up in surprise. My fingers skimmed his lips, and then I slipped one finger in his mouth. His canine teeth protruded slightly—so sharp. I knew they grew longer when he prepared to feed. I carefully drew my finger back. I'd never willingly touched him like that before.

"It is different then." His voice sounded hollow, as if he'd recognized a truth about me. "I seem more... human?"

True. He did seem more like a man. He wasn't human though, and I'd better not forget that little fact. A thousand years of whatever he called life had made him one of the most superb killers ever to walk the earth.

Would he keep his word to me? Keep his part of a bargain? He always had before. There was nothing else I could do. I hated him, and after this night I would hate him more—not to mention hating myself.

Yet, I knew in my heart someone else would hate me tomorrow.

"You still don't get to bite me, Ruelle. I'll fight until you kill me if you do."

"Very well, Maat." He laid his face against my throat. "My love."

Chapter Fourteen

Blue Ridge Mountains

Five warriors and one undervalued, uncomfortable, werewolf hunter riding in two turtles. Sounds like the opening of a drunken fairy tale. Me, Xavier, and four black shirts—only none of us wore black. We'd dressed in gray and brown, neutral colors I favored when I walked the woods. All four of Xavier's men had the look of competent seasoned soldiers. The turtles were the heavy army issue, so our biggest load was extra fuel.

I rubbed my fingers across the pockets of the ancient leather vest I'd worn for so many years. I bought it at a craft fair right after I left the Freaks. It was in the suitcase along with the Sparks that Christopher had sent with Anolia when they brought her from Avalon.

Anolia had the vest in her hands, ready to pack back in the suitcase, when the weres attacked. She'd carried it outside and dropped it when the troops rushed her up the tower, so it didn't burn.

One pocket held the small toy truck given to me by a little werewolf boy I'd allowed to escape so many years ago. The other carried an exquisite teardrop shaped ruby the size of a bird's egg Ruelle had insisted I take last night before he left me. I refused at first. I have no need of such things, and I lose them.

"Please. Keep it for now." He sounded so sincere. "You may return it when I see you again. It will remind you of our bargain."

He wasn't the only one with a gift for me. A light chain around my throat held an incredibly detailed pure silver replica of a running wolf. When I touched the pendant, I could feel the savage fury of the hunt stirring in my soul. Sabrina had come to my room right after Ruelle left. Her werewolf nose had to have recognized his lingering scent, but she didn't say the words. "I have a gift for you." Sabrina held out a small box. "My father gave me this for my ninth birthday. I can't touch it now. It would honor me if you would accept it, and remember that this werewolf asks for your friendship and wishes only the best for you."

I opened the box and drew out the pendant. Sabrina had cried and begged me to forgive her for not saving Anolia. I laid the pendant down and for the first time in my life, I knowingly embraced a werewolf. I knew Anolia would have wanted me to accede, regardless of my discomfort and personal misgivings.

"Sabrina, Xavier wanted to kill you at the market. Why?"

Sabrina's voice held genuine sadness. "When Lilly, Aaron's first wife, died, they said it was an accident. Xavier believes it was murder, and I killed her to get Aaron. I didn't. I was content as Aaron's mistress since it allowed me more freedom. Perhaps one day, Xavier will believe me."

"He's kind of…stubborn."

"Ah, but so are others. Maat, I understand your mission is dangerous." She shook her head and touched her ear. I took that to mean someone might be listening. "Perhaps when you return, we can talk more. Anolia told me so much about you, your courage, your capacity for love. I would so like to prove that you can trust me."

When Sabrina left, I cried again for Anolia. There were tears on my face when a black shirt came and said it was time to go.

We'd begun our journey heading north. Trees formed a vibrant green canopy while their roots chewed at the pavement edges as we rolled north. This paving material PBA, Perma-Black Asphalt, was not the indestructible interstate's CLT. A rugged surface, but season-by-season, nature gradually consumed these roadways. Since we were close to New Washington, we did see a few vehicles at first. By noon we were alone on the road surrounded by wilderness.

Xavier and I rode in one turtle with two of his men while two followed us in another. Such a strange silent journey. No introductions, no friendly greetings, and no one talked except for the occasional muttered curse when the road turned incredibly rough. Xavier didn't speak to me at all, which wasn't unusual. He never talked much for any reason. I had too much to think about to notice until late afternoon. We stopped before dark in the ruins of a small town and parked in an abandoned building.

Time had laid an inevitable hand on the structure. Chunks of wood siding had given way and holes peppered the roof. We'd fuel the turtles, eat, and then sleep. There would be no lights.

Xavier finally decided to formally introduce me to the four men. Santos, Mack, Terry, and Billy. Santos,

Mack, and Terry were big and muscular soldiers, without an ounce of fat on them. Lean, slender Billy was barely taller than me. He had an African heritage and the flowing movement of a martial arts fighter— quick and deadly.

Our fearless leader spread the map on the hood of one turtle. He pointed out our destination and a few details of the surrounding area. I still had no idea what we were going after. I studied the lines on the paper. "So, what are we going for?"

"Our target is a truck. We're going to drive it away." Xavier wouldn't meet my eyes.

I, of course, couldn't keep my mouth shut. "The target is a truck—or is it the truck's cargo?"

Xavier carefully folded the paper. "You mean you didn't get a detailed report from your vampire." His eyes met mine then. I saw nothing but rage.

Oh, holy hell. Damn Ruelle. I could feel fury rolling off Xavier. Yes, we'd come to a bare beginning of a warmer relationship over the last few days. But it was born of violence and tragedy, and he didn't own me.

Damn it, he did not own me!

I had always acted as I believed for the best. And I had made mistakes. Bargaining for Ty was not one of them. I leaned back against the turtle and grinned. "No report. Lying is the least of his nasty habits, anyway."

"Well, I suppose you'd know. Did…?" Xavier stopped, aware that the others around us were listening. The four men's gazes jerked between Xavier and me, as if they'd jumped in a den of snakes and didn't know which way to run. I would not flinch, nor quail, under Xavier's anger. I've made it a habit to accept responsibility for my actions and never make excuses. I wouldn't start now.

At ten o'clock, I went to Mack who was standing guard at the building's door. "I'm going out. Please don't shoot me when I come back."

I thought Xavier might try to stop me, but he said nothing. I swiftly walked a quarter mile perimeter around the building. The trees like old friends stood in the darkness, and the earth gave way beneath my feet like a fine carpet. I sensed no weres. A man and a woman quietly passed by, heading south on a well-worn trail. They didn't see me. The woman held a baby in her arms, and the man's back bent under the weight of the pack on his shoulders. I watched them as they moved away, and silently wished them luck.

Billy had taken over guard duty while I was gone. He called a soft challenge before I made it within fifty feet of the building. I thought I'd get closer. That one would make a fine hunter. Once inside, I made my way to the pallet I'd rolled out before I left. Xavier lay on his, right beside mine. Since the building was mostly empty, he'd made it obvious. *Now what? Guarding me? He knew I wasn't going to run.*

I lowered myself, unbuckled my guns, and laid down. This at least was familiar, sleeping in wilderness ruins. Tomorrow would be a better time to fight—with him or anything else that came along. That strife, while set aside for a couple of years, was familiar, too. I relaxed and immediately fell asleep.

Chapter Fifteen

I woke before Xavier the next morning. We were deep in the mountains, so we wouldn't see the sun rise, only a brightening of the sky until noon. I sat up. He instantly woke. The men around us did the same. Xavier didn't look at me. We'd folded our bedrolls and stowed them away, when I sensed a were within the far edge of my range. I raised a hand and everyone froze. These guys were good—and they knew I could sense monsters.

"Where?" Xavier mouthed the word.

I nodded to the west. We waited, long minutes, barely breathing. The were passed on. I relaxed. My companions did the same.

Xavier dug packages of bread and cheese out of our turtle and passed them around. We'd eat cold rations while on the road.

"Your guys have any experience fighting weres?" I asked Xavier as we climbed in the turtle.

"Some. Your experience is different. You've been close. Tell them what you know."

I turned to Terry and Mack. "So, how have you fought?"

Terry shrugged. "Lived in a commune when I was a kid. Adults fought off attacks a couple of times. Had a couple of workers picked off when they got careless."

Mack shook his head. He wouldn't meet my eyes. I

understood. He didn't mean he'd never fought. He meant he didn't want to explain. Xavier was right. I was different. I'd long since come to realize my life as a lone hunter was unique. I went on.

"My experience. Average male, height seven feet, six and a half for a female. Ninety percent are male. Lead bullets won't stop them except for a close, accurate heart or head shot. But it hurts. Hits them hard and slows them down. Silver kills. Often, it's not quick enough. Only sure thing is silver in the heart or brain. If you do get a solid hit, back away until it falls. Keep your knives with silver sheathed when possible. Not too many people know this, but the fuzzies are super sensitive to silver at a respectable distance. Leather will mask the silver to a degree." I'd already removed Sabrina's silver pendant and stuffed it in my leather vest pocket.

I went on with the lessons, and they asked intelligent questions.

"Wish I could see one change," Terry said. "I don't like surprises."

Mack chuckled and nodded at me. "Saw *you* once in Memphis. You stomped some big guy's ass."

"I stomped a lot of ass in Memphis. Got the shit pounded out of me a few of times, too."

One of the few true stories about me. It felt good to say that. This was the old Maat, the kick-ass monster hunter.

When we stopped at noon to refuel, Billy and Santos came to ride with us, and I went through the routine again. Both men had seen and fought live weres. Both lost family in raids. Like the other two, I gave them all the information I thought they might not have. They listened with grave, solemn faces. Santos and Billy left and joined the guys in the other turtle when we stopped to fuel again. Xavier's attitude obviously made them uncomfortable. He cautiously steered while brittle pavement crunched under the wheels. Slow going. He finally deigned to speak.

"Your uncle taught you to hunt weres. Tell me about him." Xavier sounded dispassionate—the soldier was giving orders.

Okay, I didn't want to fight. "My Uncle Jake taught me to shoot and hunt anything that moved. He was Dad's oldest brother. He retired from the army and built a cabin in the mountains, smack over a hidden arms and ammo dump. My toys and games involved explosives in one form or another."

I rubbed my hands on my jeans and stared straight ahead. "The Sparks, the gun I used at the mountain house? It was the first that was mine alone. I must have popped ten thousand rounds through it learning to shoot. Relentless ass, my uncle. Everyday, draw and fire. Then on to drop, roll, and fire. I pulled the trigger from every position the human body can take." The recoil of a pistol in my hand soon padded my palm with calluses. "I can put a hole in a four-inch stationary circle from almost any position. I'm good at moving targets too."

Xavier slowed the turtle to creep over a section of severely broken pavement. "What about your aunt?"

"Aunt Nell was a schoolteacher. College professor, even. She educated me, and she was as relentless as Uncle Jake. I tried to tell Aunt Nell all I wanted to do was kill weres, not quote Shakespeare or the periodic table. Thanks to her nagging, I do know how to set a table for a formal dinner. I can also carry on an intelligent conversation with most anyone—if I want to—which I usually don't. Nell couldn't take my mom's place, but she gave me everything she had. Ty showed me his mother's picture. He looks like her."

Xavier hit me with a big one.

"You kill Jenks?"

"What?" I jerked so hard I bumped my head on the door. He'd caught me off guard—again.

"Jenks. Did you kill him?" His spoken words full of wrath.

The turtle gave a vicious lurch. Oh, yes, Russell Jenks, the man who drove my Uncle Jake to suicide. He should have killed me, too. He wasn't that smart. There didn't seem to be any point in lying.

"Yeah, Xavier. I did him."

Xavier's voice was stony cold. "Did you watch? Did he squeal? When they ate him?"

"He squealed." How did he get those details? And what was Xavier's connection to Russell Jenks? He answered my unspoken question with that same icy tone.

"We were a militia family. Aaron, Lilly...Jenks was there too. A were bit my wife in an attack. She ran home. Jenks followed her, burned the house down around her and...the baby. She'd protected the baby from the were. She would have given him to me before..." Before they killed her. I knew, I understood. I'd killed my own mother. Xavier went on. "I went in the house, but I couldn't get to them. Aaron dragged me out."

So that's how he got the scar.

"I tried to find Jenks later, after I healed, but he

disappeared."

The pavement smoothed out, and we rode in silence for a while, and then he asked, "If Anolia had been bitten and lived, would you…?"

"Kill her. Hell no. Not if I had a choice. I'd walk away like a coward. I'm a fucking hypocrite. It's on my list of personal faults. Just below liar and thief. Knowing her…she was so brave. She would have killed herself if she thought it necessary. Would you kill your men if they were bitten?"

"No. It's happened. I sent them away where someone would take care of them. No matter how it went. I have a list of faults, too." He kept his eyes focused straight ahead and never looked at me.

I had formed a complex bond with Xavier, a bond neither of us understood nor desired. Our lives were bound by forces beyond our control. I'm not religious, but I do believe in fate. Now, someone walked beside me. Maybe for a week, a day—or the next three minutes. Tomorrow we might fight again. Xavier was angry about Ruelle, but I didn't know how to deal with that shit. I had to make my own decisions about what's best. I'm a person who should always be alone.

Xavier stopped before dark. He pulled off the road, crossed a trickle of a stream, and parked in a small clearing. It was too open to suit me, though the forest leaned heavily upon land.

We'd made fifty miles the first day while the road was decent. Only fifteen today. We'd sleep on the ground, no fire, no light. I can stomp through the woods all day and half a night easily—riding the turtle, fighting the motion, exhausted me.

Xavier produced another map of a smaller area

with precisely drawn roads and trails, along with the locations of large trees and rock formations to guide us. Ruelle had pinpointed several caves. He'd also noted their entrances and sizes, with the best approach marked. Even with his speed and precision it had to have taken a lot of time to produce that map. Whatever that truck held, the vampire wanted it—bad.

"We walk from this point." Xavier smoothed his hand over the map. "We must make each of these caves before nightfall. Maat will tell us if any weres come close."

I laid my hand on the map. "Weres yes, but more than that. Bears, mountain lions, the occasional wolf pack—real wolves. Not likely they'll attack a group if we stay close together."

"Don't shoot anything." Xavier gave an unnecessary order.

Once we hit the woods close to our destination, one shot could bring a pack of monsters down.

"The truck is here. It's parked in a barn." Xavier pointed to the map. "We'll make for this cave and watch for a while, then decide how to proceed."

I saw a problem. "If these distances are right, that cave is within five hundred yards of the barn. You'll never get that close without them smelling you. You'd be better off to drive up to the front door and knock." I bit my lip as I realized how impossible this would be. "Shit! You don't even know how many are waiting."

"Have you ever made this kind of assault?" Xavier asked the question straight, not sarcastically.

"Not since the Freaks. I work alone, or with one other person. One who knows what he's doing. I've hidden for days, watching the fuzzies and the occasional humans that ran with them." I traced the map with a finger. "I think we can make it here. With the right weather. And luck. Lots of luck." I pointed to a cave over half a mile from our destination. "If we make it there without detection, I'll go check things out. At least we'll know what we're getting into."

Xavier sighed. "I know what we're getting into. The truck is wired with explosives. That's why the Army's not involved."

My mouth dropped open. Gannett and his vampire master had sent us on a suicide mission. Would Ruelle keep his word and help Ty escape? *And if Ruelle wanted the fucking truck why didn't he have a better plan?* I knew of a few of his previous plans. Some worked brilliantly. Others were intricate failures that cost lives. The painstaking detail of his map did not translate into a bigger scheme.

Xavier went on. "We've been told the explosives are old and—"

"Unstable." I'd barely survived contact with unstable explosives a couple of times.

"We have an expert." Xavier nodded at Terry. "We just have to kill the weres before they can set it off.

Just have to kill. That's all. "Did suck-face say how many we'd have to deal with?"

"Ten one time and six another."

I rubbed my eyes. Damn I was tired. "And how big is this truck?"

"It's 26-feet long, has 10 wheels, carries up to 25,000 pounds and, if it runs, we can drive it away."

"And if it doesn't run?"

"We guard it until one of us goes for back-up that's supposed to be about thirty-five miles from here."

"Bullshit. I have a better idea. We have two vehicles that work fine. Let's blow up the truck. Then we sneak back to New Washington, kidnap Ty, and run like hell into the mountains. The vampire will follow, but I know a place where we can ambush him."

"No." The barely audible word carried weight. And did I hear a syllable of regret? He folded the map.

"Fine, Xavier. I need to check it out before crashing this little party."

"We can do that."

"We? Meaning you and me?" I gritted my teeth.

"Yes."

"You'll get us killed."

Xavier shook his head. "You were told to take orders."

"Oh, Yeah. I forgot. The dog fucker president said you were in charge."

Xavier stared at me. Then, without any inflection, any hint of emotion, he said, "If he's a dog fucker, what are you?"

I jerked back. It hurt. How the hell did he get the power to hurt me? Damn him to hell! I turned and stalked into the woods and found a soft, sheltered spot to rest. I wrapped myself in the darkness and worked ridiculously hard at thinking about absolutely nothing.

I returned when the chill seeped too deep inside my bones to ignore. I called softly to the first shift watch so he wouldn't shoot me. I wanted to run away, but I had to do this. For Ty—and to keep my word. My word to a vampire. Again, Xavier had made his pallet on the ground beside mine. God knows why.

****

Early the next morning, before light, we began our

walk up a mountain. I could see better so I led and warned them of holes, fallen branches, and rocks along the path. Xavier's men did better in the woods than I thought they would. So did he. Even with fully loaded backpacks, we made valuable time until it started to rain.

A supply of dry wood stacked in the back waited for us when we reached the first cave early that evening. We waited until dark to light a fire, and a natural chimney let the smoke out of the ceiling. We weren't comfortable, but we weren't cold, and we made it through the night. Not surprising. Ruelle rarely depended on others to take care of details. Time taught most of us if we wanted something done right, if it was important, we did it ourselves. Ruelle had a lot of time behind him.

Rain blessed us again the next day. Oh, how wonderful were these green eastern mountains. At various elevations on our climb we passed thickets of wild mountain laurel. I loved the red, orange, and yellow of wild rhododendrons and azaleas, too. I remembered the nights when I had slept in deep, fern filled rocky grottos. If I survived these next days, if I managed a future life, I prayed a kind friend would bury me here when I finished with this world. If I didn't survive, I'd be a werewolf snack, and eventually be disposed of here in a less poetic but more practical manner.

About noon we hit our first problem—or it hit us. Xavier was in the lead when I sensed a werewolf coming straight at us.

"Were! Moving fast." I spoke as softly as I could. I dropped my pack and drew my silver knife from the sheath on my belt. Xavier dropped his pack, too, and pulled a silver knife out of his boot. The others did the same.

We'd been following a steep narrow path through heavy forest that left us little room to maneuver. The mountain dropped straight down to our right. Massive boulders, slick with moss, cut up at a steep angle to our left. Santos and Billy scrambled up the slope onto the rocks above us. We hugged the embankment where the path curved around the mountain. Not much room to maneuver, but enough for Xavier and me to stand side-by-side and brace for an assault. As the fuzzy closed the distance, I realized he was in human form. He trotted around the curve and spotted us.

Xavier charged. The were didn't have time to change, but he could shout. Xavier's knife arced through the air. It slashed, swift, silent and deadly. The were's hands clutched his throat as blood gush through his fingers. I ducked under Xavier's arm and thrust my blade into the were's stomach. He crumpled, blood from his neck arteries spraying across us. I managed to get an arm up and keep it from my eyes.

Another were suddenly burst onto the scene—this one in full fang and fur. This fuzzy had been running so close after the first I couldn't separate their scents. He towered over Xavier and me. He saw us and threw his arms up. This I knew. The classic werewolf position, arms up, claws flexed, ready to slash down and tear. We'd have to fight across the fallen were's still thrashing human form body.

Billy suddenly did something I wouldn't have the guts to do. Thin and wiry, he leaped from the slope above us onto the furry were's back. He caught one hand under its muzzle. A swift arc and he drove his knife down.

The knife plunged in, but it missed the throat. Arms flailing, the monster shook Billy off. Billy twisted and rolled as he landed, then jumped to his feet. He'd hung on to his knife. He charged and jammed it into a furry back. That wasn't enough.

A howl could bring others down on us if they were close. Santos leaped for the were like Billy had. It saw him, twisted, and caught him with both hands. Our comrade's eyes bulged. Claws punched into his chest and through his heart. Good man. He hadn't screamed.

The were hoisted Santos' body higher over his head. I punched my blade into the were's heart. Xavier's silver thrust up and found his throat. A bubbling gurgle came from his mouth. No howling possible now. Santos' body came down on top of the monster. The whole scene lasted less than twenty seconds. The only sound, heavy breathing, was barely audible above the rain spattering on the forest leaves.

We all froze, alert, waiting for another attack. When it was obvious it wasn't coming, Xavier knelt beside his fallen soldier. Billy, Mack, and Terry came and stood close behind me.

Xavier rose. "Let's move."

We didn't speak as we dragged human form and fuzzy werewolf bodies to a place where a rocky crevasse split the mountainside. We threw them in, and they rolled a long way. Billy and Terry carried Santos as we walked to a spot where we could turn into deeper woods and dig a hole. We piled stones over the spot. By the time we finished, the rain had drenched us and washed most of the blood from our hair and clothes.

There are times when being soaking wet was a blessing.

We stood at the grave and listened to the insistent shower of water on the leaves. Two monsters down—a better than average score for the humans.

"Did he have a family?" I'd stood over a grave like this one so many times.

"No." Xavier stared at the grave "He wouldn't have been here if he had. Anybody want to say anything?"

Terry, Billy, and Mack shook their heads, but I'm Maat, so I had to open my mouth.

"Don't forget—ever." I met each one's eyes. "He didn't have a family. He's got us. We've got to remember him." I grabbed my backpack. I'd done this before. "Now let's go kill more of them."

Chapter Sixteen

Right before dark we reached the cave I thought was distant enough to escape detection. Thankfully, the summer rain continued. It should help wash our scent away. We had no fire this time, only a single lantern. I wanted to head out, find the barn, and survey the defenses.

"No." Xavier shot that down. "Rest. Then we make plans."

I gave up, dug out my bedroll. I woke rested a few hours later. Xavier sat staring at me. He sighed as if resigned to a mysterious thing in his life.

He woke the others with a single whispered hiss. The five of us crouched down around the map spread out on the stone cave floor. We studied Ruelle's fine-artist quality drawings in the lantern's light.

"Here's where we are." I pointed to our cave. "It's about three hours to dawn."

I never carried a watch, but I had my own internal clock that marked sunrise and sunset, no matter where I was. "I can go see how many fuzzies, how to get in and out. I'll come back, report, and then we can plan."

"I'm going with you, Maat." Xavier stood. "I have to see for myself."

I rose too. Oh, boy. Another face-off.

"Xavier? Why don't we all shoot ourselves? It's better than—"

"Damn it, I can move—"

We both broke off when we realized we'd raised our voices.

"Maat, I can't let you go alone." His voice asked me to be reasonable.

"Xavier, werewolves smell humans better than any other animal. Maybe because they can change to human shape. They will smell you. You won't get close enough to see anything."

"You're human, Maat. Unless you actually believe that *Angel of Death* crap."

"Oh yeah, I'm human." I kept shaking my head. "You're right. The Angel of Death is absolute bullshit. There's no angel, no magic, no mystery. But don't you wonder how I killed so many? You think Ruelle had Gannett hunt me down just because I can *sense* werewolves at a distance? Your dictator and his vampire didn't tell you everything. And that is fucking terrifying because you're leading this little travesty of a suicide mission.

"Werewolves can't smell me, Xavier. More important? *They can't sense my presence.* I can sneak up on them—hide from them. Don't ask. I don't know why. It's a gift...or a fucking curse."

Damn. Damn. Damn. A few days ago, for the first time in my life, I'd had a werewolf I could have asked about that little quirk. With all the other shit, I hadn't thought to do so.

Xavier remained impassive as usual, but I knew he was reassessing our situation. His secret mission, this deadly mission, and his boss had withheld vital information. What else hadn't they told him? Ruelle knew about me, of course. God knows what I told him in the days after we left New York. The days I drifted in and out of madness.

"How many have you killed?" Terry broke the tension.

"Since I was fifteen…four hundred…or more."

Billy grinned. "Exterminated 'em."

"I did my best."

Thunder rumbled outside and promised more fortuitous rain to help us move in undetected.

"How close can you get?" Xavier had recovered from my little surprise. And best of all, he'd accepted what I told him. Or at least he seemed to.

"I once crawled under an old frame house full of them. Even with holes in the floor, they never knew I was there. I planted charges and crawled back out. Boom." I chuckled at the memory. "Big ass boom."

"What's your range on sensing weres?" Xavier wanted more.

"Fuzzy weres I can get a reliable sense at three to four hundred yards. Human shape only a few hundred feet. I get a real hard hit when they change from human to beast. Like at the market. I was a little too far when they arrived. It didn't hit me until they changed. And there are variables. Psychic information is perception. It's *not* a magic voice speaking in my mind."

In the end, Xavier agreed on a simpler plan. I would go down and get close to the barn, then hide and wait. At dawn, he and the others would move in fast and attack from the front. They'd knock on the door with silver-loaded automatics. I'd hit the target from behind.

We were betting the weres would fight first and blow the truck as a last resort. It depended on how much value they placed on the damned thing. Being closer, I could come in and cut down quite a few. Not to mention, I could also get blasted into pieces of dead meat.

Some of us, like Santos, might not make it back. Disaster loomed over our heads. It was like a sign with the word *fools* written in red, and arrows pointing down. I figured even worse than my show of bravado at Avalon that ended at a rock wall. It was all we had. *Or it was all the vampire had given us. Why? I knew he could do better.*

Terry, Billy, and Mack turned away as I changed into my only clean dry clothes. Xavier didn't. He watched me with those dark, dangerous eyes. That gaze…how intense. When I finished, he handed me a gray jacket of waterproof material he'd dug out of his pack. I could shoot with wet guns, but they'd get slippery.

With any luck at all, these weres would change shape when attacked. We'd have a few precious seconds when they shifted. Then again, they might remain human shape and shoot back with guns. Or they might immediately commit suicide by blowing the truck and taking us with them.

Xavier and the boys would have to run half a mile down a narrow path and across a field. Okay, it wasn't a clever plan, but it was what we had. As I lifted the tarp covering the cave's opening, Xavier stepped up to me. He straightened the collar of my jacket. He wrapped his long fingers around a lock of my hair, tugged it gently, and let it slide free to bounce back to a tight curl. Shadows pooled under his eyes. I resisted the urge to touch him. If I did, I might give in to disaster and let him go with me.

"I'll make it, Xavier. You know I can fight. Just flex your knee and see if it still hurts."

That got me a rare smile. "We both lost that battle, Maat."

I eased into the dripping darkness.

How amazing. No matter our differences, Xavier trusted me to do my job. To be an independent warrior, not a lesser woman. So, did that mean he no longer saw my night with the vampire a betrayal? I forced myself to stop thinking about Colonel Xavier. No distractions.

Ruelle had done a respectable job on the map. Out of my undying hatred, I'd tried and failed to think of a way to keep him from getting his prize. Not without hurting Ty. Knowing the vampire, he'd hunt me down and make me watch while he tore the boy apart. I'd once witnessed the horrifying spectacle of him tearing a man in two pieces. I'd seen his rage and there was nothing I could do to stop him.

I managed a glimpse of the barn through the trees as I made my way down the mountainside. Tall and covered with gray weathered wood, it had wide double doors on the front. It was a replica of most of the barns in Appalachia. I stayed on the path until I was within three hundred yards, then cut away. The closer I came, the stronger the sense of werewolves rippled through me. Six separate entities, all males. Years ago, I'd taken out ten weres by myself with a single gun. I'd studied the area and the pack for days. And it was a big gun.

Ruelle had marked at least two entry points on the barn. They might be there—or they might not. No way of knowing how current the information was, though the description of the vegetation seemed accurate. It hadn't grown much since he'd been here.

The barn backed up against a hill, facing open fields that were once cropland. The forest quickly claimed farms like this, thanks to Gannett's anti-homesteading laws. The weres had partially cleared the land here again to allow a narrow, but unobstructed, view from the barn's wide-open front doors.

The gentle drizzle occasionally intensified to rain. It hissed like a waterfall as it hit the leaf canopy. I slipped through the woods around to the back of the barn. Good luck and I found a bit of level ground, and a stretch with enough vegetation for cover. I made it to less than two hundred feet from my destination.

Two weres in human form sat huddled by a small fire in a lean-to shelter at the side of the barn. They wouldn't be able to see the back. I saw one furry monster lumbering along where the open field met the forest. It signified an organized patrol of the perimeter, a thing I'd never seen in all my years of hunting. Sentries, yes, occasionally, but organization like this never happened. The patrol remained out of my sensory range. How many others were with him?

I winnowed my way through the brush, and from tree trunk to tree trunk to a place where I could see a back door. Okay, only another thirty feet...the door popped open. I froze and crouched low against a tree. The were who stepped out was in human form, but he was naked. I took that to mean he would soon change shape. If I could catch him right at that point...my luck held. He walked straight toward me.

He couldn't see me, sense me, or smell me. I can be extraordinarily still when my life depends on it. But he would feel it if I drew my silver blade out of its leather sheath. I'd have to wait until the last moment, then strike.

He walked to within fifteen feet, kicked aside a patch of leaf mulch, and squatted with his back to me. Thunder grumbled across the sky.

I slowly rose and allowed a few seconds for the blood to circulate in my legs. Another rumble of thunder. I wrapped my hand around the knife hilt as I moved. I'd intended to grab his hair with my left hand and slice his throat from behind, but it didn't work out that way. He heard me coming and turned. I had the advantage. His squatting position put him off balance. A werewolf's first reaction to danger is to change shape. I had those magic seconds to strike.

I whipped the knife sideways and sliced his throat from the front. That solved the noise problem, but he wasn't dead yet. He shoved himself to his feet. He staggered and lunged for me with half-human, half-werewolf hands. His jugulars gushed, and if the other weres smelled that blood…I leaped back, out of range and immediately sheath the silver blade. Hopefully none of the others had felt the weapon. He toppled, twitched a couple of times, then stilled. Death in the forest. The agony, the devastation these things had wreaked on my heart never ceased, but each monster I killed brought relief.

The relentless rain. That would keep the blood odor down. I caught him by the wrist and dragged the body across the wet slick carpet of leaves. I tucked his corpse behind a fallen tree trunk. I'd been super careful not to pick up any of his blood.

The black night had brightened to a thick gray morning, so Xavier and the troops would begin their assault soon.

My senses told me the weres inside the barn were closer to the front than the rear, and they didn't seem to be moving around. I hurried to the door and laid my ear to the wooden slats. Nothing. One hand on the Aries, I used my other hand to ease the door open. The plan, if I was captured, was to fire off a few shots to warn my team, then surrender and hope they didn't kill me right away. Distract them and I'd be rescued. Distract? I could do that. Rescue? I could always pray. Not that I'd ever had a prayer answered. Silence and darkness greeted me as I stepped inside. The stink of oil and gasoline from the farming days permeated the air and mixed with the aroma of moldy hay.

My eyes quickly adjusted to the deeper shadows. The back door was part of a room separate from the main barn. Some type of storage, where piles of junk, boards, metal, and barrels littered the floor and walls. The weres in the lean-to and those in the front of the barn hadn't stirred. I crouched low and peered around the door jam.

The truck, as Xavier said, was twenty-six feet long with ten wheels, and it covered most of the open barn space. The grill faced big open double barn doors on the front. They'd left more room to congregate there. I waited. No movement, and the only sound was rain drumming on the metal roof. I dropped down on hands and knees and scooted under the truck, and found a prize waiting for me. Five wooden boxes, each about a foot square, strung with wires, were set in a straight line down the truck's center. Crude, but effective. Not what I expected. I thought they'd be inside the truck, not exposed.

I'm not an expert, but Ajax, my demo-man friend, taught me the rudiments and virtues of blasting the shit out of inconvenient things. I crawled forward and loosened critical wires on each box. Not easy with my bare fingers and the visibly corroded connections. The manufacturer designed this type of explosive to be set off by gunfire, too. I had to move them. Thunder rolled again, and rain fell harder, drowning out everything else.

The weres in the front of the barn didn't stir, but a smaller human size door by the bigger entry doors opened and closed twice. Where was Xavier? They should have attacked by now.

I carried the boxes, one at a time, to the back of the truck—not an easy task crawling on hands and knees. They'd be safe tucked under old hay banked up against a wall. I turned to hide until Xavier arrived—and smacked face first into hairy werewolf legs. The weres weren't the only ones deafened by the rain on the roof. He staggered back. I recovered from the shock first. Since I was on my knees, he died with my silver blade punched into his guts and up to his heart.

He died howling.

I sheathed the knife, drew the Rudra, and ran beside the truck and toward the front of the barn. I'd have more room there. The smaller door banged open as the weres from outside rushed in. Two quick rounds cut one down, and I aimed at the other and—

A strike smashed me hard from the right and tossed me into the air like a cat tossing a mouse. I landed ass first on the hard-packed dirt floor. Stunned, I'd managed to hang onto the Rudra. Hands, human shaped hands, tore it away from me. A fist slammed into my stomach. I wanted to scream and vomit at the same time. Desperate gasps for air produced violent choking.

The were grabbed my wrists. He twisted them behind my back and jerked me to my feet. He dragged me to the front of the truck, slung me around, and forced me to my knees.

The werewolf in human form standing in front of me appeared to be in his sixties. Thanks to Sabrina, I knew he might be much older. His hair was chalk white. Such cold, blue eyes glared at me. In a moment of perversity, I wondered what he'd look like if he changed shape.

I gagged, and bile ran from my mouth. My stomach muscles twisted. Internal injuries? More stuff poured from my mouth—but no blood. The white-haired werewolf patiently waited for my trauma to ease.

"Who sent you?" he demanded.

"Fuck you!" I gasped out the words. *Oh, Maat, such wit and charm.*

He slapped me. A gentle tap for a werewolf. If he'd hit me hard, he'd have torn my head off. My neck popped, though. I sucked air, fighting for control. I also sucked in blood from my now bleeding nose. When I choked, he hit me again. White light flashed and then came the dark.

I woke when they poured a bucket of icy water on me. They'd tied my hands behind my back. One of them grabbed me by the arms. He jerked me up, and slammed me down on a rough, wooden box. He held me upright—otherwise, I'd have toppled over. They waited until my breathing slowed. I licked my lips and again tasted my own blood.

"Gannett can't have this." The white-haired were

spoke through clenched teeth. "You…how did you get in?"

I didn't answer. I coughed and swayed, trying to stall. Where the hell was Xavier?

The werewolf holding me locked a hand in my hair and turned my face toward him. He was a handsome man, who didn't look much older than me. He chuckled. *Oh, goody. I amused him.*

"You know her?" The white haired were seemed baffled.

"Know her? Not personally. You don't recognize her? Only one human could have come in like that—Suriel."

The white-haired were studied me. "Ah, the infamous Angel of Death. My New Washington pack went into the mountains to kill you. I told them you were nothing, not to bother." He shook his head. "Now most of them are dead and you are here to plague me. But really, I should think killing werewolves would be a nobler cause than thieving for a dictator."

I shrugged despite the pain. I managed to speak, too. "Not looking for nobility. Dictator has someone I love in a cage."

"That is not a surprise. My name is Alistair Lockerbie. Dr. Alistair Lockerbie. Did he speak of me? Did he tell you what I have?" Lockerbie leaned forward and spoke with an eager, arrogant voice. His right eye twitched, and his breath smelled of rotten meat.

"Nope. Never heard of you."

"Bastard!" Lockerbie raised his hand to hit me again. He stopped.

"Yeah, Gannett's a sorry fucker." I had to keep him talking—not hitting.

"He can't have it." Lockerbie slammed one fist into his palm. Better that than me. "It's mine. I dug it out of that vault. I worked day and night to find a decent truck. To get it ready to go. I'm the one who will change things, not him."

My mind circled, searching for things to say, to stall him.

Xavier walked in—alone.

Lockerbie froze, but the other were released me and leaped toward Xavier. Xavier shot him once. Silver in the heart, he dropped onto the barn floor, blood pulsing from a hole in his chest. The clay floor, hard packed and oil soaked, refused to accept the offering. The viscous fluid slid away in a scarlet sheet.

Lockerbie grabbed me by the throat and lifted me to my feet. No claws needed. He could tear my life away with his fingers. I couldn't breathe, choked, and to my shock, he loosened his grip. Then all I had to do was manage to stand. I couldn't go much farther. *Xavier! End this, now, please.* The man I begged silently lowered his Aries.

"Xavier," Lockerbie said. "My oh my. Gannett's butcher. How wonderful to see you again."

Xavier stepped forward. Lockerbie tightened his grip again. I gasped for breath. Lockerbie's free hand slid into his pocket, and he drew out a small square device with buttons.

"Do you know what this is?" Lockerbie asked. He held it up.

A remote trigger. Ajax had a few of those babies, too. Now we'd see if I'd disabled all the explosives.

Lockerbie released me. I collapsed on the dirt floor. I rolled so I could watch. Lockerbie held his hand out to Xavier. A thick slow laugh came from deep in his chest. "A worthy game—and I've won." He pushed the button.

Nothing happened. Seconds passed before the knowledge that his master plan had failed registered in Lockerbie's expression. Xavier fired. Cold, clean, there was no countenance of revenge or satisfaction.

The silver hit Lockerbie in the chest and slammed him onto his back. His head landed near me. Blood gushed from his mouth with his last words. "In hell, Xavier."

Silence filled the barn. Xavier stared at Lockerbie as all fell silent except the relentless rain. Terry and Mack rushed in the door. Billy walked behind them. I'd heard no shots. How did they kill the weres patrolling outside? Hand-to-hand?

The barn spun around me and with my hands tied behind my back, I couldn't move. Xavier was suddenly there and had me in his arms. Terry came to us and cut the cord holding my wrists.

"I'm okay," I said. Barely conscious and bleeding, I could lie.

One of them brought a bucket of water and a cup so I could drink. Then Xavier gently washed my face. "We'll be ready to go soon." He helped me into a sitting position.

I didn't try to stand, but I did crawl over to where the Rudra had landed when they knocked it out of my hands. My Aries had remained tight in its holster. The four men busied themselves around the truck, lifting the hood and checking the tires. I couldn't see, but the big back doors on the truck creaked as they opened and closed again. They cranked the truck engine and let it run. It hummed as smooth and level as any engine I'd ever heard. The weres had taken better care of the vehicle's maintenance than the explosives planted under its belly.

Terry and Mack approached me. Each one caught an arm and they lifted me to my feet—gently, but too fast. My head spun. Xavier was suddenly in front of me.

Next thing I knew, they relieved me of my guns and knife, had me sitting on that damned wooden box, and fastened to a post by a chain around my waist. At least my hands were free. Then they ignored me as I called them a few choice names and went on with the work of preparing our ride to roll out. What the hell was going on here? *Weren't we comrades in arms? Shit*!

The bucket of water sat beside me and with nothing better to do, I washed more blood away and soaked my wrists where the rope had chafed.

My head hurt, and I bet I looked rough as the planks covering the aging barn. That wasn't my biggest problem. The truck was secure. Xavier had it and would take it back. I'd kept my word to Ruelle. I could go. If I wanted to.

"You asshole." I cursed Xavier when he came by.

"Yeah." He sounded so agreeable. "But I need to be sure you get back to New Washington."

"You may be pissed enough to let Gannett shoot me, but I didn't think you'd give me to the vampire."

"Your personal vampire?" Xavier raised an eyebrow. "Shouldn't be a problem."

He said the words, but they lacked his previous malice. After that, he ignored me. Billy didn't. He crouched beside my box. He held his arm close to his side. He'd been bitten.

"How long do I have?" he asked softly. The white of his eyes stood in stark contrast to his dark skin.

"Maybe a month."

"What'll happen?"

I sighed. "I don't know. It may not infect you. That's possible. But if it does, I know you'll need help to get through the change the first time. Do you know any weres around New Washington?" I didn't want to use Sabrina's name, for fear it would cause her trouble.

He drew a sharp breath. "I didn't know there were…"

"I didn't either until a couple weeks ago. Sit down. We'll clean the wound. No need to add infection to everything else."

Billy removed his shirt and sat beside me. Even in his misery, he'd remembered not to approach me armed. I yelled at Terry, and he brought me another bucket of clean water. Then he came back with a jar of antiseptic cream. He wouldn't meet Billy's eyes.

When I finished, Billy left me without a word, walked to the door, and stared outside. Xavier did stop and talk to him, and that seemed to help. Billy had received a virtual death sentence. Either he'd die of infection, or he'd become a were. According to Sabrina, the chances were good he'd die during the first shape shifting, or he'd go crazy and his keeper would kill him.

Xavier came closer, but not within striking range. I'd taught him better. His expression was that of a military man, stoic, indifferent, focused on his duty.

I leaned back against the post. "Gannett's butcher?"

"You think you're the only one who can kill?"

Xavier glanced at Billy, who still stared out into the rain. "I'll send him to a place where he'll be safe."

"But a werewolf. If he survives the change."

"If he survives."

Not long after that, Terry and Mack moved in behind me. They left the chain around my waist, but they unfastened it from the post. I drew a deep breath. I'd regained a bit of strength, so I fought. Not hard. They'd been good traveling companions and respectable fighters. My main target was Xavier. He'd given the orders. He stood back so I couldn't reach him. It took them a while, but they managed to wrestle me into the truck cab and attach the chain hooked around my waist to a metal bar. Terry and Mack remained patient about the whole thing, though I bruised them both.

Xavier climbed into the driver's seat. "The guys are going back for the turtles," he said. "We should meet up with them outside New Washington."

"Like I give a shit."

"Maat? I have pain pills, if you want one." So kind, so compassionate.

"You've got a gun too. Save a lot of time if you'd just shoot me."

"Don't tempt me." Wry amusement filled his voice. He was smirking. He'd almost accomplished his mission. "I promised I wouldn't. Shoot you, that is."

"Promised who?" Arms crossed, unyielding, I stared straight ahead.

He didn't answer. From where we sat, we could see Terry, Mack, and Billy heading across the open field and into the forest. The rain had eased so I guess we waited to give them a head start for the promised meet up.

"Who was the were? The old one?"

Xavier gripped the wheel tight, his fingers white at the knuckles. Then he relaxed and gazed into the distance. "Alistair Lockerbie. A pre-war physicist. Brilliant. He designed the low-level nukes they spread like a carpet across China. Or that's what he said. He found the…property…in this truck. For Aaron. We didn't know he was a werewolf. Sabrina wasn't around then to tell us. Once he had everything secured, Lockerbie's monster buddies came in and slaughtered all the humans Aaron had sent to help him."

Xavier's strained voice said it all. He'd cared for those slaughtered humans.

"Okay, what is this…property?"

"You don't need to know that."

"The hell I don't! I risked my life for it!" I shouted and fought the urge to attack despite the chain. I did have another question. "You walked right in, Xavier. How did you know I'd disabled the charges?"

"Billy." Xavier reached on the truck dash and lifted a pair of binoculars. "He crawled a quarter of a mile on his stomach, in the rain, to get where he could see the barn. At that level, that angle, he could see a shape moving back and forth under the truck. We had a Morse code device. Small, low power battery, but he sent me the message."

"And from that little bit of shit you decided I'd disarmed the explosives?" I had to laugh. Dear God, it hurt from my head to my guts and back. "Xavier, you're a complete ass, but I never figured you for a gambling man." *But he'd trusted me. He'd interpreted information received correctly because he knew I would act.*

Werewolves moved into my psychic range. Should I warn him? Yeah. I didn't want to die trussed up like a special gourmet lunch. "Got monsters closing in from the north."

Xavier drew a sharp breath. "How many?"

"Three or four. Coming through the woods. Fast."

Xavier cranked the engine and drove out the open barn door and onto a dirt farm road. It was slow going across the slippery and muddy red clay. Fuzzy weres could outrun us at this speed.

"There's a side case in the door by your right foot." Xavier jerked the steering wheel when the truck started to slide. "Your guns and knife are there."

"Big deal. If I shoot you, I'll still die. Right?"

"Unless you can chew through that chain and outrun a were. I was hoping you'd shoot a couple of them instead. It's three miles to the pavement." He'd drawn his own Aries and laid it on the dash.

I glanced in the large rearview mirrors sticking out from the truck sides. Four fuzzies raced down the muddy road behind us. "Take this fucking chain off."

"Can't. I'm driving. The Angel of Death should be able to handle the situation."

The chain was snug around my waist and attached to a metal bar bolted to the floor up near the dash. I had enough slack to move, but shooting would be awkward. I dug in the case and dragged out the Rudra.

Xavier gave me a brief glance before his eyes returned to the road. Damn those eyes of his.

The mirrors gave me an unobstructed view of the weres racing behind us. Their distance would be deceiving. When one got close enough on my side that I couldn't see him anymore, I gripped the Rudra tight. I leaned out as far as I could. One loped beside the back wheels. I aimed, pulled the trigger…and missed. The truck hit a hole and bounced me up. I pitched backwards. My head landed on Xavier's thigh. The head of the were I'd been trying to shoot popped up in my window. His clawed hands gripped the sill. Xavier raised his right arm. The Aries he'd retrieved from the dash bucked. The were's face exploded and disappeared.

Damn, damn, damn. Someone stuck knives in my ears. The blast deafened me in the tight confines of the cab. I struggled back into a sitting position.

Xavier had laid his Aries back on the dash and was steering with both hands again. Son of a bitch was laughing—until a were appeared at his window. His right hand shot out and he jammed his thumb and forefinger straight up the were's nostrils. He pinched and twisted.

Uncle Jake had shown me how to control animals by catching them in the nose. He'd lead the meanest of boar hogs around with a special pair of pliers clamped in his nostrils. I don't imagine Jake would have thought to apply the method to monsters. He was smart enough not to get that close.

Oops. Interesting position for Xavier—steering with his left hand, while his right hand crossed over his chest and held the were. Good thing the road remained level here. Xavier's mouth moved, so I think he was shouting. I couldn't hear. Oh, I think he wanted me to shoot the were.

I leaned over and carefully popped a silver bullet through the hairy forehead. That solved Xavier's problem. The discharge slammed my ears again. I could see the pain on Xavier's face, too. Oh, well. Better bruised eardrums than a ripped open throat.

Xavier snatched his hand back as the were fell away. He grabbed the wheel with both hands and increased our speed. I couldn't see anything in the mirrors, but that didn't mean they weren't still there. I wasn't about to stick my head out the window again. Besides, I could feel them.

"Still with us," I shouted. He had to read my lips. We were both deaf and would be for a while. I pointed at his hand. I grinned and worked my mouth, so he'd understand. "Werewolf snot."

Xavier shot his hand out, locked it in my hair, and gave it a vigorous rub. Then he released me and held up his fingers. He wiggled them in my face—until a fuzzy monster flung itself on the hood. It might have come on through the windshield, but Xavier slammed on the brakes. The beast rocketed forward across the hood and down in front of us. It hit the muddy road with a mighty splash and slid, limbs thrashing, until Xavier punched the gas. The tires thumped as they rolled over muscle and bone. The truck wouldn't kill the damned thing, but it sure would hurt. The remaining monster stopped to aid his companion on the road. They didn't follow us.

It took time and miles of road to regain my hearing. Hopefully, there'd be no permanent damage. "Why don't you let me go?" I asked when ordinary sound returned. We'd reached the better smoother road. "You got the stuff. That should satisfy Gannett. Ruelle can always run me down. That way, I might have a chance to kill him."

"You had a chance to kill him the other night. You

chose something else."

"When did who I fuck get to be your business?"

Xavier drew a breath to speak and stopped. No fury this time. He hunched his shoulders and studied the road. We rode in silence, broken only by the truck's engine and the constant murmur of the tires on wet pavement. Right before dark, he slowed, made a right turn, and we entered a small community tucked in the woods. Armed men instantly surrounded us.

"Keep your guns down." Xavier climbed out, hands in the air. He spoke briefly with one of the men. Fifteen minutes later, we were in a large garage-type building, and I was sitting at a table, chained to another post. He had allowed me to keep the Rudra and the Aries. I thought he might try to take them from me when he helped me out of the truck, but he didn't. All he did was find a longer chain.

I could have escaped if I worked at it, but by then I was curious. What was he up to? Possession of my guns allowed me to keep concern at a minimum.

Men came in and fueled the truck. They whispered and laughed to each other. I guess they thought the chain around my waist was a weird sex thing. Xavier brought me food and a blanket and pointed out a bathroom I could reach.

"You won't have to shoot anyone here," he said. "Take your guns off if it makes you more comfortable."

I shook my head.

Xavier shrugged. There was that smile again. Brief but beautiful. "Suit yourself. When Ty was four, he had a teddy bear. He never let it out of his hands. When he climbed in the bathtub, he held it over his head and made his mother wash him. Security thing, I guess."

I drew the Rudra. I didn't point it, but I held it out like a bizarre offering. "This ain't no teddy bear, asshole."

Xavier laughed, low and husky, and walked away. Oh, I wanted to hear him laugh like that again. I watched him move, checking the truck. Tired, exhausted, but still graceful. Still...desirable.

I managed a restless half sleep, sitting in my chair. I woke to find Xavier, his head and arms resting on the table near me. He opened his eyes and sat up straight.

"Time to go." Was that sadness I heard? I relaxed because I knew then, whatever his plans, they didn't involve giving me to either Ruelle or the president. His fingers brushed my face. "Swollen, black eye."

I wanted him to touch me more, but he simply stood and walked away. He came back with food—bread, cheese, and apples. We ate quickly and loaded up. I still had the chain around my waist, but he didn't attach the end to secure me.

We left the small community, and about ten miles down the road he said, "Key is in the bottom of the side pocket. Get yourself loose." I wasted no time. In minutes, I was free, had my weapons checked, ready—and was more confused than ever.

With the mountains and cool forest behind us, we rolled by green pastures where cattle stared across fences at neatly plowed rows of corn and peanuts. They longed to be free to gorge themselves. More rain threatened, but it promised to be a pleasant year for the AG communes spread across the Roanoke valley.

We were fifteen miles from New Washington according to a neatly lettered road sign. I don't usually speculate about the future, but I couldn't stop speculating on what was going on with the man sitting next to me. Nothing about him or what he was doing made any sense—and I still wanted him. Wanted to hold him, to make love to him, call him mine. I couldn't figure out why, so I stopped trying.

The truck did one of those funny little jerk things mechanical beasts are prone to do. Xavier hunched his shoulders and gripped the steering wheel with both hands. He relaxed as the engine smoothed out again.

"Xavier, what about Sabrina?" It seemed an appropriate time to ask.

"What about her?"

I mumbled a curse. He knew what I was asking.

He waited a few minutes to speak. He used carefully measured words. "I don't trust her, but others do. Next couple of hours and we'll see what she's made of."

"What's with you and Parr? I thought you two were going to go at each other at Avalon and maybe that bullshit wasn't about me at all."

"I'm not sure. He suddenly appeared and moved close to Aaron fast. Suspicion is—was—my job. Not that he's done anything but help. Maybe I'm wrong. Too much shit happening too fast."

I let it go. Xavier wasn't one for explanations any more than I was. Something was happening. Unusual and unexpected, he'd surprised me once again.

Houses and shops replaced farmland as we neared New Washington in early afternoon. Xavier slowed the truck at a crossroad. Mack, Terry, and Billy were there with the turtles. They must have traveled the night while we slept. Xavier stopped the truck, climbed out, and went to them. Billy seemed stronger, so I'd guess he'd survive the bite. All he had to worry about now was the trauma of transformation into a were.

Xavier and the three men talked for a few minutes, then they did the handshake, backslap, and rough hug thing men do when they want to show affection, but don't dare do a decent job of things. Billy, Terry, and Mack waved cheerfully at me and drove away.

Xavier climbed back in the truck and started the engine. He drove into the heart of the city. He held his head high as if readying himself for battle. "Maat, for once in your life, I want you to listen."

"Me listen! You—"

"Shut up! You know why I chained you up? So I wouldn't have to argue with you. You know where our arguments lead. You do stupid things and I overreact."

He reached a hand toward me, and then suddenly jerked it back. He drew a deep breath. "Now, if I slow down and say *run*, God damn it, you jump out and run."

He reached into his shirt pocket and pulled out the trigger Lockerbie had tried to use to blow up the truck. "We loaded all the explosives, cleaned and armed them. If they come at us, try to stop us, I'll lead them away, then I'll jump and blow it up. Gannett—or his vampire—won't get this truck."

"Bullshit! We can jump and run at the same time. Like we did on the mountain."

"Better odds if we split up. One of us *absolutely must* get away. If it's you, go to the New Washington Transport Corral. Ty's there. He's leaving. Go with him. I'll catch up with you when I can. Take care of him if I don't make it. Will you do that?"

"Yes. I will do that." I glanced in the mirror. No vehicles followed us. "What should I look for?"

"The army."

"Great! Got lots of experience there."

I checked my guns again, which always made me feel better. Xavier and I traveled unchallenged through town. We passed a couple of army vehicles, but they ignored us. Then we were at the large dirt lot that served as the New Washington Transport Corral.

Every city along the interstates had a corral. Convoys formed there to carry goods and travel safely through the wilderness between population centers. The convoys came in all sizes, but they had things in common. Each carried a road crew with machinery and materials for repair. The CLT interstates might last hundreds of years, but the approaches and lesser roads wouldn't. The biggest part of the convoy was fuel trucks. The vast empty country between cities also required a troop or two of mercenary guards. I had worked my way between cities as a mercenary at times, especially after the were hunting business fell off. It was boring for an excitement junkie like me, but it got me from one place to another with few challenges from any law or military types. Commerce equaled survival in our world.

Xavier drove the truck to an empty place in the line of a waiting convoy. He didn't shut off the engine since everyone was obviously awaiting the signal to move forward. I jumped when Ty suddenly appeared at my window.

"Hi there!" Pure joy in that voice. "About time you got here. You are late. Five hours late. Let me in."

He opened the door, I slid over, and he climbed in beside me. He immediately wrapped both arms around me in a ferocious bear hug. I hugged him back. I was happy to see this kid.

"Damn, Ty, let me breathe."

He relaxed his grip. "Can I have a kiss?"

I laughed. "I haven't had a bath in a while—or brushed my teeth."

"She's got were snot in her hair, too." Xavier just had to offer that bit of information.

"Were snot?" Ty stared at me with wide eyes. His fingers traced my jaw, bruised and swollen from where Lockerbie hit me. "What happened to your face?" He glared at Xavier. "You didn't take very good care of her." Ty hugged me tighter. "I still want a kiss."

"Okay." I gave in. "No tongue."

Ty kissed me, and it was a respectable kiss, even without tongue. He glanced over at Xavier. His expression was smug at first, then concerned. "You want me to drive a while?" Xavier's exhaustion showed now that we'd reached our obvious destination. He and Ty changed places and within minutes, the convoy moved out.

"Where are we going?" A little late, but I asked.

Dust from the truck ahead of us swirled around in the air. I wasn't sure I was going with them, but I knew I couldn't stay in New Washington. I admit curiosity burned my ass right about then.

Xavier told me. "First to Memphis. Then we're headed for New Mexico. City called Salvaje."

Absolute surprise. I wanted to talk, but his hands lay in his lap, and he sounded so tired. I wanted to touch him, too, but despite our common goal of escape, the memory of the vampire still stood between us. *The vampire I screwed to save a boy who didn't need saving because his father loved and protected him.*

"And the army's chasing us." I suppose it was inevitable.

"Probably not yet. They didn't watch for, or meet us, on the way back to New Washington. That's what I would have done. That's what I expected. This is too easy, too smooth." Xavier rubbed his hands across his face. "Maybe we can make Memphis first."

"Ah…The army's in Memphis, too."

"Yes. It could be a problem. But it's not Gannett's army anymore."

I'd heard rumors about Memphis Base, but being at Avalon I'd been out of touch with true news. Xavier hadn't mentioned Ruelle, but we both knew the vampire would be on our heels soon. He'd gone to too much trouble to get our cargo to let us go.

Xavier didn't look at me when he spoke again. "You may leave anytime if you wish, Maat."

"No!" Ty grabbed my arm. "No. You promised she'd go with us."

"I promised I'd get her *here*. You have to talk her into going along for the ride." Xavier settled back. Two good reasons to go with them were, of course, Gannett and Ruelle. But the biggest reason of all sat next to me. *Yes, I had totally lost my mind, independence, and free will, over a man and a boy I'd known for about three weeks.* Werewolf hunter extraordinaire, but nothing could save me from myself.

The convoy entered the interstate approach and the vehicles rolled onto the smooth CMT roadway. I made a decision. "I'll go at least as far as Memphis. What about your black shirts?"

"Black-shirts?" Xavier frowned. "Oh, you mean my troops. I got word from Billy, Mack, and Terry when we met them earlier. Mass desertion. They took equipment with them—and they blew up the helicopter. Should make you happy. You didn't think I'd leave them or any viable equipment I had for Gannett, did you?"

I bounced and clapped my hands like a kid. "The helicopter? Boom! As in blasted into little pieces?" I started to ask for details when I realized he had fallen asleep.

"Sabrina wouldn't come with us," Ty said softly. "She did stuff, helped us get away, but…"

Xavier had said our escape was too easy. Had the auburn-haired werewolf somehow cleared our path?

"She's a big girl, Ty, and a really clever werewolf. She can take care of herself."

I wished she'd come too. She didn't stand a chance against Ruelle. No matter what Gannett wanted, Ruelle would kill her eventually.

Chapter Seventeen

The convoy moved along I-81 at a dangerous fifty miles an hour. We were late and had to make the first wayside before dark. A wayside consisted of a substantial area fenced with razor wire. Until a few years ago, each convoy carried its own silver-coated wire to set up a secondary line. It wouldn't completely stop crazy weres, but they did hesitate and were vocal trying to get through the painful barrier.

A post-war government official—a bureaucrat with no mechanical experience and acute motion phobia—decided that the safest travel speed on a smooth open highway was forty miles an hour. A convoy traveling at that rate could make 320 miles in an eight-hour day. With astounding logic, they built the waysides 320 miles apart. Unfortunately, that limited travel to forty miles an hour. If you went faster, you drove past the wayside. If you didn't make the next one by dark, you could wind up in deep shit. Packs of werewolves haunted the roadsides until they disappeared, then human bandits rose to replace them. One bunch of monsters wanted food, the other tangible property. Both were deadly enemies and neither left survivors to speak of their deeds. The resurgence of weres did not bode well for travel. Our first wayside would be where I-81 ended and I-40 began. Our fifty-mile an hour speed meant, as Ty had said, Xavier and I, and our vital truck, were late.

Xavier slept while Ty drove in silence. No sleep for me. Being this close to Xavier made my insides twist and turn like fevered children in a restless daze. After two hours, we slowed to a stop. Convoys don't stop on the road unless something's wrong.

Xavier woke instantly.

A tall, thin man came trotting back toward us. Ty put the truck in neutral and set the brake. Xavier climbed out. Convoy rules—keep your engine running until you reached a wayside or a corral. Abandon any incapacitated vehicle. Scavengers regularly patrolled all roadways, looking for doomed vehicles to tow away or strip if they couldn't.

Xavier spoke to the man and then led him back to our truck. I climbed out, too. A relief. I'd been sitting for a long time.

The man swept his hat off a head of thinning blond hair. Hard to determine his age—mid-forties or early fifties—and the deep tan skin and a network of wrinkles around his eyes said he'd spent considerable time in the sun.

"Maat." Xavier quickly stepped up to introduce him. "This is Ray Heflin, our Wagon Master."

Wagon Master, a fall back to the vintage title from the 1800s. You could easily compare the convoys of the post-war world to the great western migration. Safety in numbers and abundant firepower required. Like a ship's captain, the Wagon Master was the boss. You rode only with his permission and disobeyed him at your own peril.

Heflin offered me a slender bony hand. "I've heard a lot about you, Maat."

"You don't believe everything you hear, do you?"

He gave me what sounded like a good-natured laugh. It wasn't. An unspoken tension swirled beneath his humor. Xavier had moved behind me, standing so close his body touched mine. An invisible sphere of concern suddenly surrounded him, and it enclosed me. *It also projected an I dare you threat.* Protection? For whom? Me...or Heflin. And which of us was he threatening? Since he stood behind me, I couldn't see his eyes to know.

"We're going to pass by the wayside and drive all night and tomorrow," Heflin said. "We'll stop before dark and refuel."

"Why?" I frowned. That didn't sound right.

"I sent scouts ahead before we left. There's a troop of soldiers camped at the wayside. This close they may have radio communication with New Washington. Some do." Heflin replaced his hat. He jerked it down tight as if the non-existent wind would carry it away.

This wasn't a good idea. "Won't they come after us if we pass?"

"Maybe," Heflin said. "I'm betting that they'll be settled in for the night and not want to run us down in the dark."

I had a better plan. "There's another road. It leads to the Avalon turn-off and cuts through the mountains. There's a couple of bridges, but they were solid the last time I saw them. Not too long ago. It goes back to I-40 about thirteen or fourteen miles below the 81/40 Wayside. Farmers use it and keep it in tolerable condition."

Heflin looked at Xavier. "Paved?"

Xavier nodded. "I remember the road. It was

smooth until we started up that damned mountain. I don't know where it leads."

That damned mountain. Avalon. Home. To enforce his anti-homesteading and tax collection laws, our beloved dictator Gannett had destroyed all the interstate exit ramps except for those at the cities and a few smaller towns. That kept decent, law-abiding people from wandering around the country—or he *thought* it did. It also left it free for me and other assorted criminals.

Avalon sat close to one of the small towns. Since it wasn't one of the official registered communes, I don't know how Anolia kept it a secret. Farm? Yes. We grew what we consumed and sold the rest.

Heflin agreed to try the road. Surprised me, but the troops ahead could be a disaster. It was a lesser of evils again. Unknown vs. unknown. The convoy exited I-81 at White Pine Township and headed into the hills at dusk. Like prudent people living on the edge of the wilderness, the town folk stayed inside after dark, with curtains drawn over barred windows. None would investigate the passing of trucks in the night.

When I first came to Avalon the deficiency of security troubled me, but the confidence of the residents lulled me into what I'd now consider disastrous incompetence. The Maat of two years ago would never have let the VP, Xavier, and troops arrive and take Anolia hostage while I played around with Christopher.

****

Aaron Gannett sat and watched the oil lamplight paint radiant streaks in Sabrina's hair. After Xavier and Maat departed, heading north to get his prize, she'd begged him to come here with her. There had been no word from Xavier, but he wasn't worried. His guards wouldn't allow Ty to leave the mansion. Ruelle had disappeared on a mysterious errand, so he was free of presidential duty and could devote time to his wife.

It was to this isolated farmhouse, an hour's drive from New Washington, that Sabrina came when the need to hunt overwhelmed her. He kept a small trustworthy staff here for her, and of course, twenty heavily armed soldiers accompanied them.

Gannett smiled. He believed that she'd simply wanted him away from the vampire's influence these past few days. He'd told only Borden he was leaving. He'd instructed the general not to inform Ruelle of his location. Ruelle could force Borden to speak, but that wasn't likely.

The moment Gannett had seen Sabrina, he knew he had to have her. He had loved Lilly, but Sabrina set a fire in his soul that raged through his body—a fire that nothing but possessing her would quell. He didn't know she was a werewolf until after he'd buried Lilly and begged her to marry him. He'd had to buy her from her alpha, offering protection for her pack. That act went against all he'd lived and fought for most of his life.

As if reading his thoughts, Sabrina rose and came to him. Her robe slithered off her naked shoulders and pooled around her feet. Her soft skin glowed as she knelt before him.

"Once you wanted to see me completely change shape. Do you still want that, after all that's happened?"

He leaned forward and kissed her. When he asked her to be his wife, and she refused, she had to prove to him that she was a werewolf. He wouldn't believe her otherwise. She had allowed only her hands to transform, to become clawed weapons capable of tearing flesh and breaking bone. After that one instance, she'd never allowed it to happen in his presence again.

"I thought you didn't want me to see you as a monster." He stroked her cheek with his fingers. "Monster—your word, not mine."

Sabrina rose and held out her hand. "Come."

They went to the bed and she had him sit.

"Then you decide. Am I a monster, a wild animal, or simply a human who can change shape?"

He'd asked her once to let him join her, become like her, but she refused. She'd told him he didn't know what he was asking, and she'd leave if he found another werewolf to infect him.

She stood before him and changed. Her body kept its human shape, but it shifted like a bag filled with soft powder. He stared into her face as it lengthened and became a muzzle filled with incredible teeth. Her ears stretched to a point, and auburn fur grew as his beautiful wife's body changed in an unfathomable way. He'd been a militia soldier and commander as he gathered the power to rule the country. He'd seen the raging monsters firsthand. He knew the devastation only a few could wreak on a whole AG commune or small town. Now he loved one beyond all reason. She stared at him with amber eyes and reclined on the bed.

Gannett's stretched out beside her. His hand stroked the fur on her stomach. Fine silky hair covered her breasts. They were smaller and harder, and her nipples rolled like marbles between his fingers. He touched her face and rubbed it with his own.

"I love you," he whispered in the gentle taper of her ear.

They lay there, face to muzzle, until the sound of approaching vehicles came like an unwelcome storm.

"Now what?" Gannett muttered. "I'm sorry." He didn't want to leave her, but years of planning were coming to fruition. There would be time for love later. He kissed her and rose to deal with the interruption.

She didn't move as he left the room.

Gannett walked downstairs where General Borden greeted him. Then he learned what his beloved werewolf had done. Hadn't Ruelle warned him she was treacherous? He hadn't believed it—hadn't wanted to believe.

He stood there, silent, caught in the moment, until time relentlessly drew him back. Shaking himself out of his self-induced trance, he went to the soldier standing behind Borden.

"Give me your gun."

The soldier pulled the pistol from the holster and handed it to Gannett. Gannett checked the clip. "Silvers?" he asked. The soldier nodded.

Gannett turned to Borden. "Clear the house. Five minutes."

"Yes, sir." Borden quickly moved away.

Aaron climbed the stairs as if each footfall marked a rocky path up a mountain. When he entered the bedroom, Sabrina had changed back to human shape and donned her robe. She stood facing him. He raised the pistol and pointed it at her heart.

"Well." She shrugged. "At least I'm not an innocent like those you slaughtered simply because they stood in your way."

Gannett pulled the trigger.

He stood there as the deafening sound eased. Then

he picked up one of the oil lamps and left the bedroom, closing the door behind him. At the top of the stairs, he stopped, turned, and flung the lamp down the hall. The spilled oil caught fire immediately, spread, and painted the carpet with flame. By the time he climbed in the limo with Borden, the three-hundred-year-old farmhouse lit the sky, crackling and roaring into the night.

Chapter Eighteen

I rode in the lead truck with Heflin to show him the way. He'd asked me to, but I suspect he wanted to question me without Xavier around. I felt no specific threat, but he betrayed his uneasiness by slightly clearing his throat every few seconds.

Off the interstate and moving through darkness, we barely made twenty miles an hour. The two-lane road remained clear. The locals had repaired it as best they could, given the fact it was illegal to do so. They used it to move crops south toward I-75 and Atlanta. It's amazing the things people will do to avoid paying taxes. I turned the other way when we passed the dirt road that led up the mountain to Avalon.

Heflin drove hunched over the wheel, his eyes steady on the road. "Xavier says you're psychic. You can sense vamps and werewolves. You feel any?"

"There's a touch of were. Not strong. Probably in human form. Can't judge the distance." Of course, I still had dried were snot in my hair. Never perfect, my proficiency for sensing them could be off with the recent close contact.

"Okay. Here's the deal. We're carrying two back in the last mercenary truck. I hired them. What I meant was any around in the woods."

All I could manage was to shake my head, which I doubted he could see in the darkened truck cab. *Two monsters in the mercenary truck—hired by the Wagon Master.*

He cleared his throat more forcefully. "So, you and that vampire Ruelle. You've known him a long time."

"Far too long. Heflin, you've heard things and you don't trust me. I don't blame you. Just say what's on your mind. I'll deal with it." Heflin had misgivings—and much more information about this venture than a Wagon Master, an independent businessman, should have. He was obviously a player in this bizarre game of *why don't we steal that truck away from the werewolves, president, and vampire.*

Despite my past and more recent involvement with Ruelle, Xavier had stood behind me earlier when I met Heflin. He'd made his endorsement of my presence personal and literal. That apparently outweighed Heflin's acting on his mistrust, even if he remained wary.

Heflin slowed and eased the truck over to avoid serious potholes. "Xavier called you elemental."

"Xavier's just afraid that Ty will follow me if I leave."

"Ty? He'd go after you?" Heflin made a low grunting sound. More skepticism.

"Yeah. The kid has delusions about werewolf hunting. I won't let that happen."

Elemental? That was a more accurate description of me than those myths surrounding the werewolves' Angel of Death.

"Okay, Maat. Elemental or whatever, you need to know that Salvaje, New Mexico, where we're headed, is a free city. Vamps, weres, humans, we all live there. We kill each other for a bunch of reasons, but not because some have fangs or fur, and others don't."

"Vamps? You live with vampires?" I fondled my gun, a bad habit I'd never broken.

"We have rules. We obey those rules."

"Vampires and werewolves obey human rules?"

"Yes. But not just obey. They helped write them."

In a rare moment, I couldn't find words. I sat there and let my mind run. Sabrina had shown me a werewolf form I never expected to see. The idea of either type of monster living with humans in greater numbers without making the humans breakfast, lunch, and dinner, marched straight to unfathomable. For me, all reckoning of werewolves had to climb over a great wall of rage and sorrow for the hideous deaths of those I loved. *Anolia…ah, no. Don't go there, Maat.*

Vampires were another more omnipresent nightmare. It had eased when Emanis' head popped off but would never completely cease.

I leaned back and let thoughts settle in. I'd had too many earth-shaking ideas dumped on me since the VP arrived at Avalon. "I heard there were people in Seattle. Nothing about New Mexico, though."

"Rumors about Seattle come and go. Distance makes information unreliable. I'm not surprised you haven't heard of Salvaje. We're careful, I think you understand why."

"So, no werewolf hunters allowed in Salvaje." Was that what he was telling me? That they wouldn't let me in?

"Hunters aren't specifically banned. But it's a closed society. No one new gets in without a personal invitation from a citizen. Then that citizen is responsible for the invitee's actions." Heflin slowed the truck again as we inched across shallow dips in the road.

Now this was an interesting development. "Are you inviting me or forbidding me to go there?"

"It's an invitation."

"Why?"

"You've earned it. Xavier says he couldn't have gotten the truck without you. Things are going to get nasty around New Washington. I guess he wanted to save you from Gannett."

"Aaron Gannett is a pathetic puppet. I'm way more afraid of that vampire because I *have* known him for so long." I laughed softly. "The leech is probably pretty pissed at me right now."

My companions had manipulated me into breaking my solemn word to deliver the truck to him. Pissed, livid, infuriated, many such words would describe Ruelle. I'd fight, I'd lose, but I'd hurt him.

Heflin slowed the truck and then stopped. "I don't have time now, but as soon as we get past Memphis, we can talk more. Don't talk about the weres. My drivers know, but the mercenaries are eastern locals and they won't understand. The sudden new were attacks around New Washington have them on edge."

I didn't understand either. Why did Heflin feel the need to hire werewolves as guards when he had a whole troop of mercenaries on the payroll, too?

"Come on." He put the truck in neutral, set the brake, but didn't shut off the engine. "I'm going to do a truck check."

Really? He was going to stop in the middle of the mountains in the pitch-black dark and do a truck check? Well, it was his convoy—and I had my guns.

I followed him back along the convoy to one of the trucks. The forest around the road stood dark and ominous. Only the sound of idling engines broke its silence. The weres stood away from the truck lights, but I could see them. They weren't fuzzy, of course, but my senses reacted to their presence as I moved closer. The female looked like a librarian. Plain and unpretentious, she had the rounded body of a matron. She'd twisted her blonde hair into a severe bun on top of her head. The male was the big black-furred were who had made the trek to the mountain with Sabrina—the one who held Ty's life in his claws. I don't know *how* I knew, but I did, just as I'd recognized Sabrina in her formal black gown. I might have had the ability to recognize individual werewolves all along, but I had no reason to try. It was always a shoot first or die situation.

Heflin wasted no time on introductions. He told the weres to pace the convoy on foot. Weres can run especially fast through dense woods. They could act as moving sentries and wouldn't tire. I understood their value here, but Heflin hadn't known we'd be traipsing through the mountains off the interstate. Did he need them on the open road?

The Wagon Master collected their clothing after they undressed and changed shape. My awareness of weres grew significantly stronger. At least I still had that ability to guide me.

The first bridge we crossed was easy, but one side of the second had collapsed since I'd last traveled that way. The supports on the remaining span looked adequate, and we made it across one truck at a time. I could feel the weres, invisible to all eyes, as they ran through the woods ahead and beside us. We passed under the abandoned southern leg of I-40. Before the war, it ran through the mountains to Ashville, then on to the Atlantic coast.

We'd bypassed Knoxville's ruins by dawn and were only a couple of miles from cutting back into I-40 when we stopped. Heflin sent the road crew ahead to see if it required work to get back on the interstate. We gathered around a camp stove in the middle of the convoy to grab steaming cups of Appalachian coffee.

I'd read about real coffee, roasted beans from South America. In his eloquent moods, Uncle Jake used to sigh and call it ebony nectar of the gods, a wonderful opiate of his misspent youth. He'd cursed and said Appalachian coffee didn't taste anything like the real stuff. The caffeine rich liquid squeezed from the seeds of plants developed and cultivated after the war had its own flavor and was fine with me. But the constant rumble and smoke from the idling trucks didn't lend any ambience to a cool pleasant mountain morning.

Several of the mercenaries came to get coffee before going back to their truck. I knew two, Liz and Jimmy, both capable fighters. Jimmy, gray, worn, and grizzled as the mountains themselves, nodded in greeting. "Maat. Heard there were weres around New Washington. Surprised you're leaving."

"Got a job in Memphis. I'll be back."

Liz, a six-foot black-haired Amazon with awesome knife skills, eased up to me. "New partner? Thought you worked alone."

I figured she meant Xavier. Someone must have told her how I arrived with him. I shrugged. I didn't want to talk.

"Serious, huh?" Liz winked at me.

"What?"

Liz cackled, her laugh a sharp sound on the morning air. "If it wasn't serious, you'd talk about him. Give me dirty words on the good or bad deeds."

I snarled at her, and she backed away still laughing. She was right. I'd been known to describe my partners in detail, remarkable, mediocre, or bad. But only after five or six beers, not during my first cup of coffee in the morning.

Familiar voices, familiar friends, approached. Ty joined us from the back of the convoy, accompanied by Lowell Parr.

"Maat." Ty grinned and almost pranced along. "Look who's coming with us."

Parr suddenly caught me in his arms. He gave me a fierce hug. "I knew you'd make it. Anolia would be so proud." He released me and quickly turned away, so I couldn't see his face. I caught the inside of my lower lip in my teeth and bit down hard.

Xavier and Heflin approached. Parr wiped his eyes and joined them.

"Come on." Ty had my arm. He urged me away. "I need to introduce you to Sabrina's friends. She sent them along to help. She's the one who helped me and Lowell get past the guards and out of the mansion. Aaron locked everything down and we wouldn't have made it otherwise. She did other stuff to help, also. I think. I hope she's okay." He rubbed his hands together, and a tight frown wrinkled his youthful face.

Ty dragged me back toward one of the trucks— toward the weres. They'd changed back to human form. Heflin must have returned their clothes since they were dressed. "This is Jacob." Ty nodded at the male. Dark eyed, with an angular face, Jacob's long black hair fell to his shoulders.

"I'm pleased to meet you under better circumstances. This is Rachel," Jacob introduced the blonde, soft-featured librarian with blue eyes and a shy smile. She nodded but didn't speak.

"Who are you?" I asked, pitching my voice so only the four of us could hear.

"We belong to Sabrina's pack." Jacob offered a soft-spoken explanation. "She asked us to join this convoy. To protect Ty and help you. Heflin agreed to hire us."

Well, that answered the question of why Heflin hired them, but I knew nothing about Sabrina's part in this whole scheme or her influence on him or the players. Interesting—and scary. Werewolf hunting, I understood. Track down, outsmart, and kill. Today, I stood basking in the morning sun with two creatures I'd have slaughtered on sight only a month ago. And they were there to *help* me?

Anolia had paid the price for my admission to this bizarre dance though, and I swore upon everything I believed she'd get what she'd given her life for. Heflin broke away from the trio and headed toward the convoy's lead truck. Parr went with him. Xavier came to us. He actually smiled. Before I could be amazed at how sinfully beautiful he looked, one of the mercenaries came running toward us, shouting. "Attack from the rear."

"Drive," Xavier ordered Ty and pointed at the truck. Then he raced for the back of the convoy.

I handed Ty the Rudra after he climbed in the truck. "Try not to shoot yourself in the foot."

He laughed and picked up a handgun from the truck seat. "That's okay. I'll use this." He held up my Sparks, the gun I'd left behind when we started our truck retrieval mission. "I stole it from your room."

"Keep it, then. But still don't shoot yourself." I left him and headed toward the end of the convoy.

The last truck in line was a troop carrier. The mercenaries already had the tire shields dropped. The sides, fuel tanks, and engine had armor built in. The most heavily shielded and guarded trucks in a convoy were always the fuel trucks, but the troop carriers came second. Most convoys had three or more, depending on the number of vehicles needing protection.

The back of the troop truck had no solid doors, and only a steel shield blocked the bottom half of the opening. There were panels on the side that popped open to fire or quickly exit if necessary. Xavier and I climbed in the back, and the convoy started forward—inched forward—given the number of trucks. The shield would drop instantly if we needed to get out and attack. In the meantime, we crouched low and waited, silently urging the vehicle to move faster.

The terrain had changed during the night. This morning we drove through flatter land, where forest had given way to head-high brush. When the sound of gunfire came, it came from the front, not the rear. Then a pickup type truck and an old turtle appeared behind us. Our would-be robbers had painted the pursuing vehicles the gray, green, and brown of camouflage.

I felt Jacob and Rachel rush away from us, toward the lead trucks. "Ty brought my Sparks from the mansion," I told Xavier. "You did teach him how to shoot, didn't you?"

He gave me a look that said of course he had, and I was stupid for asking. I relaxed and prepared to fight.

An explosion shattered the air. It came from the front. Gunfire followed. The convoy kept moving so the lead mercenaries had done their job. The trucks pursuing us didn't seem in a hurry to close in. I kept waiting for more bandits to appear. This was strange. There should be more, even if there were twice as many up front as behind. The attackers weren't sufficient to take on the number of trained mercenaries in the average convoy.

I felt Jacob and Rachel approaching, running low in the bushes beside the road.

The lead pickup truck chasing us suddenly raced to within a hundred-fifty feet behind us. The armor plate riveted over the front truck window left only a small grill for the driver to see through. One bandit rose from the truck bed. He shouldered a four-foot tube like pipe.

Oh, oh, deep shit rising.

"Where the hell did they get that?" One of the mercenaries shrieked.

I knew the answer to his question. So did Xavier. "Some bitch of a thief lifted a truckload of Atlantis rocket launchers from the Chicago factory a few years ago and sold them on the black market."

Oops!

He didn't mention that the thief, in conjunction with local rebels, blew the factory to rubble afterwards. Limited supply of the Atlantis brought a better price. I'd heard they never rebuilt the factory.

Just before we could make a fast leap from our truck to hopefully avoid a deadly shot, Jacob and Rachel burst out of the roadside in full fang and fur.

They leaped onto the lead truck. I'd seen Jacob in his midnight fur, but Rachel's gleamed gold in the morning sun. Jacob grabbed the bandit with the Atlantis and tossed him like a living mannequin. Propelled by werewolf power, he and his weapon landed more than a hundred feet away.

Rachel straddled the truck cab. She tore the metal shield from the front. That exposed the driver. She thrust clawed hands inside and yanked him out. His screams abruptly stopped when she bit his head off. Blood from severed arteries gushed and splattered her golden fur. *Rachel the librarian?*

The truck careened off the road. She leaped off as it rolled and bounced like a kid's toy flung away in a tantrum. Jacob had already gone. Rachel disappeared into the bushes again. A smart move since they didn't know whether lead or silver would chase them.

I heard the mercenaries around me scrambling, and I knew they were looking for silvers. Silvers are expensive, and these days most kept them safe for special occasions. Not me. I'd always paid the price and kept them in my guns. One of the mercenaries raised his rifle, though he no longer had a target. I grabbed his arm. "Let the weres do their thing."

He shook his head. "But they're killing humans."

"Right. And those humans would have…?"

I guess Heflin thought he was protecting Jacob and Rachel by not letting the mercenaries know what they were, but that put them in danger, too. The other vehicle chasing us stopped. The raging battle that didn't exactly happen was over.

A couple of werewolves saved us from death in the form of a missile. The mercenaries around me sat silent.

They exchanged *what the hell have I gotten myself into* looks. I knew the feeling well.

A few more miles and we were pulling back onto I-40. The mercenaries in the front truck had dealt with the attack there. Those would-be thieves had an Atlantis too, but the mercs shot the carrier. The explosion I heard was the launcher firing as he fell. It went wild and hit far from the convoy. Not too many bandits involved, but they knew the missiles would give them an edge. If they'd wiped out the mercenaries, the convoy would have been theirs. It hadn't been a well-planned attack, either. My guess was that a large convoy suddenly passing through these deep mountains caught them by surprise.

Vicious thieves. Too close to home…to Avalon. I hope Christopher the prophet would warn Avalon of such if they went that way. Of course, he hadn't warned me of what was happening with Anolia, the VP, and Xavier until it was too late.

The road crew and one truck of mercenaries stayed behind to dig a ditch across the access road in case the bandits had more missiles and decided to follow and try again. Thirty minutes later we stopped on a high section of the interstate with an unobstructed view of the roadway territory all around us. That gave the road crew a chance to catch up and the fuel trucks time to make their rounds.

Xavier and I climbed out. Jacob and Rachel, in human shape, were talking to Ty. In the distance I could see Heflin and the mercenary leader having a heated discussion. I wondered what explanation Heflin would give him about the two weres. The mercenaries in the front truck had seen them too. They, like myself, had probably never considered weres anything but animals who attacked, not aided humans.

The Atlantis could have ended it for all of us in the troop truck. I owed my life to a couple of werewolves. What could I say?

Jacob saved me the trouble. "The world changes, Suriel." He spoke with conviction.

I shrugged. "It's okay. Deal. You don't bite me. I won't shoot you. We'll leave it at that for now. Do you know what's going on?"

"No." He frowned. "They haven't told us much."

"Yeah, I know what you mean." I knew nothing, and I had gone with Xavier to get that damned truck. "I guess we're just lowly hired guns and claws."

When the road crew arrived, Ty, Xavier, and I climbed in a turtle. One of Heflin's drivers took over the truck. A piece of shit turtle wasn't comfortable, even on the smooth CLT roadway, but it beat how I'd ridden for the past few days. Ty drove and Xavier moved things around in the back. He cleared out a space, so he and I could lie down. Neither of us had managed any real sleep for over twenty-four hours. He quickly fell asleep, and I lay there for a while, listening to his steady breathing. Occasionally, he reached for me like a lover, but always drew back. I fell asleep fighting the urge to touch his hand, wake him, and demand to know what he wanted. By the time I woke again, the sun was falling in the sky, and we were slowing down. My bladder sent me an urgent message as I remembered the joys of riding in a convoy.

I'd slept while we passed through Knoxville's ruined western fringes. Wilderness continued to reclaim the cities, one year at a time. So many houses, so many people, once lived here. If a person left this road and walked, they could pass through miles and miles of nothing but abandoned homes.

Before the war, MAG houses were the most desirable homes. Magnetic seals made them air and waterproof and guaranteed they would last a hundred years without maintenance.

I found a MAG house in Knoxville's ruins once, one that no one had looted. Its occupants must have left quickly since there was nothing to indicate decayed bodies inside.

Had they realized how rich they were? We had books and videos to tell us about televisions, satellites, cell phones, but it was hard for me to imagine that instant communication and information.

I sat down in front of a blank television in the MAG house and pretended for a while, and then wandered into a dining room with a table set with china and glasses. I rummaged through personal belongings, but handled each like a precious relic, a symbol of a human life. A few objects were familiar, but others gave me no clue as to their purpose. The photographs on the walls showed a man, woman, and three little girls in various stages of their lives. When I left, I had only taken the silver I found. I sold it to buy the bullets that kept me alive.

I'd always lived in the present, and that house represented another world, another lifetime. I would never see anything like it in mine. Werewolves and vampires never terrorized the people who called the MAG house home, but they found adequate enemies in their fellow men.

Chapter Nineteen

Nashville, Tennessee

Nashville's ruins stretched out as spooky as Knoxville's. The Interstate passed through them, though, and the wayside was on the western edge of town. I'd take the wilderness any day—or night. At the wayside, a larger area than most of its kind, Heflin had the trucks parked in a rough square with the armored ones on the outside. Habits from my years on the road stayed with me. I needed the exercise, so I walked the perimeter and checked the razor wire. This well-fortified wayside had a ten-foot high outer wire fence. Parr joined me.

I'd hoped he just wanted to walk, but no such luck. People often relieved their pain by talking. Others, like me, save it up and released it in violent acts. Parr was a talker. Because Anolia had cared for him, I listened.

"You know, Maat, I was something of a lady's man. There were always women in New Washington willing to crawl in a vice president's bed."

I stopped and stared at him. "Only because you're the vice president? You're not exactly repulsive." A soft night wind lifted strands of silver hair on his forehead. Yes, he was an attractive man, and women, mature like Anolia, or younger, would seek him out. Soft spoken, kind, the younger ones could have a daddy and lover all in one.

He laughed gently. Of course, he knew that. "No. Not repulsive. And the vice president vacated his position a few days ago. Please. I'm just Lowell now."

"Congratulations. That's easy enough."

"No, not easy at all. I've wanted to leave for at least a year, but I was afraid Aaron would decide I knew too much to accept my resignation graciously. My predecessor resigned on the wrong side of a firing squad."

Really? I had heard a truck *accidently* ran him down. Politics, a purely human invention, mixed with the machinations of inhuman creatures. So sad. So terrifying.

Lowell cocked his head and gave me a look that made me think he was deciding if he should tell me something. He chose to speak. "Maat, a man came to the gate late in the evening after the attack in the Bell Market. Before you and Xavier left to get the truck the next morning. Big muscular fellow with red hair. The guards called me. He said he came for Anolia, to take her home to Avalon."

I stared out into the night. "That would be Christopher."

"Did I do the right thing?" He touched my arm. "I let him have her."

"Yes, that was right. Thank you. She would want to go there."

"He sent you a message." Parr's voice held a touch of curiosity

I wasn't sure I wanted any of the prophet's *messages*.

"He said Avalon would be there for you, when you

were ready to come home."

"That's nice to know." Well, at least Christopher expected me to survive. Or he expected me to return in a coffin like Anolia.

Lowell's fingers brushed at his eyes, though I saw no tears. "I asked if he wanted to see you. It would have been difficult, but I could have arranged it for him. He said no. It wasn't time."

"That's okay."

God, why wouldn't he shut up? Failure, my failure, would break me.

"Maat, he…" Tears did form in his eyes then. "It's so far from Avalon. How did…?"

"Christopher left Avalon before she died, Lowell. He's…a seer. He knows things."

I couldn't explain the oracle, his visions, and his prophecies. How horrible that journey must have been for the kind, gentle man.

Lowell followed me in silence for a while, but as we started back to the trucks, he said, "I told this Christopher that I loved Anolia. He stared at me and said, '*Your heart will receive its reward soon.*' What do you think he meant?"

"Don't know. He spoke to you more in a few minutes than he did to me in two years."

We returned to the fortress of trucks. Heflin's cook made dried beef and potatoes into a palatable stew. He used a portable oven to bake bread. Most caravans were for profit, and their owners cut costs where they could. Rations were barely edible at times, but this was better.

After eating, I decided I needed to talk to the werewolves. I found them sitting on a makeshift bench near a small campfire. They both smiled at me as I approached.

"Come and join us, Maat." Jacob pointed to one of the nearby wooden boxes that held everyday travel items and doubled as chairs in the rugged waysides. One did not sit on the ground at a wayside. If you were lucky there were outhouses built over deep lime-filled pits. If not, you watched your step and didn't disturb the top layer of soil.

I dragged the box closer to them and sat. "Tell me about werewolves, Jacob—your version."

"Rachel would be better at that than I would. She's a historian." He reached out and stroked her butter-colored hair.

"I can give you a condensed version." Rachel spoke in a soft voice that made me strain to hear. "Before the big war and the plague, there were only a few hundred werewolves left in the world, and all of us lived here, in the United States. One pack in the east and another in the west. They'd made a pact that no more of our kind would be made." Her eyes glittered gold in the lantern light.

"And someone broke the pact?"

Rachel nodded. "I think it was inevitable. There will always be dissidents. And many of us lived in areas where the bombs fell. We lost loved ones. I do understand the desire to increase our numbers."

This was a new thing for me, werewolves as living history. "What about the vampires?"

Rachel frowned. "Information on vampires is difficult to obtain, unreliable, and incomplete. I believe there were—are—far fewer of them than us. I will tell you, we werewolves tried to live in secret, peacefully as we always had, but suddenly, right after the plague ended, wild packs appeared everywhere east of the Mississippi. They slaughtered humans and their own kind. Humans found ways to fight back. Their defense also exposed those of us who lived in peace. And so, it went on—until about five or six years ago. The rogue packs stopped attacking. They began living quietly, but increasing their numbers. I'm told they have a strong new leader, but I know nothing about him. There are rumors of Seattle, too."

I had a sinking feeling in my stomach. About the time everyone thought weres had been exterminated, they'd gone into hiding. *And a bored Maat Ferris had marched her stupid ass to a New York hell in search of excitement.*

"What about the theory that the plague, the Devil's Dance, caused a change in werewolves. It doesn't kill, they're immune, but did it cause the craziness, the craving for human flesh?"

"I don't know. I've heard elders discuss that possibility. Some believe, others do not."

"Jacob, you and Sabrina were on the mountain. Why?"

Jacob leaned forward, elbows on his knees. He laced his fingers together. "Word had been out for over a year that the vampire and the president were searching for you. You have a mystical and deadly reputation among us. They say the vampire Ruelle is obsessed with you. You are a hunter. But Ruelle is…"

"I know exactly what Ruelle is, Jacob. I'd seen evil by his hand that would give even a werewolf nightmares."

Jacob glanced at Rachel before turning back to me. "The president and his army did not concern us, but if

Suriel the Angel of Death and the vampire joined him, it would be a fearful thing. Sabrina received word from someone about a pending attack at the mountain house, and we went to help you. And help you escape if we could. She knew you were being held against your will."

I fingered the silver wolf at my throat. "Why help me? Seems to me that killing me, and you could have, would solve any problems there."

"I don't know. Sabrina is part of the leadership. I'm not. I have few details, but I know there was a debate among the packs. A few felt it was important that you live, others felt it equally important to kill you."

"And the attack at the Bell Market?"

"Again, no one told me where those came from," Jacob said. "Either you, or Sabrina, could have been the target."

I was their target according to Lockerbie. He, like everyone I'd met since leaving Avalon, could have lied. This was a mystery I might never solve.

"How old are you, Rachel? I know it's rude to ask, but I'm ill-mannered at times."

Rachel smiled. "I was bitten by one of my mother's lovers while she lay in the next room and slept off a large quantity of alcohol. It was 1975. She brought him home from a bar. He was a rogue, and a local pack had been tracking him. The pack caught and killed him that same night. They took me with them, cared for me. That's how I survived."

"Now, you answer my question, Suriel." Rachel's voice sounded amused. Her accent was Midwestern, cultured, and highly educated. "Did you ever kill a were that didn't attack you?"

"Couple of times. I loved my work."

"But when you worked, it was because someone had a problem with werewolf damage. They hired you to fix things."

"Usually. Not always. And I guess that's why I missed those like you. You didn't cause problems. And I avoided cities where I might feel you, locate you." I stood. "I need time to think." I wasn't about to justify my life or occupation to a werewolf. If Rachel was trying to rationalize a personal problem dealing with me, I couldn't help her.

I walked back to where the others sat in the light of a single lantern. Xavier was there. He had mostly ignored me after he stood behind me in a quasi-protective stance when meeting Heflin. I'd seen him talking to Liz earlier, and I suspected she had told him a few tall tales about me. Aunt Nell once made me read a psychology book. Had a chapter on split personalities.

Xavier's personality appeared split down the middle. Part of him seemed to respect me and could be approachable. Yes, my night with Ruelle repelled him, though I'd made no commitment to Xavier. I considered it his problem, not mine. Except that the rejection cut me deeply and disturbed me on a level I didn't understand. His later kindness increased my confusion.

Ty had confiscated a wooden crate big enough for two and invited me to sit beside him. Xavier sat on another crate and Parr in a folding chair nearby.

"Hey." Ty wrapped an arm comfortably around my shoulders. "Want to ask you something."

"I'll tell you a lie. How about a tall tale? How I

once snuck into an army base and stole…" I laughed and glanced at Xavier. "Better not. Might piss someone off."

"No. I need to know the truth about this." Ty's face grew still and solemn. "The same day you and Xavier left, I was going down one of the mansion's inside passages. It was daylight outside." He removed his arm from my shoulders and clasped his hands in front of him.

My stomach knotted at the word *daylight.* Only one reason to stress that word.

Ty shuddered. "I ran into Ruelle on the narrow stairs. Shit, I was scared. It's one thing when you're in a room full of lights and guns, but that close…alone."

"Did he…?" If he had hurt Ty, I could head back east in the morning. I could walk then probably hitch a ride in a couple of days. Most convoys would pick up a single person. I might encounter Ruelle on the way if he'd pursued me. Or I'd hunt him down and kill him— or die trying. Maybe the vampire and I had both lived too long.

"No." Ty shook his head. "He didn't bite me. I'd have fallen down the stairs if he hadn't caught me and held me up. *He laughed at me, Maat.* Guess he felt me shaking. Then he said, 'Don't worry little boy. Our fearless hunter has bargained for you.' " Ty shivered. "He left me there and went on downstairs."

"Ty, damn it! Listen to me." My voice exploded in fury, way too loud. "That damned fucking vampire has been meddling in my life for years." Oh, shit. I had to calm down. "Ty, he manipulates everyone with lies. It's all lies."

"No." Ty sounded older now, more like a man—a

man growing into Xavier's ferocious intensity. "You did something for me. I owe you—"

"You owe me nothing." I jumped to my feet. "I need to rest."

I stalked away but felt Xavier's eyes follow me as I went. I'd never have told him anything like that of my own will. I made no excuses for my life. I explain nothing. I owned every action I had undertaken—good or bad.

I didn't have the first watch, so I went back to the turtle and crawled in. I realized how spoiled I'd become at Avalon. I longed for warm baths and clean clothes.

I was almost asleep when Ty joined me. "Can I lie down with you?"

"All right. But don't snore."

Ty rested beside me and wrapped his arm around my waist. He snuggled close, and it reminded me of Xavier's story about Ty's teddy bear.

"Is the country all like Nashville?" he asked. "I've never been far from New Washington. The land between cities…doesn't anyone live there?"

I heard the sadness in his voice and had to remember his youth. "Most of the country I've seen is empty, ruined. But there's good things, too. Growing things and places where people congregate for safety and make new lives. Think of Nashville, all the ruins, as a skeleton. Learn the lessons, go on with life." How many lessons had we humans learned, though? The struggle against the tyranny of men seeking power and wealth that almost destroyed us in the first place continued. The only change involved the unusual predators that descended upon us.

After a few threats, Ty settled down and went to

sleep. He didn't wake when my internal clock said it was two a.m. and forced me to rise and go to the watch post. I stood staring into darkness, seeing the usual shadow and light. I felt a werewolf out there and realized it was Jacob, silently walking a perimeter around the wayside.

Ty magically appeared at daybreak with a bucket of warm water for me to wash in. He and Xavier had shaved. Most men in convoys usually went for practicality. Unless an easy and unusual opportunity presented itself, most facets of grooming waited until they reached their destination. Women made do in their own way. I'd washed between my legs under cover of a blanket countless times.

Xavier and Ty had more class than the average convoy traveler. Fact is they had more class than a roughneck werewolf hunter and self-proclaimed liar and thief.

Ty produced a small tube of shampoo, so I washed my hair too, removing dirt and dried werewolf snot. What a mess. I needed to cut it short again.

I'd let it grow at Avalon. Ty made me sit down while he applied a bit of oil. Then he combed it, carefully untangling my rough curls one at a time. Sweet boy. I'd do anything to protect him. Yes, I recognized it was profound guilt because I failed to protect Anolia. Would I do a better job with him?

Ty separated and tugged at each curl. "Lilly had arthritis in her hands, and I combed her hair for her." He spoke in loving memory.

Xavier watched him groom me in silence. He remained with us as we waited for the call to start the engines and resumed our journey.

Chapter Twenty

Memphis, Tennessee

The convoy entered Memphis at sunset, not that we could see the sun. The sky rolled with pillows of slate-gray mist. Thunder threatened from more storms in the distance, but then quieted, leaving only the soft hiss of light rain.

Two rival army factions raged a territorial war across western Tennessee in 2038, culminating in the Battle of Memphis in 2039. The clash leveled ninety-five percent of the city's already abandoned buildings and infrastructure. The remaining five percent continues to waver on the edge of ruin. People stay because of commerce, the bridge across the river, and electricity. A small power plant north of the city remained the town's redeeming element.

I knew the Memphis area better than I knew the mountains around Avalon, so it wasn't hard to guide Heflin as we left the interstate and eased through the side roads into town. He watched me, and I saw occasional glimpses of hostility in his gaze. My misgivings about continuing with this bunch had grown. Xavier be damned, I should remain here and wait for the vampire. I had no doubt he would come after us, and I did have a few allies here.

We hid the trucks in an abandoned warehouse, one

the next strong wind might bring down. Rainfall increased and hammered on the metal roof. It forced its way into the building in sporadic drips or gushing streams, depending on the size of holes it discovered.

Heflin met with Xavier and Lowell and called for an executive meeting in a corner of the darkened warehouse. He'd asked me to join them, a surprise given his mistrust. We stood close together behind one of the trucks. Jacob and Rachel guarded our meeting. With their super senses they'd hear everything we said, but no one else would. This was the first time the three men had included me in their conferences.

Heflin slouched against the side of the truck. "I want to cross the river before dawn. The army's blockaded the bridge. Just barricades, soldiers, and light arms, but they're stopping and searching everything." He'd been into town and come back with the news.

"You can go to St. Louis," I said. "It's further, but—"

"No. Damn it. We're running out of time. I have to meet people across the river." His attitude had become more anxious and irritated since we parked.

Lowell cleared his throat. "So, are you with us, Maat, or are you going to stay on this side of the Mississippi and dodge the army?"

Heflin stiffened, but he didn't speak—didn't say what he wanted. I suspected he wanted me away from him and his prize. Had Xavier not stood behind me on the road out of New Washington, he'd have kicked me to the side days ago.

I shrugged. "I don't know. Been doing the dodge game for years. And it's not me who will be dodging. They'll be concentrating on whatever is in that truck.

And Memphis is one of my homes. I have friends here."

Xavier's eyes narrowed. I knew what he was thinking. If I left or stayed behind, Ty would follow me. I stared straight at him. "He'd be safer with me than you, right now."

He looked away. Did that mean he thought I was right?

Jacob and Rachel suddenly entered the pool of light. The lantern's glow spread across determined faces and glittered in feral eyes. Now what? *This did not feel right. Should I run?*

"Draw your silver knife, Suriel," Jacob said.

No problem with that. Despite our casual conversation, he and Rachel made me nervous. Just as my blade cleared the sheath, he caught my wrist. Too slow, damn, damn. In an act of what had to be terrifying courage, Jacob raised the blade within a fraction of an inch of his own throat.

"Suriel, I bare my throat to you." Jacob's hand shook, but his voice held steady. "I renounce my pack. You are my alpha and I will follow you, obey you. I will defend you with my life."

He stood there, leaning in with vast intensity, waiting for me to act. I had my mouth open like an idiot, too stunned to respond. He must have taken that silence as acceptance of his offer. Rachel's hand closed on my wrist before Jacob released me. She didn't hold the knife quite so close to her throat, but she made the same vow. I stood silent, struck dumb by their actions. *Oh, shit! Oh, damn! Why did they do that? An oath to die defending me?*

Nothing in my life had prepared me for this. I could see myself traveling through the world with a pair of monsters trailing along behind me. Behind me? Would I turn my back to them?

"Jacob," I found my voice. "What the hell? I don't want you. Don't need—"

"We've given you our lives, Suriel. Make appropriate use of them." Amusement vibrated in his voice as he turned to Heflin. "Please forgive us, Wagon Master. We will return the money you paid us to work for you. If you wish our services, you must bargain with our new alpha."

I wanted to slap that smug self-satisfied smile off Jacob's face, but he and Rachel immediately returned to their guard positions.

Heflin wasn't amused. "Maat, I don't think I can get across the river without them. It's going to require more than manpower. We have to move those barricades to get the trucks by." The dismay in his voice told me the sudden plot twist wasn't his idea.

This travesty of a game—a game that cost Anolia her life—had changed. I had a hunch, a strong suspicion, that someone really wanted me to go west. When I hesitated, they'd coerced two werewolves to manipulate me and offer me their loyalty and lives. Heflin needed to move soon. With certain pursuit behind us, he had absolutely no time to seek alternatives. He needed the—my—werewolves. The success of this mission had suddenly dropped like a yoke on my shoulders.

I leaned back against the truck. "First, I think you should tell me what we went to so much trouble to steal. And why you're so determined to take it all the way across the country."

Heflin crossed his arms, and when he spoke, I

knew he begrudged me every word. "In the mountains beyond Salvaje, there's a functioning missile command complex. In that complex are remote launch controls for five multiple warhead nuclear missiles. We believe—we pray—they're the last in the world."

I swallowed. "And you're going to…"

"We want to disarm them, but we can't get into the complex. The army abandoned and sealed it when the war appeared to stall. We don't know why. So far, the damned thing has been impenetrable. The equipment on this truck will allow us access. Our mission now is to get it to New Mexico. Then we break in and destroy the firing controls." He blew out a breath. "The actual missiles? They could be hidden anywhere in the west. Even if we knew those locations, we have no one capable of arming or disarming them."

I glanced at Xavier. He met my gaze for a moment, before looking away.

Heflin closed his eyes. I thought he had finished, but he continued. "You met Lockerbie. He could have opened, aimed, and fired those missiles. The hateful bastard would laugh as cities died. But he had no one to help get the truck to New Mexico or get past us to the complex. So he armed it with explosives and squatted his ass in the mountains, threatening to destroy everything. We weren't concerned until the vampire arrived and joined Gannett."

I frowned. That didn't seem quite logical. "Why not blow the truck yourselves?"

"We could and we will, before we will let it be taken. But if we get inside, destroy the main controls, the missiles can sit in their holes until the world ends. But most importantly, there's a wealth of technology in

271

the complex, including an atomic generator that could power a city for fifty years."

"Pretty powerful weapons. You could use them yourselves. Rule this world."

Heflin eyed me. "No, Maat. That doesn't tempt me, nor does it tempt my comrades in this venture."

Lowell leaned forward and held out a hand. "Are you with us, Maat?"

He meant, are you and your newly acquired, loyal, and excessively valuable werewolves with us?

"Exactly, who is us?"

"Myself of course, as well as Heflin, Xavier, and Sabrina and her pack in New Washington. There's a larger network of people who pass information and work to save what's left of the country. I only joined late last year."

Larger network? A whole bunch of people who pass secrets, tell lies, and form conspiracies. I knew nothing about missiles, or nuclear warheads. I did know Ruelle. I would die to keep him from those weapons. I'm neither noble nor a hero, but I had people I loved.

Was I with them? I'd taken a significant role in the capture of their prize. Then there was the man. Xavier, who kept drawing me close, then rejecting me. The big beautiful man, with his scarred face and dark eyes, the one I'd been able to drive to a fury that almost killed me. Jacob, Rachel, and their blood oath baffled and infuriated me. I had to find out what that was all about.

Ah, but I had a bit of leverage in the game now. "My weres and I will cross the river with you, Heflin. No promises after that. I do want to go into town tonight and try to get more information. Loan me a turtle, will you? And a little money. Oath bound werewolves aren't cheap, you know."

"Sure." Heflin sighed in relief as if money and a single turtle were the least of his worries.

"What about the Memphis army?" I was curious about that. "Gannett lost it?"

"About a year ago." Lowell answered the question. "The Memphis Base Commander, Borden's equal in stupidity, has aligned himself with the democracy movement in Seattle. It's a righteous cause, but almost two thousand long empty miles from reinforcements."

I shook my head as if I could deny the savage events that brought me here. While I rested my soul in the peace of Avalon, my world had slipped into another war.

The grumble of voices came from across the warehouse.

"Damn. The mercenaries." Heflin clenched a fist and shook it in the direction of the sound. "I won't pay them until later. I don't want them wandering around town talking about us. I want—I need—to cross the river before dawn." He stalked away, cursing under his breath. Lowell went with him. He glanced back at me and smiled. I guess he approved of my decision. That left me alone with Xavier.

"Maat…" Xavier started to speak, but stopped.

Xavier wasn't any better at expressing feelings than I was. Except for rage. We were warriors who conveyed wrath with exceptional proficiency. I changed the subject and let him off the hook. "Will you come into town with me? Might need backup."

He stood very still for a moment, then nodded.

I know he didn't understand my relationship with the vampire. I didn't understand it myself. It was born during the aftermath of the horror in New York. I'd always kept a hateful connection with Ruelle, waiting for the miracle that would give me the power to rid humanity of his evil. I had only sought him once. All other times he had come to me. That wouldn't change until I dragged him into the sun and reduced his bones to ash. Or he killed me. I think I knew him better than any other human alive. It was a complex affiliation that had to end in destruction of one or both of us.

We went to the turtle Heflin said I could use, and had to argue with Ty, who wanted to come with us. Xavier refused, and I backed him up. Ty had no business where we were going. I did call Jacob aside and give him orders. If Xavier and I didn't get back in time, he and Rachel were to help Heflin cross the river before dawn.

I'm not a city person, but I could tolerate Memphis. Families, at least two thousand people, made their lives and raised their children in the area around the crumbling North Bridge. The durable CLT span held, but the support piers had broken in a few places giving it a precarious tilt. Foot traffic could easily cross, but few drivers were willing to take a chance, especially since it ended in the same place as the newer, concrete South Bridge.

By contrast, the South Bridge area had twenty-six bars, and an equal number of brothels. They hunched on the river's edge around the bridge where I-40 began its westward run.

Memphis had no official law enforcement. You protected yourself or you became a victim. Loyalty and keeping your word had as much value as gold. A smart person would have care where they laid less tangible coins down.

The South Bridge area also served the army base located on Presidents Island. I'm not sure what kind of brains it took to quarter soldiers on an island connected to the mainland by a single causeway. Defensible, with suitable existing usable buildings, yes, but all supplies came overland from the east. It would be easy enough to lay siege and starve them out.

The rain had ceased. It left the air warm, muggy, and permeated with the aroma of raw sewage and rotting garbage dumped into the river to make its way south. I'd told Ty to think of Nashville as a skeleton. Memphis was a carcass with a little bit of decaying meat left. The vultures worked hard here. They'd finish the meal soon.

****

Sabrina Gannett, former First Lady of the United States, raced through the woods like a phantom. With her clawed toes digging into the rich loam, she would cover many more miles before sunrise. Then she would hunt, feed, and rest.

The depth of Aaron's love had surprised her. She expected to die when the bullet slammed into the wall three feet to her right. Aaron had stood there with an unfathomable look in his eyes, then turned and picked up an oil lamp and walked out.

She had jumped to her feet, torn off her robe, and changed to werewolf form in seconds. She ran to the window. Out on the back-porch roof she made a running leap for the hickory tree that shaded the yard. Her claws caught a limb, she swung up to another, then across the branches to the next tree. Two hundred feet from the house, she dropped to the ground and raced away into the night.

She covered familiar ground at a steady pace, slowing only at the small cave where she kept a pack containing clothing, boots, gold coins, and other essentials she would require if she had to pass among humans.

She'd planned to leave, but hadn't expected them to discover her role in the plot so soon. It was with little hope she had stowed the pack months ago. She'd been gathering information from Aaron's office, listening to secret meetings for over a year. She'd passed the information on but when the vampire came, she knew she had to do more. Someone had to keep Aaron distracted at times, too. She had believed it unlikely that she could escape when it all went down.

Aaron's merciless acts against the people of the country had killed her love for him not long after they were married. She endured. She hadn't expected the unusual woman who suddenly arrived and turned everything upside down.

She was quite certain Suriel, the deadly, mysterious Angel of Death, could have found a way to kill a president's wife. The woman had a power beyond understanding. She had stayed her hand and allowed Sabrina to live. Now Aaron had given Sabrina another chance. She had no hope for her husband, locked in the vampire's embrace, but she wished Maat Ferris well.

She could move faster in werewolf form, and heightened senses would warn her of danger. Free.

Sabrina stifled an urge to howl her joy into the forest and hills around her. Danger waited for her in the world beyond her own. She would have to avoid strange werewolves who walked the land, and she would have to eat. And where would she go? She laughed, and the night stilled at the rumbling growl from her throat. Every living thing within the sound of her voice froze in terror. Under the light of a rising crescent moon, Sabrina began her journey west—her journey into tomorrow.

Chapter Twenty-One

Unattended vehicles soon had new owners in Memphis, so we had to use a secured parking lot. Heflin had been generous with the money he'd given me. I could pay to keep our turtle safe. Fagan's was closest to the place I wanted to go.

"Maat, welcome home, girl." Fagan waddled his pear-shaped body across the lot. He cradled a shotgun in the crook of his arm. He prided himself on never having a vehicle in his charge stolen.

"Fagan." I smiled in greeting. Fagan was rumored to be too fond of children, buying and selling. Rumored. If I had proof, I'd kill him.

Fagan stared at Xavier with narrow assessing eyes. I remembered my first sight of the scar, but the complex man beneath it intrigued me so much I barely noticed it now.

"What's with the lockdown at the river bridge?" I tried to act casual. "Deserters?"

His mouth went tight, and he shook his head. I'd never seen him so uncomfortable. "Bigger than that. Looking for something. Or someone. Nothing going west without a search."

I cut my eyes at Xavier. My guess? The Memphis Base Commander had heard about us, and by God he wanted to get his hands on our stolen truck. It's good that I'd found a place to hide it away from town. Word would go out, though. We had to get across the bridge before a troop of soldiers surrounded us, even if they were no longer Gannett's soldiers.

Fagan couldn't tell me more, so I paid him to guard the turtle and led Xavier into the dirty streets of the place that, before Avalon, I had called home. Xavier kept his hand on his Aries, and I kept mine on the Rudra. I hadn't been here in over two years. The forlorn street looked more defeated than ever. We walked past stunted, two-story buildings jammed together, parted only by an occasional dark alley. I wouldn't walk down any of those alleys with an army of mercenaries to back me up.

The usual jumble of emaciated men and women stood in dark knots away from the light. Their next meal or beating could depend on what they bought or sold in a night. None approached us. In fact, the street was almost deserted. In times past, I'd had to run a gauntlet of men staggering in and out of the bars. Most of them in an alcohol fueled goodtime way, but occasionally looking for a fight they always found.

I stopped at the edge of an alley. Too late, I questioned my own judgment in bringing Xavier with me. I didn't need anyone to guard my back in Memphis.

My hand caught his arm. "Hey, I—"

"Want me to be quiet and follow you." He grabbed and tugged a curl of my hair. I think he liked my hair, coarse and tangled as it was. "It's your town, Maat."

I released his arm and nodded, suddenly suspicious. He gave in too easy. *Memphis was my town?* Where had he heard that? Ah, bet Liz told him shit. Yeah, I projected a tough image here, mostly because any sign of weakness made you a victim. I had backed that projected image up with action a few painful times.

I punched Xavier in the arm. "Brothels don't bother you, do they?"

That got me a rare laugh. I doubted he was celibate, but I also doubted he was a man who craved multiple women—nor would he have to pay for sex. I led him down the alley to an arched entry where a light bulb cast a pool of light. The word *Sable* and a single black rose decorated a sign hanging above the door.

A hook-nosed dwarf sat on a stool by the door, smoking a cigarette. He sneered at me.

"Hey, Choppy." I grinned at him. Ah, yes. Something normal here at least. "Good to see your ugly face again."

Choppy crushed the cigarette out against the wall. "Hey, woman. Finally fucked your way back home, huh."

I laughed. Choppy was glad to see me. "Where's your little goat, buddy, you wear her out?"

"Yep. Sure did. Her ass ain't as tough as yours." He pointed a finger at Xavier. "This one's uglier than me."

"You're jealous?" I clasped my hands over my heart and opened my eyes wide with mock surprise.

"Woman, you broke my heart." Choppy slid off the stool and opened the door.

I went in and Xavier followed me, keeping one eye on the grinning dwarf, who slammed the door behind us. I let loose a sigh of relief.

"Xavier, I don't know if you'll see him again, but don't underestimate him. Choppy's a good guy, but he's hell with a knife."

"You have an odd definition of a good guy." Xavier touched his gun. "I usually don't play knife games."

I winced when I opened the door to the main barroom. Sable's place smelled of beer, sex, and unwashed bodies—and the pervasive hint of sewage.

Way, way wrong.

The Sable Rose had always been a clean house. Sable's janitor had scrubbed the wood floor to a smooth patina over the years and polished each varnished table to a dull shine.

Again, the sense of sullied surroundings had a troubling edge. Tables and chairs were scattered around the room in a haphazard arrangement—not the orderly manner I associated with the place. The mirrored wall behind the bar held less than a third of the usual array of bottles. Half the stools were missing. Uneven light spread across the floor because burnt-out bulbs hung from the chandeliers like dead flowers in a bouquet.

Two young girls made straight for us. Megan and Jan, my adoptees. I found them living in an AG commune several years ago. Their father had raped his eleven and twelve-year-old daughters and worked them unmercifully in the fields. Sable was the only person I could trust at the time. I brought Megan and Jan to Memphis and promised to send money to support them. I extracted a promise from Sable to educate them and try to keep them out of business conducted at the Rose. They might choose to go there someday. There were no other jobs here. At least they'd understand the risks. I shot their father when he arrived and tried to take them back. No great loss in this world.

"Maat." Auburn haired Jan shouted my name.

Darker Megan rarely uttered a sound. I embraced them, so happy to see them. Had I thought about them at all while I stayed at Avalon? Or was I so firmly centered on myself I didn't care? Their attention quickly turned to my companion.

"These are my girls, Megan and Jan. Girls, this is Xavier."

I couldn't call him a friend. What could I call him?

"He has nice eyes." Megan's head bobbed up and down. *Wow! Megan spoke actual words. I guess he impressed her.*

"Is he yours?" Jan twisted a bit in my arms.

"No, not mine." I didn't have time to explain. "He's traveling with me. Come on, where's Sable."

"At the show. It's Liam and Kelly tonight. It's way worse since you've been gone. It gets really bad if no one watches them." Jan's mouth twisted as it always did at the mention of Kelly. Jan wanted to talk, but I put her off with a promise for later. Megan, again silent, kept her eyes on Xavier.

"Maat?" Jan called to me as I turned to go. She nodded at Xavier. "You should keep this one a while." She'd grown into a bright pretty girl. Xavier smiled at her. Another smile? Wow.

Sable had always expected patrons to buy two or three drinks before heading upstairs with a lady. Unlike most houses, this one operated by ladies' choice and every woman had the right to refuse any offer. Most didn't, of course. That's how they made a living. Alcohol and the shows helped support the place. Ladies' choice meant Sable had the prettiest and best protected girls in town.

The place was not only dirty, but the usual energy,

noise, and cheer was missing. Patrons only occupied a third of the tables, and there were at least two women for every man, more proof of the soldiers on lockdown. The women who clustered around the few available men were not up to Sable's usual standards either. I didn't recognize any of them.

Toto, one of Sable's bouncers, stood guarding the door to the showrooms. Toto didn't like me, and his eyes narrowed as I approached. Most men took a defensive stance with arms crossed and feet spread apart. Wouldn't work with Toto. His massive arms were too short to reach across his equally massive barrel chest, so he held them at his sides like a pigeon-toed monkey. Muscle tissue extended to his thick skull, and he exercised it doing stupid things—like picking a fight with me.

Toto opened the door and stepped back. He'd learned.

We walked through the intricate, twisted labyrinth of dim hallways and stairs designed to confuse patrons. I'd walked the maze and knew each step by heart. Sable refused to allow patrons to wander around at will. The Sable Rose had always been a carefully controlled business. That's why the condition of the barroom was so disturbing.

For the first time ever, I found the showroom door unguarded. When Xavier and I entered another small anteroom, I turned and raised my hand. He was closer than I anticipated, and my palm touched his chest. Before I could move, he caught my hand in his own— and held on. My mind went blank, and we stood in the sultry darkness.

I drew a deep breath. He released me.

"Xavier, listen, when we go in, the word is *show*. Kelly is…strange. Remember that."

I opened the door and a woman's high-pitched shriek of agony poured out and enveloped us like water bathing a stone in a rushing stream. Xavier surged forward, and I wrapped my arms around his waist and grappled with him. Damn he was big. He caught my shoulders in his hands, drew deep breaths, and stared into my eyes.

"A show?" he said softly.

"Wait. Please. Something's not right here." Absolutely not right, because Kelly's scream sounded so visceral—not an act like it was supposed to be. I led him into the room, and we found a place in the shadows.

Liam and Kelly had turned pain—her extremely high tolerance for pain—into a profitable business. Kelly stood naked, her wrists stretched above her head and secured to a long bar. Her back was toward us, and her lush body swayed. Spotlights trained on her and most of the room dark, but there was light enough showcase six men sitting close in a semi-circle around the pair.

Thick muscles in Liam's bare arms and chest stood out, but the black whip in his hand drew all the attention. He drew it back and lashed Kelly across the back of her thighs. She shrieked, twisting and dancing, trying to escape the leather snake flaying her.

Xavier jerked again. I pushed my body back against him. Kelly's skin glowed and sweat streaked and matted her hair. She whimpered and cried inarticulately. No blood, Liam would never cut her, but from her shoulders to her ankles, raw red streaks created great masses of abused skin. Liam caught her body in his arms and turned her around.

He'd worked the area from her breasts to her knees too—with much greater attention to detail. That wasn't supposed to happen. By consent or not, this was too much. Sable would not permit this abomination. Where the hell was Sable?

Liam released Kelly's wrists from the bar, and she collapsed against him, moaning and crying. She wrapped her arms around his neck and held him in a ferocious grip. She rubbed her face against his chest. He held her up and started to work the crowd. I'd seen that before. He'd allow each spectator in turn to caress her bottom or thighs, stroke the hot, painful skin.

He encouraged each man to paw, pinch, and twist anywhere he wished. A few were particularly sadistic, drawing more cries from Kelly.

I was shaking by then. What should I do? This was Memphis. Spectators would be well armed. A high-power shoot-out in this confined room could have dangerous unintended consequences.

Sable's throaty bass voice suddenly rumbled as he moved out of the darkness to stand beside me. "Maat please. Wait. I'll take care of it when it's over,"

Long, black hair fell like a midnight waterfall across a lace-collared, red brocade dress. Diamond earrings, painted eyes, and cherry lips, six-feet-three with a battered hooknose, Sable was spectacular as usual. Except he needed a shave.

He laid a hand on my shoulder. His fingers gripped tight. I leaned back against Xavier, who stood so still he might have been a wall.

Liam had jerked at the sound of Sable's voice. He

scowled. He carried Kelly back and laid her on a blanket at the side of the room. She curled up into a tight ball and lay still.

With his hand still on my shoulder, Sable held me as the lights brightened and the audience filed out. They'd tossed considerable cash on the stage. I resisted the urge to terrorize them. I settled for glaring and received a satisfactory reaction, until I realized Xavier standing behind me had instilled the fear. I knew what they saw in his face as they hurried past. I'd seen it a few unfortunate times myself.

"I'm sorry, Maat." Sable planted his hands on his hips, obviously frustrated. "Things are happening and I had to go out for a few minutes. You know I would never allow it to go that far."

I knew Sable would take care of the matter, but I wasn't sure how many options he had. Liam and Kelly were popular. If he kicked them out, they'd go to another house. Sable kept them there for Kelly. Kelly was safer at the Rose since there was little hope of persuading a masochistic woman in love to leave her man.

"Liam." I gritted my teeth.

Liam grinned at me. "You gonna preach, Maat? Dog fucker like you."

No audience now. Kelly lay still on the blanket, eyes half closed, as if in a trance. I could solve Sable's problem. I drew the Rudra. There would be no collateral damage now. Xavier wrapped his arm around me and squeezed. I relaxed before I shot myself in the foot.

He released me and made swift strides to scoop up the black whip that Liam had so carelessly discarded.

He twisted the leather in his fingers.

Liam, who was gathering the patron's money from the floor, stood and faced him.

"You like hurting women?" Xavier asked the question with what sounded like genuine curiosity.

Liam's gaze flicked to Sable and me for an instant, then back to Xavier.

"Not your business." Liam was a formidable man, strong and an excellent fighter.

"No." Xavier agreed pleasantly. "It's not."

Liam's hand went for his pants pocket. The whip lashed out. It cracked like fractured ice when it caught Liam across the wrist. A small caliber pistol flew out of his hand and landed in a dark corner of the room. Liam's high, knife-sharp shriek sliced my nerves. He staggered but remained on his feet, staring at his now oddly warped wrist. Xavier raised the whip again.

He cut Liam's feet from under him as he tried to run away. With powerful strokes and slow, precise cuts, Xavier lacerated Liam's body from shoulder to ankle and back again. The welts on Kelly were raw seared skin—Liam drew blood. Liam howled, twisted, and writhed, and desperately tried to roll away, smearing the stage with red as he went. There was no escape as his own instrument of torture followed him.

I turned to Sable. My mouth dropped open at the wicked grin on his face. He reached out, draped one long arm around my shoulders, and hugged me tight.

****

Sabrina knelt beside the stream. Cold, clear water gurgled around the rocks as she used a tiny bit of her lilac scented soap to wash her hair and body. Her jeans and shirt lay spread out on a nearby bush. She hadn't worn them since she left Virginia. After she dried and dressed, she tied a scarf tight around her copper hair, carefully tucking each strand away. The color was too noticeable to remain visible, and it was time to stay in human form.

She'd crossed Kentucky and passed into Illinois in werewolf form. Gliding through the somber shadows, she'd watched the moon swell and brighten each night. She'd slept during the day, and she knew a convoy couldn't have made better time. She'd avoided the ruins of abandoned towns. Those who could not live in regular society, the most depraved, often congregated there. She had crossed the Ohio River's swift currents, swimming with her backpack wrapped in a waterproof bag and securely clamped in her fangs.

Sadness for the empty land consumed her as she followed primitive tracks and broken roads. At times, the night wind grew heavy with the ghosts of a dead world. They whispered through the trees and urged her to be gone. The deep green forest brought peace, though, after the years of discord with Aaron.

Humans did traverse the wilderness, as did other werewolves. Men she avoided with ease. The slightest scent of a fellow were sent her running. She had no desire to join or be torn apart by a strange pack. Yesterday, she'd come upon a sign when she crossed an abandoned roadway. St. Louis—thirty miles. Now in human form, she walked in the trees parallel to that road, moving west. The stillness of dawn surrounded her, so she heard them before she saw them.

"Jenny, please." A man's voice coming from the woods made what sounded like a desperate plea. A man's desperate plea echoed from the woods.

Sabrina froze. She started to turn and move away when he spoke again.

"Change back, Jenny. If someone sees you…"

His answer came as a giggle, then a weak growl.

Intrigued, Sabrina crouched, dropped her backpack, and eased silently through the trees. A small creek cut a three-foot gully across the forest floor. The man stood on the far side. A dark-haired boy of seven or eight stood beside him. A fitful breeze brought the werewolf scent to her. A little girl in furry form scampered around on Sabrina's side of the creek. She ignored the man's plea.

Sabrina ached for her—and hated the evil that possessed man or werewolf to do such a thing. Even with care, those children rarely lived to maturity. This one, maybe five years old, was in grave danger. Worse, she was a danger to anyone who tried to protect her.

"Come on, Jenny," the boy cried, fear in his voice. "You stupid little…"

Again, Sabrina started to turn away. She had her own problems.

"I'll stay with her, Eddie. You go on." The young boy spoke with the clarity and resignation of a grown man who'd made a bitter decision. He was afraid, but he'd do the right thing.

Sabrina smiled. Such courage. It wouldn't hurt to help a little. She eased closer, stepped out of the brush, snatched the little girl up by the scruff of her neck and shook her—hard.

"What do you think you're doing, little wolf?" Her question purposely couched in an alpha's demand.

The little werewolf girl whined. Her eyes wide. She suddenly changed back to human form. Sabrina lowered her and looked up into the barrel of a pistol. The man had crossed the creek.

They stared at each other.

Sabrina spoke first. "Are you going to shoot me?"

Eddie, that's what the boy called him, shook his head. He lowered the pistol but it remained in his hand.

"May I talk to her?" Sabrina gestured at the girl lying between them.

"I won't let you hurt her." This man was a protector, not an aggressor.

Sabrina dropped to her knees, lifted the girl, and turned her so she could stare into her eyes. As an adult werewolf herself, she had the ability to send the girl certain messages and impressions. She sent one of what men would do to her if they caught her. The girl refused to accept, closing herself off completely.

"That won't work," the boy said. He'd crossed the creek, too. He stood close to the girl. He'd understood what Sabrina tried to communicate to Jenny.

"Why not?" Sabrina reached out and touched him.

"She knows." He gave a little sob. "She won't think about it 'cause it scares her too much." His voice carried sorrow a child should not have to bear. "Mom died."

"I found them with their mother," Eddie spoke quietly. "She'd been caught in a trap. I buried her. I couldn't leave them to starve."

Sabrina sighed. Overwhelmed by terror, Jenny had rejected her visions of slaughter and had withdrawn from the rational world. The odds were against her survival.

A strand of pale blond hair fell across Eddie's forehead, and his blue eyes narrowed with worry. His stocky, muscular body reminded Sabrina of a workman. Not a handsome man, but sturdy and dependable—and incredibly compassionate to care for dangerous werewolf children. She wondered if he had a woman waiting for him. Sabrina had known she'd have to attach herself to someone eventually if she traveled among humans. A woman alone, obviously not a mercenary, would attract too much attention.

Sabrina eyed his gun.

He put it away.

Sabrina gathered an unresisting Jenny in her arms. "Her clothes?"

"At my truck," Eddie said. "She stripped and ran away. Who—"

"My name is Sabrina. I'll try to help you with her, but I'm not sure what I can do." She turned to the little boy. "What's your name?"

"Joe," he replied.

Eddie shifted uncomfortably. "I got to get back to the truck. My son, Terrell, he's there alone. He's only twelve. Traffic's been passing all morning. I told him to run if anyone stopped."

Sabrina asked Joe to retrieve and carry her backpack.

They hadn't gone far when Sabrina suddenly halted. Joe's eyes widened in alarm. Eddie couldn't hear the faint sounds she could as a werewolf.

"Stop, Eddie."

He obeyed. Good. This man accepted her alpha authority. She laid Jenny on the ground. Jenny whimpered and tried to cling, but a hiss from Sabrina silenced her. Like a wolf puppy, she curled into a ball and lay very still. Sabrina wanted to leave Joe with her, but she might need his eyes and ears.

Eddie, alarmed now, started forward. Sabrina caught his arm. "We need to see first."

He nodded, and they eased forward together, crouching low. The thick brush made it easy to get closer. It took all of Sabrina's considerable strength to hold Eddie back and keep him quiet when he saw what had happened. When her fingers dug into his arms and pinned him down, he turned and met her eyes. If he didn't know she was a werewolf before, he did now.

Eddie's large, delivery-type truck sat in a clearing with both doors opened wide, and the cab's contents scattered on the ground. The steady clank of metal on metal came as two rough-looking thugs tried to beat the lock off and open the big doors on the back. A third was probably supposed to be standing watch, but his eyes were on the adolescent boy lying tied and gagged on the ground. The thug nudged him with his boot, and the boy struggled.

Eddie drew his pistol. "Oh, God, Terrell," he whispered under his breath. "I shouldn't have left him alone."

"Wait," Sabrina whispered in his ear. Eddie would go down before he could shoot all of them. Sabrina drew Joe close and gave him instructions. He nodded and slipped quietly away through the brush.

"I'm going to attack with you. You won't hesitate?" Sabrina whispered in Eddie's ear. "You will shoot, won't you?"

He nodded. Cold anger flashed in his eyes.

Sabrina gently squeezed his thick muscled arm.

They eased closer to the clearing. The two thugs at the back of the truck had given up on the lock and walked toward the one guarding Terrell.

"Need a bigger bar," one of them said. He rolled the boy over with his foot. "Better, bet this little shit knows where there's an extra key."

Sabrina allowed her hands to change from the elbow down. She heard the sharp intake of Eddie's breath, then a sigh. Howling and screeching burst from the other side of the clearing. All three men turned and drew their weapons.

Eddie and Sabrina charged out of the brush.

Sabrina threw herself on the closest man. One arm went around his head, and she ripped out his throat with the claws of her other hand.

Eddie shot the second one, and he instantly dropped. Good aim. He aimed at the third and…click. The gun jammed. Eddie stared at it in disbelief.

Sabrina dashed toward the third man, knowing it was too late. He'd already aimed. Her body passed between him and Eddie as he pulled the trigger. The bullet hit her mid-chest, but it didn't stop her momentum. She slammed into the thug, and he screamed as she disemboweled him and rolled across his body—dragging out bloody guts locked in her claws. He screamed again, gurgled, and blowing blood, finally relaxed in death.

The bullet wasn't silver. Sabrina knew that when it hit. Damn, it hurt though. Her body convulsed, the smell of meat…blood…she couldn't stop. Her clothes tore apart as she completed the shape change. As she did, the chest wound closed and healed.

Joe suddenly appeared beside her. He'd changed to full were form too. Little Jenny came running out of the woods to join them. They wallowed against Sabrina, blood streaking their fur, their small tongues licking her muzzle, nuzzling, whimpering and crying. She heard them in her heart and in her mind. Mommy, Mommy…

Sabrina glanced up to see that Eddie had untied his son and lifted him to his feet. He held the boy in a rough embrace. She gently pushed Joe and Jenny aside and stood, but they clung desperately to her legs as if she had become their sole source of life and nourishment. Her torn clothes and shoes lay on the ground. Blood and pieces of human organs clung to her auburn fur.

Eddie stared at her, an unfathomable expression on his face. He'd taken in the two children, buried their dead mother, but to stand face to face with a grown werewolf…. She soared a foot and a half taller and outweighed him by a hundred pounds. His gaze traveled up and down her body.

"Are you…would you like to come to St. Louis with us?" Eddie's voice wavered. Despite his shock, he tried to smile. "This is my son, Terrell."

Sabrina, feeling a bit evil, grabbed his shoulders and held him tight. A man who could tolerate weres. Perfect. She'd have to be the strong one, the alpha of her little pack, but she could do that. Sabrina opened her mouth and with one flick of her long tongue, licked his face from chin to forehead. His eyes popped open wide in such astonishment she did it again.

Chapter Twenty-Two

Xavier continued to flay Liam. I grabbed Sable's arm.

"Should I do something? Xavier is—can be—intense at times." Intense? Xavier was a killer. A brutal, terrifying killer. My offer was a joke. I couldn't stop him, and I knew it.

"No." Sable's deep voice turned hard. "Don't get between them. "Don't trouble yourself, either, love. I've put up with Liam for her sake. It keeps getting worse. He'd injure her if some asshole gave him enough money." He nodded at Kelly, who still hadn't moved. "That's an unusually strong man you have there, my darling, Maat. And where have you been? I was afraid you'd finally become part of a carnivore's nutrition plan."

Liam's screams ceased. Xavier stared down at the unconscious man's torn body for a moment. He dropped the whip onto the floor. His dark eyes stared straight into mine. His presence pushed against me and at the same time, warmth spread between my legs and twisted along my nerves. I broke into a sweat.

"This is Xavier." That's all I could manage to choke out for an introduction.

Sable studied him. "I thought our intrepid hunter worked alone."

"She made an exception for me." Xavier's voice

sounded calm, pleasant. I knew better.

"Does she treat you well?" Sable grinned. His eyes were too shiny and bright. He had recognized Xavier's dangerous rage and was using humor to defuse the emotion. Sable knew the nature of violence all too well.

"I suppose." Xavier spoke in a lighter voice. "She stabbed me. Pushed me off a mountain. Tried to drown me. Should I expect better?"

Sable threw his head back and laughed, low and deep in his throat. "Lucky man. I think she's in love."

"Cut the crap." Oh, hell, did that sound bitchy? "We don't have time for this. Where's my demo man? Is he in town?"

Sable sighed deeply, and his voice filled with false scorn. "Over at Lucky's. Lucky has twins, both about two-fifty, two-seventy-five. I can't compete with that. He'll stay there until he runs out of money."

Yes, that was Ajax, my longtime friend. I explained to Sable that I was only passing through, guarding a convoy, and that I planned to cross the river in the morning.

"Well, my dear, you arrived just in time. Everything's packed and ready. The Sable Rose is closing. We'll be gone before midnight."

Okay, that explained the place's condition.

"Why? What's happening?"

"I'm not certain. The soldiers from the base talk about a war with New Washington. They've blocked the river bridge. Searching everything. Mass desertions there, too. Things have been getting steadily worse over the last six months. A mercenary came in a few hours ago and said a big convoy of troops is in Nashville. They'll be here by noon tomorrow, and I'm not going to be part of the welcoming committee."

Xavier and I eyed each other. The president had obviously missed us, but other things had been happening, too. Memphis Base's traitorous commander might have pushed things too far.

"Do you want to go with me?" Sable sounded hopeful.

"Where are you going?"

"North to St. Louis, then west to Seattle. I don't know exactly what's there, but I've heard good things. There's nowhere else to go now. I'm adaptable, you know that. Come on, girl. Another great adventure."

Should I go? It was one option, but Ty…who was I kidding? Xavier had moved close enough for his arm to brush mine. His body tensed. Was he waiting on my decision?

"Sorry, Sable, scheduling conflict. I'm already booked for one adventure this month. You go on. Seattle sounds good. I'll find you later."

Xavier relaxed. No, not relaxed, merely less stiff.

"What do you want me to do with your half?" Sable asked the question, but he knew the answer. He'd asked it for years and it had been the same.

"Take it with you. Let me have a hundred full-gold, now, though. What about…" I nodded at Kelly, still lying unmoving on the floor.

"I'll take her with me. He'll probably follow, but I'll do the best I can." His painted mouth pursed, and his eyes narrowed. "Or maybe I'll solve the problem before she wakes up."

Sable grabbed me and hugged me tight. "Be careful, Maat." He eyed Xavier as he spoke. *Yes, Sable. I knew the danger.*

I returned the embrace. Sable released me and hurried away. He stopped to scoop Kelly up in his arms before he left the room.

"Your half of what?" Xavier stood too close. His hand brushed down my back but stopped before he caressed anything lower than my waist.

"Half of the Sable Rose. He likes his diamonds, emeralds, and dresses, but he's an ex Tennessee militia officer—mean and smart as hell. He and I lifted an army pay truck in Atlanta once upon a time. We were flush. I gave him my half of the take. Told him to invest the funds. He manages money better than me. He built this place." I took a chance and laid a hand on his arm. "Hey. Where'd you learn to use a whip like that?"

He seemed fully relaxed now. "It's a long story. Maybe I'll tell you on the way to New Mexico."

"I haven't decided on New Mexico. Let's cross the river first." Okay, that was a lie and we both knew it.

Back in the main barroom we sat at a table, and I signaled the bartender for a couple of beers. The bartender had dirty hands. A sticky film coated the outside of the glass, maybe the inside, too. I'd had worse.

I took a sip of mediocre beer. I'd bet Sable had loaded the best brew on a truck to fortify them on the journey. Sable was, among other things, a master brewer. He'd make more when he settled. Might as well enjoy what I had right then, though, since I didn't know when I'd get another.

I turned to Xavier. "So, they're after us."

"We expected pursuit eventually. Not this soon, though. Borden may have been assembling a strike force to attack Memphis Base and had it ready to go. I warned Aaron to watch him. He's a cagey old soldier. He should have retired twenty years ago."

One of Sable's bouncers came by our table and dropped off a leather pouch filled with full gold coins and another with half-golds. I rarely needed money. I usually bartered for life's requirements and stole what I couldn't trade for. My usual situation didn't apply here. We finished our beer, seeming to want the last luxury of civilization to linger with us. Only Heflin knew what lay ahead.

The streets had emptied while we were in the Rose. Maybe they'd heard the news about the army's pending arrival and decided they should lay low until the shooting stopped. Then they could emerge to congratulate the winners.

Lucky's place sat two blocks over on Acorn Street. At least he had a front door and we didn't have to weave our way through the alley. I asked Xavier to keep watch at the entrance. To my surprise, he agreed.

Lucky sat at a table in the empty barroom. Rough banging noises and muted voices came from the back. I assumed he'd received word and decided it was prudent to leave Memphis, too. Three girls carrying suitcases rushed down the stairs and toward the backdoor.

Lucky greeted me with his usual contemptuous snarl. "Better run, Maat. 'Spect you're pretty high on the army's list."

His pinched face, small-boned body, and rank odor made me think of a ferret—or a rat. My dealings with him were always straight, though. I anticipated no trouble now.

I sat across from him. "On my way out. Ajax here?"

"Maybe."

I dropped one of the gold coins Sable had given me on the table. It lay there like a single yellow eye.

Lucky grinned and flashed black, broken teeth. "Upstairs."

"Can you keep him here until daylight?"

"Maybe."

I dropped another gold coin.

"No problem. He paid for the whole night with the twins anyway. First room on the left at the top of the stairs. Anything else?"

I shook my head. "Be careful, Lucky. You might be on a list, too." I added another coin to the table, so he'd remember me.

Ajax was my friend, my demolitions expert, and I had a feeling I'd need him. I knew I had to get him out of Memphis before the army arrived. Like me, he had a reputation. I wondered if Gannett had a thick file on him, too. By the time Xavier and I headed back to the turtle, the pace of foot and vehicle traffic had increased, though not by much. Noon tomorrow was twelve hours away.

Heflin met us as we drove into the warehouse. I gave him the unwelcome news. "There's an army battalion outside Nashville headed this way. Supposed to be here at noon tomorrow. You should warn the mercenaries." The army and mercenaries rarely moved in the same circles, and I felt a kinship with my fellow soldiers-of-fortune.

Rachel and Jacob returned. Heflin had asked that they scout out the bridge. Unfortunately, they addressed their report to me, their new alpha. Heflin's expression turned as sour as persimmons before the first frost.

"The approach is clear." Jacob rubbed his hands together in what I took to be anticipation. "Concrete barriers block where the span starts, forcing everything through a single gate. They're searching anything outgoing. No actual confiscations yet. We saw at least twenty soldiers, but no guns heavier than rifles. Couldn't detect any silver. Rachel and I can take care of men and rocks."

The 2033 battle of Memphis blasted the original twentieth century bridges to a muddy grave. The current newer concrete span was laughable by comparison. Government engineers built it half a mile south of the old one. It was too low, and the rising spring river often covered the surface, keeping away any who would approach.

The truck engines fired up at four in the pre-dawn morning. Three cargo trucks and two turtles slowly rolled down empty streets. Everything else, including the fuel trucks, a small fortune in vehicles, had gone with the lucky mercenaries.

"I've got more trucks and fuel waiting on the other side," Heflin said with a shrug. A lot of planning and money went into this expedition. New Washington to New Mexico, a vice president, the president's top security man, werewolves—and a vampire. Too much still didn't make sense, but my options were few, and so far, I'd dealt with events. Or at least survived them.

I rode in the lead turtle with Heflin, Rachel, and Jacob. We passed the alley to the Sable Rose. The sign was gone. The door stood open revealing an empty black cavern. They'd left on time.

When we reached Lucky's place, it appeared abandoned too. I told Heflin to stop. He raised an eyebrow and frowned. I climbed out before he could object, and I knew he wouldn't leave without me. All the other vehicles stopped behind us.

"Rachel, you and Jacob come with me." Yes, the alpha gave orders. "I need to collect a friend. I can't leave him for the army. Be careful. This one *does* have silver." The pair swiftly obeyed. It sent a thread of amazement through me. Werewolves obeying my commands—damn!

Only the light from a single, second floor window gave any sense of life.

I eased in through Lucky's open door. Jacob and Rachel followed with less caution. Well, I had warned them. The hollow, empty building picked up and amplified any sound. Our footsteps sounded like a hammer striking metal.

"No one is here," Rachel sniffed the air like a hound on a fox trail. "Except..." She nodded at the stairs.

We climbed the stairs as quietly as we could, but the steps squeaked under Jacob's weight. I knew Ajax wouldn't come with me without prolonged explanation, so the situation required direct action. I had it well planned, which always guaranteed things would go wrong.

I stood away from the door and knocked. "Ajax? It's Maat."

Silence.

I reached out and cautiously turned the doorknob. Locked.

"Ajax." This time I pounded on the wood. "It's Maat. Come on man, answer me." With Ajax, it was best to be careful until you knew he recognized you.

We waited. The soft whisper of our breath sounded loud.

"Shit," Jacob said. He stepped up to the door.

Before I could say no, Jacob lashed out with his foot. The door popped off the hinges, sailed into the room, and crashed to the floor. A shotgun blast hit Jacob square in the chest and slammed him back against the wall. Another tore into him as he crawled away. Not silver thank God. Manufacturers stopped making the labor-intensive silver shotgun shells years ago. If Ajax had used his pistol, we'd have been minus one werewolf. Jacob curled into a tight ball, knees to his chest, and his face twisted in pain. Lead hurt, even if it wouldn't kill him.

The violent roar of gunfire fell to silence.

"Ajax," I screamed. "Stop shooting. It's Maat."

"Maat?" Ajax sounded a little confused. Hung over—or drugged if Lucky felt it was necessary to keep him there.

"Can I come in?" I wasn't about to move until I was certain he knew it was me. He didn't answer, and I heard him reloading the double barrel.

"Maat?" Ajax sounded more coherent this time. "Come on in."'

"You okay." I mouthed the words to Jacob who sat on the floor on the other side of the doorway. He nodded, but his expression said he still hurt. His clothes hung in rags, shredded and burned.

"Wait till I call you," I hissed at him. Maybe he'd learned to listen to me.

I stepped through the open door into a shabby room furnished with a single outsized bed and a table without chairs. Ajax stood naked in the middle of the floor. He swayed a bit, but the shotgun barrel remained pointed downward.

If I had to describe Ajax, I'd use the word *whipcord*. A tall man, six-five, he was lean and hard with tight sinewy muscles. Blessed with striking ebony skin and a razor-sharp mind, he was one of my first and few loyal friends. We met in the Freak Squad and they kicked us out on the same day. I had Ruelle take me to Ajax when he carried me out of New York. I weighed less than a hundred pounds and came as close to death as I ever had. For six months, I lived in a fog of pain and insanity. Ajax fed, washed, and cared for me like a child until I recovered.

While my life revolved around killing weres, Ajax obsessed with ample women and blowing things up. The bigger the better for both. I knew without a doubt *he* was on the army's shit list. Behind Ajax, his *twins* struggled to dress.

One was lemon-haired and pale, and the other had mahogany skin, a shade lighter than Ajax. I guess you could call them twins. Both had the substantial bodies that excited my demo man.

"Let's go," I said.

"Go?" Ajax held the shotgun in one hand and rubbed the other over his face.

I grabbed Ajax's bag and dug out a pair of pants. His boots sat beside the bag and his handguns lay on top. He had taught me that long ago. Being naked is great, but always keep your stuff ready to go. In a tight, you can snatch, run, and dress later. "Come on." I tossed the pants at him.

"Where we goin'?" He caught the pants and laid the shotgun on the table.

I glanced at the twins. "You girls better get out of here. There's probably going to be a big fight tomorrow."

They looked at each other, and then back at me. "But Lucky said we could go with Ajax." The blonde's lower lip quivered as she spoke. "He said someone paid him enough money for us."

Oh, shit. That's all I needed.

"My ladies go with me," Ajax grumbled. Of course, they would. He liked women and treated them well. He protected them too, when necessary. He'd just gotten his pants on when Jacob, his tattered burned clothes flapping around him, walked into the room. The werewolf who'd sworn I was his alpha, whom he would defend with his life, didn't like taking orders.

"What the—" Ajax stared at Jacob.

"Something's coming." Jacob pointed at the window.

A long, escalating whistle filled the air. It ended when the pre-dawn world erupted in a flash of light, followed by a massive explosion. I ran to the window. Another blast, then another. The building shuddered, and debris rained down on the trucks below.

Fully alert now, Ajax grabbed his bag, boots, and shotgun. "Damn it, Maat. Every fucking time you show up, I wind up with—"

More explosions, louder and closer, hammered our ears. We rushed out of the room and down the trembling stairs. Heflin met us at the door.

"I think the army's arrived early." Heflin had to shout over the din. Our Wagon Master was a master of understatement.

"This is Ajax and his twins." I pointed at the trio.

"They're going with me." Heflin didn't look happy. Too bad. He'd accept Ajax, or I'd leave with people he needed following me.

After a minor struggle, Ajax, his twins, and what little they carried, filled the entire wide backseat and we were on our way. Rachel and Jacob would continue on foot. I glanced back at Xavier behind the wheel of the following truck and saw Ty had joined him. Ty's wide-eyed face glowed with the excitement of a grand adventure. Xavier's tight grip on the wheel said he understood the deadly turn of events. And, of course, I'd royally pissed him off—again.

We headed for the bridge with Jacob and Rachel trotting beside us. They loped along with the effortless grace of animals. The bombardment eased, and when we turned a corner, I saw why. A double line of armored cars and troop trucks plowed down the street less than a quarter mile behind us. *Oh, shit.* That was artillery on the bigger trucks behind them. General Borden and his army had vastly improved his portable munitions while I was out of circulation. I turned in my seat to look at Ajax. At least we had enough room his ladies didn't crush him. I really was happy to see him. "Ajax, my man, glad you could come along."

He draped one arm around the blonde twin's shoulder. "This is Mary."

Mary gave me a shy smile.

"And this is Giselle." He grasped the dark twin's hand and raised it to his lips.

Mary was pretty in an uncomplicated way, but doe-eyed Giselle crossed the line into beautiful. Both silently gazed at Ajax with adoring expressions.

Ajax's deep-voice laughter boomed through the

vehicle.

"So, someone's shooting at us. Let me see. That ain't happened since…last time you was around, Maat. Who we running from now? Anyone I know?"

"The President of the United States."

"President! Damn, woman! That's one up. What did you do? Why didn't I get to help?" He released the twins and leaned forward, eyes bright with interest.

I reached back and patted his cheek, just to touch him. "Short story? I got…" I started to say kidnapped, but changed my mind. "I was un-ceremonially drafted by the president for a secret mission. I deserted the president and took up with this bunch of thieves. They seemed like more fun." I nodded at Heflin. "I'm pretty sure…almost sure…maybe…this falls under the category of noble causes instead of highway robbery. Not that I've ever objected to highway robbery."

"It's salvage, damn it." Heflin grumbled. He gave Ajax a sour glance but said nothing else.

Ajax stared out the window at Rachel and Jacob, in human form, but easily trotting along keeping pace with us. "What…?"

"Werewolves." I sighed. "My werewolves. Unfortunately. It was not my idea, but please do not shoot them unless I say so."

"Live weres? With you?" The turtle rocked with his booming laughter.

Since the artillery barrage had stopped, there was no horrendous damage yet, but the residents of the South Bridge area were in a panic and pouring out of buildings and into vehicles. Vehicles crowded the streets in front of us and behind. They'd slow the army too, and we had our own version of heavy moving equipment. Heflin said he planned to blow a small section of the bridge after we crossed if he had to, so no one could follow us right away. That would hurt the locals and their day to day commerce, but he'd determined that he was saving the world. Justifiable to him.

Rachel and Jacob took advantage of the slowdown to strip off their clothes, Rachel threw hers in the turtle, but Jacob's, shredded by Ajax's shotgun blast, went in the street. They changed shape.

Ajax drew a sharp breath. "Son of a bitch," he muttered. Two ordinary looking people melted and became monsters. They never missed a step in a fluid, effortless transformation. As many as Ajax and I had seen and killed, together and separately, it remained a terrifying sight. A were changing shape always gave me a psychic hit, but it doubled this time. Was it because of their vow that named me their alpha? I didn't know, but my stomach knotted, and all the nerves under my skin burned.

Jacob caught the side of a pickup truck that pulled in front of us. The incredible strength they had in human shape made an enormous leap when they turned fuzzy. He flopped the truck on its side. A gentle action, since he could have sent it and its occupants rolling down the street. It screeched along the asphalt as he shoved it aside.

The brightly lit bridge approach lay ahead of us. Soldiers lined up behind concrete barriers were ready to fire. Rachel and Jacob swooped down on them, tossing them around like toys. Rachel finished with hers and tore the steel gate from its hinges as Jacob rammed enough obstacles aside to let us pass. The path across the bridge was clear—and another artillery barrage shattered the dawn. Explosions blasted the air and pulverized buildings around us. It was only a matter of time before they got lucky. As Heflin started across the span, I opened the door and jumped out.

"I'll catch the last truck." I slammed the door behind me. Ajax started to argue, but Heflin had the turtle moving before he could grab me.

I don't know why I wanted to be last, unless it was my need to finish things—see them through. I had to say good-bye. I might not burn the bridge behind me when I crossed the Mississippi River, but I was closing a door. I would not come this way again. Rachel and Jacob, damn it to hell, stood waiting for me.

Xavier slowed his truck as he passed me. "Go!" I shouted at him. "This is my town, remember."

He snarled but went on. He knew what his truck carried. The other trucks passed one at a time until the last turtle came. Jacob stopped the vehicle with a single hand.

Daylight had advanced and I could see as the first line of armored cars roared down on us. *Mistake, mistake. Too close. We'd never escape in time.* They'd roll over us and be snapping at the convoy before it reached the western bank.

Jacob had changed back to human form. He tore the turtle's back door open and dragged out a long Atlantis tube. "I picked it up in Tennessee." He hefted it on his shoulder. "Personally, I think fangs and fur are overrated."

Jacob ran a short distance toward the armored cars, aimed the Atlantis at the first row, and fired. Four of them exploded in a blinding ball of orange fire. So close, the sound and fury knocked me down and onto the vibrating concrete pavement.

Rachel's arms closed around me as she jerked me to my feet and hauled me to the turtle and shoved me in the passenger seat. The Atlantis explosion had shattered all the windows and multiple cuts decorated the driver's face. His breath came in gasps, but he managed to drive. We rolled onto the bridge with Rachel and Jacob running ahead of us, and the roar and devastation of burning vehicles—and burning men—behind. Pursuit had stopped for the moment.

The bigger guns blasted again, but with no direction, no precision. The shells went wide, sending great geysers of river water roiling into the air. White flashes lit the sky from another direction. Memphis Base had joined the battle. From the concussion and ear blasting sound, they had bigger guns than Borden's toys mounted on trucks.

I could see the far side of the river. Wonderful. Everything moving okay—until the bridge span, weakened by the relentless pounding, dropped away in front of us, leaving a twenty-foot gap. The driver slammed on the brakes, but the turtle skidded off the concrete and into the air, thirty feet above the muddy Mississippi River.

Chapter Twenty-Three

We hung in space for one gut-wrenching instant, then the turtle tipped, engine first, and plunged down. Impact cumulated, not in water, but in a stupendous crash. It flung me forward, and I would have hit the windshield if the Atlantis' blast hadn't already taken it out. The doors popped open and the driver either fell or jumped out.

The turtle had landed on a pylon, its front bumper smack against an angled slab of concrete torn from the bridge span. Pylons braced the slab too, but it wouldn't hold long under the earthshaking inferno of battle. The immediate furor of artillery blasts thundering through the air in great drumming waves of sound battered me like a lightning storm on a mountain.

I couldn't move. The turtle's dash had punched in and down. My right leg was clamped in a bizarre steel-toothed vise. I sat there for an indeterminable time, stunned. Then the shock wore off. I shrieked as massive bolts of agony surged through my body.

The only way I knew to fight the torment was to accept the pain. I drew in deep breaths and let it flow over me, through me for eternal minutes until I could think. *Sure. Calm down, Maat.* No way. Pain driven panic, the need to escape overwhelmed rational thought.

I laid shaking hands on the dash and pushed. It

moved, but not enough to get me free. I pushed again. It lifted off my leg. My arm muscles failed, and it slammed back down with the vengeance of a great, metal-jawed monster. The world dissolved into a wave of white fire. It sent me wandering into a maze—into madness. Oh, sweet serenity, there was no pain—if only the voices had left me alone.

"Come with me," Anolia whispered.

"Come with me," my mother called.

"Come with me," Emanis cackled in her burn-scarred voice. "To hell. Come. Come…"

Emanis stood in front of me, holding her severed head in one hand, eyes dripping blood, and the finger nubs of her other hand locked in my shoulder.

My eyes popped open.

"Come on, Maat," Xavier roared in my ear. He had my arms and was dragging me out the front window. Pain rushed in again, but not the blinding force that tipped me out of reality. While my mind had danced with the dead, Xavier had freed my leg. Blood soaked my jeans from the knee down as it leaked in steady streams from puncture wounds. Pieces of the dash had impaled it like knives. Tears in the material meant lacerations, too. I would probably never walk again on that furious mass of tortured flesh and bone.

Helpless, I flopped around as Xavier dragged me off the turtle's hood and onto the angled slab of concrete. Everything grayed out as I hit the solid surface. Another agonizing swell washed over me, and again, the world faded away. I only heard one thing this time. Ruelle's laughter. I would have welcomed death at that moment. But the vampire? No. I forced my mind back to the world—and the pain.

The slab's angle wasn't so steep that I couldn't have made it with two good legs. My quaking body begged me to give up and die. An explosion hit the river near the bridge, sending a deluge of rust colored water to drench us. I choked and spit the muddy stuff out, but my eyes burned. A constant barrage roared through the air, battering it in great huffing waves.

Xavier grabbed my hands one at a time and jerked them to the chain he'd obviously used to climb down to me. I grabbed hold, but there was no way I could lift myself.

I didn't have to because someone pulled from above. Hanging on, with Xavier's arm around my waist, we started to ascend. A lull came in the battle and other sounds became audible: small arms fire, pitiful after the major bombardment, the scrape of clothing on concrete as our bodies inched up. We made great targets.

Xavier breathed in gasps, and my only contribution was to keep my balance by holding the chain. Skin peeled off my knuckles and hands. I didn't feel them. The torn, punctured leg took up all the space my mind allowed for agony. It overwhelmed all else.

I could hear voices above me now. Another three feet—the chain suddenly loosened. We dropped. The slide stopped with a jerk. Then we were on our way up again, faster. I banged against the slab. Pain lashed a more ferocious assault on my leg. Again, the crackle of gunfire and small arms fire came directly over my head.

In a final, intense jerk, those above hauled us over the slab and onto the flat concrete of the remaining bridge span. A pair of dark muscular arms scooped me up.

"Oh, hell. You really did it this time, babe." Ajax held me close as he carried me away at a jarring run. Before he did, I turned my head and saw Jacob tossing large chunks of concrete aside and then kneeling beside the battered, crushed body of Rachel, the werewolf who pledged me her life.

****

"How's Maat?" Heflin laid a gentle hand on my shoulder. The first kind gesture I'd ever received from him. The injury that crippled me seemed to have eased his concerns about my loyalty. Or, more likely, eased the concern that I would leave with my remaining werewolf and Xavier would follow.

"Been better, Heflin."

With the broken span behind us, there would be no immediate pursuit.

They'd wrapped me in blankets. Ty had stood behind me and held me up while Ajax cut off the leg of my jeans to clean and bandage my wounds. I wouldn't allow anyone else to touch me. At least I'd stopped bleeding. Or Ajax said I had. He wouldn't let me see, but I wasn't soaking through the bandages. My lacerations burned, and the entire leg throbbed with each heartbeat. The punctures worried me the most.

Ajax stuffed pills in my mouth. I didn't ask what they were. The wonderful drugs beat the pain down enough I could at least think. My fingers traced small cuts on my face and brushed over a swollen mouth. My face had taken more abuse in the last few weeks than it had in my last five years as a hunter. The oily gunk my companions smeared on my abraded hands smelled foul, but they didn't hurt anymore. We all knew the big danger was infection. I had a respectable immune system, though, and I'd survived worse in New York. I survived because in New York they'd fed me vampire blood.

I sat in the cab of a truck while Lowell, Heflin, Xavier, and I watched the further destruction of Memphis from a hill safely out of artillery range. Buildings already on the verge of collapse surrendered to gravity under the relentless barrage. Half the city was on fire. My former home would not rise again for many decades.

There wouldn't be any immediate pursuit. A two-hundred-foot span in the middle of the South Bridge now rested in the river's main channel. It wasn't the only break. Concrete supports protruded from the water like tombstones climbing out of a liquid grave. Men on foot might cross the North Bridge, but anything heavier would have to go upriver to St. Louis.

"Borden did better than I expected." Lowell shook his head as he contemplated the destruction like a philosopher pondering life. "Don't know how he got cross-country so fast."

Heflin was more animated. "Borden couldn't find his dick if he didn't have to piss occasionally. Genius at organizing. Laughable in action. Build a perfect army and march it in the wrong direction." He chuckled and spoke as someone who knew Gannett's army commander well.

"Memphis Base gave a passable fight." Xavier offered his expert solider man-speak opinion. "Heavy losses, both sides, I'll bet. Base is gone. So is the city. Maybe they'll build a New Memphis."

"Shame." Lowell crossed his arms and sighed. "And here I stand, observing history. That's what politicians—and dictators—do best, though. Watch from a safe place while we kill men, destroy homes and families."

Heflin grunted. "Okay. Enough about our wasted lives. Let's get on to Little Rock. I'll get Maat antibiotics there." He left and headed for the trucks at a quick pace.

Xavier came and stood in front of me. I wanted to lean against him, needing to experience his strength. I rarely felt so vulnerable. No such luck.

"You went back. Damn it, we were rolling and you…" He sucked in a breath, whirled, and marched away. Oh, well, we were back at it again. Maybe *pissed off* was our normal.

Ajax sauntered up. He planted his hands on his hips and stared across the river at the columns of smoke painting a dull, sepia haze across the rising sun. "A whole fucking city. New York was only a couple of blocks. That was Memphis, babe. Our Memphis. You outdid yourself this time."

"Hey! They started it, not me."

He gave the retreating Xavier a speculative look. "Been kinda' boring without you. Heard you joined a convent."

"Commune, asshole, AG commune. Convent? Shit!" Ajax was going to start mouthing off. "Be nice, man. I saved your ass—again. If it weren't for me, you and your cows would be chopped meat by now."

"Hey, hey. Don't be insultin' my ladies. They're sensitive." He kept looking east across the river where the sun made a dirty red umbrella of the smoke and dust of destruction. His hard-lined face held a rare look of sadness. "Long way from the Freaks, babe."

A long way, yes. In my short lifetime our world had evolved from the scattered militias battling bands of werewolves and each other, to the formalized tyranny of a standing army. Not long ago, we believed that all the furry beasts were dead. That our hunting prowess had eliminated them. Three weeks ago, I'd believed with the certainty of a religious zealot that there could be no such thing as a good werewolf. Such arrogance—and willful ignorance.

Ajax laughed, but I heard irony, not humor. "Don't worry, babe. You've got guns and silver. I got magic fingers." He flung his hands out. "You shoot true, I make big booms. The world may change, but there's always work for first-rate killers like us."

Unfortunately, he was right.

When the call to load up came, Ajax gathered me in his arms and carried me to a turtle. He and Ty did their best to make me comfortable.

Xavier came back, but Heflin stopped him close to the turtle. They spoke, but their voices barely registered until Heflin raised his. "Come on, man. I'll get her meds in Little Rock. I…we need you in Salvaje. You can't leave now. It's no further to Little Rock than St. Louis."

Xavier's sharp words cut the air. "And what if there is nothing in Little Rock? There's a hospital in St. Louis."

Their voices lowered again, and the pain meds let me drift off.

I woke when Jacob returned shortly before the convoy moved out. He'd carried Rachel's body away to bury her. He knelt beside the open turtle door, and I laid a hand on his shoulder. "I'm sorry, Jacob. I wish I'd known her longer."

Jacob's hand brushed mine. "We knew the danger when we made our vows in Memphis. We pledged our lives to the Angel of Death."

"I don't remember asking for any promises." Suddenly cold, I drew my blanket tighter around my body.

"I meant to comfort you, Suriel. I blame only those behind the guns." He left me to take his place in another truck.

****

Sabrina knew the sound of artillery when she heard it, even if it was 250 miles to the south. It had started at dawn. She'd watched Aaron and his war games too often. Faint thunder, yes, but werewolf ears took note as they drove into East St. Louis near noon.

The truck was comfortable enough. Sabrina rode in the front with Eddie, while Joe and Terrell sat on boxes behind the seat. Jenny had curled up on her lap. Sabrina glanced back and smiled at Terrell. Eddie's twelve-year-old son wasn't unfriendly, but yesterday's traumatic events marked him. He'd seen her change shape and disembowel a man.

She glanced over at Eddie. "Are you going to cross the river?"

"Eventually. Depends on what it costs. I may have to stay on this side and work—"

"I've got money." Sabrina lifted her backpack from the floor between her feet. "We need to get across." Either she communicated her sense of deep urgency or he completely accepted her as alpha. Either way, he didn't argue.

East St. Louis seemed prosperous enough. Didn't

smell too bad either. They pumped the sewage into the river downstream, not in town. The locals had obviously scavenged the surrounding ruins for building supplies, so some places appeared almost new. Shops, markets, commerce made it far more prosperous than New Washington.

Signs pointed the way to the bridge and marked it as the property of the City of East St. Louis. The City of West St. Louis across the river owned and marked its side too. They'd have to pay a toll for each. She sighed with relief when she saw the posted amount. She could easily afford the fee. As a werewolf, she'd been able to carry a significant amount of gold in the bottom of her pack without strain.

Of course, the toll man demanded a little extra over the posted fee for himself and his armed companions. His eyes narrowed when he saw Sabrina. She thought he might insist on a physical bonus. It had been years since she'd had to pay attention to the trouble caused by men's desire. A horn blasted behind them. The line of vehicles waiting to cross had grown longer, and greed won out over lust. The toll taker motioned them on. At the western tollgate, she hugged Jenny tighter, and kept her face averted.

"Mommy." Jenny snuggled against her.

Sabrina Gannett, werewolf, former first lady of the United States, left her past life behind her when they crossed the river. She could still hear the big guns' faint rumble to the south as they rolled away from the western tollgate. What was Aaron doing with his army? And the hell-spawn vampire? What were they destroying?

"Do you think things will be better here in St.

Louis?" She asked mostly to take her mind off the guns.

"Don't know." Eddie grinned at her. He smiled often. "Won't have to stay long. I hope. My brother, he's in Seattle. Sent me a letter. That's where I'm going."

Seattle. According to Aaron, rebels and traitors ruled Seattle. Sabrina had gleaned a bit of information at the mansion, but her focus was on other things. She rubbed sweat from her face. The heat and humidity near the river were sharp contrasts to the cool forest she had traveled through recently.

Eddie located an abandoned garage-type building to use as makeshift quarters for his unusual family. He apologized to Sabrina about not finding a house. He couldn't take a chance on letting his truck out of sight again. The building was adequate though, three side rooms, and with minor repairs, running water and a functioning toilet. Sabrina agreed with his choice, especially since it was close to where the forest encroached on the ruins. Purchasing too much meat would rouse suspicions. She could survive on regular food, but she'd have to hunt occasionally for Jenny, Joe, and herself to satisfy other needs. They worked into the evening to make their place clean and habitable.

After they finished, Eddie cooked supper over a small gas stove. This was the first time they'd been able to talk. "I'm a good mechanic. I got tools in the truck. Got a lot of standard spare truck parts. Machinist too. Get me a little steel and I can make things."

He could make things. Sabrina wondered if Eddie realized exactly how desperately the world needed him and his tools. It would change, eventually.

Mechanization and industrialization would come, but for now, a skilled craftsman would have a trade to survive and prosper.

Terrell sat on makeshift furniture across the room playing with Joe and Jenny. The older boy seemed to have accepted them, but he eyed Sabrina with suspicion occasionally. She suspected he was a bit jealous. Sharing his father with a couple of strange kids was bad enough but sharing with a woman might be too much.

"I'm surprised they let you leave Chicago," Sabrina said. "I'd heard mechanics and other skilled workers were guarded." She knew they were, because Aaron had told her. Slave labor by any definition. Without guards, they'd all have run away like Eddie.

Eddie's sly sideways grin said so much. "There was an…accident. Lots of accidents in Chicago, especially in the factories. A big one happened and I had access to this truck already loaded with spare parts. I was supposed to be sending it to New Washington the next day. I decided to take the chance. I loaded all the tools I could lift, and me and Terrell took off."

Jenny made her way across the room. "Mommy." She grasped Sabrina's arm. Sabrina hugged her and sent her back to play. Jenny had shoved the horror to the back of her mind and transformed the available female werewolf into her mother. It worried her. Such a fragile child remained in peril.

Neither she nor Eddie needed the dangerous burden of two orphaned werewolf children, but neither had the heart nor will to send them to certain death. Sabrina had already decided she liked Eddie. Aggressive alphas, both human and wolf, had filled her previous life so she had lived in constant chaos. Chaos would reign, it was the nature of their world, but with Eddie she might find pockets of peace.

"Terrell's mother?" Sabrina kept her question soft and not urgent.

"Left me five years ago. Went home to Atlanta." He shrugged. "She left Terrell. Said he was better off. Guess I'm kind of...boring. Bet your life hasn't been boring." Eddie glanced at her, but quickly averted his eyes.

Sabrina smiled. What could she say? *Well, I'm a runaway, too. Wife of the President and Dictator of the US. I used to live in a mansion and...* In a way, she was more of a danger to him than Jenny and Joe. "No, Eddie. My life wasn't boring. Not safe either." She needed to change the subject. "What's in Seattle?"

"Freedom. Law. Order. You know. Or at least they're trying. Don't know how well it's going. Rico, my brother, he's a cop. That stuff at the bridge, robbing people needing to cross the river, pisses him off big time."

"Democracy?"

"That too. No dictator, and..." He wet his lips and eyed her. "He says Vamps and weres are...citizens. Vote and everything. Hold elections from noon to midnight so the vamps can, you know, vote. How .'bout that?"

"Interesting." And disturbing from what *she* knew of vampires.

He turned off the stove and gazed at her. "I figure, maybe I can fix a few trucks here, show what I can do. Couple of months and it shouldn't be any problem joining a safe convoy. I won't have to pay up front to get in or carry my own fuel. Fuel's expensive." The silence hung between them for a moment. Then he said, "I didn't thank you. The money at the bridge. Promise, I'll pay you back when I can."

"That's okay. I could ride to Seattle with you. If you don't mind. I'd like to go there. See something new."

He gave her a shy smile. "I'd like that."

Sabrina shook her head. "It'll be dangerous, Eddie. I don't know about Seattle, but there are people who would find silver and shoot Joe, Jenny, and me if they knew. And kill you for being with us."

"They can try." The tone of his voice suggested he might be less placid than she thought. In certain situations, anyway. He hadn't hesitated to kill in the woods, and while her shape changing had surprised him, he hadn't panicked. She appreciated that he hadn't quizzed her about her past. She'd tell him eventually, but it was safer for now that he not know.

They barricaded every access to the garage. Eddie opened the back of the truck and dragged out mattresses. He made beds for Sabrina and the kids in one of the rooms off the garage. A mattress for himself went into another room to the side. Sabrina waited until she was sure the children were asleep, and then she eased out to join him. He wasn't asleep.

"You don't have to." But his hands reached for her, and his arms drew her close.

"I don't like to be alone either," she said. "It doesn't bother you that I'm…"

"No." He slipped his arm under her neck, caught her face in his hand. "I never saw a woman like you before. You're so beautiful."

Eddie's mouth tasted warm and sweet. The dark

held no mysteries for her, but the room had one high window, and the full moon offered light for him to see. Sabrina gently drew away and undressed for him, listening to his breath grow ragged as she removed each piece. Then she peeled away his shirt and jeans. Kneeling beside him, she ran her hand from his chest to his stomach. She stopped short of where she knew he wanted her to go. "You look very…strong," she said softly.

He swallowed and licked his lips. "Not as strong as you. The bullet…"

"It wasn't silver. You can't hurt me, Eddie. I must be careful not to hurt you, so I may seem a bit passive at times. It's difficult to explain."

He rose to sit beside her. "Then show me."

Sabrina did show him, and while he was reluctant to apply the pressure she needed at first, he did learn to caress her trembling body until they both found satisfaction.

"You know, that wasn't what I call passive." Eddie's breathing slowed.

"No. We seem to be suited to one another, don't we?" She kissed him. "Your wife said you were boring?"

Eddie grinned. "Well, sex wasn't boring."

Chapter Twenty-Four

Little Rock, Arkansas

Heflin had won the battle of direction. We went west, not north to St. Louis. Halfway between West Memphis and Little Rock, I developed a fever. Suddenly hot and cold from minute to minute, I grew delirious as infection rapidly progressed. Thick pus oozed from the holes in my leg. The last time I saw it, I passed out. I knew nothing after that until I woke on a narrow bed in an expansive but dimly lit room—filled with the sound of quiet breathing and the scent of old petroleum. The fingers on my left hand twitched and touched hair. I had a bit of a time focusing, but I turned to face that way. Ty slept, crouched on his knees, his head on the bed by my side. Across the room, Ajax and his twins covered a king-sized mattress on the floor. Ajax's head rested on Mary's ample breasts while Giselle curled up against his back.

I turned again toward a faint noise on my right. Xavier sat close in a chair, staring at me. The light from a single lantern glittered in his eyes. Ty woke with a jerk. Xavier rose and slipped away. Ty made so much noise he woke Ajax and the twins. He held a cup while I sipped water. I learned we were in Little Rock and I'd been unconscious for three days. More people came, and exhaustion claimed me before I saw everyone who wanted to be sure I was okay. I'd never been so popular in my life.

The room fell quiet as my visitors drifted away. I worked a quick inventory of my body. I was in decent shape—considering. The bandaged leg ached and the rest of me felt sore, but the pain was tolerable. I held up my hands and stared at perfect knuckles. Had I dreamed the concrete scraped them to the bone?

Ty sat in the chair Xavier vacated, watching me. A shadow lurked in his eyes, and I wondered what he had seen—what he knew. The sweet boy from New Washington was growing up fast.

"What happened, Ty?"

"You started shaking. We had to hold you down. Your heart stopped. Heflin and Lowell did that thing with their hands, CPR. It started beating again. But it took so long they worried about brain damage." He shuddered, and tears formed in his eyes. "You died and I…" he hesitated. "Could I kiss you?"

"Sure. No tongue."

"Darn."

He gave me a sweet lingering kiss on the mouth. It had nothing to do with desire and everything to do with love. Then he cried, and I held him in my arms as best I could.

How long was I dead? Brain damage? Worse than it already was?

Ty made his bed on the floor beside me, and I fell into a dreamless sleep.

****

I thought I'd talk to Xavier the next day, try to make peace with him, but he seemed to have disappeared. The trucks were parked in a fenced area outside the shabby West Little Rock warehouse lot. Lowell called me and Ajax into an office that offered a semblance of privacy. "It's going to take longer here than we thought, but Heflin says we should be ready day after tomorrow." Lowell smiled as he spoke. "He's waiting on another fuel truck, and others are coming to form a larger convoy"

"Suits me," I said. My leg still ached, but I could walk. An amazing thing considering the damage I'd felt and observed, and the trauma they said stopped my heart.

The pair stared at me. Something was up.

Ajax kept shaking his head.

Lowell sighed. "I'll do it. Maat, I…we…have something to tell you. When we arrived here, you were dying. You did die once. Heflin bought antibiotics, but they didn't help. You kept getting worse. So…" He swallowed. "Heflin asked around, and found people who'd seen a vampire. He, Xavier, and Ajax found the vamp and persuaded him to donate you a little blood."

I flung out my arm to hit Ajax, but my leg twisted. I yelped at the searing pain. He and Lowell had their arms around me before I hit the floor.

"Fuck it, Maat. You was dying." Ajax didn't sound a bit repentant.

"You! You're the one who knows—"

"Yeah, yeah." Ajax flipped his hand to mimic talking. "You'd rather die than drink vampire blood again. That's bull. That's Maat's shit mouth. We poured it down your throat, and you didn't know. Lowell's the one who said we had to tell you. I damn well know what you been through, but ain't you glad to be alive?"

He was right, but I could not forget the horrific time when all I had for nourishment was Emanis' blood. Later, Ruelle used his to keep me alive. It had changed me forever.

"Wait. How did you *persuade* a vampire to give me blood?"

Ajax wouldn't meet my eyes. "Heflin bargained. Said we had to get used to living around vamps. Had to barter."

"Barter?" I choked on the word.

"Yeah, barter." Ajax spit on the floor. "Vamp gave you blood, Xavier and me gave him some in return. Vamp said he'd been eating rats and stray dogs. Heflin's going to let him ride to Salvaje with us, too."

I wasn't happy, but it pleased me that they cared enough to make that harrowing sacrifice. In New York I'd watched the utter hell of vamps draining and killing a couple of humans they'd captured. I thought I might go that way, but Emanis wouldn't let them bite me. I remained her personal toy, her plaything until Ruelle rescued me. I seriously doubted this vamp's tale of sucking rats and stray dogs.

Later that afternoon, I spied Xavier across the room. The minute he caught me looking, he turned away and went out the door. He'd risked his life for me and now he avoided me. What the hell. How did I feel about him? Certainly, I desired him. I knew him well enough now to know there was a passion in him that matched my own. Love? I loved people. Ajax, Sable, my friends at Avalon…Anolia. Ty had wormed his way into my heart like perfumed oil.

I'd loved a man once, years ago. My first and deepest love. Werewolves had taken him, too. Xavier troubled me, and I knew I'd better work things out. I came across Lowell sitting in the shade of a tarp stretched across several plastic pipes.

"Maat," he said. He offered me a glad to see you, good-natured smile as he turned over a wooden box and dusted it off. "Sit down."

I sat and got to the point. "Tell me what you know about Xavier."

He pursed his lips and waited a little too long before answering my question. That meant I'd only get a partial on the truth. He frowned, then his face smoothed, and the usual thoughtful diplomat appeared.

"I've only known Xavier for about three years. He keeps to himself, so I can't say I know him well. Aaron discouraged any companionship between us. I know Xavier and Aaron were orphans, raised by the same family. I know he once cared for Aaron, respected him.

"Two years ago, Aaron started ordering attacks on civilians, and it escalated into massacres. Xavier couldn't stop it, but I never heard of him participating. As I understand, the threat, using Ty as hostage to control his father, had been there since before I arrived."

"Xavier doesn't like Sabrina."

Lowell nodded in agreement. "Hard to say on that one. We wouldn't have made it out of New Washington without Sabrina's help, though. You should ask Ty. He's only a boy, but he's a careful observer."

I laughed. "I wanted reasonably unbiased information."

Lowell scratched his mane of silver hair. None of us had been able to bathe completely since we left New Washington, and vermin tended to be a road hazard.

"Yes, I've seen that. But you mother him." He tilted his head and gave me a wry smile.

"Mother? Me?"

"Yes. And he's a willing participant in the game. The boy's lost his mother and foster mother. He's been over and under protected. He's maturing nicely though, if a bit late."

"Thank you for rescuing him and bringing him along. I don't know about mothering, but I do care for him."

Lowell's smile grew wider. "Xavier wouldn't have left without him. Tell me, fearsome werewolf hunter, are you in love with Xavier?"

I shrugged and stared down at my hands. "That's what I'm trying to figure out."

"Maat, it required great courage for a man like Xavier to give blood to a vampire, even to save someone he loved. At the bridge when we saw the turtle go down—everyone thought you were dead. He wouldn't listen. He jumped out of the truck and ran back. And your friend Ajax was right behind him."

"And right now he avoids me like I have boils on my ass. He's been doing that ever since I met him. One minute he was trying to kill, or at least damage me. The next he'd be making me want to grab him and never let go."

"Maybe he's trying to figure things out too. It troubled him that you let the vampire stay with you that night. Vicious monster."

I drew a breath to protest, and then let it go.

"Maat, I think Xavier is torn between suspicion, jealousy, and guilt. You made a sacrifice for Ty. An unnecessary sacrifice. But you didn't know. And your prior relationship with Ruelle made all of us conniving conspirators nervous, too. We didn't know if you could be trusted."

"I had to do something for Ty. I thought steal the truck and run away was a suicide mission. I still do. Sorry if it offends, Lowell, but I live my own life. I'd made no commitment to Xavier the night I'd stayed with Ruelle. I traded my body for what I wanted."

He chuckled. "Fate made a suitable, if somewhat violent, match with you and Xavier. Though, without a doubt, you have the strangest courting ritual I've ever seen."

I shrugged. "Strange. Yeah. But if I see suck-face vampire again, I'm going to go in guns blazing, knife swinging—and praying for a miracle. No conversation, no sex."

Parr frowned. "Perhaps you should be more cautious. Ruelle is quite mysterious, and to say that he only values your body for sex…"

I laughed, and his face turned red. Was the great politician embarrassed?

"My body's not all that great, huh?"

He recovered quickly. "Your body is nothing compared to your spirit, Maat. Your soul is a powerful thing. To win your heart, your desire, would be a prize for any vampire, or man for that matter."

"My soul. Now you sound like Anolia."

Parr turned his face away.

"Sorry. I don't know when to shut up." I stood and hobbled away.

****

Little Rock proved to be much like Memphis, except that there were fewer people. Scavengers hadn't completely looted all the abandoned buildings. It would take decades to rebuild here. Heflin had bargained with local mercenaries to act as guards, and Ajax bargained for other things.

"You got any money?" Ajax cornered me as I limped around the warehouse, trying to exercise my leg so it wouldn't freeze up on me.

"Some. How much do you need and for what?"

"Pulp and Powder." He grinned. "Make a big boom."

Stupid question. Big women and big booms, the sum of Ajax's life.

"So, Ajax, are you going west with this bunch of hijackers?"

"Aren't you?" He winked at me. This was my old familiar Ajax.

"Yeah. Should be interesting."

I went to the turtle and dug out most of the remaining gold coins Sable had given me. I'd already paid Jacob for his service. Whatever Ajax needed from me he could have.

Pulp and Powder are slang names for two chemicals invented and produced in massive quantities during the war. Pulp being an oatmeal-textured semi-liquid and Powder being exactly that. Mixed together in the correct proportions, they made a stable, but destructive explosive. Get the formula wrong by half an ounce and they produced Pink, an incredibly volatile gas.

After I healed from my injuries in New York, Ajax and I went back with barrels of Pulp and Powder, and a truckload of fuel we could pump in the building to make a fire. But then he accidentally created Pink. We imploded an entire block of New York City's already unstable ruins. That was our intention, of course, but we planned to be farther away when it happened. That was the day I learned I could outrun the demo man.

I handed Ajax the coins, and he tucked them in several pockets of a leather bag. "I suppose I should thank you for giving the vamp blood in exchange for him to heal me. I wish there had been another way. I'll thank Xavier too, if I can get him to stop avoiding me."

"Wasn't bad. And Xavier..." He winked at me, then chuckled.

Five hours later, Ajax returned to the compound with a heavy truck. He had a whopping *I'm the man* grin on his face. The truck seemed road worthy and should make any trip with ease. A fuel trailer attached to the rear meant he wouldn't have to buy gasoline. The twins expressed their admiration of his business acumen with lavish hugs and kisses. He strutted and accepted the tribute with the arrogance that I so loved in him—and hated in others.

I'm not sure what Ajax told Heflin, but the Wagon Master raised no objection when the truck joined the convoy. That much Pulp and Powder together on one truck, even in separate containers, made me damned nervous. They'd scaled it in hundred-year barrels, all dated forty years ago, but a pinhole leak, a few grains...big, big boom.

"How'd you find so much of that here?" I asked him.

"Didn't have to find, babe. Knew where it was. Came across and hid it last year. I needed the money for the truck and fuel trailer." *Came across* was our code for major theft.

Ajax suddenly grabbed me and pulled me close. I held onto my wonderful dark man for a while. His friendship had been one of the few constants in my life. I thought of Anolia and I hugged him tighter.

Heflin gathered the new mercenaries together that evening and told them Jacob was a werewolf. He strutted around the room, staring his would-be soldiers in the eye. Then in a deep voice that made me shiver, he said, "I'll crucify the man or woman who *accidentally* kills this were."

When he finished his pep talk, I knew I had one other thing to do. I went to Heflin. "I want to talk to the vampire."

Heflin rubbed his hands on his pants. Still guarded, still wary. The Wagon Master thrived on control. He knew he couldn't control me.

"I promised him safe passage to Salvaje, Maat. He's acting as a night guard, too."

"I won't kill him. I only need to meet him."

"Why? You have to tell me."

"I thought you lived with vamps in Salvaje."

"Not exactly *with* them. They stay in the same city. We're not intimate."

This was going to be great. I leaned a little to ease the ache in my leg. I wanted to explain but would not speak of how what happened in New York set me free of a vampire's ability to control my mind. There was another separate issue involved. "When a human drinks a vampire's blood, it gives that vampire a certain connection to that human. Yeah, the vamp's blood healed me, but now he has a connection to me."

All the other vampires who have given me blood, in the past, are dead, except one. Unfortunately, the one was Ruelle.

"So, you're linked to this vamp. By his blood in you."

I nodded.

Heflin sighed and ran his hand through his thinning hair. "I didn't know, Maat. And wouldn't care if I had known. I had to do something. You were dying, and I had three men and a werewolf going crazy on me. Come on. I'll take you to him."

Wow! Xavier, Ty, Ajax, and my werewolf Jacob, all demanding a miracle from Heflin to save my life. Now, that was interesting. And I'm sure it was damned alarming for the Wagon Master to learn how much they valued me. Heflin's words left me filled with a sense of wonder. My mind kept repeating two thoughts. *How did this happen? What was I going to do about it?*

One sizable question in the back of my mind, given my blood link to Ruelle, was why it had taken him so long to find me at Avalon. The strength of the people around me and their link to the earth and living world might have created a shield. Christopher was the only Oracle, but others did have psychic abilities. Loretta could predict the weather weeks in advance, and Mitchel could control animals by looking in their eyes. Maybe Anolia's prayers, her loving spirit, and deep love of the place hid me from the most diligent of vampire searchers.

We drove across the crumbling asphalt of what had once been a wide highway. A faded sign with the words, Westside Mall, etched in metal marked it as an icon of another era, another lifetime.

Heflin stopped at the gaping midnight hole where doors had once secured what Uncle Jake liked to call a *palace of capitalist consumerism.* The entire building, like ninety-nine percent of the buildings in the country, stood on the verge of complete collapse.

Heflin nodded toward the ruin. "A local told us they thought a vamp was sleeping here during the day. Xavier and Ajax went in, found him, and I talked to him. Got me a respectable new guard out of that little talk."

My mouth dropped open. "You're kidding. They went in there? With a vampire? Ajax knows better, even if Xavier didn't."

"Not my fault. All I did was locate." He had his unhappy face on again.

Yes, Heflin. I know you would have kicked me aside east of the river if you'd had a choice.

A soft rattling sound came from inside the building. A vampire eased into my psychic range. As with Ruelle, I experienced a sense of recognition. I carried his blood as I carried Ruelle's and that of the hell bound Emanis. Emanis would trouble me no more in this life, but this vampire—and Ruelle—I'd have to live with for a while. The sun had dropped below the horizon, and he stepped into shaded half-light.

I clenched my fists. "God, I hate vampires."

The vampire hunched his shoulders and stuck his hands in his pockets. He didn't look at me. "Are you going to kill me?"

A victim, he'd been a boy, no more than fourteen when they made him. With pale blue eyes, an angelic face, and lustrous amber hair, some pervert vamp had created him as an eternal toy.

"No, I'm not going to kill you." Yes, he was a vampire, and deadly to humans. But I'd be long dead before he grew strong enough to harm me. He reminded me of another facet of vampires. When one vampire creates another, it creates a far stronger bond than drinking blood.

"Who made you, and where are you from?"

"I'm Cody. I saw you in New York." He came closer as the sun faded. "My Master had taken me away before you destroyed all the others. I ran away from him last year. His name is Gunnar." Cody shuddered. "He…"

I reached out and gripped Cody's shoulder, and our connection grew stronger. "He can follow you. Probably already is."

He nodded.

"Hey, Hef. I can kill vamps in Salvaje if they attack me, can't I?"

"Yes, Maat. You may always defend yourself. Let's go back. Others need to meet Cody if he's going to travel with us. We leave in the morning."

We went back to the convoy, and Heflin led Cody away. A couple of hours later, Cody came back with Jacob. I was trying to relax and wondering if there could possibly be a beer in this God forsaken place. I didn't like the gleam in Jacob's eyes, but I was glad to see him moving around more since Rachel's death. He'd loved her, and that I understood.

"Cody says he's bound to you, too," Jacob said. Smug ass werewolf was up to something.

"So?" Damn, I didn't like this.

Jacob gently pushed Cody forward.

Cody drew himself up and stared me in the eye. It would take him a hundred years to gain enough power to glamour and freeze a strong-willed human. "Suriel.

You carry my blood, and like Jacob, I pledge you my life. I'm yours."

"Which means it's my responsibility to save your ass when that blood sucking pervert, Gunnar, comes looking for you." I intended to do that anyway, just on general principles, but I didn't like a werewolf manipulating things. That werewolf who still wouldn't tell me who ordered him to make sure I went west with the convoy. "You know, Cody, pledging me your life puts you in pretty monstrous company. There's me, the terrifying Angel of Death, and my pet were," I gestured at Jacob.

Jacob frowned.

I slapped my hands on my knees. "Hey, we're a bunch of thieves, mercenaries, and outlaws in general. We have to stick together like…like blood brothers…and sisters. You hungry, Cody?"

My vamp's eyes lit up.

"Well, since Jacob pledged himself to me, I think we should keep such delicate matters in the family. He could probably spare a little blood. I'd do it, but I'm weak from my injuries—"

"You're making fun of me." Cody sounded like he was going to cry.

"What?"

The monumental expression of shock on his face floored me. "Suriel, don't you know how *horrible* werewolf blood tastes? It's like acid or poison."

My mouth dropped open. No, I didn't know how *horrible* werewolf blood tasted. Acid? Poison? Wow!

A hearty laugh bubbled up and warmed me. It brought a pure simple joy so rare these days. It was the strangest conversation I'd ever had in my life. I laughed so hard I had to wipe the tears from my eyes. When I looked up, the pair had wisely disappeared into the night.

****

Aaron Gannett stared at Herman Borden's crumpled body. The general's hand still grasped the gun he'd used to splatter his brains across the tent wall. He'd taken the honorable escape from failure. Gannett would truly rather have had a living incompetent. Borden was the last of the old guard, the ones like Heflin and Xavier who had come up with him from the beginning. From the militia to ruling the country. Now he'd lost them all.

"Your general did not wish to face you?" Ruelle spoke from behind him.

Gannett turned to face him. "I suppose not. I wouldn't have…" He stared at Borden's junior officer standing behind the vampire. "What happened?"

"Sir." The officer's voice sounded dull and muted. "The scouts located the convoy, and the forward column spotted it before it reached the bridge. General Borden contacted the Memphis Base and ordered them to stop it, keep it from crossing. There was a miscommunication and our artillery commander ordered a barrage. Memphis Base returned fire as if they were attacked."

"I see." Gannett sighed. He shook his head. What a fiasco. "What's our status?"

The officer paled and swallowed. His eyes kept cutting to Ruelle. "We lost over half, maybe three quarters, of the troops and equipment."

"And Memphis Base."

"Mostly destroyed. The troops who survived

retreated downriver in boats. The city's gone. We can patch the bridge, but nothing heavy will cross."

Gannett and Ruelle left the tent and walked into the night. Ruelle had greeted Gannett when he'd arrived in Memphis at sunset. Gannett wondered how the vampire traveled or where he slept. He didn't ask.

"Borden thought he was doing the right thing." Gannett tried to make an excuse.

"Perhaps. But I remember you distinctly gave him orders to follow, but not capture, the convoy. To wait on us to catch up. He not only pursued and tried to capture it, he did so with all your new artillery equipment—which is now useless since most of it is damaged beyond repair."

Gannett shrugged. He'd heard the wrath in Ruelle's voice, but it made no impact on the swell of regret and loneliness that filled his mind. "Borden was the last. From the old days. Heflin, Xavier…all gone. Lilly…Sabrina…I'm alone now."

"Alone? Humans should not use words like alone. It's as meaningless as saying forever." Ruelle stopped and stared at him with a twisted smile. "Why don't you find a place to hide Mr. President? It's demeaning for the Commander of the Army to cry in front of his troops."

Gannett wiped his eyes. Was he crying? He'd received nothing more than he deserved.

Chapter Twenty-Five

I-40 West

We left Little Rock with the rising sun at our backs, and a clear western sky ahead. Our destination for the day? Fort Smith. Heflin, obviously a man with an ample supply of gold coins, procured three more fuel trucks with twice the capacity of the ones he'd left with the mercenaries in Memphis. Three troop carriers with troops and munitions, because he said the road west was incredibly dangerous. He procured another road repair truck with crew, two more turtles, and ten fully loaded cargo trucks from other merchants with material goods bound for Salvaje. It made a respectable convoy. It would never fit in a wayside, which didn't matter, because there were no waysides west of the Mississippi anyway. I rode with Ty and Xavier in a turtle. We didn't talk much. Really, there was nothing to say. Xavier kept his gaze away from me.

We crossed the Arkansas River to Fort Smith the next morning and again parked at a warehouse with a chainlink fence compound. Repurposed, pre-war warehouses, well-built reinforced steel, sheltered much of the country's commerce these days.

The city itself could be a duplicate of Knoxville and Nashville, with square miles of abandoned buildings surrounded by empty suburbs. I saw only an occasional sign of human activity in any of the ruins here. There was nothing of a convergence of people that would constitute a town. Not long after we settled in, the Wagon Master approached me.

"I have to fuel up. Will you ride shotgun?" His face was tight and serious.

"Sure." He expected trouble. That I could deal with.

The new mercenaries he'd hired spread out around the compound—apparently not a place to relax. Jacob and Carlos, the mercenary troop's leader, joined us.

"There has been trouble here," Heflin said. "Ill equipped scavengers mostly, but some gangs. The locals to the north have banded together and set up a small militia. They confiscate any weapon they can find, and they've done an effective job. What's left out there are the poorly armed, but desperate and hungry."

He scanned the group. "Carlos, be sure you secure the warehouse. Let Jacob be your eyes and ears."

Carlos nodded, but he cast a nervous glance at Jacob. Good. Heflin had warned him. Heflin would punish anyone who deliberately hurt my were—if I didn't get there first. *Oh, how my world had changed.*

I rode in the lead turtle with Heflin driving—again. He either liked my company, or still had qualms and wanted to keep an eye on me. Xavier brought up the rear in another turtle behind the three armored fuel trucks. Lowell drove. Gut instinct told me Lowell should stay behind and let one of Heflin's regular experienced drivers take the wheel. I liked the former VP, but he'd be a liability in a fight. Xavier would have to protect him. It also concerned me that Heflin had left all the mercenaries on guard behind us. He talked about the danger here, then moments later disregarded his own words. Had he suddenly become a believer in the wild tales of my fighting prowess? I didn't know. I did know he was an annoying, contradictory man and hoped his ambiguities wouldn't kill us. With three fuel trucks, I'd have brought another turtle and a bunch of mercenaries to guard. I wasn't Wagon Master, though. I didn't make those decisions. I had to presume he knew this place and what he was doing.

"We're actually north of old Fort Smith." Heflin drove us carefully through the extensive ruins. Eyes focused on the road, he didn't seem nervous. "Life congregates around the interstate here but once you leave, there's a lot of empty land. No waysides, no occupied towns. There's a rule in Salvaje. Every truck that comes in must have at least enough fuel to get back to a fuel source. No one accidently gets stuck in the city. If they do, equipment gets confiscated and owners put on the next convoy out."

Salvaje, a closed society, full of vampires and werewolves. Why the hell was Maat Ferris headed there? One reason? I didn't have anywhere else to go. *Another reason sat in the turtle following the fuel trucks—still pretending I didn't exist.*

Once out of ruins, the trucks rolled over a remarkably well-maintained four-lane road. We topped another hill and before me lay a spectacular sight. At least a hundred enormous circular tanks appeared ahead. They squatted in a vast battlefield of cleared, ravaged land, and smoke blackened the sky as it spewed from tall pipes and other less discernible sources. The air sliding in the turtle's windows filled it with the stench of sulfur.

"Is that…?" I'd seen pictures, but this went beyond my imagination.

"An oil refinery." Heflin slowed the turtle.

"Who owns it?"

"Don't know. I buy my gas and diesel with gold and keep my eyes straight ahead. No questions, no answers."

"Where does the oil come from?" I leaned forward and studied the amazing scene ahead.

He shrugged. "I've heard Oklahoma. Maybe Texas, too. I think there may be at least one underground pipeline that still flows, maybe more."

I stole a fuel truck from the army once. A monstrous clunky liability, I quickly disposed of the beast. I asked Heflin a question that had rarely crossed my mind. "The fuel in the east, where does it come from?"

"North Florida. There are a few permanent platforms out in the Gulf of Mexico that never stopped working during the war. There's a refinery in a secret location along the coast. And it's possible some of this goes east, too."

I'd been through Ohio. I had made sneaky trips through the president's military factories to plunder viable goods. My country was evolving in myriad ways. Gold coins remained the primary mover, but anarchy still ruled most everywhere. Would the United States ever be whole again? Only if a robust, resilient leader came along, one the people could and would follow. Aaron Gannett, intelligent by most accounts, might have been that leader had he chosen to rebuild rather than rule the country as a tyrant.

"I don't know exactly who owns or runs this

place." Heflin flipped his finger in the complex's direction. "Near as I can tell, they're only loyal to gold coins. Take 'em from any hand that offers. If I were young, I'd consider getting involved here." He sighed. "I'm not young."

We rolled closer. I knew a military complex when I saw one. A small army guarded in front and behind a high chainlink fence topped with razor wire. Patrol vehicles slowly rolled by that fence in a constant cycle, searching for intruders. From casual observation, I'd call it well-armed, well-disciplined. The games I'd played in the east with Gannett's troops would have gotten me killed here. Heflin stopped on a low hill a distance from the complex and ordered me out. I joined Lowell and Xavier by their escort turtle.

The fuel trucks had stopped and idled behind us. Heflin drove slowly to the complex gate, exited the turtle, and walked forward. He lifted and held his hands away from his sides to show he wasn't armed. He spent time in a small building by the gate. He came out, faced us, and did some odd arm waving. Our fuel trucks passed us and headed his way. Soldiers stopped and searched each vehicle, then allowed them past the fence.

While Xavier, Lowell, and I waited and watched, ten heavily guarded tankers, each twice as big as Heflin's fuel trucks, entered or left the refinery. Open troop trucks ran before and behind each tanker, each filled with well-armed soldiers dressed in sand colored combat gear.

"You ever seen that uniform?" I asked Xavier, the military man.

Xavier shook his head. His hands clenched into

fists. "This…God damn it! I oversaw intelligence. Not one word, not a hint. Shit about Seattle, rebels in Atlanta, sabotage in Ohio, but nothing about this."

Gannett's former Chief of Security was a bit perturbed. At least he hadn't directed his irritation toward me. Lowell leaned across the turtle's hood. "What would Aaron do, what would he be, if he had this?" He laughed out loud at the irony. "No way to take it by force. A battle would destroy everything. But what a prize."

My mind went to the vampire now unofficially in charge of the U. S. government. This place could offer easier lives and a way to rebuild the country. Enough had come out in the last hour to run the east for a month. Where did it go? Gasoline was always in short supply where I lived. Always had been.

Ruelle wouldn't care for human lives. He considered us parasites or play toys. He thought he could live forever. I had taught Emanis *forever* was a false god.

I climbed into the turtle to take weight off my leg. Lies, mistrust, political power games. Personally, I preferred a simpler life. Not as simple as Avalon, but this refinery was part of the stinking mess that got us humans in real trouble in the first place. Technology added to human nature equaled mega war. Arrows, swords, and spears of ancient times killed efficiently, but not on the scale of the bombs or the artillery that leveled Memphis.

Heflin returned cursing. He'd acquired the fuel, but pumps kept malfunctioning and it took too long. We'd barely make it back before full dark. We remained road wise, however, and lowered all the armor over the fuel truck tires and fixed plates over the windows.

The ruins we'd traveled when the sun stood high hadn't seemed so ominous as they did in the near dusk shadows. The whine of engines wavered and then echoed louder through crumbling buildings. Speed up, slow down, thick tires thumped in potholes. Whole walls had collapsed, and debris had fallen into the street, leaving only narrow lanes. Okay to weave through at noon, but oppressive on the return. Heflin bared his teeth and gripped the steering wheel with white fingered hands. He leaned forward, as if he could push the turtle to a greater speed by his will alone. His discomfort made me check my Aries in its holster.

Gunshots popped behind us.

Heflin jerked the wheel to the right and jammed the brakes to stop. The massive fuel trucks passed us. They had orders. Keep moving, never stop.

We waited. Five seconds…ten…too long. Lowell wasn't a pro driver, but he was less of a shooter. I jumped out of the turtle and headed back. Heflin was right behind me, shotgun in hand. He cursed under his breath. He'd expressed enough vulgarity to fill a book since we left earlier in the day.

We crouched low and crept through and around piles of concrete blocks and wood rubble. A soft breeze brought the faint smell of smoke from a faraway fire. The falling sun cast shadows among broken buildings. We saw why Xavier and Lowell hadn't followed.

Concrete blocks lay scattered in the narrow opening between debris piles. Probably tossed at the fuel trucks. The reinforced trucks rolled right over them. Unskilled driver Lowell had hit one and it wedged under the front wheel assembly.

"Scavengers I'll bet. They may be running low on ammo." Heflin kept his voice subdued.

Gunfire slowed to sporadic shots. Just enough to keep Lowell and Xavier pinned down.

Two men belly crawled over the pavement behind the turtle. Xavier and Lowell hunkered low behind the doors. The turtle, an old army model, had armor plated sides. The blown-out windows littered the pavement around it with a sheet of crystal pebbles. We inched our way closer. My leg throbbed as it withstood the bend and flex of maneuvering across unforgiving rubble.

The two men crawling came along side the turtle. Others jumped out of hiding and charged forward. Heflin and I were on Xavier's side, so we couldn't see Lowell.

One of the crawlers jumped up, reached through the turtle's window. Stupid bastard grabbed Xavier's gun arm. He shouted. "Shoot, Shoot, Sho—"

Xavier's knife slashed his throat. His last word poured out with a red flood. It splashed the turtle's door panel like an abstract painting. The ones he shouted at to shoot hadn't heard him. I shot one and Heflin took out the other. Damn. Shotguns make a mess.

Heflin and I raced toward the turtle in time to see the last three scavengers drag Lowell away. They'd hauled him out while Xavier was killing their companion. They bunched close around him, using him as their human shield.

Xavier joined us. He wiped the blood off his knife and sheathed it in his boot. I glanced at his face and backed away. I knew *that* look. He'd burned the image into my brain at Avalon. It was the same when he sliced Liam to shreds in Memphis. Xavier had his killing face on.

We rushed after the men who held Lowell and trapped them in a partially blocked alley. Blood ran down Lowell's pale face. Barely conscious, his body swayed. They had to drag and support him. The three kidnappers faced us, all lined up behind their hostage.

"Let him go and we'll let you leave." Heflin took the lead—but he kept an eye on Xavier. Let them go? He might. But Xavier? I wouldn't take any bets there.

The biggest kidnapper was a giant, at least six-seven. He had a powerful build and an odd bullet-shaped head. His thick nose flattened against his face, so he breathed through his mouth like a fish opening and closing its gills.

The one holding Lowell had his arm around his hostage's neck. His wide eyes darted back and forth. His free hand held a knife poised to puncture Lowell's stomach. Crazy. Fear and anger can be rational occasionally. Crazy not so much.

The third was a boy not much older than Ty. Dressed in rags, the kid had stick-thin arms and a glassy expression on his face, as if he didn't quite comprehend the events around him.

Bullet-head stood behind crazy and his hostage. Desperate men. They had a plan. They had everything to win—or lose.

"Okay. Okay." His flattened nose gave his voice a permanent *I've got a bad cold* sound. Bullet-head flexed his fingers. He stared straight at me. "You. Bitch."

I raised the Aries and pointed it at his forehead.

He didn't blink. "All of you. Back up to the wall and lay em' all on the ground." Bullet-head raised his arm and pointed at Heflin. "The shotgun. Bring it to me. Butt first."

Heflin straightened and turned to me. "Do it, Maat."

I backed up, laid the Aries and Rudra on the broken ground, then stepped to the side so I was in the best position to fall and snatch them up again. That's a move Uncle Jake had me practice on all manner of terrain.

Xavier removed his Aries. In a gesture that seemed so casual, he laid it on the ground too. There was an odd stillness about him. He was like the midnight hour of a winter night—cold, silent, and deadly. Xavier had offered me hot, burning rage, but nothing like this frozen fury. The only words that came to mind were Alistair Lockerbie's. *Gannett's butcher*.

Bullet head pointed at Xavier. "You. Back up."

Oh yes, I had backed Xavier up at Avalon. Disarmed him, too. *And that had worked so well*. Xavier stepped away up a few paces, but his eyes never left the trio.

"Bring the gun," Bullet-head said to Heflin. "Slow. Hold it out in front of you. One hand."

Crazy's knife wavered in his shaking hand. They'd either give him to Heflin and run or stick him and run. Heflin stepped forward, shotgun in one hand, but he held it in a way that would make it difficult for bullet-head to immediately grab it and fire. I prepared to drop and grab my gun. I could fire straight from a prone position.

When Heflin got within four feet of them, Crazy tossed Lowell at him like a rag doll.

Bullet-head squawked like a chicken. "No. Not yet!"

Heflin caught Lowell, but fell backwards, dropped the shotgun, and they went down together. Bullet-head grabbed for the shotgun.

Crazy and the boy bolted for me—for my guns.

Xavier suddenly stood between us. I thought only a vampire could move that fast.

Xavier's booted foot swept up and slammed into Crazy's throat. Crazy fell back—wheezing and choking, his windpipe crushed. The boy backpedaled. He tripped on his own feet, fell, and kept scrambling away.

Bullet-head had managed to claim the shot gun. If he'd had any sense, he'd have run immediately. Whatever smashed his face must have addled his brains, too. He fumbled with the gun, trying to get it into a firing position. Didn't he know how it worked? Xavier grabbed the barrel, twisted it, and tore it away like taking a toy from a kid—or a gun from Maat at Avalon. He tossed it out of reach.

I grabbed my guns and re-holstered the Rudra. The Aries I kept in hand.

Bullet-head and Xavier circled like predators challenging each other over a kill. The big man fought. Xavier played with him. His expression never changed. Everywhere Bullet-head turned a fist or boot battered him. The thick sound of pounded flesh and bone filled the alley. Finally, the big man dropped to his hands and knees. He toppled over onto his back.

Xavier casually walked around and kicked him in the balls.

Bullet-head screamed. It came out more like a squeal from his bleeding mouth. He rolled across the concrete.

Xavier followed. Oh, shit. His eyes.

The man was down, damn it. Probably dying. Yes, he would have killed us, but I wanted to shout at Xavier to stop. Just kill him damn it—get it over with. I glanced at Heflin, who stood holding Parr on his feet.

Xavier's next kick slammed into bullet-head's ribs. Bones cracked, snapped like dry sticks. One pierced a lung, and Bullet-head's scream bubbled to a gurgle. His body sagged. Dead I hoped.

Someone whimpered.

The boy. Dear God, he hadn't had the sense to run. Backed up against a wall…what was he waiting on?

Xavier moved in fast.

"Please," the boy cried. He choked and hunched down. "No, no."

He held out one hand, but his eyes were on the knife in Xavier's hand. Xavier grabbed him. His arm drew back and up. The blade slammed into his chest. The boy choked and sagged. Xavier released him and shoved him away. His body collapsed on the concrete. A wide red stain pool spread from his chest like an opening fan. The familiar odor of blood filled the alley.

Xavier turned to me. Not Heflin or Parr. Me. The killer still filled his eyes, but another thing lay veiled there. So heavy, that unexpressed emotion. *Familiar. An old companion. I had lived with it searing my heart and mind. It stood over my shoulder when I listened to Russell Jenks moan and scream as werewolves ate him alive. A complex and turbulent thing, a love of violence, of danger—the tempest. The blood lust I recognized. The thing that sent me fleeing to Avalon. The lust, the need to kill, that so terrified me, blazed like a torch in him. It was part of him.* Xavier sheathed his knife, picked up his Aries, and stalked out of the alley.

"Help me." Heflin had his arm around a swaying Lowell.

I grabbed the shotgun, caught Parr by the other arm, and together we led him out of the alley and to the turtle. Darkness closed in fast, and we needed to be moving. It was easier to put Lowell in the front seat, but that meant I had to sit in the back with Xavier.

He sat on my right. We hadn't gone far when his hand streaked out and clamped the back of my neck—a hand that could crush my spine. He dragged me across the seat to him. Heat radiated from his body, as if his killing fury transformed him to a furnace, barely constrained by human will.

Xavier grabbed my hand and forced it between his legs. Oh, damn. He was big and hard. Part of me wanted him, but another part recoiled. I'd screwed a vampire with less revulsion than I felt right then. I got a little high when I killed weres. Revenge was sweet. But sex—I didn't get off on killing anything. Sex was recreation—sex was life.

Only my ragged, labored breath broke the near silence as I twisted and struggled to get away. Everything in me demanded that I fight. I don't know what Parr and Heflin thought, but they didn't speak or turn to look back. Smart men don't get between two armed struggling fighters.

Xavier released my neck and used both arms to crush my body against his. That gave me the chance to draw my knife. The sound, metal across leather, alerted him. He grabbed my wrist in another bone-bruising grip. The blade flashed between us. He froze, and for an instant, his eyes fixed on the silver.

"We can go to hell together, Gannett's butcher." I spoke low and heavy, and I wanted my voice to carry my revulsion.

From one breath to the next, he relaxed and released me. I threw myself away. I sucked in deep breaths and scrunched my shaking body against the far door. I kept the knife free.

We rode through a more populated area, now closer to the interstate. Barrels filled with wood burned on an occasional street corner and cast fitful light on assorted people of the night. Men and women moved in and out of shadows.

"Stop here." Xavier's voice came low and flat. I couldn't conceive of what he might be thinking.

"What?" Heflin hit the brakes and slowed, but he didn't stop.

"I said stop."

It seemed the air would ignite in a killing blaze at any moment.

"We have to—" Heflin turned in his seat. Whatever he saw on Xavier's face made him punch the brakes and stop. Xavier opened the door, climbed out, and slammed the door behind him. Three obvious prostitutes immediately closed in on him. He slung his arm around the one who reached him first, and dragged her into the darkness. I closed my eyes as Heflin drove on, leaving him there—a predator on the dark streets. I'd bet our Wagon Master was reassessing his relationship with his old friend. The man he was taking to Salvaje. To his home.

When we arrived at the compound, I had to spend an hour lying like hell to assure Ty that Xavier was okay. I couldn't fool Jacob, but he accepted it when I told them there was nothing he could do—for Xavier or me.

We patched Lowell up and put him to bed. Mostly serious bruises and small cuts, he'd be sore for a few days. Heflin gathered men and went back to recover the damaged turtle. Said he'd have it ready to roll again by morning. He didn't mention Xavier. Jacob came to me and told me Lowell wanted to see me.

"How do you feel?" I knelt beside Lowell's cot.

"Fine." He managed an unconvincing smile. "More important, how are you?"

I frowned. "I'm not hurt."

Lowell reached out and grasped my hand. "Yes, you are. I'll make a little speech, and then I'll let you go." He chuckled and I could hear the irony, the self-loathing. "Speeches are apparently all I'm good for these days. This is a brutal world we live in, Maat Ferris, and you, of all people, should understand. You've killed men and slaughtered a legion of werewolves to become a mythical Angel of Death. You can fuck a vampire, then look him in the eye and tell him you're going to kill him. For God's sake, woman, this vicious, deadly life shaped you—and Xavier."

"You're saying we're both killers and deserve each other? The perfect couple. That I'm a hypocrite?"

He released my hand, and his fingers brushed my cheek. "I'm saying you are a survivor. You want the man. And he wants you. Don't lose him over principles neither of you believe in—or live by. *There are few innocents in this time and place.*"

He turned his face from me. I left him there and made my way back into the main warehouse.

Lowell was right.

Maat Ferris and Colonel Xavier, Gannett's butcher, were both competent killers. Xavier might be a psychopath, but Maat was an utter hypocrite. I'd fight any man, vampire or werewolf who attacked me. Sometimes I'd strike first. I have my guns, my knives, and my wits. I have psychic defenses most humans will never have.

While the specter of Xavier's violence far outweighed mine, it was not a stranger. I could accept the peril—or leave. I found a dark corner, sat down, and for the second time in my life, cried over a man. At least this time, I wasn't crying over his grave.

I sensed Xavier approach later in the night. He didn't try to enter the compound. Nervous guards had quick trigger fingers. I didn't see him when he came in at daylight, but I heard the whispers that swirled around his appearance. I took a deep breath and went to find him. The knowledge of his presence led me to a small room at the end of a dirty hallway. The door stood open, but I stopped outside. He knew I was there.

"Come in, Maat." Oh, that deep heavy voice drew me like a magnet.

I stepped into the doorway.

A shaft of sunlight from a high window illuminated the grubby room. It danced across his bare chest and arms. Such a big man, so fierce, so intense—not so deadly this morning, but that storm inside always threatened. He'd washed and shaved, and the shirt he'd worn the night before lay at his feet, bloody stains turning brown as it dried. I stared at it, then into his eyes.

"You have to kill her?"

"I didn't kill her." He chuckled, low and husky.

"She needs a new pimp, though."

I turned to go. He reached out and caught my arm. "I didn't fuck her either."

"It's your life."

Xavier dragged me closer to face him. He held my arms in those powerful hands. I wouldn't fight him. If he wanted to take me, right here, now, on the floor, against a wall, I'd let him. If he rejected me, I would leave, walk away forever. I would never fight him again. He released me.

Why the hell did he keep dragging me close then shoving me away?

A hollow, fragile, bubble of silence formed around us, filled with unspoken anguish. He rubbed his hands on his jeans, a nervous gesture, so out of character. Colonel Xavier, the strong man, the leader—how could he be unsure of anything? He drew a deep breath.

"I'm not good with words, Maat. *You* find them. You can do that, can't you? Run your mouth. Say something for both of us. Anything. I'll agree."

Hell yes I had words.

"Okay. I'll say it." I didn't hesitate. "I love you. I love you and I hate it. And yes, sometimes I hate you."

"Yeah, Maat. I knew I could count on you." He smiled. Such a wondrous thing. The smile faded. "We're proficient and well-practiced at violence, you and I. But I'm not as strong as you are. I lost myself last night." He had my arms again, drawing me closer. "I love you. And I'm afraid. When that black blinding rage takes over…each time I say never again. What if I hurt you? I couldn't live if I…"

Parr was right. Xavier and I were creatures of a violent world. We would protect what was ours at all cost, and we wouldn't wait until something or someone attacked. We would strike first. "We'll deal, Xavier, just as we always have."

Time stopped, and caught us in an alternate reality, a place where only he and I existed. He held me there and his lips brushed across my cheek. I flattened my palms on his stomach, ran them up his bare chest and around his shoulders. Those wonderful lips, so soft, found my mouth. Our bodies fit perfectly, so close, so right. This was an intimacy I'd never experienced.

The wildness in him from the previous evening had slowed to a massive surge of desire, languid but inevitable. He kissed me with deliberation, with the control and command that would create the potential for battle, even at the most intimate of times. Potential…not certainty. We might find a rhythm, a way to quench the wildfire that filled our lives.

I can remember times when I wanted sex badly, but someone as personable as Christopher could handle that. A take it or leave it situation. I never wanted a man as I wanted Xavier. He had the power to evoke emotions I didn't know existed. Xavier's arms slid around me, and his hands grabbed my ass. His fingers dug in, and he jerked me against him. Oh, could I get any closer?

One of love's liabilities is rampant stupidity. While Xavier and I reveled in delicious sensation, Ty had come to stand in the doorway. If he had been an enemy, we'd be dead. I jumped and tried to pull away when I realized he was there, but Xavier didn't let me go.

Ty leaned against the door jam, his face a sulky pout. "Heflin says we leave in twenty minutes."

"We'll be ready," Xavier said, holding me tight.

Xavier had to exert ownership. Ah, men. Ty turned away and disappeared down the hall.

"Xavier, he's just a kid. You don't have to rub it in."

"He'll get over it if you stop encouraging him."

"Encouraging! I don't…you're jealous." I shoved him, and he released me.

"Am not." He turned and grinned at me. "I know what's mine."

Xavier kicked his bloody shirt aside and grabbed a clean one hung on a nail in the wall.

He left me standing there alone—again. Arrogant bastard.

My declaration of love ended in a piss-off. Life was easier when all I had to do was grub potatoes or face a fuzzy monster every day.

Chapter Twenty-Six

We left Fort Smith that morning and soon rolled past the old monument sign that marked the Oklahoma state line. I again rode with Heflin in the lead turtle. I still wasn't certain whether he was beginning to enjoy my company, or he still felt he needed to keep an eye on me. I couldn't turn back now. We made two-hundred and fifty miles with no stops or breakdowns. By three o'clock, we'd crossed two rivers. The bridges still stood, but Heflin made us cross one vehicle at a time. Our country, though in sad shape now, retained technological building blocks. I could see what I had not seen before. The future—or futures.

We passed south of the Oklahoma City ruins. There were no waysides here. Every night we would be vulnerable. I could see why Heflin wanted Cody to accompany us. We had Jacob, but Cody could go faster and farther without tiring. Outlaws might strike, but we'd know they were coming.

"Is it usually this dry?" I asked Heflin.

"No." He studied the parched red land around us. "Going to be a drought again, I suppose. Same as last year. Pretty empty, though. Only the animals to notice."

I didn't like this place. With a sun powerful enough to scorch the earth and the straggling bushes that speckled wind-raked hills, the oppressive air seemed ready to explode.

"Someone once told me humans might become extinct." I closed my eyes, remembering the green mountains of Tennessee. "War, plague, weres, vamps. You believe that, Heflin?"

He didn't answer for a moment. Then he said, "Plenty of people around seems like. Lots of babies. Another war, though, another plague, a flu epidemic, maybe not the whole world, but the United States? Yes, it's possible. Other countries might not be as bad. Or worse. Who knows?" Heflin's somber voice spoke what he believed.

Human extinction would mean the end for human changelings, too. Vampires would starve since they shun werewolf blood. Weres might last for a while but since they're sterile hybrid creatures, time would run out eventually.

"Maat?"

"Yes, Heflin."

"I want to tell you about Xavier. He, Aaron, and I started out in the militia over twenty years ago. Teenagers. We were going to make the world right." He stopped for a minute or so and I waited. His jaw worked as if he were rehearsing what he would say. He finally decided and went on. "Aaron and Xavier? They've both changed. I have too, but not so much. The years with Aaron have scarred Xavier as much as that fire scarred his face. He's always had that explosive temper, but it's easier to trigger now. I don't think he'd intentionally hurt you, but…"

"He could hurt me and be sorry later." I didn't need his warning. I was fully aware of the danger of loving Xavier. I had no intention of talking to Heflin about my personal relationship.

"Heflin, I know you won't believe it, but if you ever liked Aaron Gannett, you should feel sorry for him now. Did you know, Ruelle—maybe all vampires—drive humans crazy if they stay close around them too long? Gannett is already showing signs."

"No. But you…"

"Yeah, I've been around Ruelle and other vampires more than most humans. Maybe I'm crazy. I'm told I act that way at times."

Heflin suddenly slammed his hand against the steering wheel. "Shit!"

I saw it too. Another of those walls moving out of the west—only this one was dirty red. Dust! The sun behind it gave it a fiery halo.

Heflin knew the road, and he pushed the convoy on to the ruins of a small town. No wayside but he parked the trucks and protected the engines with tarps. We stood guard, scanning the flat empty land until the sandstorm hit. After that, nothing would move until the wind died.

Xavier, Ty, Cody, four mercenaries, and I stayed with the most important truck in an abandoned garage. Ty dug around in the litter, uncovering old tools. He turned up a rattlesnake. Cody caught the snake with his hands and lifted it to stare into its eyes. It froze, held spellbound. It didn't struggle or make a sound. How amazing. He released it and after that, the mercenaries didn't want to sleep on the floor. They braved the sand to find a reptile free building. I wished them luck.

I spread a blanket near one of the truck wheels, sat, and leaned back. The wind blasted outside. At times a whisper, then rising again to a static crackle of sandpaper rubbing away at the remains of the town.

While the building's steel frame stood steady, sand seeped through generous cracks in the walls and sifted down from holes in the roof.

Xavier and Ty joined me as we huddled in the lantern's light and ate a prepacked supper of cold pasta, mixed with unidentifiable chunks of what might have been vegetables. Not too gritty if you didn't chew hard. Heflin came in and produced a bottle of passable wine and four paper cups. If you didn't slosh the cup around the sand settled to the bottom.

I had questions for Heflin. "Tell me a little more about Salvaje."

"Salvaje isn't a big place." Heflin found a box to sit on and slouched comfortably, elbows on his knees. He seemed more relaxed than I'd ever seen him. Maybe it was the wine. "Only about three thousand in all. And that includes the herders living in the hills."

I laughed. "Counting weres and vamps, too?"

"Counting weres and vamps."

"You think I'll be recognized? As Suriel. What about Xavier? His association with Gannett."

"The politics of New Washington are nothing there, except for a few of us who have contacts in the east. Xavier will be fine. I have heard stories of Suriel, though, so others may have too. But no one should know it's you unless you tell them. There's the Asha too."

"The Asha?" The word sounded familiar.

The wine had seeped into my system, and I leaned comfortably against Xavier. Heflin shifted and poured more wine. "The Asha is the pact between humans, werewolves, and the vampires of Salvaje. A vampire wrote it, and my signature is on the original document."

Heflin grinned. "I'm proud of that. Like the Constitution. Anyway, it's a set of rules, rights, and responsibilities that are supposed to keep us from killing each other on sight. If one group starts a fight, the other two join forces and destroy the aggressor. Not an *original idea*, but it works. We make it work. The rules are important. One of the vampires said Asha meant—"

"A creed of righteousness." I remembered where I'd seen the word. "My mother studied history. I watched her crawl through a crumbling library to rescue books."

Heflin's face grew serious. "You and Xavier are humans—entering Salvaje as my guests. If any werewolf feels he has a serious enough grievance, he or she must issue a formal challenge to fight. Since you're human, you can choose a werewolf as a champion to fight for you. Jacob would tie most of them in knots. As for the vampires, they keep to themselves."

I drained my cup. "Sneaky bastards, those vampires. If they have a grievance against you, you disappear."

Heflin didn't disagree. He poured more wine. "Salvaje vampires don't play games. Their leader has complete control. He's highly intelligent and quite dangerous, but not overly aggressive. He's shown no proclivity for grand power schemes. He signed the Asha, too. As far as I know, he enforces it on his people."

After Heflin left, Xavier told Ty to climb up in the truck and sleep on the seat.

Cody had been sitting in the shadows. He had the silent way of vampires. I suspect only I would notice him there. I reached out with my aura and touched him. He rose and came to me.

I patted the blanket beside me. "Would you tell me how you became a vampire? Don't have to if you don't want to."

Cody gracefully lowered himself. He leaned closer to touch me, to make that physical contact. "I don't mind telling you. It seems so far away now. It was 1992." His eyes glowed in the lamplight. "My mom and dad, me and my little sister—she was four—we went to the beach. We had to go home the next day and Mom wanted to walk on the shore in the moonlight."

Cody sat silent and I was sorry I asked him to explain.

"Gunnar," he said finally. "He killed my dad first. I jumped on him, and he knocked me away. Mom screamed, picked up my sister, and ran... She didn't get far. Gunnar smashed her head open with his fist."

Oh, God. What had I done? "Cody, don't. I shouldn't have asked—"

"No. I want to. I've never been able to tell anyone. No one cared."

Outside, the barbaric wind rose to a furious howl, and we waited until it spent its wrath and returned to a pulsing moan.

Cody leaned closer, his shoulder still touching mine. "When Mom went down, I grabbed my little sister and ran. I ran so fast I didn't hear him behind me. The motel lobby, full of light and people, I was within a few feet when he snatched us back. He knocked me out. When I woke up, I was in a basement—with him."

I wanted to tell him to stop, but his loss was my loss now. Cody raised his eyes to meet mine. A trace of tears puddled there. "Never saw my sister again. I can remember she was four years old, but I can't remember her name. It's so strange. Since I've been with you, I feel almost human. I'd forgotten that, too." Cody lifted himself to his feet in one agile move. "Jacob said he and I could hunt if the wind died before daylight." He stepped back and faded into the shadows.

Until a few weeks ago, I'd considered all werewolves to be raging beasts. My rational mind had always known they'd been human once. I'd known that they could take human form to walk among men. But reality then was my mother and all the other victims I'd buried over the years. I would do well to remember, though, Cody was not the teenaged boy he appeared to be. He had spent years dwelling with the vilest creatures in the world.

Xavier drew me into his arms. "I love you." He spoke softly in my ear..

"I love you too, Xavier. But I want you to understand. New Washington was your town, Memphis was mine. In Salvaje, we stand back-to-back when we need to, but if I must fight alone, that's how it will be."

I didn't want Xavier to try to take care of me. One of our problems from the beginning was his insistence on trying to control me and my constant battle for independence. In truth, I wasn't willing to give a man, no matter how much I loved him, that kind of control of my life. No relationship was perfect, and there would likely always be a power struggle between us.

"So, Angel of Death, I should let you take on an army of weres or vamps single-handed?" Xavier's voice was light, but his eyes serious. "I'll try to restrain myself."

My fingers traced his lips. We lived in a brutal world, but joy laced our time occasionally. It was something to live for—or die for.

Xavier dug out a couple more blankets and spread one out beside him. He folded another as a pillow. I wanted to kiss him, but then I'd want more. We'd have to wait until we reached Salvaje.

I fell asleep with him softly stroking my hair. Each touch was a caress from a hand that could easily kill. Had almost killed me. Safe. This night he made me feel safe. At least as safe as one could be lying by a sleeping tiger.

More treacherous miles lay ahead of us on our journey to a strange city, one like we'd never encountered before. Soldier, hunter, demo man, all humans, one secretive werewolf, and a young vampire. We'd grown into a pack of deadly misfits. Beware Salvaje, here we come.

A word about the author...

Lee Roland is a writer of urban fantasy and paranormal romance. She lives in Florida with her family.

http://leeroland.com

~

Other books by Lee from the Wild Rose Press...

Bone Dance

Thank you for purchasing
this publication of The Wild Rose Press, Inc.

For questions or more information
contact us at
info@thewildrosepress.com.

The Wild Rose Press, Inc.
www.thewildrosepress.com

To visit with authors of
The Wild Rose Press, Inc.
join our yahoo loop at
http://groups.yahoo.com/group/thewildrosepress/